Dream Defender

Knight Flyers Book 2

Ann McCune

Dream Defender, Knight Flyers Book 2
1st edition

Ruby Gulch Enterprises LLC
P.O. Box 64
Craig, CO 81626

Edited by: A Fading Street

Cover by: Anelia Savova AKA Ann_RS

For Jessica,
"Those who don't believe in magic will never find it"
-Ronald Dahl

Chapter 1

A knock at my door made me blink at the page in my calculus book I had been staring at for the past twenty minutes. "Come in."

"Liz, are you going to go to bed soon? It's getting late," my mom asked, sticking her head inside my room. "Tomorrow's a big day."

I stretched my arms over my head. "Yeah, I want to get this last problem done."

"I think you've been studying too hard. You always look dead on your feet." She stood behind me and looked over my shoulder.

"I know, but I don't want to mess up my GPA." I hated lying to her about why I was tired all the time, but if she knew the real reason, she would pack up everything and move us to the other side of the country, not that it would help and plus, I loved where we lived. Twisted Pines, Colorado, in the heart of the Rocky Mountains, was a great place to grow up, and I didn't want to think about spending my senior year of high school at a new school even though goblins, or mares, tormented my dreams whenever Shawn or Heather couldn't keep me company.

Shawn, my boyfriend, and Heather, his sister, were Knight Flyers, part of a group with special powers that allowed them to fight the mares and keep them from sucking the souls out of people while they dreamed. They had moved to Twisted Pines during spring break with a division of Knights Inc. because there were so many mares in the area.

After they had arrived, I learned that my bio-dad, Victor Robinson, was one of them, and I had inherited his ability to manipulate my dreams and fight mares. Shawn's dad, Jon, the leader of Knights Inc. in Twisted Pines, had been best friends with Victor until their vision for the future of the business diverged. Jon had refused to let me train to be a knight until he watched me fight off a group of dream zombies on prom night and the mare who created them. I had come close to begging him to let me train, but I got what I wanted. My training would start the day after Memorial Day.

"You won't get straight A's if you fall asleep in the middle of your final." Mom gathered my waist-length blonde hair in her hand and began to braid it.

"Fine," I shook her off, turned my desk lamp off, and pushed my chair away from my desk. I yawned and stood up, fumbling with my watch band.

"Liz," Mom whispered, looking at my wrist as I took my watch off and stared at the angry lines of the brand Stalker, as I called him, a mare who wouldn't leave me alone, gave me before prom.

"What?" I asked. We both knew there was nothing I could do about the brand except close the gateway between the mare's dimension and ours, then send them back. With the gateway closed, they wouldn't be able to come back and harass me or anyone else.

"I'm sorry, I'm just worried about you." A tear streaked down her cheek. I went to her and wrapped her in a hug.

"I know Mom, I'm worried too." I pulled back. "But everything's fine. I'm sleeping with my dreamcatcher, and I'll be able to protect myself before you now it." I went to the door and held it open for her.

"I don't know what I would do if I lost you, Liz." She stopped when she reached the door and squeezed my hand.

"Don't worry, everything will be fine." I closed the door after she left, leaned against it, and stared at my bed. I wished Shawn wasn't working, and that Heather was back from Trinidad. I'd already been on my own for four nights in a row. I woke myself up when the nightmares were too bad, but then I wouldn't go back to sleep, and I was tired. I shrugged; I would be useless the next day if I didn't take what sleep I could get.

"Please, just leave them alone," I cried. My face was wet with tears as I watched the two mares who'd been harassing me for the past month pour gasoline over Mom and Dad. We were in our dining room and they were sitting back to back, bound and gagged. Mom was sobbing and Dad was telling me with his eyes to run while he awkwardly held Mom's hand. I stood in the doorway and as much as I wanted to untie them, I wouldn't reach them in time, and even if I did, I couldn't fight off their attackers.

"Why, would we?" The mare I called Pigskin asked, as he lumbered around, emptying the gas can over my parents. He was short with bowed legs like he spent most of his time riding an elephant bareback. His head was shaped like a football, with the pointy ends where his ear holes were. He didn't have any lobes to speak of, and he had a few wisps of white hair on his head that reminded me of laces.

"You won't fight us, and we can't hurt you, so we need to keep ourselves entertained somehow," his partner, Twiggy-Squatch, said, holding a box of matches. He was tall, covered in dull brown fur, and emaciated. I could see every bone in his face, and his arms were so thin they resembled broom handles. No two mares were the same, except for their eyes, or lack thereof. Instead of eyes, they had black gaping holes, and sometimes I thought if I looked into them too long, they would swallow me, and I would never wake up.

"What are you going to accomplish by setting my parents on fire?" I asked as Twiggy-Squatch lit a match, threw it on the trail of gasoline, and took a step back, laughing. "No," I screamed, falling to my knees. I couldn't watch my parents die again. It felt like my insides were being torn out every time the mares did this. Closing my eyes didn't help as I still had to listen to their screams of pain as the fire reached them. The worst part was, I couldn't help them.

"As good as your soul would taste, watching you suffer is more satisfying since we get to do it night after night," Pigskin said, trying to kick me, but his foot bounced off the protection bubble my dreamcatcher created, and he cursed. "When are you going to give up and come to us without protection?" he yelled, leaning in as close as he could without touching my bubble while the muffled screams of my parents made me want to jam ice picks in my ears so I wouldn't have to listen to their cries of pain.

"Don't worry, the time will come." I got to my feet and wiped the tears from my eyes, doing my best not to look at the inferno spreading up the walls as it silenced my parents' screams. When I finished my training and became a Knight Flyer, I would make them both pay.

They laughed at my words and nodded. "We can't wait." Twiggy-Squatch went over to the charred, still-smoking bodies of my parents and kicked them. They dissolved, covering the floor with black ash.

"Who should we kill next?" Pigskin asked.

I screamed in frustration; I couldn't watch them kill anyone else. I had to wake up.

I blinked and stared at the clock next to my bed. Four-thirty, better than the night before when I had woken up at three. I sat up and rubbed my face; it was wet with tears. I'd been crying in my sleep again.

I hurried out of bed, tiptoed to stand at my parent's door, and listened hard. At first, all I could hear was Dad snoring but then I heard Mom tell him to roll over. They were fine. Another nightmare. They were alive, and I almost crumpled to the floor with relief. I always convinced myself that whoever the mares killed in my dreams weren't really there, but I never relaxed until I knew everyone was okay.

I went back to my room, closed the door silently, and leaned against it. It was too late to go back to sleep and too early to get ready for school. I sat at my desk and opened my calculus book. My last day of junior year would start in a few hours and I would be lucky if I didn't fall asleep halfway through my finals.

Chapter 2

"Liz, are you up?" Mom asked, opening the door, and peeking inside my room.

"Yeah, I've been cramming for a while." I spun in my chair and looked at the clock. It was seven ten. Where did the time go? "Crap," I jumped from my chair and ran to my closet. With no time to shower, I put on a pair of jean shorts, grabbed a Red Hot Chili Peppers T-shirt off the hanger, then ran to the bathroom.

"Hurry, you don't want to be late for finals." Mom followed me. "I'll make you a burrito you can eat when you get to school."

"Thanks," I called as I picked up my toothbrush and squirted toothpaste on it while grimacing at the bags under my eyes, and the red spider-web-looking lines surrounding my blue eyes. I needed a good night's sleep in the worst way. After I brushed the tangles out of my hair and put it in a ponytail, I went back to my room, threw everything I needed into my backpack, swung it over my shoulder and headed downstairs.

I was ready to grab my breakfast and run for the door when I reached the kitchen, but I stopped in my tracks when I saw a long narrow box sitting on the bar between the kitchen and the dining room with a Mylar balloon floating above it that read, 'Happy Birthday'.

"No way." I slowly walked toward it like the box contained the Holy Grail and I was King Arthur.

"Do you like it?" Mom came around the bar with a travel mug and two paper bags.

"You got me the light bar?" It was the best birthday present ever. It was going to be amazing on my *new to me,* Jeep Wrangler. A moose totaled my old Jeep over spring break.

"Happy birthday, Liz." Mom grinned as I ran my hands over the box.

"Thank you so much," I twisted around and hugged her. "It's so cool."

"Be careful, don't spill your coffee." Mom laughed, hugging me back. "You better go."

Right, finals. I let go, wishing I had time to install it right then. I took my breakfast and lunch bags from Mom and stuffed them into my backpack then took my coffee cup. "See you later, Mom. Thanks again." I ran into the mudroom, shoved my feet into my Chucks and ran for the door.

"Drive safely, no speeding," Mom yelled as I shut the front door and ran to my Jeep, trying not to spill my coffee.

I got in and shivered. It was the end of May, and the sun was out but it was still cold. I reached under my seat and pulled the Red Bull out, hoping it hadn't frozen. I was going to need more than coffee to get through the day. I started the Jeep and cranked up the heater before I pulled onto the dirt road that would lead me down the mountain to the highway.

I arrived at school with minutes to get to my first period class. I ran, not bothering to stop at my locker and took a seat just as the bell rang. Opening my backpack, I looked longingly at my breakfast; but it would have to wait. I had a final to take.

The rest of my morning wasn't any better. I finally ate after first period but then I was almost late to second. My only saving grace was that I'd been studying for weeks and felt like I did okay on the tests.

I caught up with Shawn at lunch, he was the first one at our table. "How was work last night?" I asked, taking the seat next to him.

"Busy, I got three mares on my own. Did you sleep at all?" He frowned, no doubt noticing in the bags under my bloodshot eyes.

"Yes, but it wasn't restful." I gave him a tight smile and ran my hand through his short blond hair.

"I'm sorry, we'll close the gate soon. Oh, hey Billy." Shawn tensed but smiled as my best friend took the seat across from me.

"Hey, Billy." I watched him to see if there was any sign that he had overheard Shawn. When he didn't respond, Shawn winked at me, and I took my sandwich out of my sack while waiting for Billy to wish me a happy birthday.

"What?" He frowned at me.

"Nice haircut." I wiggled my eyebrows at his new summer buzz cut, leaving only stubby brown hair poking out of his scalp. "Thought you weren't going to let your mom touch your hair?" *Did he forget what day it was?*

"Yeah well," he ran his hand over the stubble making a sound like sandpaper on wood. "She said I get a choice when I pay my own rent."

I could not keep the laughter inside of me. He hated it when his mom cut his hair. "Hey Jo," I said to Billy's girlfriend and Shawn's best friend, as she sat down next to Billy.

"Happy last day of school." She sat next to Billy and pushed her chin-length, strawberry-blonde hair behind her ears.

I slumped in my seat when she said *happy.* I thought Billy must have told her what day it was.

"Hey, what's wrong?" Shawn nudged me with his shoulder.

As much as I wanted to tell him it was my birthday and everyone forgot, I didn't want to be that girl. "Long night and crappy day."

"I'm sorry." He put his arm around me and gave me a squeeze. "I have good news though."

"Really?" I perked up, thinking he had something planned for us.

"Heather will be back this weekend."

"Thank God." If they were coming back from Trinidad, maybe Shawn wouldn't have to work six nights a week and I wouldn't have to deal with the mares. "How has your day been?"

"Good, only one final left, right?"

"And it's history; it'll be cake, but shop class will suck. All we are doing is cleaning." I glanced around the table. Sam and Tommy had joined us while I talked, and I gave them a wave. "So, what are we doing tonight?" Billy, Tommy, Sam, and I always did something on the last day of school.

"Sorry, Liz, we're leaving right after the final bell for

Denver. Our parents are taking us to a Rockies game." Tommy glanced at Sam then Billy.

Billy cleared his throat. "Yeah, Jo and I made plans to go to Spruce for dinner and a movie."

I gave Shawn a tight smile, waiting. "I'm sorry, I have to work. Dad wants me home right after school." He shifted in his seat refusing to meet my eyes

It took everything I had not to storm off. I even considered blowing off my last two classes, but I wasn't mad enough to mess up my GPA. I didn't blame Jo or Shawn for not knowing it was my birthday, I'd only known them for a few months. But Billy, Tommy, and Sam had no excuse, I'd known them my whole life. The warning bell rang, I got up, saying nothing, and gathered my trash.

"Liz, you can come with us to Spruce if you want," Billy offered after Jo whispered to him.

"What?" I spun around. "No, that's okay. I'll figure something out." I didn't want to be a third wheel to that make-out fest. I walked away from our table with Shawn trailing behind me. I loved having our last two classes together, but right then I wanted to be alone and wallow in self-pity.

"Liz, wait up," he said as I reached the trash can and tossed my bag in. "What's going on with you today?" He took my hand as we took our time walking to Auto Shop.

"I'm just tired. It's been a long week." Between the mares and studying for finals, there hadn't been a lot of sleeping, and I didn't function well on three or four hours of sleep.

"I'm sorry. Now that the mare outbreak in Trinidad is under

control, things will go back to normal." He gave my hand a squeeze.

"I hope so, I don't know how much more of this I can take." I looked at my wrist and the edges of the brand. Jon, Shawn's dad, was right, it was like a homing beacon for mares. I had sent the one who gave it to me back to his dimension, but it hadn't taken long for others like Pigskin and Twiggy-Squatch to find me and pick up where he left off.

Shawn let go of my hand and put his arm around my shoulder. "It'll get better Liz; I promise." I wanted to believe him, but I was so tired, physically and mentally. I didn't know how much longer I could deal with it.

Shop class dragged as our teacher had us sweeping the floors and putting tools away for the summer. Everyone was laughing and joking around, excited for summer break, but I wasn't feeling it. *Maybe I should tell Shawn about my birthday,* I thought, pushing the dust in front of the broom into the parking lot. *No, it would only make him feel guilty for not being able to hang out with me tonight.*

After shop, Shawn and I went to our last class of the school year, history. Billy was already there when we arrived. He was sitting in his normal seat, typing something on his phone.

"What's going on?" I asked, taking the seat next to him.

"What?" Billy jerked his head up and flipped his phone face down on the desk. "Oh, not much. Let's get this over with." His voice was higher than normal and, as he looked past me, I turned following his gaze, but didn't see what he was looking at.

"What's going on with you?" I asked.

"Nothing, just nervous about the test." Billy tapped his hands on the desk to a nervous beat as the bell rang and Mr. Anderson came around his desk holding a pile of paper.

"All right everyone, you know the rules. Good luck," he said, passing out the tests.

After class Billy disappeared without saying goodbye. He was probably finding Jo so they could leave for Spruce. At least Shawn hadn't ditched me yet.

"I'm sorry I have to work. It feels like the only time we get to see each other anymore is here," he said as we exited the school and walked to my Jeep.

"It's okay. With Heather and everyone coming home we'll get to see more of each other, right?" I tried to sound hopeful.

"Yeah, there is no other option." When we reached my Jeep, I leaned against the driver's door not wanting our time together to end.

"Shawn," Mary called from his Rubicon parked on the other side of the lot. "Come on let's go."

Shawn rolled his eyes. "I'll find you if I get done with work early."

"Okay." He leaned down and kissed me. As his soft lips met mine, I melted into him and wanted to ask him to blow off work so we could continue, but the safety of the town was at stake and I couldn't bring myself to be that selfish.

"Bye," he said, finally pulling away from me and jogging over to his ride.

When I got home a half hour later, I unloaded my backpack and put everything away. I went downstairs and opened the box with the light bar in it. I took out the directions and read them. It was going to be a major job to install it and I started a list of what I would need.

"Hi, Mom," I said when I heard her come in through the garage door and take her shoes off.

"There's the birthday girl." She came and gave me a hug. "What are you doing home? I thought you'd be out with the boys since it's the last day of school." She let go and made her way to the stairs.

"Shawn has to work, and Billy forgot it was my birthday, I don't know what his deal is." I followed her upstairs.

"Billy forgot your birthday?" She sounded stunned. "I'm sorry, sweetheart. I figured you would be out with your friends tonight, so your dad and I made plans to go to dinner with the Andersons." She stopped outside the door to her bedroom. "I guess I could call and cancel."

My face fell, and I felt tears well behind my eyes. Even my mother hadn't planned anything for my birthday. It shouldn't have been a big deal; it wasn't like I was turning eighteen or anything but come on. "It's okay Mom, I can just hang out on my own tonight." I ran into my room, slamming and locking the door behind me.

I went to my computer and opened my music player; I needed something loud and angry to match my mood. I pushed play, cranked up the volume, and fell onto my bed, trying not to cry as Rammstein's wailing filled the room. It was just a birthday, so why was I letting it get to me? Because it felt like everyone was so wrapped up in their own lives, they couldn't be bothered to help me celebrate. Getting old sucked.

Chapter 3

I jerked awake and took in my dimly lit bedroom; I had fallen asleep and was dreaming of Billy being beheaded by Pigskin when I forced myself to wake up. I was shaking and covered in sweat, and someone was knocking on my door. I rolled over to stare at the ceiling. I didn't want to answer it; I was still mad at everyone for blowing off my birthday.

"Liz, open the door," Dad said from the hallway. I forced myself off the bed, unlocked the door, and went back to my bed. My dad, Burt—he was really my step-dad, but he was the only father I'd ever known—followed me inside.

"Hey, Dad."

"Mom told me what happened." He sat on the bed next to me. "This is just part of growing up. People get busy. They won't always have time for you. Today was the day I helped bring you into the world, and it will always be important to me, Mom, and you, but for everyone else, it's just another day." He put his arm around my shoulder.

"I still can't believe Billy forgot. He's never missed my birthday." I rested my head on his shoulder. *I would not cry.* I made myself take a deep breath and stand up.

"Well, once he remembers, I'm sure he'll make it up to you. Come on, we brought you takeout." Dad went to the door.

I wanted to stay in my room and hide from the world, but my stomach growled; I was hungry. I followed him downstairs and was headed for the kitchen when Mom called from the deck, "Liz, can you come out here for a minute?" She sounded angry, and I wondered if it was my fault as I followed her voice to the deck.

"What, Mom?" I wondered why she was out there in the dark.

"Surprise!" I staggered back a step as ten people yelled at me and the lights came on.

"What?" I blinked until my eyes adjusted to the light and found Billy, Jo, Shawn, Heather, Sam, Tommy, and my parents waiting for me to say something. "You didn't forget?"

"How could I forget?" Billy came over and gave me a hug. "Shawn planned this whole thing," he whispered in my ear before letting go.

I went to Shawn and wrapped my arms around his waist. "How did you know it was my birthday?"

"Facebook, and Billy." He kissed me on the cheek before letting go.

"How were you able to sneak in without me hearing you?"

"You had your music loud enough to wake the dead." Mom walked around me with a tray of burgers ready for the grill. "I don't know how we would've managed if you didn't do that."

She laughed and handed the tray to Dad.

"Speaking of music, this is a party," Billy called, tapping a few buttons on his phone before the outdoor speakers came on and Green Day began playing.

I spent the rest of the night eating, drinking, and laughing with my friends. When it was time for presents, Billy gave me a new dreamcatcher to hang on my rearview mirror, Heather brought me a new hoodie from Trinidad, and Jo gave me a key chain with a dreamcatcher on it. Then Shawn dug out a small velvet box from his pocket and put it on the table.

"Shawn, what did you do?" I held the box with two fingers, not sure what to make of the soft velvet. I didn't wear a lot of jewelry, and I wasn't sure how I felt about Shawn giving me something that looked expensive. I thought it was too big for a ring box, but I never really paid attention to that kind of thing.

"Just open it, and you'll find out." He ran his hand through his hair like he was nervous.

I opened it and peeked inside. I smiled and pulled out a silver bracelet with a single charm on it, a dreamcatcher. "Shawn it's awesome." I undid the clasp and tried to get it around my right wrist but couldn't seem to get the two ends together.

"Here let me help." Shawn took my hand and rested it on the table while he connected the clasp. "It's a charm bracelet, you can add as many charms as you want."

Once he had the bracelet on me, I held my hand out to admire it. "I love it, thank you." I leaned in and gave him a kiss.

"You're welcome," he said, pulling away and gazing at me like I was the only person in the world. I think he wanted to say something else when Billy interrupted.

"What should we do now?" he asked, getting to his feet, and putting his hands on his hips.

My dad stood up and checked his watch. "It's getting late. I think we should call it a night. I'm sure your parents are wondering where you all are."

"Dr. Lawson, you're no fun." Billy picked up the half-eaten cake and took it to the kitchen.

"Sometimes, ending the fun before it gets out of hand will ensure everyone's safety," Dad said before leaving us to clean up the mess.

After we took out the trash and wiped down the table, everyone left except for Shawn. We were standing by his Rubicon holding hands. "Thank you for this." I rested my forehead on his chest. "I really thought everyone forgot."

"I'm glad we surprised you. You know how big Billy's mouth is."

"No kidding." I laughed then drew back from his chest. "Are we meeting tonight?"

"Yeah, we'll meet in my padded room in about an hour?" Shawn's padded room was a place in his dreamscape where mares couldn't enter, and only people he invited were allowed, so nothing could bother us there. It started as a place for him to hide from his dad but morphed into our favorite spot to hang out while we were together in our dreams.

"That works for me." I took a step toward the house.

"Where are you going?" He pulled me to him and kissed me like it was the last time we would see each other, and he didn't want me to forget him. Every time we kissed like this, with his arms around my waist and mine around his neck, clinging to each other like we may never see each other again, I never wanted it to end. My parents were probably watching from the window, but I didn't care. When we finally pulled away from each other he left, and I went to bed, dodging my parents as best I could.

As soon as I entered my dream, I thought of Shawn's padded room. The floor was spongy, more like a wrestling mat than carpet. The walls were padded and tufted into squares. There were no windows and no doors, and everything was white. My surroundings morphed until I was staring at Heather, Jo, and Shawn. They were sitting at a glass table, in white leather chairs.

"Hi, did you start without me?" I took the chair next to Shawn.

"We were just talking about what we haven't been able to get done since we last met." Jo rolled her eyes and drummed her fingers on the table.

"I know, this past month sucked." I reached under the table and grabbed Shawn's hand. "Where should we start?"

"Where did we leave off?" Heather twirled around in her chair causing her honey-colored blonde hair to swirl around her shoulders.

"We were all supposed to research places with mares and see if there were any similarities we could use to narrow down the location of the gate in Twisted Pines." Shawn stared at the notebook in front of him while turning the pages with his free hand.

"Did your notes show up?" I was curious, if you took notes in your dream, could you bring them back in another dream?

"No." He laughed and closed the book. "But it was worth a try."

"Moving on." Heather got to her feet and strode around the table, her long legs eating up the distance. "Was anyone able to get any research done?"

"No, between finals and training I had no time." Jo leaned back in her chair and put her feet on the table.

"Me neither, too much has been going on." I felt guilty, but between studying for finals and helping my boss find my replacement, there has been no time for research. Plus, I was exhausted most of the time.

"I've been on duty almost the entire time you were gone. I've had no time." Shawn leaned forward and rested his chin in his hand.

"You guys calm down." Heather moved to the head of the table. "This isn't school or work. We have to take care of our other obligations before we work on finding the gate. Let's start over. Get a fresh take on this. What do we want to know?"

"How and when the gate opened, which means we need to find an event that might correlate to it opening," I said, squeezing Shawn's hand.

Heather rested her hands on the table, her blue eyes so much like Shawn's staring me down. "Liz, you were going to research Twisted Pines, right?"

"Yeah, hey, wait a second. Why wasn't a team of knights closer to Trinidad?"

"The mares just showed up there. We had a team of knights from New Mexico and Colorado meet there. What's the big deal?"

"What will happen now that you're back?"

"We added it to both New Mexico's and Colorado's monitoring system. Between the two clans, we will have the area covered. I don't understand what you are getting at."

"If there had never been mares there before and suddenly there's a bunch, wouldn't that point to exactly what we are trying to find?" I tightened my ponytail. Jo crossed her arms over her chest. Shawn smiled and Heather put her hands on her hips.

"You think a gate just opened?"

"It would make sense wouldn't it?"

"Let's say you're right." Heather nodded her head. "What should we do with the information?"

"I think we should check it out. Was there an earthquake or a flash flood? I doubt it popped into existence of its own accord. Check the newspaper, the police blotter, Facebook, YouTube—people put everything on the internet. There has to be an account of it opening."

"Let's say we find it. What do we do then?" Jo took her feet off the table and leaned forward. "Try to close it?"

"That would be ideal, but I don't think our parents or Jon would let us road trip to Trinidad, but it might help us find the one here."

"It's not a bad place to start." Shawn nodded his head.

"I wish I would've thought of it while I was there. It's a boring town during the day. We still need to dig into Twisted Pines history though. If we don't find the gate here, finding the one in Trinidad won't help us." Heather put her hands on her hips.

"Okay, I'll start next week, the library isn't open this weekend because of Memorial Day, and I want to start with the newspaper. They don't have the editions from the eighteen hundreds online." My mind was filled with the possibilities of what I might find.

"I'll see what I can find online about Santa Fe, but like Liz said, it might be something we need to be there to see." Jo got to her feet and stretched her arms above her head. "How were the mares down there?"

"They were the same as anywhere, but one was strong. He reminded me of your stalker, Liz." Heather sat down, leaned back, and laced her fingers behind her head. "Is he back terrorizing you yet?"

"No, I haven't seen him since prom. I think he's afraid of me, but it hasn't stopped a bunch of other ones from harassing me."

"And you're sleeping with a dreamcatcher?" Heather raised her eyebrows at me.

"Yup, it sucks. They lit my parents on fire last night and there was nothing I could do to save them." I stared at my hands. "I have to deal with it until I'm a knight, I guess."

"I'm sorry, I can't imagine." Heather stared at the table.

"It sucks. With you and Shawn working so much, they've done nothing but pester me. When I wake up, it feels like I haven't slept at all."

Heather drummed her fingers on the table. "Now that I'm back, hopefully, you won't be alone in your dreams as much."

"That's the plan." Shawn raised his eyebrows at me. "If, Dad gives us good schedules."

"Good luck with that." Jo stood and walked around the room. "You know how he feels about you dating Liz."

My heart sank, I hated that Jon didn't like me. "Well, I'm praying for a miracle." I traced the intricate lines of the brand circling my wrist with my finger. We had pored over every book we could get our hands on, looking for a way to remove it but found nothing. Most of them had said to put me out of my misery, at least then I'd get to keep my soul. I let go of Shawn's hand and stood. I'd been sitting too long and thinking about being 'put out of my misery,' gave me goosebumps.

"You start training on Tuesday?" Jo leaned against the wall.

"Yeah, I'm so nervous." I folded my arms over my chest. "What are they going to make me do?"

"You're a special case." Heather sat up and drummed her fingers on the table. "Who knows?"

"Don't worry, my dad's in charge of training. He'll go easy on you." Jo glanced at her watch and I wondered if it kept time while dreaming. I was about to ask her when Heather started.

"Oh, did you hear who is spending the summer up here?" She wiggled her eyebrows at Jo and Shawn.

"No who?" Shawn got up and rested his hand on my shoulder.

"The Valdis's." Heather let the name float on the air.

"Why?" Shawn's voice dropped, and he frowned.

"Magnus is evaluating our clan, and there's a rumor they might move here."

Shawn stiffened beside me, and Jo looked back down at her watch. "Would you look at the time? I have to go." She disappeared without a goodbye.

"What's so important about the Valdis's?" I asked, my gaze shifting between Heather and Shawn.

Shawn opened his mouth to say something but stopped and pushed on the inside of his ear before glancing at Heather, who was doing the same thing. "Copy that base, we're on our way."

"So much for a night off," Heather said. "See you later, Liz." Heather disappeared, and I turned to Shawn.

"Ivan is calling for back up. I'm sorry, we'll find time to spend together soon. I promise." He kissed me quickly then disappeared, leaving me alone in his padded room without answering my question.

Chapter 4

I closed my eyes, thinking of my bedroom, but when I opened them, I was in the clearing with the creepy mineshaft. Nothing had changed since last time I'd dreamed of it. The grass was short, brown, and dry, the sun beat down on me, and I felt a drop of sweat run down my back. The wind hadn't picked up yet, and I didn't hear the pleading for help I normally did. It was dead calm; there were no birds, no animals, and best of all, no mares, at least for the moment.

I didn't know why my dreams kept bringing me there. I'd never seen the clearing in real life, but since my first run in with Stalker, I came to this place at least once a week. There was something dark in the mineshaft. Shawn and I decided that whatever it was could stay down there.

I was about to go back to my bedroom when the scratchy voice of Stalker called from somewhere behind me. "Elizabeth, when are you going to realize there is no escape?"

I thought of a 1911 Colt. "You're back." I tried to sound like I didn't care. "Took you long enough." Stalker, the mare who gave me the brand, was standing fifteen feet from me. He was tall and thin, wearing a pair of cargo shorts and a black T-shirt. His hands were in his pockets like he was just hanging out with nothing better to do. He looked human until you started really looking. His arms and legs were a little too long for his torso, and his grayish skin made him appear sick. When his mouth was closed, it looked normal, with thin, almost pink lips, but as soon as he opened them to speak, his razor-sharp teeth sent chills down my spine. His eyes were just like Pigskin and Twiggy-Squatch's, gaping holes of blackness. He made me want to scream and run, but that was what he wanted me to do. What he wanted humans to do. He was a mare, he fed on fear, and he literally scared his prey to death.

"Oh, lamp chop I've been back on this plane for quite some time." He walked around me, giving me a wide birth. "I've been busy though and haven't had a chance to check on you."

I moved as he moved around me, keeping my sights leveled on him. I wanted to shoot him, and I could try, but with my dreamcatcher over my bed, the bullet wouldn't hurt him, and he couldn't hurt me. "What have you been doing?"

"Regaining my strength. I found an untapped town and feasted. I'm almost as strong as I was before your boy-toy killed me the first time." He jerked his head microscopically. Not trusting him, I glanced over my shoulder and ducked when I saw another mare running toward me. I let him come, bracing myself in case the dreamcatcher decided not to work. With less than a foot between us, he hit my bubble, bounced off, flew through the air, and landed on his back.

"You brought friends tonight?" I pointed the gun at him again.

"Just one, I wanted to confirm what the others told me when I returned. They were right, you can't hurt us, and we can't hurt you." His steps around me became quicker and harder. "This is not what I wanted, no, not at all. I can't afford to lose any more power." He stopped and cocked his head to the side like he was listening to something far away, then he disappeared.

"Liz, what are you doing?" Shawn asked from behind me. I spun with my gun up; the mare had tried to trick me with Shawn before, but as soon as Shawn showed me his blue eyes, I knew I was safe.

"Just having a chat with Stalker." I searched for the one who ran into my shield, but he was nowhere to be found. Damn, I would've loved to watch Shawn kill him for me.

"What happened? Is everything okay?" I walked over and took his hand.

"Yeah, Ivan, one of the knights requested back-up. Heather and I went, but they already had the situation under control." He scanned the clearing and shivered. "Can we get out of here?"

"Please." I shivered too, letting him pull me into his arms. "Where are we going?"

He tightened his grip. "You'll see." The clearing morphed into a beach with turquoise water lapping at the shore. I let go and took in the long expanse of beach with the whitest sand I'd ever seen.

"Have you been here before?" I wanted to know where we were because I wanted to move there as soon as possible.

"I wish, I found it on a calendar a few years back." He ran a hand through his hair and gave me a tight smile. Something was bugging him, but I didn't understand how since we were standing in paradise. "I think it's an island in the South Pacific."

"I want to move here, find the calendar so I'll know where to forward my mail." I wiggled my eyebrows at him then thought of my bathing suit because I wanted to see if the water was as warm as it looked.

"I'll see if I can find it." He chuckled and his eyes widened when he saw my suit. "What are you doing?"

"Beach, turquoise water, it's in the eighties, you can't expect me to pass on swimming." I move to let the bath-tub warm water splashed my feet. "This is amazing. I'm so moving here." I took a few more steps into the water until it came to my knees but stopped when realized I was alone.

"Liz, wait we need to talk." He sat down in the sand and stared at his feet like they were about to grow wings and he would turn into Hermes.

"What's going on?" I could tell by the tone of his voice something was wrong. I walked out of the water, sat beside him, and bumped my shoulder with his.

"It's the Valdis's," he said, still not making eye contact with me.

"I knew something was wrong when Heather mentioned them. What is it? Did your parents arrange a marriage with their daughter or something?" I meant it as a joke, but when I peered at Shawn, I wanted to take it back.

"No, but close." I waited while he seemed to be arranging his thoughts. "Their daughter, Kristina, and I have dated on and off since we were fourteen." He trailed off like he didn't know how to tell me that he wanted her back.

"I get it." I got to my feet and backed away. I wanted to run and hide but then I thought about how Shawn left when Billy kissed me. I wasn't going to go down that road again. I mentally pulled up my big-girl panties, stood my ground and waited for him to continue.

"No, you don't." He stood and grasped my hands. "We spent the summers together, and when you're training, there isn't that much to do. Magnus and my Dad worked together a lot before he was promoted so we always seemed to end up together." He ran a hand through his hair. "It seemed like a natural thing."

"Are you trying to tell me you want to go back to her?" I pulled my hands out of his and held them up in a stay back motion.

"No, God, I'm saying this all wrong." Shawn stood up and walked to the water's edge. "That was before, Liz. It was before I met you; before I knew what I wanted to do with my life."

"What do you want?" I watched his shoulders slump.

"I want you." He twisted and moved toward me. He pushed a piece of hair out of my face. "But it won't be easy. Kristina is determined when she wants something and, based on the number of instant messages she's been sending me, she wants me back."

"Are you sure you don't want her?" I felt like an idiot, standing there in my bathing suit while we talked about his ex and if he wanted her back or not.

"God no, she's too high maintenance for me. I'm worried because I don't think she'll take rejection from me lightly, and it doesn't help that my dad and her parents want us together."

"Why do they care?"

"We are both strong knights, we would make strong baby knights." He gulped, looking anywhere but at me.

"They are trying to arrange a marriage then." I moved away from him and stared at the horizon. I didn't know how to feel, he didn't want Kristina back, but if his parents and her parents pushed them together it would be hard not to go back to her, and what did it mean for me? Shawn's dad already hated me; he thought I wasn't good enough for him. What would happen with Kristina here?

"No, but as I told you before, we marry our kind." I heard Shawn get to his feet. "Liz, I'm with you." He wrapped his arms around me from behind and I leaned back into him. "I'm telling you this, so you're prepared when you meet her. I'm not going back to Kristina and I'm not letting you go. Whether you like it or not."

I twisted and met his eyes. He was telling me the truth, and the fact was, the more time I spent with him the more my feelings of liking him were morphing into something closer to loving him. I wanted to tell him but what if he didn't feel the same?

"Oh, before I forget, we're having a BBQ on Monday afternoon. Will you come?" he asked, dragging me out of my mushy thoughts.

"Yeah, as long it's okay with your parents."

"My mom will freak out if you don't come and, who cares what my dad thinks."

I smiled, I loved his mom. "Okay, what time?"

"I think food will be ready around three."

"I'll be there." I stood on my tiptoes and kissed him, trying to tell him with my kiss how I felt about him. He picked me up so he could have better access and starting walking as I wrapped my legs around his waist.

When the water hit my legs, I broke the kiss and let out a startled yelp. "Shawn, what are you doing?"

"You wanted to go swimming, right?" He threw me into the air, and I screamed before the water stopped my fall and I came up spluttering, wanting to be mad but laughing instead.

"You're going to pay for that." I ran at him and tried to pull him down into the water, but all I did was force him to take a step back.

"Is that all you've got?" He crossed his arms over his chest and laughed.

Not giving up, I hooked my ankle around his calf and pushed him hard. He lost his footing and crashed into the sand, landing on his butt. "No, you haven't seen the half of it." I ran away from him as he got to his feet and he chased me down the beach.

Chapter 5

The weekend went by in a blur. Shawn was busy with his parents and worked every night, they needed all-hands-on-deck since it was the biggest tourist weekend of the summer, and tourists were notorious for not sleeping with dreamcatchers. I spent the weekend going with my parents to graduation parties and BBQ's at their friend's houses. It wasn't a great weekend, but I got to spend time with Billy, and my parents were cool the entire weekend.

Monday morning, I rolled over and gazed out the window. The sun hadn't peeked over the mountains yet. I closed my eyes and rolled to face the wall. I hadn't slept well since Friday night. Since Stalker was back, he picked up right where he left off harassing me. I tried to go back to sleep but every time I closed my eyes all I saw was Billy hanging by his neck from a rope.

I lay in bed thinking about how nice sleep was before I had been branded. I didn't have anything to do until Shawn's BBQ, so after breakfast my Dad and I installed my lightbar. I didn't know what time it was when we finished, but I had plenty of time before I needed to be at Shawn's. After I showered, I saw the notification light blinking on my phone.

Liz, where are you? It was from Jo and I pursed my lips thinking; we didn't have anything planned.

I'm at home why?

Didn't Shawn tell you about the BBQ? I thought you would be here already.

Yes, he told me to come by around three. I checked my watch; it was barely one.

Jackass, it started at noon.

I'll be there as soon as I can. I didn't know what the big deal was but, I ran my brush through my wet hair hoping it would air dry by the time I got to Shawn's and put on a pair of jean shorts and a plain black, V-neck, T-shirt. I ran down the stairs, passing Mom as I grabbed my keys off the hook.

"Where are you going?"

"Shawn told me the wrong time for the BBQ and now I'm late."

"Okay, sweetie just don't drive too fast."

"I won't." I closed the front door and ran to my Jeep. As I drove, I wondered how Shawn got the time wrong. I didn't care, at least I got to see him. My phone beeped as I drove, but I waited to check it until I reached the stop sign. It was a message from Shawn.

I'm an ass, please hurry, everyone wants to meet you.

I put my phone on the seat next to me and pulled onto the highway wondering who *everyone* was.

The party was bigger than I expected, considering the

parking lot at the Freeman Mansion was close to full when I arrived. I parked, got out, and noticed thunderheads stacking up in the west. I hoped I'd have enough time to eat before the storm rained out the party. I walked toward the residence entrance when I heard someone call my name.

I turned to the back of the house and saw Billy jogging toward me. "Liz, where've you been?"

"Shawn told me it didn't start till three." I crossed my arms over my chest.

"Yeah, Shawn said he must have told you the wrong time. His mom is pissed but come on, he needs you."

"What's going on?" I asked as we quickly walked around to the back of the house.

"His ex-girlfriend won't leave him alone, so you need to mark your territory." Billy held open an eight-foot-tall wrought-iron gate, attached to a matching fence. It ran from the house thirty feet up the mountain then across the length of the house before it came back down to meet the other end of the house. The lawn was thick and freshly cut. Blue Spruce and Douglas Fir trees were sprinkled around the yard. I thought they were new since they were all the same size. Against the house, there was a huge concrete patio with round standing tables spread out, and there was an outdoor kitchen with a five-foot-long grill smoking with food cooking. There was a set of long tables set up near the grill filled with bowls and platters of food. People stood around talking, the adults with red plastic cups or beer bottles in their hands. Kids were playing tag on the lawn and the teenagers were standing in small groups, looking bored, with pop cans in their hands.

I scanned the crowd for Shawn. He was standing next to a girl who made every other girl in Twisted Pines look like Medusa, well except Heather, no one could compete with her. This girl was tall, at least five foot ten, her platinum blonde hair so light and shiny it had to be natural. She had high cheekbones and a button nose, combined with her bowtie lips she was a knockout, and I wasn't into girls.

Shawn and the girl were talking to Jon, Shawn's dad, and another man I didn't recognize. Shawn was smiling at whatever they were talking about, but it didn't reach his eyes. As I watched, the girl would move closer to Shawn, and he would move away and scan the crowd. When his eyes finally landed on me his whole body seemed to relax and he gave me a real smile. Not the polite one he had been giving his dad and the other man. He said something, then left the group, coming straight for me.

"Who's that?" I asked Billy before Shawn reached us.

"Kristina, the one I was telling you about." Billy took a step away as Shawn approached.

"I'm sorry, my mom is so mad at me." He put his hands in his pockets and stared at the ground. "I don't know why I told you three. Thanks for coming." Shawn glanced at Billy, then at me. Billy didn't know what the Knight Flyers really did, and we all wanted it to stay that way, but it was hard not talking about it when he was around.

"Shawn, it's okay, I'm here." I reached for his hand, and he met me halfway with a grin before pulling me in for a hug.

"It's about time you got here," Jo said from behind me.

"You should have been here an hour ago."

"Shawn told me three." I pushed away, he was squeezing me a little too tight.

"Way to go Shawn." Jo punched his shoulder. "Are you hungry? There's a ton of food and it's all fantastic."

"I could eat." My mouth watered at the mention of food, I hadn't eaten since breakfast.

"I hate to eat and run, but I have to go mow my parents' lawn, or I'll be grounded for the rest of the summer." Billy took a step toward the back of the house.

"Oh, bummer." Jo gave him puppy dog eyes. "I'll walk you to your car. Shawn, get Liz something to eat, and I'll be back."

"The girl you were talking to is Kristina?" I asked, waiting for him to lead the way to the food.

"Yeah, and she won't leave me alone. I told her I have a girlfriend, but it's like she's deaf or something."

"Well, let's see if she's blind too." We walked over to the food table and I tried to ignore the eyes I felt following me. I picked up a plate and was about to put a spoonful of fruit salad on it when Jenny, Shawn's mom, stopped me. "Liz, you made it," she sang, giving me a hug. I was glad I hadn't put any food on my plate yet, otherwise it would've ended up all over her. "Yeah, sorry I'm late." I pulled back from her.

"It's not your fault from what I hear." She squinted at Shawn.

"Things have been a little crazy." Shawn stared at his feet.

"Yes, well, in any case, I'm glad you made it. Get some food; there're drinks in the trough over there and enjoy."

"Thank you for having me," I said to her back as she left us to talk to other guests.

I filled my plate with a bit of everything then sat at an empty table. Shawn got us each a soda then sat by me. "We haven't had a lot of time to talk this weekend. How is everything going?" I asked, taking a bite of pasta salad.

"The nights have been crazy busy, I can't believe how many people come up here without dreamcatchers." Shawn ran his hands through his hair.

"I wish Stalker would've found someone without one." I stared at my plate and kept my voice low.

"I'm sorry, we're going to get our schedules soon, then Heather and I will come up with a way to keep you company when you aren't in dream training." Shawn reached across the table and took my left hand.

"Yeah, thanks, I wish there was a way to get them to leave me alone." I took another bite of food.

"We'll figure it out." We went silent, lost in our own thoughts after that. I thought about how nice it would be not to wake up more tired than when I went to bed. Shawn's eyes were darting around, and I thought he was probably keeping an eye out for Kristina.

Finished with my food, I people watched. "Is everyone here a knight?"

Shawn nodded his head. "Or they work for Knights Inc. Do you want to meet them?"

"Well, I'm here, and I'll be working with them, it would be nice if I learned their names." I was nervous but meeting them now would be better than my first day of work. I wondered how many of them knew my bio-dad, Victor, and if they liked him or not. I hoped they wouldn't hold him leaving the clan against me.

"Let's go." He took my plate and stood.

I followed him to the trash can then faced the crowd. Jo was standing nearby, talking to her parents. They had been at Shawn's before we left for prom, but I hadn't really met them.

Shawn took my hand, and we joined them. "Hi, Jo," I said as we came to a stop forming an informal circle.

"Liz, these are my parents, Tom, and Tina. Tom is the head trainer, you'll probably be spending a lot of time with him."

"Liz, you're Victor's daughter, right? Jo's told me so much about you." Tina offered me her hand.

I took it awkwardly and shook it. "That is what I'm told. It's nice to meet you."

"Jo told me you have a lot of Victor's talents. I look forward to seeing them this week." Tom nodded his head at me.

"I hope I live up to the hype," I said, trying to get a measure on my new boss? Teacher? Knight? I wasn't sure what to call him yet. He looked like most of the people in attendance, light skin, light hair, and light eyes, the wrinkles around his eyes and mouth when he smiled told me that he smiled a lot and I smiled back at him.

"You will. I'll see you tomorrow morning around eight?" he asked, scanning the crowd.

"Sure." I cocked an eyebrow at Jo as she smiled from ear to ear for some reason.

"Shawn, is this Liz Robinson?" A woman in her forties asked, joining our circle.

"Lawson, actually," I said, giving her a tight smile. I wondered how many other people would call me by Victor's last name and not my real one.

Her smile faltered for a second then she gave me a hug. "Your father was one of the best people I've ever known."

I patted her back lightly, silently asking Shawn to save me. Finally, the woman stepped back. "Forgive me I'm Stacy, Shawn's aunt. Your dad and I spent a lot of time together as teenagers."

"Wow, I bet you could tell some stories about him." I wanted to know if she knew about any of the research he did on the gate.

"I sure do, but not while Jon is around." She gave Jon and the man I had seen with Shawn when I arrived a tight smile as they approached.

"Hey Dad, Magnus." Shawn pulled me to his side, leaving his hand on my waist.

"This must be the girl you were telling me about, Victor's daughter," a man in his mid-fifties asked. He was built like a linebacker, thick and stout with very little fat. His hair had probably once been thick and blond but now it was thin and gray. His bushy eyebrows drew together as he assessed me. "She looks like him, but are you sure she has the gift?"

I wanted to put this guy in his place. Who did he think he was to judge me without even introducing himself? I was about to open my mouth when Shawn squeezed me in warning.

"I've seen it, and she has some talent considering she hasn't had any training." Jon gave me a tight smile.

Had Jon just paid me a compliment? "Thank you."

"Have you tested her in the simulator yet?" Magnus eyed me up and down again.

"No, her mother wouldn't let her begin her training until the school year ended." Jon's eyes moved back and forth, giving me the impression that he was uncomfortable with Magnus around me. Heather said he would be evaluating the clan, maybe Jon wasn't as confident as he let on.

"Hi, Daddy," the girl I had seen Shawn with when I arrived said, popping up next to him from out of nowhere it seemed. "Shawn." She dipped her head and batted her eyes at him. I glanced at Jo as she rolled her eyes and I held in a giggle.

"Kristina, this is my girlfriend, Liz." Shawn squeezed me tighter to his side. A flash of lightning caught my eye before the crash of thunder echoed off the mountains. Jon and Magnus frowned. Kristina's smile fell for a split-second before it was back in place, and she extended her hand to me.

"Always nice to meet one of Shawn's girls," she said as I took her hand to shake it.

I really wanted to tell her to keep her hands off my man, but before I could Magnus started speaking. "Why don't we test her now, just to get a baseline? I'm sure everyone would enjoy watching Victor's daughter."

Jon gave me a worried look, which surprised me. I thought he wanted me to fail. "Of course, Liz, why don't we get a jump start on your training? Shawn, go get Brandon to boot up the simulator and we'll be there shortly."

Shawn winked at me then glanced at his dad. "On it." He let go and went toward the house.

"The simulator?" I stared at Jo waiting for an explanation.

"Don't worry, you'll kick ass," she whispered as Jon whistled to get everyone's attention.

"Since a storm is going to force us inside, I've arranged for some entertainment," Jon said as everyone turned to see what the whistle was about. "As you know Liz Robinson-Lawson, is joining the Squires this summer and she hasn't had her baseline test yet. If you would like to watch her first go around in the simulator, we'll start in ten minutes. If she is anything like her father, we'll be in for a treat."

There was some cheering and murmuring as everyone moved their eyes from Jon to me. I smiled, wanting to roll my eyes, I couldn't believe how two-faced Jon was. Why was he being so nice to me? The last time I'd seen him he called me a distraction and tried to bribe me to break up with Shawn in exchange for admittance into the Air Force Academy.

I didn't want to do this. I hated speaking in front of people. I had to do something with the simulator while all these people watched? I shook my head, trying to think of a way to get out of it.

"Jo, why don't you take Liz inside and get her set up," Tom said, wiggling his eyebrows.

"Sure, Dad, come on Liz, let's get in there before

everyone else." She hurried toward the door and I jogged after her but not before noticing the frown on Kristina's face.

Once we were clear of the partygoers, Jo slowed down to a walk. "Magnus is such an ass, I'm sorry you have to do this today," she said as we walked down a dark hallway.

"What's the simulator?" My stomach twisted into a knot.

"It's a computer program that simulates dreams. It's not that bad. You'll forget about everyone watching once you're in the program. You will fight mares, but they aren't real, just a computer simulation. It'll almost be like fighting them in your dreams.

"Why almost?" It had been a while since I'd fought a mare. If Jon wouldn't have made me sleep with a dreamcatcher, I could have been killing mares almost every night for the past month.

"There's a lag time from when you think of a weapon and when it materializes, and you can't jump to different locations, the program decides where you are."

"What kind of lag time are we talking about?" I drew my eyebrows together. I was used to weapons manifesting almost instantaneously.

"A second or two. It depends on how hard you concentrate on them."

"Great." My heart started to race as panic took over. *Why did I agree to work for Knights Inc. again?* I stopped and bent over, taking huge breaths.

"Liz, I'm sorry I didn't mean to scare you." Jo rubbed her hand in a circle on my back. "You're going to be fine. You go in, kill as many mares as you can, and you're done. It will be easier than prom, I promise."

"Really?" I straightened, taking a deep breath.

"Yeah, you'll be fine." Jo moved her hand and walked me the rest of the way to the training room.

Chapter 6

"This is the main training area," Jo said as we entered a massive room. The ceiling went up two floors above us and there was a balcony with white wrought-iron spindles surrounding the room. It was divided into sections. Across from me was a boxing ring and next to it was a gym with treadmills, stationary bikes, and free weights. There was a partition wall blocking the view from half the room, and I wondered what was behind it. Across from the boxing ring I found Shaun standing by a computer workstation sitting next to a bed. He was watching another guy clicked buttons on a keyboard. He laughed at something the man working on the computer said and looked up to see us.

"Hey, are you ready?" he asked after jogged across the room meeting us halfway.

"No, this was is the last thing I expected to happen today." I stared at my shaking hands. "I'm not ready for this. I haven't practiced in a month and with all the knights watching. . ." I trailed off as I heard people begin to file in behind me.

"Liz, look at me," Shawn took my hands and bent to meet my eyes. "You will be fine. Just remember what you did prom night. I believe in you."

"You do?" I gave him half a smile.

"Yes," he bent his head further and pressed his lips against mine, making me forget about the room full of people and the simulator. When he pulled away, I smiled as someone nearby cleared their throat. I looked up finding Kristina staring at us with her mouth hanging open. I cocked an eyebrow at her trying to say *he's mine, back off,* with my eyes.

"I don't want to let you down." I blinked then looked at Shawn.

"The only way you could let me down is if you are too scared to try it." Shawn led me over to the bed.

Jon joined us, standing behind Brandon at the computer and cleared his throat. "Let's get started. Liz, take your shoes off and lie down." Jon pointed at the bed behind me.

I sat down on the bed with my hands under my thighs to hide their shaking and taking my shoes off. "Is this going to hurt?"

"No, I'm going to attach these electrodes to your face, hands, feet, and the top of your chest. Then you'll put on the virtual reality goggles and we'll see what you can do." Shawn showed me the electrodes then took the backs off and placed them on my hands and my feet. He put one on my collar bone and one on each side of my face. "Bring your head up for me so I can help you with the goggles." I tipped my head up, and he secured them around my head. "How are you doing?"

I was in complete darkness, and even though I knew I was lying down I was having a problem with my balance. "This is a little disorienting."

"Give Brandon a chance to start the program and it will be better. I'm going to put the earphones on you now. I'll be right here if you need something." Then the noise of the room filled with people was gone. I was in the dark and I couldn't hear anything. I was about to call out for Shawn when I blinked and suddenly, I wasn't in the dark anymore. I was in the high school gym. It was empty and all the lights were off except for one in the middle of the room. It beckoned me and I ran, wanting to stand in the light like it would save me from the monsters.

Once there, I made a slow circle, I was alone. There was no noise, no movement. I was about to ask them to start the program when something ran toward me. I quickly thought of a twelve-gauge, semi-automatic shotgun. I didn't care what was coming for me, I was going to kill it. Jo was right, it seemed to take forever to manifest the gun and the mare had almost reached me by the time I had it at my shoulder. I aimed at his knees and squeezed the trigger twice, once for each knee. My aim was on and the mare fell to his knees screaming in pain but, not giving up, he crawled toward me. I switched to my dad's 1911 Colt .45 and shot him at point-blank range in the head. He fell, dissolving into nothing before he hit the ground.

I heard a noise behind me and found a zombie ambling toward me. Using the .45 I blew a hole in its head and it dissolved like the first one. I turned in a slow circle, wondering how many I would have to kill before I was done.

Something grabbed me from behind and pulled me backwards. I thought of a scalpel, wanting to stab it in the ribs and cut it as deeply as I could but the lag time manifesting it was killing me, literally, the monster was squeezing the air out of my lungs. I didn't give up but, by the time the knife was in my hand, I couldn't reach him. My vision was going dark. I had to do something. I lifted my foot and stomped on his as hard as I could. His grip loosened enough for me to get a lungful of air and I swung around to see what I was up against. I screamed when I saw it. It was covered in long black fur, it had pointy ears, a long snout with a black nose and sharp teeth to match. *Wait were werewolves real?* I shook my head, *Stop thinking and fight.* I plunged the scalpel into the side of his neck and pulled it across his throat. The mare's grip loosened, and I pushed him away from me as another one grabbed my ankle.

I glanced behind me thinking of a machete and twisting, brought it down on the monster's arm, but it reared back before I made contact and I only scratched it. It reminded me of Pigskin, and I took half a second to revel in the idea that I was finally going to kill one of my tormentors. While I thought, he got to his feet and charged me. The machete was too long for what I needed so I thought of my Buck knife and pushed it into his gut when he was within range. I tried to yank it up his torso to gut him, but he tripped me, and I fell hard on my back dropping the knife. Before I knew what was happening, his knees were on my chest and I couldn't breathe. He lowered his mouth to mine and sucked what little air I had left out of my lungs and I swear I felt my soul leave as everything went black.

Chapter 7

I sat up quickly, taking in a lungful of air. I pulled the wires off and fumbled with the goggles as I fought off the nausea trying to work my lunch up my throat. An arm went around me, steadying me. I opened my eyes and gave Shawn a weak smile. "You're okay," he whispered into my hair. "You did great."

The room exploded with applause, and I glanced around, remembering I had an audience. I felt myself turn red, and I let my hair form a curtain, hiding my face from the crowd. "Are you sure that was your first time?" Jo came over and gave me a one-armed hug. "Cause, damn, you're good."

"I am? I lost to the fourth one, how is that good?" I backed away from her. Mad at myself for losing after only killing three, I should've had the fourth one.

"It keeps going until you lose," she laughed at me. "It took me years to kill one."

"Really?" I couldn't believe I was better than her.

"Years. I got past my first one last year and I train on the simulator three times a week. You're making us all look bad."

"But I probably have more practical experience." Shawn was looking at the corner of the room. I followed his eyes. Kristina was standing next to her dad and a woman. Kristina had her arms crossed over her chest and was staring at me with a frown.

"What's that about?" I asked Shawn, jerking my head toward them.

"After you killed the first mare, she made a fuss, she thinks you were cheating." Shawn shrugged. "Do you know how long it took me to kill my first one?"

"No." I ran my hand through my hair.

"Three years." He tilted my face toward him by my chin with his fingers. "You're going to make history."

"Well, I'm older than you were when you started, and I have experience." I kept trying to rationalize why I was good. It wasn't talent alone.

"Stop. Look at me," Shawn said as I refused to meet his eyes. "You have a gift that all of us wish we had. Stop making excuses for being good at something."

I peeked at the mark on my wrist, I could just see the outline next to my watch band. If I lived long enough to celebrate my eighteenth birthday, I needed to be the best, not just better than a bunch of newbies. "Thanks, but I need to be better."

"You're just starting, give yourself time." He put his arm around my shoulder. "How are you feeling?"

"Fine, I don't think I'll fall over if I stand up now."

"It takes a while to get used to." Shawn helped me to my feet. "Come on, the rest of the crew want to meet you." He walked me over to a group of people standing near the boxing ring.

"Back in my day we didn't have the simulator, we threw you to the mares as soon as we thought you were ready and hoped you survived," an older man said, laughing as we approached. "Congratulations young lady, just like your father." He clapped me on the back. "I'm Ivan, if you need anything, call me and I'll do what I can to help you."

"Thanks." I gave him a genuine smile. Behind him, Jon was talking with Magnus. Our eyes met for a second. He shook his head so slightly that I was probably the only one who noticed, and I looked away. His facial expression didn't change, and I didn't know if it meant I should have done better or if I'd done something wrong, either way, I didn't think it was a good thing.

"You remind me so much of Victor," Stacy said, taking my elbow, and leading me away from Ivan and the others.

"Really?" I wanted to feel honored, but if Victor and her parted like he did with Jon, it may not be a good thing.

"Yes." She laughed. "He always came up with the most interesting weapons."

"You mean the scalpel?"

"Yes, I never would have thought about it, but in close quarters it would work, and they are about the sharpest thing made."

"That's what I was thinking too. That and Pet Cemetery."

She looked at me confused for a second. "The Achilles tendon. You're right, I see why you thought of it now." She glanced at her watch. "Listen, I have to go, but I would love to get together sometime and talk to you about your dad. There are things you need to know."

I felt my eyes go wide. Did she know what he was trying to do before he died? "Yes, please. I don't know what my schedule is yet, but here let me give you my number and we can get together."

She entered my number into her phone and left, glancing over her shoulder a few times before she reached the door.

I spent the rest of the afternoon listening to the knights talk about their training experiences and what they thought I should concentrate on. Ivan said guns and munitions were the best but since I already had a good handle on them, I should stick with pointy objects. Morten, Jeff's dad, said I should work on my reflexes, you never knew what weapon would work better on what mare, so being able to change weapons quickly was key. Fredrick said hand to hand was the most important because if your mind shut down, your body would know how to protect itself. After what felt like days, Shawn dragged me away from the group with the excuse of his mom wanting to talk. I had a list as long as my arm of things I needed to practice before I was ready to become a knight. Shawn led me through a door at the back of the room and took the stairs up.

"I thought you might want a break." He stopped on the landing between the first and second floor.

"Yeah, I was nervous about tomorrow, but now I feel like I need to study and practice twenty-four-seven if I'm going to become a knight soon."

"Don't let them get to you." Shawn continued leading me up the stairs. "They don't talk to squires unless it's to tell them what they are doing wrong. You impressed them.”

“What about your dad? He gave me a weird look.”

“I’m not sure. He was standing by Brandon while you were testing. He didn’t say anything, just watched. I think he’s impressed but doesn’t want anyone else to know since he was against training you.”

“I hope you’re right. Where are we going?” We stopped climbing when we reached the third floor and went down the hall.

“To my room, I haven’t had you alone in weeks,” he wiggled his eyebrows at me, and I giggled. It had been a long time since we were alone together in reality. Not that hanging out with Shawn in my dreams was a bad thing, but it wasn’t the same as real time. We jogged down the hall, glancing behind us every few steps, to make sure no one was following us. When we were inside his room, he shut the door and pounced on me. Well, he didn’t jump on me, but he had me in his arms in seconds and my lips were locked with his a half a second later.

It had been a long time since I kissed him with abandon, not having to worry about anyone watching or interrupting us. His tongue probed my lips asking for admittance and I opened them letting our tongues duel in a sword fight neither of us wanted to win.

I didn’t know how long we stood there before a loud knock at the door broke us apart and I gazed at Shawn, pleading with him to ignore whoever it was. They knocked again. “Shawn, I know you’re in there. Heather saw you come this way,” Kristina said from the other side of the door. Shawn shrugged, let me go, and opened the door.

Deflated, I took my flip-flops off and sat cross legged in the middle of the bed. Was I staking my territory? Maybe, but he was my boyfriend.

"Kristina, what can I do for you?" he asked, sounding forcibly polite but invited her in.

"Your dad needs you, he asked me to find you." She batted her eyes at him again. I was glad I didn't have to flirt with Shawn to get his attention, I think it would have made me dizzy.

"What does he want now?" Shawn looked up as if he was asking God. "Don't leave. I'll be right back."

"I won't." I didn't have to fake my affection for Shawn or pretend it was anything other than what it was. Shawn kissed me on the cheek then ran out the door, leaving Kristina in the doorway. She was staring at me with her eyebrows raised and her eyes narrowed.

Ignoring her, I stared out the window at the rain coming down, thinking about how much I enjoyed kissing Shawn and pretending Kristina wasn't there.

Not taking being ignored well, Kristina strutted further into the room, stopping in front of me, blocking my view. "So how did you do it?" She put a piece of gum in her mouth and dropped the wrapper on the floor.

"Do what?" I got off the bed, picked up the wrapper and put it in the trashcan, then reclaimed my spot.

"Cheat on the simulation. No one kills a mare their first time, let alone three."

"Sorry to ruin your day, but I didn't cheat. I'd never been in the training center. I wouldn't know how to cheat if I wanted to. I have fought mares though."

"Fine, don't tell me, I will figure it out." She walked

around, looking at the posters on the wall. "I wouldn't waste my time with Shawn if I were you." She snapped her gum.

"Good thing I'm not you then." I wouldn't let this girl get to me as Tiffany had.

Kristina's face fell for a second before her fake, too bright smile was back. "He's just killing time with you. Shawn and I are meant to be. Our parents have been waiting for us to be old enough to get married and have kids since we were five."

"Why would what your parents want matter?" I rolled my eyes. "Last time I checked this was a free country." If she was trying to warn me away from Shawn, it wasn't working.

"Do you know how hard Jon can make your life?" Kristina crossed her arms over her chest.

"Do you know how hard he has already made it?" I got to my feet. I didn't like her looking down on me. "Kristina you have no idea what my life has been like since Knights Inc. came to town. You will not come between me and Shawn, so back off."

"Is that a threat?" She moved her hands to her hips like she was trying to channel her inner Wonder Woman.

"Only a warning." I left my arms crossed. She wasn't going to scare me away.

"Hey, what's going on?" Shawn asked, coming in and frowning at me, as Kristina's face crumbled and she squeezed her eyes shut before letting out a sob and holding her hand in front of her face to hide her tears.

"Seriously?" I moved to the door. "She was just telling me to stay away from you. I tell her to back off and she starts crying." I wasn't going to apologize.

"Shawn, I'm scared. I think she wants to beat me up." Kristina clung to him and while he hugged her, she opened her tear free eyes and winked at me.

I rolled my eyes. Shawn was playing right into her hands. "Right, like I could beat her up." I walked out, heading toward the stairs. I wanted to go home. She was a knight, which meant she could probably beat the crap out of me with one hand, while she put her makeup on with the other. But if Shawn thought she needed comfort, I would not stand around and watch. I stomped down the hall until I reached the stairs, then ran down them only to have Jon stop me at the bottom.

"Leaving so soon, Liz?" Jon grinned at me like Batman's Joker, his lips pulling at the sides of his face so hard it looked painful. It was like he knew Kristina was messing with me and Shawn.

"Yeah, my mom wants me home early since I start work tomorrow."

"Where's Shawn and Kristina?"

"Up in his room." I couldn't let Jon know how upset I was. It was exactly what he wanted.

"Liz, I can tell you're falling for Shawn, but be careful with your heart," he said softly almost like he cared.

"What is that supposed to mean?" I was stunned as my anger turned to hurt.

"Shawn and Kristina have been on again off again since they were old enough to take an interest in the opposite sex.

Since she's moving here, they will probably take things to the next level."

"What?" I asked, the anger draining from my body. It felt like my heart was being ripped from my chest instead. "I thought they were just here for the evaluation."

"Yes, but if Kristina wants to stay at the end of the summer, I'll let her. She's eighteen, so she can work wherever she wants."

I stood there like a statue; I didn't know how to react. Jon would let her stay? Maybe Shawn and I were never meant to be together, but I would not let Jon know how much the thought of it freaked me out. "Well, I guess we will have to see what happens."

"Like I said, I don't want to see you get hurt." Jon bowed his head slightly and walked away, leaving me standing in the entryway on the verge of tears.

Chapter 8

I stood in the foyer, staring into space, my mind blank until I heard someone coming down the stairs. I glanced behind me and not seeing anyone I ran for the door, I didn't want to talk to anyone. The rain was coming down by the bucketful and I was soaked by the time I made it inside my Jeep. I started it and flipped the defroster on to evaporate the fog condensing on the windshield. Through my rearview mirror, I saw Heather at the door watching me. I didn't want to talk to her. I put my seat belt on and left, pretending I didn't see her when she waved.

Too much had happened too quickly. I couldn't believe Shawn automatically took Kristina's side. It didn't matter what their history was, I was his girlfriend, he should've at least listened to my side.

I drove toward home, but I didn't want to go home and deal with the thousands of questions my parents would ask. Instead, I drove to the meadow where Shawn and I spent prom. I needed to be myself and figure out how to handle everything.

I parked where Shawn had on prom night and gazed out the windshield. The rain slacked off, and I turned my radio off to listen to the random drops falling on the roof. The meadow was green with grass intermingled with a few pockets of blue and yellow as the first flowers of the year bloomed. I wanted to forget about the BBQ and just enjoy nature, but I couldn't get the image of Shawn hugging Kristina out of my head.

Kristina was going to be a bigger problem than Tiffany had been. She knew Shawn better than I did and who knew how close they were before they broke up. Had he loved her? Was Jon right? Were they killing time until Shawn finished school? Shawn was my first boyfriend, I didn't how to act. I wished I had someone to talk to about it with, but Billy wouldn't know what to do, Jo was his first girlfriend. My mom would be of no help. Jo and Heather were biased toward Shawn, not that I could blame them. I was on my own.

Was Shawn worth fighting for? I thought about all the firsts I had with him. He had been my first kiss, had taken me to my first dance, he had been the first person who made me feel loved other than my parents. I didn't know if he loved me or not but even though we had seen little of each other lately, I was falling in love with him. In a lot of ways, he knew me better than even Billy did. Would it better to let him go before I fell harder for him or hold out and hope that our relationship was more meaningful than what he had with Kristina?

The rain stopped, and the sun came out, framed between two peaks. It would set soon, and I wanted to stay and enjoy the quiet for a little while longer. I touched the rune hanging from my neck. Stacey wanted to talk to me about Victor. I wondered if she knew what he had been doing before he died. Maybe he told her how to close the gate. We needed a hint or a direction to go. If we didn't find it, I would live my life exhausted until I couldn't take it anymore and let the mares have me.

I shook my head, I couldn't think like that. I would figure out a way to close the gate, and I would live a normal life. I thought about the simulator; the mares hadn't been that hard to kill. Stalker was a lot harder to kill in my dream than the mares in the program. Maybe Kristina was right, maybe someone rigged it.

I was pulled out of my thoughts as the sun sank behind the mountains, shifting the blue sky into a canvas of color from midnight blue to an almost electric pink and every color in between. It was amazing how staring at something as common as a sunset could make me forget about my problems.

After Mother Nature's performance, I went home in the dark, using my light bar to light my way and made some decisions. I was going to fight for Shawn. I was going to find out if someone messed with the simulator. I was going to close the gate, and, in the meantime, I would become the best knight, Knights Inc. had ever seen.

My phone exploded as soon as I was back in cell phone service, and I pulled over to see what was going on. I had text messages from Shawn, Billy, and my parents, and I had three voice mails. I opened the message from Shawn first.

Call me when you get home. Then **Where are you? I just called your house and your mom said you weren't there.**

I leaned back in my seat and closed my eyes. Not this again. I put my phone on the passenger seat ignoring the other messages. Everyone was freaking out about where I was just like prom. I drove the rest of the way home wondering if my parents had called the sheriff yet.

Every light in the house was on when I parked, like I could find my way home from the lights alone. The front door opened, and Mom ran outside. Dad stood in the doorway with his phone to his ear.

I took my keys out of the ignition, grabbed my phone, then got out, mentally preparing myself for the lecture waiting for me.

"Elizabeth Lawson," Mom started as soon as my door opened. "Where have you been? Shawn called two hours ago for you."

I rolled my eyes while I shut the door. "Mom, calm down. I went to the meadow to watch the sunset. There isn't any cell phone service up there." I walked by her, wanting to escape to my room.

"You can't do that, Liz. You need to tell someone where you're going." Mom trailed behind me as I edged past Dad.

"Yeah, she's home and safe. I'll tell her, Billy." Dad ended the call and followed me into the kitchen. "Billy has been out looking for you for an hour."

"Everyone freaks out way too easily. Can't I have a place to be by myself and not have an Amber Alert issued?" I went to the cabinet and got a glass out.

"Sweetheart, you can but you need to tell us where you'll be." Mom stood behind the bar with her arms crossed over her chest. "What if you hit another moose, and we didn't know where you were?"

I filled my glass up with water and rolled my eyes again without them seeing. "I'm sorry. Next time I'll call." I gulped my water down wanting to go to bed.

"That's not good enough." Dad blocked the doorway when I tried to leave. "What's going on with you? Ever since you started dating Shawn, you've changed. You're tired all the time, you go places without telling anyone and Mom said you were almost late for school on Friday. Are you pregnant?" He had his arms crossed over his chest staring me down.

I glanced at Mom. I wanted to ask her for help. She knew why I was tired all the time, and we would not tell Dad. "How can I be pregnant when I'm still a virgin?" I carefully put the glass in the sink instead of throwing it at the wall. "I'm tired because I haven't been sleeping well. It has nothing to do with Shawn. I didn't realize I needed to tell you everything I do."

"We are your parents; your wellbeing is important to us."

"Do you want me to tell you everything? What time I went to the bathroom? What I ate for breakfast?" I put my hands on my hips.

"I don't think she's responsible enough to work for Knights Inc." He narrowed his eyes at me.

"It's too late for me to quit. I already quit my old job and there aren't any others." I wasn't giving up on Knights Inc. I didn't care if I had to sneak around to do it.

"She's right, Burt, she can't quit now." Mom's voice was soft, and her eyes were sad. She knew what would happen if I didn't train.

"Fine, but I expect you to tell us before you go anywhere out of cell range."

I wanted to roll my eyes again, but I would probably end up grounded. "Fine, can I go to bed now? I have work in the morning."

"No." Dad left the room, and I gaped at his back. *What now?*

I stared at Mom with wide eyes. "Why not?" I went to follow him, but he was back with the phone in his hand.

"You need to call Shawn, he's worried sick."

I took the phone from Dad and went up to my room calling Shawn's cell on the way. He picked up on the first ring. "Did you find her? Is she all right?"

"I'm fine," I said a little too harshly as I closed the door to my room.

"Why did you leave?" His worried voice grew sharper becoming angry, he sounded mad now.

"You had your hands full." I wanted to fight for Shawn but that didn't mean I was going to let the stunt Kristina pulled go.

"What did you say to her? You really scared her, Liz."

"Seriously? You're buying her drama queen, fake tears performance?" *Why did I want to fight for him again?* "She said you guys were going to get back together, and I said I doubted it." I sat down at my desk and stared at the crescent moon rising over the mountains. "I told her to back off. Do you actually think I would have a chance in a fight with her? She's a knight and I've had almost no training. She would kick my ass."

He was quiet for so long I thought the call dropped. "God, I'm an idiot." He blew out a breath and I pictured him running his hand through his hair.

"Why?" I wasn't following his train of thought.

"Because I fell for it hook, line and sinker. She manipulated me again. Liz, I'm sorry, Kristina knows how to push my buttons and I fell for it."

"So, you're not mad at me?" I asked, smiling. At least he believed me.

"I'm totally mad at you." His voice went hard again.

"Why? What did I do?" My smile faded, and I stared at the wood grains on my desk.

"Where do I start?" It sounded like he was pacing. "You leave without saying goodbye, then you take off who knows where and ignore your phone."

"To start with, you didn't care I left, and I wasn't ignoring my phone. I went to the meadow. There isn't any service up there."

He blew out a breath. "Were your parents pissed when you got home?"

"You've no idea, Dad doesn't think I'm responsible enough to work at Knights Inc."

"Is he going to make you quit?"

"No, and even if he did, I would find a way around it. Plus, Mom knows how important it is." I got up and paced around the room.

"Hey, are we okay?" His voice was soft again like he was worried about what my answer would be.

"Yeah, but Kristina and I aren't." I stopped and glanced at the clock. It was getting late.

"That makes two of us. I have some not so good news."

"What now?" I sat down on my bed.

"I got my schedule for June."

"You did?"

"Yeah, I'm working Mondays, Wednesdays, Fridays, and Saturdays."

I closed my eyes and reminded myself that it wasn't his fault. "That's a lot." A lot of nights I would be on my own with Stalker to keep me company.

"It gets worse." He paused as if trying to find the courage to tell me. "My dad is partnering me with Kristina."

"He is pushing you together. I'm sorry, Shawn." I needed to pretend to be supportive. Jon was going to do whatever he could to keep us apart, but we would struggle through it.

"Me too, but you haven't heard the worst yet."

I bent over the bed and rested my elbow on my knee. "How much worse could it be?"

"Your dream training will be on Tuesday and Thursday nights."

I wanted to scream and stomp my feet. Not only was I not going to see much of Shawn in my dreams, but if I was training on the nights he had off, Stalker would have even more time to torture me.

"Liz, are you still there?"

"Yeah, we'll figure it out and we can do stuff in real time right?"

"Yeah, we will work it out. Listen I have to go, or I'll be late."

"Go, be careful," I said, closing my eyes.

"Okay, sleep tight, and I'll see you tomorrow." He ended the call and I stared at the phone. This was going to be the worst summer ever.

Chapter 9

I opened my eyes and let out a relieved breath. I was in Shawn's padded room. It was weird since he said he would be working, but I didn't care. A break from Stalker and the other mares was what I needed. I looked around; I was alone? I could find my way to Shawn's room, but normally he had to be there first. It didn't matter, being there was safer than being anywhere else.

"Alone at last," Shawn said, popping into the room with his back to me.

"So, she thinks we're working?" Kristina asked, materializing next to him.

"Yeah, bought the entire thing." He grabbed Kristina's hand, pulled her into him, and claimed her mouth. There were no other words for it, he looked like he was sucking the air from her lungs taking it all for himself. I stood frozen with my mouth hanging open, as I watched them. I needed to move, to say something, to leave, do something. All I could do was replay the phone call we shared less than an hour before.

Kristina jumped and wrapped her legs around Shawn's waist without breaking the kiss, he grabbed her thighs and walked over to a white leather couch he materialized. He sat down and Kristina broke the kiss and stood up. "Lay down," she commanded. Once Shawn was on his back, she lay down on top of him. "God, I missed you."

"I missed you too." They started kissing again.

I tried to leave, to go anywhere else because anywhere else would be better than watching them, but my mind was blank, it was like I was in a trance. I couldn't look away or even move. I don't know how much time passed before they came up for air. "What did you tell Liz?"

"She thinks I'm being forced to work with you." He smiled and laced his hands behind his head gloating.

"It's too bad we need her; wouldn't it be easier to give her to the mares?"

"Yeah, but you saw her today. She's amazing. I need to stay on her good side until it's too late for her to leave Knights Inc. If I let her go now, she'll quit and go to the Air Force Academy. My dad said we need to keep her happy."

I cocked my head. Since when had Jon thought he needed to keep me happy? He had done nothing but try to get rid of me.

"But, Shawn," Kristina whined just like she did in Shawn's room earlier. "I don't want to wait for us to be together."

"I think your boyfriend is going to leave you for her," Stalker whispered in my ear. I jerked, finally coming out of my trance, and searched the room for him, wondering how he got there, but no one was there. I wanted to know where his voice came from, but I wanted to hear the rest of Shawn and Kristina's conversation more.

"She thinks I'll be working when she isn't. We'll have tons of time together. Plus, Tom will keep her busy during the day. She'll have no idea what I'm doing. As long as we get together out of town she won't find out."

"Okay, but when you break it off with her, I want to be there. I want to see the look on her face when you tell her you've been playing her all along." Kristina sat up and pulled her shirt over her head.

I couldn't take it anymore. I stormed over to them, stopping just short of the couch. "What the hell, Shawn?" I yelled as Kristina bent to kiss him. They ignored me. "Seriously? Don't ignore me. Your plan's been foiled. I can't believe I fell for your act." Still, they pretended like I wasn't there.

"What are you going to do? Are you going to let them get away with it?" Stalker asked from behind me.

I needed to get out of there, I closed my eyes and thought of my bedroom, I didn't care if Stalker followed me there. I wanted to be away from them, but I couldn't get the picture of Shawn and Kristina on the couch out of my head.

"Come on now, Lamb chop, don't you want to watch?"

I opened my eyes as realization struck. Why hadn't Shawn noticed a mare in his padded room? Mares couldn't go in there, plus, Shawn would never ignore a mare, no matter what he was doing.

"Shawn, Kristina, you know there's a mare in here, right?" I tapped my foot waiting for them to respond. When they didn't, I grabbed Kristina by the shoulder and yanked her off Shawn, only it wasn't Shawn.

"You did this, you staged this whole thing just to get under my skin."

"How did you figure it out?" Stalker asked, as his costume melted away and the room around us dissolved into the clearing with the mineshaft.

"I'm not going to tell you; do you think I'm stupid?" Mares couldn't access Shawn's room, plus he didn't talk about the gate. If Shawn was leading me on, they would have talked about the gate and what a wild goose chase it was.

"I wish you would. Do you really think they aren't screwing around behind your back? He'll leave you for her, then what will you have to live for? Why do you want to throw your life away chasing me when you could end it now and go to paradise?"

"Somehow I don't think your version of paradise and mine are the same, now if you will excuse me I have somewhere to be." I closed my eyes and moved to my bedroom.

I opened my eyes in my bedroom, free of Stalker, and ran to my bed. I cried like everything I saw in my dream was true. It wasn't, Shawn was with me because he wanted to be, not because he thought I would leave Knights Inc. if he left me. When I finished freaking out and doubting everything Shawn and I had, I dried my eyes and thought about the more terrifying thing I learned from the dream.

How did Stalker know about Kristina and more importantly how did he know about Shawn's padded room? And, if he knew about all that, did he know we were trying to close the gate?

Chapter 10

I parked outside the mansion at seven thirty the next morning with butterflies in my stomach threatening to become a full-blown panic attack. I watched Shawn walk toward my Jeep. I forced myself to shut it off and get out, trying to forget about the dream from the night before. I closed the door and forced myself to smile. I wanted to tell him about it, but I was scared, a small part of me wondered if it was true. "Hi."

"Are you all right? You look like you didn't sleep at all." Shawn took my hand and led me to the main door instead of the side door I used when I visited him.

"I slept, but Stalker tortured me in the worst way possible." I pulled my backpack up higher on my back.

"What did he do?" Shawn stopped and stood in front of me.

"I don't want to talk about it. It was a long night." I tried to move around him. I didn't want to be late on my first day.

"You always tell me what happens in your dreams, Liz. Did it have something to do with me?" He stepped in front of me when I tried to go around him.

"Yes." I blew a strand of hair out of my face that had come loose from my bun.

"Liz, come on tell me, please." He held his hands out.

"Fine, but you won't like it. I thought I was in your padded room."

"You know he can't get in my padded room, right?" He drew his eyebrows together.

"Yes, and I realized it during my dream but not until the damage was already done." I glanced up as a cherry red Subaru WRX screeched into the parking lot. I rolled my eyes then looked back at Shawn who was also following the car with his eyes. "Anyway," I said, waiting for him to take his attention off the car. "You and Kristina were there on a couch."

"Kristina?" he asked glancing behind me.

I spun to see what he was staring at and I rolled my eyes again, of course, my arch nemesis drove the one brand of car I hated above all others. "Kristina," he yelled and waved her over.

I couldn't deal with him treating her as a friend after my dream, so I walked around him and started for the front door. I was halfway there before he caught up with me.

"Hey, why'd you leave?" he took my hand as Kristina walked on his other side.

"I don't want to be late." I sped up a little, hearing my internal clock tell me it was getting close to eight.

"Are you nervous?" Kristina asked, acting like our conversation from the previous day never happened.

"Yes." I kept my eyes from going in her direction, if I did, I might do something stupid like remember her playing tonsil hockey with my boyfriend and try to rip her tonsils out.

"There is nothing to worry about, my dad isn't even here. Jo's dad will love you." Shawn gave my hand a squeeze.

"Is he less of a hardass than Jon?" I asked as we reached the main entrance and Shawn held the door open for me.

"He's a hardass, but he isn't as bad as my dad. You'll like him."

We walked in, and I took the room in. I hadn't been in this part of the mansion since before Knights Inc. renovated it. The entrance was very businesslike. The original stone floor shone like it was newly waxed. An art deco area rug lay in front of a faux-rustic reception desk. Along one wall was a chocolate-colored leather sofa, and two matching chairs were along the opposite wall. A woman sat behind the reception desk, her dark red hair was up in a severe bun, and a headset rested just in front of it. She had a white sheer blouse on and barely glanced at us when we walked in.

"Yes, Mr. York, I'll have Mr. Ericson call you when he returns. Have a good day." She hit a button on the phone and looked up.

"Shawn, Kristina are you here for your debriefing?" she asked, reviewing a paper.

"Yes, but it's Liz's first day and I wanted to introduce you. Kristina go on back, I'll be there in a few minutes." Kristina shrugged her shoulders, took out her ID badge, and waved it in front of a locked door to the right of the reception desk. Shawn brought me closer to the desk. "Liz, this is Marcy, Jeff's mom."

"Hi, nice to meet you." I offered her my hand.

"You're Victor's daughter." She took my hand and shook it. "It's nice to meet you. I knew your father a long time ago."

"I never met him." I wondered how many times I would hear about the man who helped make me but whom I never met.

"I'm sorry, he was a wonderful man, just don't tell Jon I said so." She picked up a clipboard and handed it to me. "I need you to fill out these papers, then Tom will come and get you."

"Thanks," I took the clipboard and the pen she offered then went over to the couch. It was straightforward. Name, address, social security number, emergency contact. Typical new hire paperwork. When I was done Shawn put his hand on my knee.

"I have to go. Derick will want to get this over with." He stood, and I stood with him. "I'll try to meet you here after work, okay? I want to hear about the rest of your dream."

"Sounds good." He bent and gave me a chaste kiss on the lips before going through the door Kristina had gone through a few minutes before.

I took the clipboard back to Marcy. "I think I filled it out correctly."

"I'll look it over, if you're missing anything, I'll track you down later. Have a seat, and I'll let Tom know you're here."

I sat back down, laced my fingers in my lap, and hooked one foot behind the other. I stared straight ahead and tried to say calm. My pulse was pounding in my ears and I wasn't sure why. Tom seemed like a nice guy the day before, but that could have been non-work Tom, and work Tom might be terrifying. Plus, I had no idea what I would be doing. How did you train to fight monsters in your dreams?

"Hi, Liz, looks like we didn't scare you off with the simulator yesterday," Tom said, coming out the door to Marcy's left and offering me his hand.

I got to my feet and took his hand. "No, it will take a lot more than that to scare me away." I shook it then let go.

"Well, come on back and we'll talk about how we will do this." He went back to the door, scanned his ID badge, and held it open for me. He stepped through after me then led me down a narrow hall with cubicles on one side and a partition wall on the other with doors every ten feet. "After watching you yesterday I can tell you inherited a lot of your father's gifts."

"I guess, I can manipulate my dreams, but I have a long way to go before I am as good as Shawn or Heather."

"You'll pick up everything quickly. Victor was the strongest knight we had in decades."

"That's what people keep telling me. I hope I can live up to his legacy." I pulled my backpack up higher on my shoulder as we stopped at a door halfway down the hall.

"This is my office. If you need anything feel free to stop by. We will start in here, go over some basics then I will give you an official tour of this side of the mansion. You saw most of the training area yesterday, but this time I will explain what we do with what you saw." He opened the door to his office.

There was a large desk with a monitor sitting on top, a cushion desk chair sat behind the desk and two less comfortable chairs sat in front of it. Framed photos lined the walls, most of them of Jo and Tina, and a picture of four boys in their teens in front of a lake. I wondered if it was the same one I had found in Victor's things.

He moved around to the back side of his desk and sat down. "Please take a seat; do you need coffee or water?"

"I have water, I should be all right." I pulled my water bottle out to show him.

"Okay then, let's get started." Tom leaned back in his chair, folded his hands together, and rested them on his chest. "I don't know how much you know about our organization, so I thought we would start with our history." I took my notebook out of my bag ready to take notes. "I don't think you need to take notes, there won't be a test."

"Okay." I closed my notebook but kept it out in case there was something I wanted to remember.

"The first known plague of the *sleeping death* as they called it happened around 200 AD. No one knew where the mares came from or how to stop them. Shawn told me he told you about the first time our ancestors had to deal with them and how we learned to fight them. They thought if they killed them all it would be over, but mares are a fact of life, much like Pandora's Box, once they were released into this world there is no way of keeping them out.

"We spent most of the middle ages and until the 1960s working day jobs and killing mares in our sleep. A few clans tried to sell their protection as a tonic or a powder during the dark ages, but it never took hold. Some people can remember their dreams and us saving them, but they write it off as a dream.

"That's how I found out I was one of you," I said,

remembering the first time I had met Shawn. He was being a cocky-ass, but he had just saved my life. I held it against him for a while, but now that I knew what he did, he had a right to be cocky.

"Really? Jo never told me about this."

"I don't know if he ever told her. I was the first person he saved after he became a knight."

"And he figured you out when you remembered him from your nightmare?"

"Yeah, it freaked him out, then I freaked out because he was in my dream."

"I can only imagine." He laughed. "To continue, over the years our numbers grew until we had at least one clan on each continent, but as our numbers grew so did the number of mares throughout the world creating an endless need for knights."

"Wait, what happened in the 1960s?"

"There was an outbreak of mares when they started building NORAD in Cheyenne Mountain. Jon's father was stationed there at the time. He somehow convinced the general that the USSR had a way to invade our dreams and were killing people in Colorado Springs in their sleep. I still don't know how he convinced them, but they wanted someone to contain the threat. Knights Inc. was incorporated soon after. It was easy to create an umbrella organization in all NATO nations. Since we were no longer dependent on day jobs, we worked on research and training. Before then you fought mares with only the knowledge the other Knights could give you. We had a very high mortality rate until we were able to develop the simulator.

"We currently have bases within three hours of all the major cities in the world. Each continent is broken up into areas. Jon is the head of the North American Western Territory. It covers from Nebraska to the west coast, half of Canada from Saskatchewan to B.C. and from the Northwest Territory to Alaska then down to Guatemala."

"Weren't you in New York before this though? And why Twisted Pines? It's in the middle of nowhere."

"Jon was promoted when the prior head of this territory retired. They did a big swap. The old headquarters was in New Mexico, and none of us wanted to move there. This place is far enough off the beaten path that no one will look too closely at us, but still close enough to the big city that we can travel when we need to. Our excuse is that we want to be on a different power grid than Denver for our cover."

"How many teams do you have in this territory?" It seemed like a lot of ground to cover.

"There is at least one team in each state, there are six teams in Canada, eight in Mexico, and one in Guatemala."

"So, you're able to cover the entire state with the people here?" I asked not seeing how it was possible.

"For the most part Twisted Pines has the biggest concentration of mares, but there are others around the state. With the computer programs we have, along with information from a few satellites, we can travel anywhere in the state."

"Then why did Heather and the others go to Trinidad?"

"There were a bunch of mares and it's easier to travel there when you have to fight in the same place night after night.

It takes time to travel there in dreams, due to the rotation of the earth, but minutes can mean life or death. They went in, took care of the problem, and now they are back home."

"What if the mares come back?" I didn't know if Tom knew mares never really died. Instead, they were sent back to their own dimension. Then they found a gate and came back through.

"They will, but probably in smaller numbers which will make them easier to take care of from here or Santa Fe. There aren't enough to have anyone move there, at least at this point."

I wished we would've realized that a gate had opened there before Heather went down there. We would have had a better chance to find it, or at least find out how it was opened. I shook my head, I was here to learn to be a knight, I could figure out how to close the gate later. "How is my training going to work?"

"That's a good question. You're a special case. We are going to throw you in with the rest of the squires in your age group. Some of the training will be over your head, and from what I saw on the simulator yesterday some of it will bore you. Once I see where you are at, we'll work one on one or with Jo on things you're behind on."

"Can I ask you something about the simulator?"

"Go for it." Tom leaned forward and clasped his hands together.

"Well, on prom night Shawn and I fell asleep in a meadow and I had to fight my first mare. Anyway, I killed him, but it was hard. I shot him, stabbed him, lit him on fire, and then dismembered him before he finally died. The mares I fought in the simulator were easy to kill compared to the real thing. Did someone change the program to make it easier?"

Tom leaned back in his chair and scratched his head. "It took that much to kill one mare?"

"Yeah, I think Jon watched most of it happen." The way he asked made me think he didn't believe me.

"I only ask because I've never come across one that strong. I think you're lucky to be alive." He smiled at me. "The simulated mares you fought were as strong as most of the mares we face."

"Really? So, I didn't cheat?"

"No, you did very well for your first time. Almost as good as your dad."

"How many did he kill?"

"Four, but the fourth one was pure luck." He laughed. "Come on let me give you the official tour." Tom got to his feet, came around the desk and opened the door for me. We stepped out into the hall but did not move any further. "Here we have our training classrooms and offices for the administrative employees and staff." He continued to the other end of the hallway. "You will have dream training Tuesday and Thursday nights. Then I think you should plan on spending half the day here Monday through Friday," he said before we went through a pair of double doors. "You'll remember this from yesterday, this is the training room even though there is more than one room."

I scanned the room, remembering everything from the day before. "As you can see, we have a weight room and dojo." Tom continued walking as he talked pointing at the weights and the boxing ring.

I kept hoping I'd see Shawn, but he was nowhere around. I wondered what he had planned when he was done with his debriefing, *probably hanging out with Kristina or something*. I gave myself a mental slap, it was just a dream. I trusted Shawn.

"You remember the simulator from yesterday. You'll spend a lot of time on this. I'll show you how to use it later this week. I'm sure you want to get through your training as quickly as possible. You will have to qualify to take the final test on this. And the test is on the simulator, so the more experience you have with it the better. Once you know how to use it, there's a sign-up sheet to schedule time to practice on it."

Tom led me to a prone figure lying on the bed I had used the day before. It was Jeff, he would be a sophomore this year and always rode to school with Shawn. He was hooked up just like I had been. He looked like he was fighting for his life and I wondered if I had looked as scared as he did.

"Over here," Tom said pulling my attention away from Jeff. "This is where we watched you yesterday." We stood behind at a set of monitors where a technician was watching and clicking a mouse. On the monitors I watched Jeff shoot a goblin, but it wouldn't go down. Jeff dropped the gun, and the goblin advanced, he pulled out a machete and met the goblin halfway bringing the machete down on the goblin's head. It must not have been sharp enough though because it bounced off. The goblin sunk his teeth into Jeff's arm and the screen went blank.

"Damn it." Jeff sat up, pulled the goggles off then started on the wires until he saw us watching and his face turned bright red.

I glanced away, understanding. It was bad enough to fail, but to fail while the head trainer and a newbie were watching was much worse.

"What did you do wrong?" Tom asked, moving around to stand in front of Jeff.

"I didn't make sure my machete was sharp," he mumbled, meeting Tom's eyes before lowering them to stare at his dangling feet.

"This is why we have the simulator, it allows you to fine-tune your manifesting skills before you are out in the field where one small error could easily mean death. Jeff, you'll get there, don't give up. Why don't you work with a machete for a while? Reacquaint yourself with the weapon. Cut yourself with it if you think you need to. If you remember the cut, you might remember to make it sharp next time." Tom patted him on the back. "Let's go check out the weapons room."

We walked to the partitioned wall I noticed the day before. We went through a door on the left and my mouth dropped open. They set it up in sections. In front of me was a wall covered in everything sharp, from knives to broadswords. The wall to my left was covered in blunt objects, hammers, maces, and nunchucks. To my right was firearms.

"This is awesome," I whispered, walking around the room, letting my fingers run over the weapons.

"You are going to spend a lot of time in here getting acquainted with weapons. We were all impressed when you were able to manifest a fully functional firearm, but we expected more when you brought out the machete and the knife." Tom gave me a smile and leaned against the one bald spot on the wall.

"So far it seems like anything I have real-life experience

with is easy. Swords and stuff like that is where I have issues."

"Well, you did very well yesterday, you even impressed Jon, and that doesn't happen very often."

"He didn't look impressed; he looked upset."

"Let me rephrase that. Jon was surprised at how well you did. I don't think he thought you would get through the first mare let alone three and almost four."

"Well, I've already had to fight them, maybe that made the difference." I stopped in front of him after walking around the room and rubbed my mark. Tom glanced at it and cocked an eye brow. "This is a very cool room." I let go of my wrist and spun in a circle trying to draw his attention away from my wrist.

"It's one of my favorites too." He gave me a sad smile then stared at my wrist. "Liz, Jo told me about the mark. I'm sorry."

I grabbed my wrist, thankful I had my watch on. "Yeah, it sucks knowing there's a good chance I won't make it to my eighteenth birthday."

"You will be fine, between dreamcatchers and training you'll live a long and happy life."

"I hope so, but the dreams are killing me. I wake up more tired than when I go to sleep most of the time."

"What do you mean?"

"If I don't meet up with a knight in my dreams, the mares stalk me, they won't leave me alone. They can't hurt me, I'm protected by my dreamcatcher, but I can't hurt them either. They follow me around and kill the people in my dreams and force me to watch. Do you know how many times I've watched them murder my parents?"

"I'm sorry, what do you think they would do if you didn't sleep with your dreamcatcher?" Tom stared at his feet like he was thinking hard.

"I don't know, maybe if I killed one they would back off."

"But then there is a chance that you wouldn't be able to beat them."

I glanced around to make sure we were alone. I didn't know if my rune was a secret or not, but I was going to trust Tom. I pulled the rune out from under my shirt and held it out for him to see. "I found this with the few things my mom had left of Victor."

He glanced at it then at me and gave me a smile. "It works?" he asked like he already knew what it was and wasn't surprised I had it.

"Yeah, prom, Stalker had me pinned, and he tried to suck out my soul, but he couldn't. Did you know Victor had it?"

"Yes, and when I found out he was dead I hoped that it didn't get buried with him. It's something to be passed down. You're special if it works for you."

"Shawn and I tried to find information on it, but we didn't find much, only that it chooses who it protects and once it has chosen, it won't work for anyone else until that person gives it away or they die."

"True, no one knows where they came from but there are a half dozen floating around the world right now. Most of the knights who have them are in the top ten of mare kills. Did you show it to Jon?"

"Yeah, he tried to take it."

"He should've known better; it won't work for him since it already chose you."

"That's what I thought too. Should I even be telling people about it?" I asked as the door opened and Jeff came in.

"No, let's keep it between us for now." He took a step toward the door. "Let me show you the operations center."

We went back to the main training floor. He walked along the wall and opened another door. The room was bigger than the weapons room, but it felt cluttered with a half dozen empty workstations. They each held two monitors and faced a large wood desk with detailed scrolling on the sides. There were two monitors on the massive desk as well, but they were off to the side so whoever was sitting there could keep an eye on the rest of the room without moving. It was eerily empty at the moment, which made sense as it was daytime, so they probably didn't need to have anyone on duty.

"This is where we locate the mares and pinpoint where the knights need to go." Tom walked around the desk. "Typically, there are three people searching for mares, while the other three are in constant contact with the knights on duty. We normally have four knights on duty, with others on call in case someone gets hurt, or the mare is too big to take on by ourselves."

It wasn't what I expected. I always thought it would resemble the communication room you see in a NASA movie, with fifty people all watching what was happening on a movie screen.

"You can't see what is happening in the dreams?"

"No, but we are working on the technology to do it. It will be similar to what we use in the simulator, using the knight's brain waves to give us a visual." Tom led me back through the training room.

"Where do the knights sleep while they're on duty?" I hadn't seen any beds other than the one by the simulator.

"At home in their own beds. We don't need them until they are asleep, and we wired the technology into their homes as soon as they bought them."

"Sounds expensive."

"It is, but the benefits far outweigh the cost. It helps us keep a low profile and they sleep comfortably in their own bed."

"What does everyone do during the day?" I still wasn't sure how everything worked. You fought all night then did what during the day?

"We have twelve knights currently on active duty. If they aren't in school like Shawn, we split the time. They normally work two or three nights a week, then after each shift, they come in to be debriefed. Then they file a report on their shift. They are also required to put in at least ten hours of training a week. Most of them split it between working out and practicing with weapons."

"What about everyone else who works here, are they all Knights?"

"No, but they are all related. Not everyone born in the clan are knights. Some don't want to be, while others never completed their training. They make up the admins and communications specialists."

"So, if the knights aren't here during the week full time,

what do they tell their neighbors and friends?”

“The truth, they work part of the time remotely. Let’s go back to my office.” Tom led me back to his office.

“I’ve been thinking about your problem with not getting a restful sleep.” Tom leaned back in his chair. “Why are you still sleeping with a dreamcatcher?”

“Because Jon and my mom said I had to, and it’s part of my contract. I don’t think they realize how much it hinders me. My mom doesn’t know what the rune does, and I don’t know if she would believe me if I told her.”

“I don’t want to overrule what your mother says, but what if you went without it one night and see what happens.”

“Will Jon fire me if he finds out?”

“Stay in your dream, don’t jump to anyone else’s and he never has to know.”

“Hey, I don’t know why I just thought of this, but the mares have been harassing me every night since prom. How come none of you helped me?”

Tom stared at his desk then past me. “Don’t take this the wrong way. Jon has to watch out for all of us.” He met my eyes. “He told us to ignore any mares bothering you. He still thinks you are a lost cause, and he doesn’t want to lose any of us protecting you since you’re marked.”

I took a deep breath and stared at the ceiling before closing my eyes. It was going to be a constant battle between me and Jon, and I didn’t know if I had the strength I needed to deal with it day in and day out. I wanted to live though, and if Tom and the rest of the knights could teach me how to protect myself, I would stay until I was a knight.

"That's what I thought." I had to take my dreams into my own hands if I wanted a good night's sleep when Shawn and Heather weren't around. "What's next?"

Tom checked the time. "Why don't we stop for the day? Tonight, we have dream training. Make sure you're asleep by ten then find me. Tomorrow, we have a group training you will love."

"Sounds good, I feel like my brain is going to explode with information as it is."

"Good, Marcy should have your ID badge ready by the time you get here tomorrow. Once you have it, come on back, and we'll meet in the classroom across from my office."

"Thanks for answering all of my stupid questions today."

"No problem, it's not very often I have to explain how things work. It was kind of nice for a change. See you tomorrow."

When I got to my Jeep, there was a piece of paper under the windshield wiper. I plucked it out and got into the driver's seat.

Hope you had a good first day. Mom has me doing yard work. I'll call you later.

Love, Shawn

It was the first time he had written me a note using the 'L' word, and I held the note to my chest like I was in some teen rom-com movie. I didn't care, it made me feel all warm and gooey inside, especially after my dream the night before. I opened my glove box and put the note inside. I took my phone out and sent him a text message:

Would love to see you when you get done. Call me at

home.

I started my Jeep, rolled the windows down, turned the radio up, then sped out of the parking lot.

Chapter 11

When I got home, I called Billy to see if he could come over and help me take the top off my Jeep. It was summer and driving with only the windows down wasn't working.

"How was the first day?" Billy asked as I took a bite out of one of the sandwiches I made us for lunch.

"Pretty boring, mostly orientation stuff. History of the company that kind of thing." I wanted to tell Billy what my job really was, but Knight Flyers were a national secret. Plus, why would he believe me? Even if I showed up in his dream and showed him everything I could do, he wouldn't remember it the next day. "How was mowing lawns?"

"It wasn't too bad. It's not hot yet." Billy worked for a landscaping company in the summer. "Did you see Jo?"

"No, I'm not sure what time she was working today, besides she's already been through orientation."

"That's okay, we are going down to the lake later. Are you doing something with Shawn tonight?"

"Yeah, he left me a note saying he wanted to get together, he'll call when he gets done doing yard work." I hoped Kristina wouldn't show up.

"Is there something going on with you two?" Billy asked, putting his sandwich on the table, and leveling a look at me.

"Why would you think that?" I pushed the crumbs on the table into a pile.

"Because when something is bothering you, you get this look, you think no one notices but I've known you too long. Spill, what's going on?"

"Well, Kristina, his ex, wants him back. He told me it was over, and I believe him, but ..." I stared at Billy and sighed.

"Do you think he is going to dump you for her?"

"No, but when she had me alone, she said I shouldn't get used to Shawn, he would go back to her. That they were all but engaged."

"Really and you believe her? What did Shawn say?"

"Well I kind of threatened her, and Shawn heard me, and she played the damsel in distress, I'm talking fake tears and everything. Shawn went to her, and I left. I talked to Shawn about it later and I think we are all good, but even his dad thinks they are going to end up together."

"What do you mean?"

"I ran into him on my way out yesterday, and he said since Kristina was moving here, he thinks Shawn and her will get serious."

"Liz, all that matters is what Shawn wants, and he wants you. Don't overthink it." Billy put a hand on my shoulder.

"I want to believe he won't ditch me for this prima

donna, but it's hard when I hear so many people telling me they are going to end up together. Jon even put them on the same schedule at work."

"That's messed up, but you and Shawn will work it out. You just have to stay positive and pretend like this girl doesn't bother you. Shawn isn't the type of guy who gets off on a jealous girlfriend."

"Okay." I blinked back a tear that wanted to fall. I would not let Kristina or Jon get to me anymore.

"Come on let's get the top off." Billy got to his feet and took my plate to the sink.

"Yes," I needed something to take my mind off the drama my life was becoming.

Billy and I spent the next two hours working on my Jeep. When we finished, we put the top next to the garage, and I grabbed us bottles of water. "I thought it would be easier since it was a newer Jeep, but it still takes way longer than it should."

"No kidding," Billy took a long swig of his water then checked his phone.

"Do you have to go?" I missed hanging out with Billy, I could talk to him about almost anything and it seemed we were seeing less and less of each other as we got older.

"Yeah, but can I talk to you about something first." He sat on the bumper of his truck.

"What's going on?" I moved to stand in front of him so I could see his eyes.

"It's Jo," he trailed off like he didn't know where to start.

"What about her? I thought you guys were going good. You're taking her fishing tonight, right?"

"Yeah, but I feel like she is keeping something from me. Something important, like she has some terminal disease, and she doesn't want to tell me. Like she's afraid I'll dump her or worse, feel sorry for her."

I schooled my face, I couldn't let Billy know I knew what she was keeping from him. "Oh, Billy are you sure? Or just being paranoid. She has never mentioned anything to me." I didn't know what to say, and I hated lying to my best friend.

"Are you sure?" He looked at me with his eyes squinted like it hurt to think about Jo breaking up with him.

"Yes, she's crazy about you. If there's something she isn't telling you, I'm sure it's nothing to worry about. Everyone has their secrets. You need to let her have hers until she is ready to tell you. She isn't dying. I'm sure she would've told you if she was." I turned away from him afraid he would see the guilt in my eyes. How was I going to keep this from him?

"Will you tell me if she tells you anything?" Billy asked, jumping off the tailgate.

"I'm sure she'll tell you first but if I can I will."

"Thanks, Liz. I better go, I'll see you later." He got in his truck.

"Bye." I got up and gathered up the tools we used then put them away. Just as I finished, the phone rang and I ran inside to answer it. "Hello?"

"Hi, Liz," Shawn's deep voice rolled over me, and I closed my eyes to savor it.

"Hi, what time is it? Are you done?" I checked the clock.

It was only three, maybe he was getting off early.

"No, that's why I'm calling. Mom is going crazy with the landscaping. I'm sorry, I'll have to break our date tonight." He sounded like he was trying not to be mad.

"Oh, all right." It wasn't all right with me at all. I needed to talk to him, be with him to reassure myself that my dream the night before was just a dream.

"What's Billy doing? You can always hang out with him."

"He has a date with Jo. I'll figure something out. I need to work on that research project we talked about, anyway." Meaning I needed to dig into Twisted Pines' history.

"Tomorrow night? I promise. I'll come up with something special." He sounded distracted. "Tell your parents you have plans."

"I will."

He laughed. "Good luck at training tonight."

"Thanks, enjoy your night off." I hung up the phone, grabbed my bag, tried not to be bummed that I wouldn't see Shawn later, and took off for the library.

The weather was improving every day. The mud was gone, the road was dry, and my tires kicked up a trail of dust behind me as I wound my way down the hill from our house to the highway. When I reached the pavement, I headed to the library, located in the heart of Twisted Pines, right across from the county building. I found a parking place and thanks to Shawn teaching me how to parallel park a few weeks before, parked on my first try then went inside.

I loved the smell of books. New or old, it didn't make a difference. The written word was always a way for me to escape from my world. I was on a mission though, and I was not after pleasure reading. I needed information on the sleeping death and who opened the gate between dimensions in Twisted Pines.

I went to the help desk and waited for the librarian to notice me. "Hi, Liz, what can I help you with today?" She closed her book giving me her full attention.

"I'm researching the gold rush in Twisted Pines. Can you point me in the right direction?" The sleeping death started somewhere around then from all the stories I had heard.

"We have a few books and all the newspapers are on microfiche. If you don't find what you want there, you should check out the gold rush museum."

"Thanks, I totally forgot about the museum." I went over to the Colorado section and pulled down the one book about Twisted Pines, found an empty table and read. It only had fifty pages and most of it was pictures.

The Ute tribe were the original inhabits of the area. Living in wickiups, they hunted and fished the area. Foraging and planting small crops kept them going through the harsh winters, one paragraph explained. Once the gold rush hit, most of them left, not willing to battle with the white man over the gold. A few stuck around to work for the miners but the book said nothing about the local lore, which might have helped me.

Fredrick Freeman was the first miner to find gold in the area. He had a huge stake with one of the biggest gold seams in all of Colorado. He built a mansion on the hill now known as the Freeman mansion. I hadn't thought of him in years even though

Shawn was living in the mansion he built. I got my notebook out and took notes. The book didn't have a lot of information, but it gave me some ideas on where else to check.

After I finished the book, I went to the microfiche and pulled newspaper clippings for as far back as I could. I sat down at the projector and read. I scrolled through articles about what was happening in Denver, and DC, and an upcoming election, nothing seemed to jump out at me until I came across a headline: 'Town Founder's Wife and Children Dead.' *Jackpot*, I thought. The article said Mr. Freeman got up in the morning and he couldn't wake his wife. He went into the nursery and that found his two had children also died in their sleep. Mr. Freeman was beyond himself with grief but no foul play was suspected.

I scrolled to the next day's paper, twenty people died of what they were calling the sleeping sickness. I kept scrolling, the obituary section grew larger each day until the paper stopped being published. Their final paper had one article, a farewell. From what I read almost everyone who lived there were dead or moved away. The sleeping sickness killed the town.

I jotted some notes down. The deaths began on May 9th, 1887, which meant the gate had to have been opened near that date. I didn't know if it would help me, but it was somewhere to start. Next, I needed to find out if there were any natural phenomena reported in the area around the date.

"The library will close in ten minutes. Please take your selections to the front and proceed to the exit," a voice said over the loudspeaker.

I didn't have time to re-read the paper for clues or read Spruce's newspaper. It might have more information about what happened. From what I read no one seemed to know what was going on. Which posed another question: how did they find out about dreamcatchers?

"How was your first day?" Mom asked over dinner later that night.

"Good, a lot of orientation stuff. We toured the facilities and went over the employee handbook." I bit into the hamburger covered in cheese, catsup, and mustard.

"Are you going to like it?" Dad asked.

"Yeah, and I'm going to learn a lot once we get past orientation." I picked up a forkful of coleslaw.

"Did you see Shawn at all?" Mom asked, then remembered. "Weren't you two supposed to go on a date tonight?"

"I saw him for a minute this morning when he walked me in. He had to cancel tonight, his mom had him working in the yard. Hopefully, we'll get to hang out tomorrow." Something was always coming up, and now that school was out and he was on duty almost every night, I didn't even get to see him in my dreams.

"That's good. What are you going to do?" Dad asked, he still wasn't used to me having a boyfriend.

"I don't know. I think he has something in mind."

"Just as long as he doesn't keep you out too late." He frowned. "Just because you are dating the boss's son doesn't mean you can slack off."

"I will, Dad. I have so much to learn it would be hard not to give them everything I have."

Chapter 12

I went to bed after dinner, claiming the day had drained me. I lay in bed staring at the ceiling, trying to will myself to go to sleep, but I was nervous and excited. Nervous because I was starting my training with a bunch of kids who had already been training for years and excited because I was starting my training. At least, with Tom there, Stalker would leave me alone.

After I fell asleep my dream began in the clearing again, but I thought of Tom and as soon as I opened my eyes I moved to the middle of Main street in downtown Twisted Pines. It was the middle of the day, in the summer; the sky was clear, and it was warm. The street was empty except for five kids and Tom. I recognized Jeff, Mary, and Jo right away, but I didn't know the other two. I went to stand by Jo.

"Am I late?" I asked in a stage whisper.

"No, we haven't started yet. Are you ready?"

"Yeah," I said. "But scared too."

"You will do great." She twisted and glanced at Tom who was watching our exchange.

"Now that we are all here, let's get started." He gazed at us all standing in a semi-circle around him. "Jo, Jeff, Mary, you've already met Liz. Steve, and Brent this is Liz. She will be joining your class this summer." I thought the two boys were a few years younger than me.

I gave the two younger guys a nod, and they nodded back. It wouldn't be too bad, I thought, thinking I was glad Kristina was already a knight until I thought of her and Shawn working together.

"I know most of you were at the BBQ, but I don't know if you saw Magnus." Tom paused as Mary and Steve groaned. "It's evaluation time. It's not what we want, but we can't stop it. Let's be prepared and show him our best." Tom rested his hand on his hips. "He will test you on your manifesting skills. He will tell you what he wants you to manifest then he will time you to see how long you take to manifest it. So, we are going to spend most of tonight working on manifesting weapons. Questions?"

"Do we know when he will do the evaluation?" Jeff asked.

"No, which is why I want you all to practice as much as you can."

"What will happen if we fail?" Mary asked, glaring at me.

"Nothing." Tom licked his lips. "It's just to gauge where you are with your training."

I had a feeling Tom wasn't telling us everything. Which made me wonder. If we didn't do well, would he get in trouble?

"Any more questions?" When no one spoke up Tom walked around the circle. "Let's start with something easy. How about a Bowie knife?"

I wanted to ask what a Bowie knife looked like, I'd heard of it, but I didn't think I had ever seen one. I thought of a knife, a big one with a sharp point and a wood handle. Instead of a knife, I manifested a machete. I frowned and glanced at Jo's knife, my machete was nowhere near what hers looked like. It was long, with a ten-inch blade, the last three inches of the top swooped down to the point. The handle was wood and easily fit in her hand.

I wanted to copy her and change my machete into something closer to hers, but it was too late. Tom was standing in front of me holding his hands out. I placed it in his hands. "I'm sorry, I didn't know what a Bowie knife looked like." I stared down at my shoes refusing to meet his eyes.

"It's not what I asked for, but," he flicked his thumb over the edge, "it's sharp. You could fight a mare with this."

"Thanks," I whispered as he moved to inspect Jo's.

"Nice knife," Mary whispered and giggled at my machete. I wanted to slap the smile off her face. *It was my first day.*

I watched and listened as he critiqued each person's weapons. Everyone produced something that at least looked like a Bowie knife, except for me. Some weren't sharp though, and Jeff's was rubbery. Tom seemed to find something wrong with everyone's knife. Most of them looked perfect to me and I wondered if he expected perfection from everyone.

"Okay, you all have work to do. Let's move onto a short sword," Tom said when he finished talking to Steve.

That's easy, I thought and imagined a short sword I'd seen in the movies. When I opened my eyes, I shook my head in disbelief. I was holding another machete. This one had a sword hilt, but the shape of the blade was all wrong.

"Can you manifest anything other than a machete?" Mary asked, peering at my version of the blade.

"Get over yourself, Mary. It's her first night," Jo said, sticking up for me. "You couldn't manifest anything on your first night if I remember correctly."

"Yea, but I was just a kid."

"That's enough," Tom said, ending the conversation. "Let's try something a little more challenging" Tom caught my eye and I swear I saw him wink. "A 6mm Mauser with a ten-power scope and sling."

I had never seen a 6mm Mauser, but the inner workings and the looks of most rifles were the same. I needed to make sure the barrel was a 6mm and it had a scope. I imagined every detail from the color of the stain on the stock and the barrel to the sighted-in the scope and a full magazine. It might have taken me a little longer than I wanted to manifest it, but I wanted it to be perfect.

The rifle I held in my hands a moment later was the most beautiful rifle I had ever seen. I automatically pulled the bolt back to see if it was loaded. Tom was inspecting Steve's gun and jerked his head up. "Problem Liz?"

I started, then realized no one else checked to see if their guns were loaded. "No sir, just gun safety 101, checking if it's loaded."

"In the future, I'll check that for you," he said with a shake of his head. I nodded my head. "Was it loaded?"

"The safety is on and there's a bullet in the chamber." It would be really hard for me to break the habit of checking to see if a gun was loaded as soon as it was in my hands.

Mary narrowed her eyes at me and pursed her lips. Tom took Mary's gun from her. It was a gun, but it was missing the trigger and binoculars were mounted where the scope should have been. I wanted to laugh but I was the one who couldn't manifest a knife.

"Mary, you have work to do here." Tom handed the gun back to her. "Fix it and I'll come back around."

Tom checked everyone's gun like he did with the knives, explaining what needed to be fixed before they were safe to fire. Guns were hard for everyone it seemed. No one had one that was safe to fire on the first try. "How did you think you did?" he asked taking the gun from me when it was my turn. He pulled the bolt back and checked the chamber.

"It should be good to go."

"Let's see, shall we?" He gave the gun back. "There's a target at the end of the street, let's see if you can hit it."

"Okay." I gulped and squinted at the red target two hundred yards away. I dropped to one knee, brought the rifle up, and sighted in using my knee to brace my left elbow. I adjusted the scope then locked on to the target. I exhaled and squeezed the trigger. The boom and the recoil surprised me, but I shook it off and looked through the scope to see where I hit.

"Did you hit it?" Tom asked as I got to my feet.

"If it was a squirrel, it would have exploded." Tom extended his hand for the rifle and I handed it over. He held the gun up and looked at the target through the scope. He brought the gun down and pulled the bolt back ejecting the spent shell and loading the next one.

"You were a little off with your aim, but I agree the squirrel wouldn't have stood a chance." He clicked the safety on and gave it back. "Good work."

"Thank you." I smiled, relieved that I could manifest something right. I watched Jo give Tom her gun and took a step back when I realized everyone was staring at me. I wanted to stick my tongue out and sing 'na-na-nana I'm better than you at something' but Tom caught my eye and shook his head stopping me.

Tom went back through the line making sure everyone's rifles were safe to fire before letting them shoot at the target. It felt like it took forever since everyone still had issues, but Tom was patient and helped everyone do it right.

After everyone shot their gun Tom called us to stand closer to him. "That's it for tonight, but I expect to see you all tomorrow morning." I relaxed, I had made it through my first night of training. I gave Tom and Jo a wave then went to find Shawn.

He was in his padded room, the last place I wanted to be, lying on the same couch as the night before, but he was alone this time. "Hi, how are you?" I asked, taking a few steps closer to him. When he didn't respond I took a step back. If Stalker was messing with me again, I was going to scream. "Shawn," I said a little louder.

"There you are." He sat up and patted the seat next to him. "How was training?"

"I'm good." I held my hand up. What happened the night before wasn't real, but it didn't mean I wanted to sit on the couch where I thought he and Kristina had been making out. "Training wasn't as bad as I thought, but I still suck at a lot of things." I reached behind my head and tightened my ponytail.

"What are you talking about? I'm sure you impressed Tom." He got up and put his hands on my shoulders.

"I didn't know what a Bowie knife was, all I could come up with was a stupid machete. You should've heard Mary, she loved watching me fail." I shook my head and stared at his chest.

"It was your first night. You probably did better than all of them did on their first night." Shawn took my chin and forced me to meet his eyes.

"I got the gun perfect on my first try, no one else did." I smiled, I had something to be proud of.

"See now, it's not that bad. You'll be better than them before you know it, especially since you have access to the weapons room now." He took my hand and drew me toward the couch, but I stopped. "What's wrong?"

"You know how I told you I dreamed about this room?"

"Yeah, about me and Kristina in here." Shawn pulled his eyes brows together. "You know Stalker was just messing with you."

"But I still saw what I saw and most of it was on that couch."

"What did you see?"

"You and Kristina were talking about how you were leading me on so I wouldn't quit and that you two were really together. Pretty much my worst nightmare." I wiped at a tear that snuck out of my eye.

"Oh, babe." He hugged me. "I'm so sorry. It wasn't real. She drives me up the wall. I don't know what I ever saw in her."

"I'm just glad it was a dream." I stepped away and met his eyes. They were so blue it almost hurt. "How's work been?"

"Okay, but I wish I was working with Heather. Kristina is a good knight and she does her job, but Heather and I are a better team." Shawn pulled away from me but took my hand and led me to a red couch on the opposite side of the room.

"Much better." I laughed at how insecure I was being.

"Anything for you." He sat then pulled me into his lap. "God this schedule will kill me. How was the rest of your day? I hated not seeing you. I think we saw more of each other when we were in school."

"No kidding." I told him about my training with Tom and what I found at the library.

"Sounds like we need to meet and talk about everything, but it's so hard with our schedules."

"I know, your dad is doing everything he can to keep us apart."

"Yeah well, at least we'll be together tomorrow morning." He leaned his head back and stared at the ceiling.

"What do you mean?" I had training and since Shawn was

a knight, I didn't think we would ever see each other at work.

"Tom didn't tell you?"

"No, he said we had group training, not that you would be there. What's going on?"

"I don't want to ruin the surprise, but we get to spend the morning together. If things go our way, maybe we can sneak out and spend the rest of the day together too."

I was so excited we could spend the morning shoveling horse manure and it would still be worth it if I got to hang out with him for more than five minutes. "Now I'm really excited for tomorrow." I leaned in and kissed him. He drew me closer and ran his hand up and down my sides. I wrapped my arms around his neck and we enjoyed the moment until my alarm buzzed waking me up.

Chapter 13

The next morning, I woke up rested and excited about spending at least part of the day with Shawn. When I arrived at the mansion I had to park at the very end of the lot. I'd never seen as many cars parked there at one time before. I checked my watch, I was ten minutes early which was how I liked it. Shawn must have been waiting for me because he ran out the side door as soon as I was out of my Jeep.

"Hey." He ran his hand through still wet hair when he reached me.

"Hi, did you oversleep?" I tucked a strand of hair behind his ear.

"Yeah, I forgot to set my alarm." He bent and touched his lips to mine before grabbing my hand and dragging me to the business entrance.

"Why didn't you wake up when I did?" I shook my head as we walked.

"Because I live here and I'm a guy, its take me no time to get ready."

"Are you going to tell me what we are doing today?" I asked as he held the door for me.

He gave me a sly smile. "You'll see."

We stopped at Marcy's desk and she gave me a key-card with my name on it then Shawn led me down the hall to one of the larger classrooms. The room was filled with people, some I recognized from the BBQ and some I didn't.

"Shawn, I'm glad you made it." Stacy came up to us and hugged him.

"Me too Aunt Stacy." He patted her back and rolled his eyes at me.

"Liz, I'm sorry I haven't called yet." She took my hand and squeezed it.

"No problem, I've been busy too." I had forgotten about her but as soon as I saw her I remembered. Maybe she knew something about the gate and how he planned to close it.

"We better find seats," Shawn said, checking out the people who hadn't sat down.

"I promise I'll call you before the week is over." Stacy waved at me as Shawn led me deeper into the room.

"Okay." I smiled then turned to see where we were going.

Shawn led us to the center of the room where Jo was waiting with an empty seat on either side of her. "Thanks for saving us seats," Shawn said as I took the seat to her left and he took the seat to her right. "Kristina," I heard him say and I leaned forward to see where she was sitting. The blonde was sitting on the other side of Shawn, with perfect hair and makeup. *It was only a dream, I have nothing to worry about. Kristina can try to steal him all she wants, but he's mine,* I thought, giving her a tight smile when she made eye contact with me.

"What did you think of your first night training?" Jo asked, pulling me out of my thoughts.

"It was fun but, I have a lot to learn," I said as Tom cleared his throat at the front of the room, and everyone settled down.

"Now then on to today's workshop." Tom pulled a sheet off a cart I hadn't noticed before, revealing well I wasn't sure what it was. There were two cylinders on the cart, they almost reminded me of scuba tanks, but the bottoms were cone-shaped. The tops had valves with hoses hooked up. The hoses led to a big and blocky gun, reminding me of a 1960s science-fiction movie. "This is the Inferno 5000, better known as a flamethrower." Tom waited while the class oohed and aahed over it for a minute. I sat there stunned. Was he going to teach us how to use a flamethrower? "This one is powered by propane instead of napalm though. At full power, the two, three-gallon tanks should give you a good five minutes of flame-throwing before you need to charge the tanks. It has an automatic lighter, meaning when you pull the trigger the flame will light, and you will be roaring. They have also added a guard around the trigger and the grip to help prevent flash burns. You can adjust the flame length with the valve here." He pointed at a small nob on the side of the gun before he lifted the tanks, stuck his arms through the backpack straps, and shouldered the tanks, then he picked up the *gun* part of it and showed us the new features.

"What kind of delay is there between lighting it and throwing flames since there isn't a pilot light?" A man in his mid-forties asked.

"Less than two seconds."

"What kind of range does it have?" Kristina asked.

"Forty feet, this is an epic weapon. If there aren't any more questions, let's head to the training room. I will demonstrate how it works, then you can handle it to get a feel for it, and you can use the simulator to practice with it." Tom put the weapon back on the cart and went to the door. He propped it open and pushed the cart through. Everyone stood and followed him to the training room.

"It won't be that hard to manifest," Kristina said, walking with me, Jo, and Shawn down the hall.

"There's a lot of components to remember," Shawn said, looking dazed. "It will take work."

"Yeah, it will take me years to figure it out," Jo said, biting her lip.

"What about you Liz?" Kristina asked, cocking an eyebrow at me. "Heard you had some trouble last night."

How did she know I had a tough night? Narrowing my eyes at her, I imagined slapping the snooty grin off her face, but I resisted. "I don't know, Shawn's right, there's a lot to it. I guess we'll see."

A few minutes later we were arranged in a semi-circle behind a pane of fireproof glass in the training room. Tom had changed into a fire suit and had put the tanks on his back. It didn't look like an efficient weapon, it took too long to put on, but if you could manifest it on your back, and you had a gym full of zombies coming at you, it would get the job done.

"What do you think?" Shawn asked, and I raised my eyebrows.

"It would've been nice on prom night."

"No kidding, it would have made it easy." He nodded his head as Tom stepped forward. "Here we go."

I focused on Tom. He was standing with his feet shoulder width apart and his knees slightly bent, like the tanks on his back weighed a lot. When he pulled the trigger, it was hard to focus on him while fire streaking across the room, but I kept my eyes on him as he moved his arm slowly back and forth creating a wall of fire. It looked like if he moved too fast the fire would go out. Even behind the fireproof glass, we could feel the heat from the flames.

He released the trigger, and everyone clapped as he went over to the cart and took the flamethrower off followed by his helmet. "If you want to try it on, please form a line. You won't get to live fire it, but the techs are ready to hook you up to the simulator, so you can try it in your dreamscape.

I moved over to the line. I needed to get my hands on every weapon I could. I was good at materializing things I was familiar with, the more things I could hold the better.

"Liz, you're up first," Tom said, and my heart thumped against my chest as I moved to the front of the line. "For those of you who do not already know Liz, her birth father was Victor." There were a few murmurs at his statement. "We didn't learn of her existence until we moved here. Please welcome her as she moves through the training cycle with the other squires." I moved out from behind the fireproof glass and approached the cart tentatively. "Don't be shy everyone wants to try it on and see how it works."

Chapter 14

When I reached the cart, Tom opened his arms, indicating I needed to put it on myself. I pulled the backpack-like straps out and threaded my arms through them. It was heavy but not so much I would fall over backward. I attached the waist belt and adjusted the straps. Once it was sitting comfortably on my back, I picked up the gun with the hoses attached to it. I brought it up to aim. It was heavier than anything I had handled before. I adjusted my grip and put my finger on the trigger. I squeezed it, I would need to keep the trigger engaged to keep the flame going. I walked around a little bit and tried to spin around, earning myself some chuckles from the line of people waiting. I swallowed hard, feeling my face heat and went back to the cart.

"What do you think?" Tom asked as he helped me take it off.

"In certain circumstances, it will be awesome." I unbuckled the waist strap and unloaded the tanks.

"Remember if you need to use it you should be able to manifest it right on your back. Head over to the simulator and the tech guys will get you set up for training with it."

"Thanks." I went to the computer station, waving at Shawn as I passed him. He gave me a thumbs up before Kristina grabbed his arm. I rolled my eyes, wondering if he would ever tell her to leave him alone, then smiled at Brandon.

Five minutes later, I was lying on the bed with a bunch of electro pads stuck to me and VR goggles over my eyes. "Okay, Liz, just relax and pretend you're dreaming. Let your mind take you where you need to go," Brandon said before I put the headphones on, deadening the noise of the knights and squires around me.

The darkness slowly faded from my vision and I tried to figure out where they put me. The gym. I wondered if it was the only location they had. Zombies appeared and ambled toward me with their arms parallel to the floor. They were moaning, and I had to hold in my laughter. They took them straight from Night of the Living Dead. I thought about the flamethrower, the tanks, the hose going from the tanks to the gun, the heavy feel of it in my hands, the flash guards to keep me from being burned. I materialized it, but it took a long time and the zombies were almost on me by the time I pulled the trigger, and nothing happened. I stared at the gun, then kicked a zombie away when he got too close. I ran through everything that made it work: propane, hoses, and gun. I pulled the trigger and the lighter clicked like it wasn't getting gas.

"What am I doing wrong?" I needed to turn the gas on. I kicked another zombie while thinking of turning both the valves to the on position with my mind. I pulled the trigger again, relieved when flames shot out of the tip of the gun.

The zombies nearest me caught on fire. They screamed

and tried to escape but not before running into their friends and lighting them on fire. I moved around the room moving my arm back and forth, careful to only light the zombies on fire. I didn't want the gym to burn down with me in it. I loved the weapon. A minute later the zombies were all gone, the wires were being removed from my body and I took the goggles off, feeling proud of myself.

I pulled the headphones off and the room erupted with applause. I smoothed my hair back and blinked to help my eyes adjust then tightened my ponytail. It took me a minute to realize they were clapping for me and I wanted to run away and hide.

Tom gave me a smile. "I want you to watch everyone else now Liz."

I nodded then moved away from the bed, wanting to hide from the attention. "No one ever gets it right the first time," Brandon said, explaining the applause. "You're your father's daughter."

"Thanks." I moved to a spot where I was out of the way but still able to watch the monitors. My gaze traveled up to the balcony overlooking the training floor and I watched Jon walk away.

"Show off," Mary whispered as she walked by me to try the machine on. I rolled my eyes. The only reason she didn't like me was because I was with Shawn. She had an epic crush on him.

"Nicely done." Shawn stepped up next to me as we watched Brandon hook Jo up to the computer. "Not very many people get it on their first try."

"Thanks," I murmured, staring at the knights either waiting for the simulator or to try on the flamethrower. "I guess it gives me hope that someday I'll be good enough to be a knight."

"You need to stop doubting yourself," Shawn said as the screen showed Jo standing in the middle of a street. She was in a city surrounded by skyscrapers.

"Hey, nice job, Liz," Heather said, joining us.

"Thanks," I said, keeping my eyes on the screen. Jo was wearing the flamethrower now and an army of trolls were running at her. "Come on Jo," I whispered. I didn't want to be the only squire to get it on the first try. As the trolls got closer, I kept waiting for her to pull the trigger, but the flames never came. Jo held the gun across her chest and stared at it. It wasn't working. *Oh, no*, I thought as the first troll reached her. "She needs to turn the valves on, I forgot too," I whispered to Shawn.

It was too late though. The troll ripped the gun out of her hand, the simulation ended, and Jo pulled the goggles off. "That sucked." She pouted yanking the wires off.

"What happened?" Tom asked.

"I thought I had everything set. It should've worked, but when I pulled the trigger nothing happened."

"Did you hear the gas hissing?"

"No why?"

"Did you make sure you had full tanks?" Tom crossed his arms over his chest waiting for her to respond.

"I'm an idiot." Jo shook her head and stood. "I totally forgot to make sure I had propane." She moved over to stand with us. "I don't know how you do it, Liz."

"Do what?" I spun to look at her with my eyebrow raised.

"Remember everything you need when manifesting

something." She put her hands on her hips while we waited for the next person to get hooked up.

"I forgot to turn the propane on at first. I'm far from perfect."

"That's why you kept kicking them." Jo nodded her head. "Kristina thought you were too scared to pull the trigger."

I rolled my eyes. "So I kicked them instead. I don't get it."

"Hey, what are you guys doing after this?" Shawn asked.

"I have no plans, why?" Heather asked.

"Me neither, I'm supposed to hook up with Billy at some point but he's working most of the day," Jo said.

"Hum, gross," I said, glancing at Shawn. "Hanging with you I hope."

"Liz is right," Shawn made an ugly face at Jo. "I never want to hear about you and Billy *hooking up* ever again."

"That's not what I meant." Jo's face turned red and she punched Shawn in the arm.

"Whatever. Anyway, can we meet to talk about what Liz found yesterday?" Shawn asked just loud enough for us to hear.

"Yeah, but where?" Heather asked.

"We can meet at my house." I volunteered, Mom and Dad wouldn't be home till late.

"Sounds good," Heather said as we stopped talking to watch Jeff took his turn in the simulator.

We watched everyone go through the simulator. Besides me only a few of the older knights made the flamethrower work correctly. Poor Shawn forgot about the trigger guard and caught his shirt sleeve on fire when he tried it.

Kristina was one of the last to go. She started in downtown Twisted Pines. A bunch of teddy bears were chasing her. I had no idea where they came up with the targets for the simulations but seriously, teddy bears? They were cute and cuddly not scary, soul-sucking monsters. One moment Kristina was standing there with her arms at her sides confidently, the next she had the flamethrower on her back. She pulled the trigger and fire erupted from the barrel. The teddy bears burned, but her fire kept getting longer. I didn't know what she was trying to accomplish but as she spun to get the bears behind her the buildings caught fire. By the time she made one rotation she was surrounded by fire. Her confident expression was quickly replaced with panic, she was sweating and looking around for an escape. She dropped the gun, but the fire didn't go out. Instead the gun spun like a firehose shooting flames in a circle, catching her pants on fire.

"End it," Tom said to Brandon then ran to Kristina's side and pulled the goggles off her face. She was covered in sweat and shaking. She pushed Tom away and ripped the wires off her body.

"Are you all right?" he asked, offering her a hand. "You were doing well until you let the flames get too long."

"I'm fine." She pushed him away and jumped off the bed. "Maybe next time you give us a demonstration you can show us how to regulate the flame and turn the damn thing off," she said, pushing her way through the crowd.

"Okay, I think that does it," Tom said, ignoring Kristina's comment. "Squires let's go back to the classroom for a minute.

Everyone else, thank you for joining us today. We will do this once a month now that we are settled in.”

“She needs to pay better attention,” Jo said as we walked back to the classroom. “I remember Dad told us how to adjust the flame, and turning it off is easy, release the trigger.”

“Yeah, she must’ve messed up manifesting it,” Shawn said, taking my hand, and walking with us back to the classroom. He stopped outside the door and let Jo go in.

“Have fun. I’ll meet you at your house,” Shawn said leaned in.

“Okay, I’ll see you in a little while,” I said before he kissed me briefly then let go of my hand. I went into the classroom and took a seat next to Jo.

Tom was standing at the front of the room waiting for everyone to stop talking. “Everyone did a good job today. Don’t worry if you weren’t able to manifest it completely. It takes time and practice to create something as complicated as a flamethrower. Tomorrow we’ll work on fighting skills and basic weapons training. Tonight, in your dreams I want you to practice manifesting a weapon you’ve had a hard time with, be it a gun, the flamethrower or something else. Any questions?” He paused then continued when no one spoke up. “Okay, see you tomorrow night, same time same place. Liz, can I see you for a moment?”

After everyone left, I went to the front of the room, wondering if I was in trouble.

“You did well today. My question is, why can’t you do that with other weapons?” He leaned against the desk and put his hands in his pockets.

"If I can see how it works, what its components are, handle them, then I can. I'm not as good with weapons I'm not familiar with. I didn't know what a bowie knife was. You know?"

"So, you are telling me you can manifest a flamethrower after seeing it and touching for a few minutes, but you can't manifest a broadsword you've seen in movies?"

"Not until I study it. I've been able to create a sword, but I really have to think about it since I've never used one."

"We will spend a lot of time in the weapons room then, starting tomorrow." Tom nodded his head in understanding.

"Thanks." I went to leave.

"Don't worry, your dad wasn't good at everything either."

I spun around. "Thanks, after today it feels like everyone thought of him as a god or something."

"Some might have until he left, but we trained together. He had areas where he needed help too. Have a good afternoon."

"You too." I left the room, feeling better about how things were going. The hallway was empty, and I quickened my pace, wanting to get home. I heard a door behind me open and I glanced back. It was Jon, I didn't know if I should greet him or not. I nodded my head without breaking my stride and almost made it to the front door when he called my name.

I stopped and faced him. "Yes, Jon?"

"Can I see you for a moment?" He opened the door nearest to him. I didn't know why he asked, it wasn't like I could tell him no.

"Sure." I followed him into the classroom but didn't sit down.

"I watched you in the simulator today. You did well," he said after closing the door and standing in front of it, blocking my escape.

"Thanks." I crossed my arms over my chest, not trusting his compliment.

"Just because you are good at manifesting functioning weapons doesn't mean you will make a good knight." He put his hands on his hips.

"I never thought it would. I know I still have a lot learn." I didn't understand what he was trying to tell me.

"Good, it won't all be easy for you and I just wanted to remind you of the contract you signed. You can't quit if it gets too hard, or things don't work out."

I stared at him for a minute, trying to translate what he said into something that made sense. "You mean if Shawn and I break up? You think I'll want to quit?" Why did he think we were going to break up?

"Well he has been spending a lot of time with Kristina." He was baiting me, and I couldn't help rolling my eyes.

I clenched my jaw. "He's been spending time with her because you are making them work together. Don't try and turn this around on Shawn." I moved my hand to my hips.

"I'm just trying to do what is best for my son." His voice grew louder as he spoke.

"And I'm not it?" I couldn't help my voice becoming as loud as his.

"No, I don't think you are. You have too many strikes against you."

"What strikes?" What had I done?

"You've been marked, you weren't raised with the clan, you don't understand how we do things. Then there's your father." He stepped away from the door and paced with his hands clenched behind his back, staring at the ground.

"Really? You are really digging at the bottom of the barrel there." I went to the door, done listening to him. I put my hand on the door handle but stopped. "When I say I'll do something I don't back down. If Shawn and I break up I'm not going anywhere." I opened the door and stomped to my Jeep. I wanted to get away from Jon before I did something that could get me kicked out, like taking a swing at him.

I drove home, fuming about what Jon had said. The entire conversation didn't add up. First, he says I can't quit but then he went on about how I wasn't good enough. He didn't know me, he hadn't even tried to know me. He was judging me based off a man I had never met. I wished there was something I could do to make him back off, but until I proved myself, he would be waiting to drag me down every chance he could.

Chapter 15

"Sorry, guys," I said, flipping through the keys on my key chain until I found the one for the front door.

"What took you so long?" Shawn asked from behind me.

I glanced over my shoulder debating on whether I should tell him about his dad. "Tom wanted to talk to me after class, then I ran into Jon on my way out."

"What did Dad want?" he asked as I opened the door and led him, Jo, and Heather to the dining room.

"What he does best," I said, putting my backpack on the table. "Tell me that I'm not good enough, same old, same old."

"I'm sorry, Liz." Heather pulled out a chair and sat. "When someone does him wrong, he never forgets it."

"I get that, but I think he's taking it too far. My dad left a long time ago." I took my notebook out of my bag and sat down. "Anyway, who wants to go first?" I glanced around the table.

"I'll go first," Shawn said, holding up a blank paper. "I have nothing because I've had no time to do any research. If I'm not working, Mom has me helping her."

"Excuses, excuses." Heather rolled her eyes. "Jo what did you find?"

Jo opened her notebook. "Not as much as I would have liked, but I found something. I think the gate opened a month before the Native Americas revolted against the Spanish in 1680, but I didn't find anything pointing me to how, why, or where the gate opened. The Native Americans blamed the Spanish for the sleeping sickness, and vice versa but the natives were largely unaffected by it and no one knows why. Most of the information I found was on the internet, but I have a request in with Knight Inc.'s archivist. There's a chance we have records on file about what was going on at the time, but who knows when he will get to it."

"Did he ask you why you wanted to know?" Heather asked.

"No, thank God, I don't know what I would have told him if he asked."

"It's a good starting point," I smiled at Jo. "Heather were you able to find anything about the gate in Trinidad?"

She blew out a breath and opened her notebook. "Not really, I found nothing saying, we found this weird gate and opened it, now everyone is dying." She ran a hand through her hair when we didn't reply. "So, I went through the newspapers, online and print, checked the USGS, there were no earthquakes reported. I checked with fish and game to find out if there were any lost hikers. Nothing out of the ordinary had been reported in Trinidad for weeks before the first person died."

"Bummer," Shawn said, glancing at me. "Well, Liz, you're up. What did you find?"

"Not any more than you guys did." I told them about everything I found in the old newspapers, how it started with Freeman's kids and spread from there.

"Do you think there is a correlation between where the deaths started and where the gate is?" Jo asked writing something down in her notebook.

"I don't know but it might give us a place to start." I glanced at Heather. "Do we know who died in Trinidad first?"

"Yeah, or at least I can find out, what then?" She drew her eyebrows together.

"It's just a hunch, but I think we should plot all the deaths on a map to see if there might be a pattern." Shawn nodded his head at me, understanding where I was going while Jo and Heather shook their heads in confusion. I was about to explain more when I heard a truck pull into the driveway. "That sounds like Billy's truck." I jumped up from my chair and ran to the window. Sure enough, Billy was headed toward the front door. "Billy's here, we need to come up with an excuse and quick." I crossed my arms over my chest and glanced at Jo.

"I got it," she said, moving to join me. "We are working on a project for work, we needed somewhere quiet to work."

I watched Billy approach the door and ring the doorbell for the first time in his life. I opened the door after a second. "You rang?"

"Jo, what are you doing here?" he asked ignoring me when he saw her. "I saw Shawn's Jeep in the driveway and didn't want to walk in on anything that would scar me for life."

"Good idea," Jo said, making kisses noises. "We were just finishing up a project for work and needed a quiet place to work." She walked back into the dining room and Billy followed her like a puppy. I rolled my eyes and followed them, sitting in the chair I had been in before Billy arrived.

"What kind of project?" he asked nodding at Heather and Shawn.

"A top secret one." Heather glanced at her phone and stood. "Shawn I've got to get home. I have plans tonight."

"Yeah, okay. Let me just say goodbye to Liz. Jo are you still riding with us?"

Jo glanced at Billy and he shook his head. "No, I'm pretty sure Billy will get me home eventually."

"Okay, I'll meet you outside. Later Jo, bye Liz," Heather said, going out the front door.

"Bye," Jo said, going to Billy's side. "Come on let's blow this joint I'm over work for the day."

"See ya, Liz," Billy said as he picked Jo up in a fireman's carry. She shrieked and pounded on his back as he walked out.

"I wish I could stay and hang out longer, but Heather hates being the third wheel." Shawn got to his feet and came around the table.

"Can't blame her," I said, depressed he was leaving.

"Hey, why don't we plan on a hike Saturday morning?" He dragged me to my feet and hugged me close.

"Sounds good, just you and me."

"Just you and me" He bent his head and his lips met mine

in a kiss that was too short.

"I'll see you tomorrow." He headed for the door.

"Be careful tonight," I said, following behind him.

"You too, don't let the goblin get to you." I shut the door behind him just as the phone rang, and I ran to grab it before the machine answered it. "Hello?"

"Hi Liz?" a feminine voice I didn't recognize asked.

"Yes?"

"This is Stacy from Knights Inc."

"Oh, Stacy, hi." I walked with the phone to my ear into the living room and sat on the couch. "Sorry I didn't recognize your voice."

"That's okay, sorry to call your home phone. Your cell went straight to voicemail, and I wasn't sure when you would check it."

"No problem, what's going on?" I was dying to ask her if she knew anything about the gates, but I didn't know if I could trust her yet.

"I was wondering if you would like to go to lunch tomorrow. We can talk about Victor and I'll answer questions you don't want to ask Tom about us."

Going to lunch with her would be a great way to get a feel for her and maybe she would tell me more about what my dad was doing before he left Knights Inc. "Sure. I don't know what time I will be done with training though."

"Let me give you my number and you can call me when you're done." Stacy gave me her number, and I promised to call her the next day.

I lay back on the couch and thought about it. The way Stacy had acted made me think there was something she really wanted to tell me that she couldn't talk about at the office. I fluttered my feet in the air. It had to be something about Victor's work, what else would she not want to talk about around other people?

I sat up and looked at the clock, with any luck by this time tomorrow we would have the clue we needed to find and close the gate. In the meantime, I needed to work on something, it was too late to go to the library, it would be closed by the time I got there. I drummed my fingers on my knee thinking for a second then went up to my room and searched the internet for anything on Freeman. Even though he found one of the largest deposits of gold in Colorado, he wasn't very popular, even his Wiki page only had one paragraph.

I put my computer away when Mom got home and helped her with dinner, then I spent the rest of the evening with my parents wondering if Shawn and I would ever have some time to ourselves. My parents wondered where Shawn was when they got home and eyed me when I said that his dad was making him work. It almost felt like they didn't believe me, or Shawn.

When it was time for bed, I decided to take Tom's advice and take down my dreamcatcher. Maybe if I killed a few mares they would leave me alone.

Chapter 16

I climbed into bed and rubbed my rune; I was going against everything I agreed to when I signed the contract with Jon, but he didn't understand how the mares were terrorizing my dreams. I thought about what Tom said, how Jon told them not to help me in my dreams if a mare attacked me. I was beginning to think that not only did Jon not want me around, but he wanted to help the mares kill me before Shawn fell in love with me.

I tucked the rune under my T-shirt feeling the cold weight of it rest against my skin. I had found out on prom night that the rune kept the mares from taking my soul while still allowing me to fight them, unlike the dreamcatcher that put an invisible wall between me and the mare. Nervous about fighting Stalker, I lay in bed for a long time before sleep took me.

I was in a kayak on the lake near the shore when my dream began. I paddled along without a care in the world when I saw two people talking in the parking lot next to the beach. One had long blonde hair and the other was bald.

There was only one person I knew with long blonde hair that light, and I wondered if this was my dream or if I was in her dream. I thought of Kristina and moved to the parking lot about fifty-feet from her. I ducked behind a car then crawled forward to see who she was with.

"I know, I want the bitch dead too," she said. The wind carried their voices to me.

"Maybe we can come to an agreement," Stalker said. Why wasn't Kristina trying to kill him?

"I'm not killing her, there is no way I would get away with it." She crossed her arms over her chest.

"I'm not asking you to. She has some kind of protection or force field around her when she dreams. If you can get rid of it, I will get rid of her." Stalker paced a few steps, staring at the ground with his hands on his hips.

"It will be risky, but I'll see what I can do." She tapped her foot on the ground then twirled a lock of her hair around her finger.

"Good, if you do this for me, I'll make sure the others of my kind stay away from you." He stroked his chin. "How will you get rid of her protection?"

"I know where it comes from, I'll have to break into her bedroom while she's sleeping and take it down."

"You need to tell me the night before, so I'll be ready." He looked up at her

"I will, now if you will excuse me, I have other things to do." Kristina disappeared.

I knew Kristina didn't like me because of my relationship with Shawn, but I didn't think she would resort to meeting with the enemy to not only break us up but to kill me. I closed my eyes, I wanted to find Shawn and tell him what I saw, but he was working, and Kristina had probably just joined him. I doubted he would believe me after he took her side at the BBQ. I pushed my fear back and stood. *Stalker wanted to fight me without my dreamcatcher, tonight he would.*

"Hello, lamb chop, how are you this evening?" Stalker asked as I came out from behind the car I'd been hiding behind. I thought of my Colt .45 and brought it up taking aim at his head. "What did you overhear?" He laughed at the gun. "Why do you even bother? You can't hurt me." He walked around me in a slow circle.

"Can't you go bug someone else for the night?" I ignored his question and began shaking. Maybe sleeping without my dreamcatcher wasn't such a good idea. The thought of fighting him terrified me. If I shot him, and it didn't kill him, we would end up fighting, and I didn't know if I could beat him again.

"You are my favorite person to bug, though." He tapped his finger on his lips. "You didn't answer my question, which means you know what I plan to do." He looked at his fingernails then rubbed them on his T-shirt. "It matters not. If she succeeds, I will get you, then I will get her. If she fails, I will get her and eventually you."

Double crossing ass. It wasn't for me to judge how Kristina should pay for her plotting.

"Liz, help me," Billy yelled, bringing me out of my thoughts. Stalker was standing next to Billy with his arm around him like they were best friends, but Billy's face was pale, and his eyes were wide with fear.

"Please Liz, just do what he wants. I'm too young to die." As he spoke Stalker moved his arm around Billy's neck and squeezed, cutting off his air. Billy tried to pull Stalker's arms away, but it was too late, Stalker was too strong. I screamed as Billy's face turned blue and the whites of his eyes turned red before they bulged out of his head.

I brought my gun up, no longer caring if I could beat the goblin or not. I couldn't stand by and let Billy die, even if it was only a dream. I sighted in on Stalker's head and pulled the trigger. My aim was true, as soon as the bullet hit him with his head the momentum caused Stalker to fall backwards forcing him to let go of Billy, who crumpled to the ground.

"Billy are you all right?" I ran to him, bent, and put a hand on his back.

"Yeah, I'm fine, but you're not."

I glanced down at Billy, only it wasn't Billy anymore, a mare had taken his place. I had never seen this one before. He was short with shaggy chestnut hair. His face was similar to Stalker's, but he had a long scar that ran from his eye socket down to his chin.

I jumped to my feet and thought of the flamethrower. The tanks were on my back and the gun was in my hand ready to fire in the next heartbeat. I made sure the tank was on and pulled the trigger. Flames exploded out of the gun and shot toward the furry mare. He tried to get to his feet, but the fire caught too quickly thanks to his fur and he collapsed to the ground shaking as the flames ate through his skin and devoured his body.

I liked this weapon almost more than the chain saw. I spun, searching for Stalker, but I was too slow. Something hit me from behind and I fell forward onto my knees. I let the flamethrower disappear and rolled onto my back with my Colt in my hand ready to fire.

"You came out without your protection. I won't need that twat after all." Stalker took a step closer to me showing me his razer-sharp teeth. "It's too late now, I called my friends. You're not getting out of here alive."

I squeezed the trigger hitting him in the chest, he jerked backwards and laughed. "Your guns can't hurt me lamb chop. Now stop fighting and let me end it quickly for you."

I let the gun disappear and ran through the weapons I could manifest. Something had to work on him. He was close, too close. I needed something for close quarters fighting. He was on his knees, then reaching for my hands to stop me from fighting him. I thought of my flay knife, I jerked my hand out of his reach as the knife manifested, praying it was sharp I plunged it into the side of his neck and sawed back and forth while ugly black blood covered my hands. He screamed and jerked away from me with the knife sticking out of the side of his neck.

"You little bitch." He pulled the knife out and threw it at me. I rolled away, easily missing the projectile but not fast enough to dodge his foot aimed at my ribs. I screamed, feeling something crack when he connected. He laughed and kicked me again as I crumpled into a fetal position. "You think you can beat me? You have no idea how strong I am." He swung his leg back to kick me again, but I rolled out of the way, allowing him only a glancing blow.

I had to stand up, I couldn't lay there and let me him kick me to death. I coughed and tasted blood. Had he punctured a lung? I struggled to my knees then shakily got to my feet. I thought of the short sword from the night before and it was in my hand. "Come and get me you piece of shit."

The goblin laughed and ran toward me with his own sword, only it was twice as long as mine. He swung at me and I brought my sword up in time to block his. The impact jarred my arm all the way down my side. I held on to the sword, but my hand went numb and my side was killing me. This was not how I wanted the night to go.

"Grab her boys," Stalker said, looking behind me. I glanced over my shoulder, Pigskin and Twiggy-Squatch were behind me. They each grabbed an arm and forced me to drop the sword.

I had to do something, I could still die in my sleep even if he couldn't take my soul. Stalker came toward me with a switch blade in his hand. "Now stand still, or I will cut you." He held the knife under my chin and pressed his cold, sticky lips against mine forcing them to open.

No, I would not go down this way, I thought to myself. Ignoring the pain in my side, I used the mares holding my arms for leverage, and I kicked up and hit Stalker in the chest. The mares behind me let go as my feet hit the ground, and I thought of a chainsaw. With it running in my hand I spun holding it at arm's length, keeping the mares away from me if nothing else.

"Come on boys, there is only one of her and three of us," Stalker said, lunging at me as I tried to catch his hand with the saw.

"Come and get me," I said between coughing fits. My mouth was filling with blood and I was light-headed; something was wrong. Pigskin lunged at me and I swung the chain saw in his direction, but I was slow, and the chainsaw was getting heavy, I didn't know how much longer I could hold it.

Someone pushed me from behind and I lost my footing. I was falling right on top of the chainsaw, I closed my eyes, imagining a pillow instead of the chainsaw, and right as I felt the displaced air from the chain buzzing under my nose, my face hit the softest pillow I had ever felt. I coughed, and blood covered the pillow. One of them, I didn't know who, grabbed my arm and flipped me onto my back a second before Stalker sat on my chest, flashing a knife. He was so heavy I couldn't get a lungful of air. My mouth filled with blood again and I spit it at him.

"I'm done playing with you now." He leaned over my mouth, ready to suck my soul out and I wondered what he would do to me when realized he couldn't. I stared over his shoulder at the blue sky and puffy white clouds. I was floating away, and I didn't care. A dreamless sleep was all I really wanted and maybe to see Shawn one more time.

Shawn, I thought to myself closing my eyes. I felt Stalker's lip on mine for a second, and then he was gone.

"Get away from her you devil," Shawn said, and I opened my eyes. I was in a large room on my back. Cubicle walls were on either side of me, I must have been in an office building. Someone was screaming and someone else was calling for help. Shawn was a few feet away trying to cut the head off of a mare with a pair of pruning shears.

I tried to sit up, but my head was spinning, and everything looked fuzzy. "Shawn?" I asked, trying, and failing to get to my feet.

"Liz, what are you doing here?" He ran to me, taking in my injuries. "What were you doing sleeping without your dreamcatcher?" He took my head in his hands and stared at me with his brow furrowed.

"Tom said I might be able to scare them away if I killed one or two." I whispered as my heart fluttered and I felt something drip out of the corner of my mouth.

"Shawn," Stacy yelled, then the rat-tat-tat of a machine gun sounded, and I wondered where Kristina was. "Little help here."

"Liz, wake up or you'll die." He stared into my eyes and I understood his concern. "Wake up."

I jerked and sat up in my bed. I ran shaky hands over my body. I was alive, nothing hurt and there wasn't any blood, but I could still taste it. I had to get the taste out. I got out of bed and brushed my teeth. With fresh breath I went back to bed and looked at the clock. It was four in the morning and I was alive.

I dug my dreamcatcher back out and hung it over my bed. I didn't think I could go back to sleep, but at least if I did, I would be safe.

Chapter 17

I never made it back to sleep, there was something wrong, and I didn't think it had anything to do with my nightmare. I couldn't put my finger on it. Maybe it was because Kristina wasn't with Shawn after she met with Stalker. Everything from that part of the dream was hazy, like I missed something. I had been close to death in my dream and I felt like an idiot for not remembering to wake myself up. How pathetic was I? Not able to kill a mare on my own, then go cry to my boyfriend, when I should've just woken up.

How was I going to make an example of a mare if they kept tag teaming me? It was hard enough to bring Stalker down; I needed to be a lot better if I wanted to beat three at a time.

Then there was Kristina. How was I going to keep her from taking down my dreamcatcher? We locked the house, but not all the time, and mostly only when we were gone for the day. I can't remember anyone ever locking up at night. What was I going to tell my parents? *This girl I work with wants to kill me in my dreams by taking down my dreamcatcher, so can we please make sure the house is locked up at night?* I rolled over and checked the time. My alarm would go off in a few minutes. I turned it off, got up and ready for work, trying to figure out the best way to tell my parents about Kristina.

Mom was in the kitchen when I made it downstairs and I didn't want to look at her. I felt like she would know I almost didn't wake up by looking at me, then she would freak out and put an end to my training.

"Morning," I said, trying to sound chipper as I went to straight to the coffee pot.

"Morning sweetie, how did you sleep?" she took the skillet off the stove and split the scrambled eggs she had been cooking between two plates.

"Oh, ah, good. How about you?" I asked, sitting at the bar as she put one of the plates in front of me. "Thanks for breakfast."

"I slept good. Listen Liz," she started but then stopped until I met her eyes. "Are you sure working for Knights Inc. is really what you want to do?"

"Yes, I'm already learning so much and we're trying to find the gate, then everything will be fine." I didn't mention that there were gates all over the world. There was no need to make her worry more.

"I'm just worried. I heard you tossing and turning in your sleep last night."

"Oh, that was nothing, just training."

"Please be careful." She glanced at her watch as she ate the rest of her eggs. "I've got to go."

"Yeah me too," I said, pushing the eggs around on my

plate. I wasn't hungry, but I picked up a forkful to make her happy. I would talk to her about keeping the house locked up later.

"See you tonight," she said, running out the door.

I finished my eggs not wanting to waste them then locked the doors and all the windows on the first floor before I left for work.

Shawn wasn't in the parking lot waiting for me when I arrived at Knights Inc., and I wondered where he was. He had met me every morning since I started, and it was weird without him. It wasn't the end of the world, but I missed him especially after what happened in my dream the night before. I wanted to make sure everything was okay.

Marcy was sitting behind the desk with red-rimmed eyes when I entered. "Marcy are you okay?" I stopped at her desk. She glanced up from her computer.

"No, but Tom is waiting for you and you don't want to be late." She pointed to the door, and a knot formed in my gut.

I swiped my card and dashed down the hall to Tom's office. His door was open, so I walked in. "Morning," I said tentatively.

Tom looked up from his computer and nodded. "Come on, we've been summoned to Jon's office." He stood and walked around his desk.

"Tom, what's going on?" The knot in my stomach tightened more as he led me down the hall and through the training room to Jon's office.

"Jon will explain." His voice was tight, and I couldn't figure out if he was mad at me or if something else was going on.

"Tom, I took your advice last night and didn't sleep with the dreamcatcher, but it didn't go like we hoped." I was trying to come clean, I didn't want to get in trouble.

Tom stopped and faced me. "Liz, I can't talk about it right now. We have to get to Jon's office."

My mouth went dry as he continued across the training room. I messed up, maybe Shawn or Stacy had to tell them I showed up almost dead and Jon was going to fire me for breaking our contract.

When we reached the door to Jon's office, Tom knocked once then waited until we heard Jon tell us to come in. Tom opened the door, ushering me in. Jon was sitting behind his desk reviewing some paperwork. Shawn was sitting in a chair on the right side of Jon's desk, and he glanced at me then away like he wanted nothing to do with me. Magnus, Kristina's dad, was sitting on the far left of the desk leaving two empty chairs for Tom and me in the middle.

"Tom, Liz please have a seat," Jon said, finally glancing up from the papers on his desk. Tom held his arm out to me, waiting for me to take a seat before he took the one next to me.

"It has come to my attention that you broke your contract last night," Jon started and looked between Tom and me.

Tom was about to speak but I put my hand up to stop him. "You're right, I slept without my dreamcatcher last night." I sat up straighter in my chair. I wouldn't let Tom take the fall for me.

"I told her not to sleep with it. The mares are tormenting her, and she isn't getting any rest. What happened last night wasn't her fault," Tom said, fisting his hands and resting them on his legs.

"That is beside the point." Jon spun his chair to face me. "Tell me what happened in your dream."

"I didn't sleep with my dreamcatcher because I wanted to kill a mare thinking if I did, they would leave me alone for a while. You don't understand what they are doing to me every night."

"Stop beating around the bush and tell us about your dream," Magnus said, furrowing his brow, and raising his voice.

I wanted to tell about Kristina and Stalker, but they wouldn't believe me. Kristina was perfect in their eyes and there wouldn't be anything I could do to convince that she was going to help Stalker kill me. Instead I told them I was doing my homework when Stalker showed up, that I attacked him, then his buddies showed up and kicked my ass. "I was hurt badly, I think I had a punctured lung. I wasn't thinking straight, and I didn't know what to do so I went to Shawn. I realize now I should've woken myself up, but I was dying and scared."

Magnus crossed one leg over the other, then did the same with his arms. He didn't believe me. Jon stared, shook his head, and pinched the bridge of his nose. *Great, I'm going to get fired*, I thought.

"Kick me out if you want." I looked at Jon then Magnus. "It won't stop me from fighting them. I'm already on my own since you won't let anyone help me." I was getting mad. Yes, I had broken a rule, but it wasn't like someone died or anything.

Jon opened his mouth to speak but Tom beat him to it. "This is ridiculous, this isn't her fault Jon, and you know it." Tom folded his hands together. "It's her first week. You know the mares won't leave her alone. Why is she forced to put up with them night after night? She needs protection, not a court martial for trying to save herself."

"She's marked, Tom," Jon shouted, surging to his feet. "We've never given anyone marked protection, they are a danger not only to themselves but everyone around them." He stomped around his desk, forcing us all to crane our necks to keep him in our line of vision. "What happened last night is exactly why I didn't want to train her in the first place."

"How is me getting my ass kicked and asking for help the end of the world?" I got to my feet ready to leave. Everyone else would bow down to Jon, but I couldn't sit there and let him treat me like I was less than dirt.

"Stacy died last night because Shawn was too busy helping you when he should have been covering her back," Magnus bellowed, and the room went silent.

My stomach roiled, and I thought I was going to vomit. I breathed through my nose and closed my eyes trying to remember what happened with Shawn the night before. Stacy had said she needed help, Shawn told me to wake up, and I left. Had the minutes I'd been there cost Stacy her life? "I'm sorry, I didn't know. No one told me."

"Liz, if you want to become a knight you have to follow the rules," Magnus said, his voice calm.

I wanted to yell at him, what right did he have to tell me what to do? Maybe he should worry about his daughter instead of me. I held my tongue though, I needed to be an adult about this. "What happens now?" I returned to my seat and tried to catch Shawn's eye, but he was looking anywhere but at me.

"If I had my way you would be out. We would cut all ties with you and you would be on your own to ruin your own life." Jon came back around to his desk and sat. "But the council does not agree with me. You have too much talent to be excommunicated. You will resume your training and sleep under your dreamcatcher until you pass the final test. I don't care how tired the mares make you, you have to follow the rules."

"Very well." I stood, wanting to be by myself. "Is there anything else?"

"No, you may go." Jon dismissed me. "I would ask you three to stay, we need to make arrangements, and Jenny is in no condition to make them right now."

I got up and walked solemnly to the door. Once I was on the other side I ran for my Jeep. I needed to get away from everything including myself. It was my fault Stacy was dead.

I somehow made it to my house through a stream of tears and a snotty nose. How could I be so selfish? I knew Shawn was working when I was battling the mare. I should've remembered to wake myself up and I would have been fine. I should've never gone to bed without my dreamcatcher and now someone I knew, who I wanted to get to know better was dead because of me.

I walked into the house in a daze. It was Thursday, which meant my parents wouldn't be home till after five. I took my phone out of my pocket and clicked it on. I had no messages, Shawn probably hated me. I set my phone on the bar in the kitchen and went to the window to stare at the lake.

I had no idea what to do, but I couldn't just sit around feeling sorry for myself. I felt like I would go insane if I sat in the house one more second. I ran up to my room and changed into a pair of shorts and a tank top. I put my hiking boots on, grabbed my hiking pack and checked the contents. I hadn't been for a hike since October and I wanted to make sure I had everything I needed. In the main compartment I had a stocking hat, gloves, toilet paper, parachute cord, an aluminum foldup shovel, and some stale protein bars. I took the bars and threw them in the trash, grabbed two new ones out of the pantry and filled up the water bladder, then I checked the smaller compartments. One had my knife, water proof matches and a compass. The other one held my tissue paper and charcoal I used to take rubbings of the random tombstones scattered through the mountains. With everything I needed in place I took off toward the trail near my house. Maybe getting back to nature would help me clear my head.

Chapter 18

The trail started about a quarter mile from my house. It wound its way around the hillside, circled through a meadow then came back around to meet the road where it started. It was only two miles, but I didn't care. I needed to get away from everything and nature was the only thing that would help me. There was a car parked at the trailhead, which meant I would probably run into people, exactly what I wanted to avoid but there weren't any other trails nearby and I didn't want to go home, get my Jeep the drive somewhere else.

I started up the trail, trying to forget about the night before and the meeting with Jon, but I couldn't stop thinking about how Shawn wouldn't make eye contact with me and that he said nothing through the entire meeting. I didn't expect him to defend me, but it would've been nice for him to say something. He was probably blaming himself just as much as I was, but it wasn't his fault, it was mine. Why didn't I think about waking myself up? I should've waited to sleep without my dreamcatcher until I was a better fighter. All I wanted was a good night's sleep.

They hadn't kicked me out, but it was a close thing. I made it sound like I knew what I would do if they fired me during the meeting, but the thought of being on my own every night terrified me to the point of tears. I wiped them off my cheeks and gave myself a shake. *Keep it together Liz, they didn't kick you out.*

I was coming down the back side of the mountain where the trees gave way to the meadow. It was early but the blades of new green grass were working their way through the yellowed flattened grass from the year before. The aspen trees were full of new leaves and the birds were singing the sounds of summer from above. The meadow was as beautiful as it had been the year before and I smiled at the wonders of Mother Nature without realizing it.

I walked, taking everything in when I saw a trail I'd only dreamed about. It was a two-track leading into the forest. I stopped and looked around; it hadn't been there the year before; I had hiked the trail I was on almost weekly the prior summer, then Dad and I had hunted deer there in the fall. I would've remembered a well-used trail like the one in front of me. But I'd seen it in my dreams. I had dreamed of it not long after Stalker started showing up in my dreams. I wanted to know where it led but it could go on for miles without ending and I wasn't prepared for a hike like that. I continued down the main trail, thinking I would explore it with Shawn if he still wanted to see me.

The crying of a baby and angry voices ahead of me made me stop. A man was yelling at a woman while their toddler cried in her arms. A dog was running around barking probably scaring the small animals nearby. The last thing I wanted to do was talk to them.

Decision made, I took the two-track a little quicker than I normally would, but it was better than listening to the couple argue over who had to cook dinner when they got home. As the trail left the meadow and led me deeper into the woods, I breathed in the clean air that smelled of pine trees, earth, and sunshine. It was hard to see where I was being led as the trail twisted and turned around gnarled pine trees, but I wasn't worried, it was a good trail and I would be able to find my way out as long as I didn't go off trail. The terrain got steeper, and I had to stop to take a sip of water. I kept thinking I was getting close to the end but then the trail would turn and there was no end in sight.

I was about to turn back when I noticed the forest had gone quiet. The birds stopped singing, and the squirrels were tucked away in their nests. I could've heard a feather fall to the ground it was so quiet. A branch broke behind me. Startled, I took off at a sprint, my flight or fight instinct taking over and I couldn't stop my legs from racing up the trail.

All I could hear was the pounding of my heart, the fabric of my shirt rubbing as I pumped my arms, and the sound of my feet hitting the ground. I ran for a long time and I was tiring. I would have to stop soon but I didn't want to face whatever was behind me. My energy was almost gone when I saw it, a break in the trees- sunlight and safety were a few hundred feet ahead. I pushed my legs to go a little faster and pumped my arms harder. When I burst through the trees and into the sunlight, I dropped to my knees and put my hands on the ground. I took deep breaths and calmed my racing heart.

When I could breathe again, I stood up, wiped the sweat off my face with the hem of my shirt and took in my surroundings. My mouth hung open when I recognized where I was. The grass was short and yellow, with no sign of new growth. The dirt was dry and dusty and there was a mineshaft in the middle of the clearing. I almost fell back to my knees. This was where my reoccurring dream always took place. I had never seen this place before the dreams started.

I walked toward the open shaft with my eyes on the ground. There were no footprints or sign of animals, but when I reached the opening to the shaft there was fresh, coffee ground colored dirt piled around the opening. I knelt and picked up a handful then let it slide through my fingers. It was moist compared to the dirt I walked through to get to the shaft. I moved closer to the opening in the ground, careful not to disturb any of the dirt piles. I didn't want to walk through them, someone or something had put them there and I didn't want them to know I had been there.

I stared into the shaft. It was so dark I couldn't see more than a few feet into it and a cool breeze blew out of it caressing my face, making me think it was really deep. I had a flashlight in one of the side pockets of my pack and as I fumbled for it, I heard someone running behind me. I twisted around to see who it was but was too late. Hands shoved me toward the opening. I reached out, latched on to the support beam and yelped as I almost lost my footing and splinters of wood gouged my palm. I stared into the black hole, panic freezing me in place for a second before I scrambled to get my feet back under me. I turned to see who pushed me, but no one was there, and the clearing was empty.

My whole body shuddered, and goosebumps broke out

along my arms and legs. It was time to go. I pushed away from the mineshaft and sprinted across the clearing to the trail. The forest was still deadly quiet and knowing someone or something was out there trying to hurt me made my legs move even faster than they had before. I was breathing hard and my legs were cramping by the time I reached the meadow and the main trail. I forced myself to stop to catch my breath when I got there. There was something very wrong with the trail and the clearing.

When I could breathe again, I stood and noticed the sun was low in the sky. It was late, but I didn't understand how. I checked my watch for the time, but it was frozen with all of the dials pointed at twelve and a shiver shook my body. I hadn't been gone more than two hours, three at the most and it was before noon the last time I checked my watch, if the sun was right, it was past seven in the evening. I rubbed the back of my neck then walked back to my house slowly, digging the slivers of wood out of my hands and listening to the birds singing and the crickets chirping.

I was almost back to the road when I heard a car start. I doubted it was the family I'd seen earlier, which meant it could have been whoever pushed me. My legs were killing me from my run down the mountain, but I needed to find out had followed me. I jogged up the last bit of hill obscuring my view of the road. I reached the top just in time to see a cherry red car drive around the curve leading down the mountain. The dust it kicked up made it impossible to make out the model or the plates, but after last night's dream, I knew who it was. What I didn't know was, what to do about her.

Chapter 19

As I approached my house something wasn't right. There were enough cars parked in the driveway to make me think my parents were having a party, except as I got closer, I recognized Billy's truck, Shawn's Jeep, and Heather's Subaru. What were they doing at my house? I picked up my pace even though it felt like my legs were going to fall off. *What now*?

I opened the front door and voices drifted to me from the dining room. I took my backpack off and left it by the stairs. "What's going on?" I asked, joining the group huddled around the table looking at something.

"Liz?" Billy almost yelled, wrapping his arms around me. "Where have you been?"

I hugged him back and winced at the concerned faces of my parents and friends. "I went for a hike, I was just going to do the loop but—" Before I finished Dad yanked me out of Billy's arms and shook me.

"Why didn't you leave a note?" The worry in his eyes stabbed me through the heart. "You know better than to just take off without telling anyone where you're going."

"I'm sorry, like I said, I was just going to do the loop when I found a new trail." Before I could say any more Mom took me into her arms.

"Why were you hiking alone?" She squeezed me tight, as if she thought she would never see me again.

I stared over her shoulder at Shawn standing on the other side of the table with his arms crossed over his chest. If his eyes were lasers, I would be headless. "What happened?" His voice was tight.

I stepped away from Mom. "There's a new trail that shoots off the loop." I glanced around, everyone was looking at me like I was crazy. "I'm serious, it's a two-track on the far side of the loop. It leads up into the trees and comes out in a clearing with an old mineshaft."

"Why would you take a trail you've never been on by yourself without telling anyone?" Dad asked, crossing his arms over his chest.

"I'm sorry, Dad, I guess I haven't been making the best decisions lately." I nodded my head at Shawn, he got it.

"I think you all need to leave now." Dad glanced at my friends. "Thank you for coming, but I need to have a long talk with my daughter."

"I'll walk you out," I said, moving toward the door with Billy, Jo, Heather, and Shawn following me.

"Five minutes, Liz," Mom called from the dining room.

"Okay," I called, holding the door.

Once we were at the edge of the driveway Billy started. "What is going on with you Liz?" He paced back and forth between his truck and the edge of the driveway. "This is the second time this week you've gone AWOL, and I'm tired of getting the call to look for you."

How could I make him understand? "I'm sorry. Everyone is always so worried about where I'm at I can't go to the bathroom without Dad sending out a search party."

"It's because we care about you." Jo crossed her arms over her chest and narrowed her eyes at me. "There's a lot of other things going on that you aren't in the middle of right now."

I put my hands on my hips. "You think I did this for attention? After what happened last night, all I want is to be left alone. You don't believe me?" I asked as Jo and Heather snickered. "Look at my watch." I took it off and gave it to Heather. "I swear I was only gone for two, maybe three hours and I left at ten till noon."

"Wait, what happened last night?" Billy asked, stopping his pacing to stare at me.

"Your watch stopped," Heather said, rolling her eyes, and giving it back. "It proves nothing."

"Not now, Billy," Jo said, raising her eyebrows at me.

"I don't know how to prove it to you guys. Please, you have enough going on with Stacy, the last thing I want to do is cause more trouble than I already have." I ran my hand over my face. *Could I make things any worse?*

"Fine, whatever I need to get home. Mom's a mess," Heather said, stomping over to her car.

"Me too, Billy, are you ready?" Jo asked, taking a step toward his truck.

"Yeah, look, Liz." He wanted to say more but stopped. "We'll talk later, okay?"

"Yeah." They got in his truck and left. Shawn was standing behind me and had been oddly quiet. I turned, afraid of what I would see in his eyes.

"Hey, it's been a long day. I know you're sorry, you didn't mean for any of this to happen, but we have to deal with it." He pulled me into his arms and gave me a squeeze. "I have to go." He let me go refusing to meet my eyes. "I have to help Mom and Heather."

"Okay, Shawn, I'm sorry I never meant for this to happen." My eyes burned with unshed tears. I had so much I needed to tell him.

"I know. Let's meet when you're done with training?" He pulled my chin up, finally meeting my eyes.

"Please." I sniffled, trying not to blink, and let the tears escape.

"Stay out of trouble till then." He leaned in and touched his lips to mine before walking over to his Jeep. "We have a lot to talk about."

His comment about having a lot to talk about made my stomach twist as I watched him backed out of the driveway. I wondered if it would be the last time he was at my house, the last time he would kiss me, the last time I could call him mine. After Shawn's taillights disappeared around the corner I went inside, wondering if I could sneak up to my room without my parents noticing, but as soon as I closed the front door Dad called me back to the dining room.

"Liz, sit down." Mom pointed to a chair. I sat down and stared at the table, afraid of the disappointment I would see in their eyes.

"Liz, we're worried about you." Dad stood and paced around the room. "Ever since you met Shawn you've changed and not for the better."

"It's not Shawn's fault, at least most of it isn't," I mumbled and snuck a glance at Mom. She was frowning at me with her hands clasped together so tight her knuckles were white. I wouldn't get any help from her.

"Then whose fault is it?" Dad stopped, put both hands on the table, and leaned toward me.

How did I answer his question? I couldn't tell him about the mares, but would he be able to tell if I lied? "Stacy, Shawn's aunt died in her sleep last night." I figured Mom would understand what really happened. "They canceled work, and her death hit me hard. I met her on Monday at the BBQ. She wanted to talk about Victor. We had planned to go to lunch today."

"That's horrible." Mom put her hand over her mouth. "What happened?" She was about to start crying.

"They don't know yet."

"I'm sorry Liz," Dad put a hand on my shoulder. "But it doesn't give you the right to take off and not tell anyone where you're going."

"I'm sorry." How many times did I have to say it?

"I don't think *sorry* will do it this time." Dad started pacing again.

"What do you want me to say? What do you want me to do?"

Dad glanced from me to Mom. "From now on I expect you to text us whenever you leave the house and tell us where you are going. Then I want a text when you've reached your destination and another one when you leave."

I closed my eyes and tightened my ponytail. He was acting ridiculous. I wanted to fight him on it, but I didn't want to lose my Jeep. "Fine, if that's what you want."

"It's our job to keep you safe." Mom wiped a tear from her eye. "Next time you have a bad day, find someone to talk to or come to work, I always have time for you." Mom buried her head in her hands. "You have no idea how scared I was when we couldn't find you."

"I need to tell you about something else." It was now or never.

Dad crossed his arms over his chest. "We're waiting." He tapped his foot on the floor.

"There's this new girl at work and I guess she dated Shawn a while ago. Anyway, she hates me because I'm with Shawn, and I have the feeling she's going to try to do something to me."

"Aren't you being a little paranoid?" Mom tisked.

"She threatened me and tried to push me down a mineshaft today."

"Who's her father? I'll have a word with him." Dad sat up straight and puffed out his chest like a mad papa bear.

"I don't want to go there yet. I just think we should make sure we lock up the house when no one's home and at night."

"Do you really think she would break in?" Mom asked.

"Yes, I do. Please? Just for a little while."

"If it will make you feel better then we will." Dad got up and went to the patio door and put the wood slat in the bottom so it couldn't be opened.

"Thanks."

"It's a terrible world we live in." He hugged me back.

"I'm sorry," I said for the millionth time that day. "If you're done lecturing me, I'm going to go to bed." It was early, but I didn't want to deal with life anymore. Dealing with the mare would be better than dealing with today.

"When was the last time you ate?" Mom asked as I got to my feet.

"This morning, but I'm not hungry." I started toward the stairs.

"I'll make you a sandwich and leave it in the fridge if you get hungry later," Mom called after me as I grabbed my pack and went up to my room.

"Thanks," I called, already knowing I wouldn't eat it.

Chapter 20

I took a shower then crawled into bed and stared at the ceiling. I didn't know what to do. Everyone was mad at me either for causing Stacy's death or making them worry while I was on my hike. What made me mad, was where the time went, there was no way my hike lasted six hours. If I had only been gone for the two or three hours, no one would have known I went anywhere and now I had to tell my parents everywhere I went and everyone was mad at me. It was going to be a crappy summer.

I rolled over. I was physically and mentally exhausted from my day, and as much as I was ready to fall into a dreamless sleep, I had training, and I wasn't looking forward to it. Word about how Stacy died had probably made its rounds thanks to Jon and I hated that Jo was mad at me. She and Heather were the only girls I considered friends, and I didn't want to lose them. How could I make it up to them?

Shawn had said we needed to talk before he left, and I was more worried about that than anything. I didn't want to lose him, but I would have to go along with what he wanted. It was my fault his aunt died. I would move on if he didn't want to be with me anymore, but I didn't know how while working at Knights Inc.

Unable to fight my exhaustion any longer I fell asleep thinking of Tom. When my dream started, I was in the training room. Tom and Jo were already there talking in low voices.

I didn't think Jo wanted to talk to me, but it didn't matter I needed to talk to her. "Jo, can I talk to you for a minute?"

She rolled her eyes and walked over. "What?"

"I'm sorry about everything. I never meant to make everyone worry or make it all about me."

"I don't think you did it on purpose, I think you're so wrapped up in everything going on in your life that you're ignoring everything else." She crossed her arms over her chest and cocked her hip.

I opened my mouth then closed it. I didn't know what to say. Was she right? Was I so wrapped up with the gate and Stalker that I was missing things? "Jo, I'm s…"

"Don't bother, we're all tired of hearing you say you're sorry." She cut me off then walked over to Mary when she joined us.

I glanced around the room, almost everyone was there, and I wanted to talk to Tom, but he was talking to Jeff. I leaned against the wall, instead trying to ignore the looks Jo and Mary were giving me.

"Okay, now that we are all here, please gather round," Tom said, standing in the middle of the mat with his hands on his hips. We moved to form a loose semi-circle around him. "It's been a tough day for us all. Losing a knight is never easy, but it's something we all learn to deal with." Everyone's eyes shot to me as he spoke. I looked away refusing to meet their eyes. "During this time of mourning, emotions are high, but I expect you all to focus on the task at hand." He gazed around at us until his gaze settled on Mary who was still staring at me. "Mary, are you with us?"

She jerked her head to Tom. "Yes."

"Good, we're going to work on hand to hand combat tonight. Now I want you to break up in pairs and spar. This is a dream, so it's full contact, we will have a three-minute round then switch."

The only sparring I had done was with Heather and it had been months before. I wasn't very good and with the way everyone was staring at me I had a bad feeling about what was about to happen. "Liz, come on I'll go with you first," Jo said, grinning at me with an evil glint in her eye. Tom blew the whistle and my suffering began.

Three minutes later Tom blew the whistle and Jo offered me a hand up for the tenth time. "Isn't there a way to upload how to fight, like in the Matrix movies?" I asked between breaths. I was covered in sweat, my ribs hurt, my face hurt, and my arms hurt from blocking the few punches Jo had not landed on my face and torso.

"Yeah, I wish. You have to learn to fight just like everyone else." Jo rolled her eyes. "It takes more than talent to beat a mare."

She thought everything came so easily to me? Maybe she was right. I had a lot of talent, but I would put the work in and learn to fight. I didn't have a choice, no matter what happened with our friendship I had to learn to take care of myself.

"Okay if you're outside the circle move to your left to face your next opponent," Tom called. Jo moved to Jeff, and Mary moved to stand in front of me.

"This will be fun." She cracked her knuckles and waited for Tom to blow his whistle.

As soon as he blew it, my suffering continued. I blocked most of Mary's punches and kicks, but when she swept my feet out and jumped on top of me, I didn't know how to defend myself. It felt like she whaled on me for an hour instead of three minutes. When Tom finally blew the whistle, she climbed off me, and I wiped the blood from the corner of my mouth.

"Oh, you're bleeding, are you going to run to Shawn for help?" Mary asked, stepping over me to move to the next person she was slated to fight, and everyone laughed.

I rolled onto my stomach and made it to my hands and knees. My whole body hurt, how was I supposed to beat the mares when I couldn't hold my own with someone two years younger than me? I made it to my feet and found Tom standing in front of me.

"Are you all right?" he asked, giving me a once over.

"Yeah, I'm good, just need more practice." I stared at a spot on the wall over his shoulder, not ready to make eye contact with him. "Are we still working tomorrow?"

"Yes, we have a lot of work to do." He walked to the middle of the circle. "That will do for tonight, but I have an announcement. If your parents haven't already told you, Stacy's funeral will be at ten, at the mansion on Saturday. I expect you all to be there to honor a great knight."

Everyone murmured their affirmatives before leaving. I

was glad training was over, but I wasn't sure I was ready for what I had to face next. I didn't want Shawn to break up with me, but could I blame him? I all but killed his aunt.

Not wanting to face him, but knowing I had to, I thought of Shawn and popped into his padded room. He was sitting on the couch staring at the ceiling. "Hey," I said, walking over to him, and manifesting a padded armchair to sit on.

"Hi, holy crap what happened to you?" He jumped to his feet and he gently cradled my injured face in his hands.

"Hand to hand training tonight. You are seeing the work of Jo and Mary." I jerked away from him when he touched a sore spot.

"I'm sorry." He pulled his hand away and returned to his seat on the couch.

"It's okay, I deserved it. Plus, I need to learn how to fight." I slumped in the chair.

"What do you mean you deserved it?" Shawn bent to meet my eyes.

"After everything I've done. Stacy, making everyone worry about me..." I trailed off, not making eye contact. *Don't cry, don't be the attention whore Jo thinks you are.*

He stared at his hands. "Liz, about last night."

"Shawn I'm sorry, I won't ever forgive myself for what happened."

"Liz, stop." Shawn reached out and took my hand. "It wasn't your fault, my dad is..." he paused as if trying to find the right words, "he's protecting me by blaming you."

I blinked, "What? Shawn, what really happened last night?"

"After you left, I went to help Stacy, and we were doing fine. The mare was one of the strongest ones I've seen. We tried everything from guns to broadswords, but nothing seemed to take him down. I decided that we needed to bomb him. I thought Stacy was behind me when I threw the grenade, but she was behind the mare trying to sever his spinal cord. I didn't see her until it was too late." He hung his head. "It's my fault she died."

I moved to the couch and wrapped my arms around him. "Shawn, I'm sorry." He leaned into me and sobbed. I held him in my arms staring at the wall and patted his back, trying not to show my relief. It wasn't my fault. I didn't kill Stacy. I felt the weight I had been carrying around all day leave me, and Shawn let out another sob. I knew how he felt, I'd been feeling it all day. I wanted to ask him what Jon was protecting him from, and why he went along with blaming me in the first place, but Shawn needed time to grieve. We sat there for a long time until eventually his sobs quieted, and the tears stopped. He moved away from me, avoiding my eyes. "Are you all right?"

"I don't want you to see me like this." He wiped his hand across his face.

"Well, it's too late, and it's okay." I reached for his hand and he grabbed mine giving it a squeeze.

"Thank you, I don't know what I would do without you."

"Can you tell me what happened after?" I didn't want to finish the sentence.

"Yeah, what do you want to know?"

"Why is your dad blaming me?"

"I told him the truth Liz, I promise I did, but he said I couldn't afford to have her death be my fault. I told him no, I would take responsibility for my actions, but he said if I told the truth he would transfer me to Mexico."

"He could do that? And what do you mean when he said you couldn't afford to have Stacy's death be your fault?"

"He has plans for me. He wants me to take his place when he retires and thinks it would look bad on my record. If he can spin it so I was helping you when it happened, then it doesn't look as bad." Shawn rubbed his eyes and stared into the distance.

"Does he treat everyone who isn't family like this?" I had never wanted to punch someone so badly in my life.

"No, he doesn't think you will survive long enough for it to matter," he mumbled.

"With him in charge, I'd believe it." It was bad enough I had to constantly worry about the mares, and while I never trusted Jon, I thought, since he was letting me train, he would not try to get me killed. Between him, Kristina, and Stalker my list of enemies was becoming unmanageable.

"You're not mad at me?" he asked as I got to my feet and paced around the room.

"What? No, I get it, you don't have a lot of options. Would I rather not be blamed, and have you shipped off to Mexico? I'm not sure, but I understand why you went along with it. Does Magnus know?"

"No, as soon as I woke up Dad was waiting for me and gave me my options. What am I going to do?" He leaned forward and rested his elbows on his knees.

"I think I can deal with everyone blaming me, if you think your dad will send you to Mexico, but can you at least tell Jo and Heather what really happened?" I could deal with all the knights and squires hating me, but I didn't want to lose Jo and Heather.

"Why? Have they been mean?" He drew his eyebrows together.

"look at what Jo did to me." I pointed at my face. "And, based on what Heather said at my house, she is too. I don't want to lose them." I sniffed and wiped a tear that escaped the corner of my eye.

"Liz, I'm sorry. I didn't think." Shawn jumped to his feet and took me in his arms. "I'll fix it. I promise." I looked up in time to see him lowering his lips to mine. As much as I needed to affirm our feelings for each other, Mary had hit me hard in the mouth and pain shot through my lips when they met his. I jerked away, wincing from the pain.

"Oh, I'm sorry, did you get hit in the mouth too?" Shawn asked.

"Yeah, Mary kicked my ass."

"No kissing for the rest of the night then. So, you really found the mineshaft?" He pulled me down to sit next to him on the couch.

"It is just like it is in my dreams." I pulled one knee up and twisted so I could see him.

"And you're sure you've never been there before?"

"No, like I said, the trail wasn't there last summer, and I always stay on the trail when I'm hiking alone. It was weird, there was all this freshly turned earth but there weren't any footprints."

"How do you know an animal didn't do it?"

"When I say there were no footprints, I mean human, animal, bird. There was no sign of anything in the clearing. When I tried to see how deep the shaft was, someone tried to push me into it, and I ran away."

"You're kidding." Shawn straightened. "Did you see who it was?"

"No, but I have an idea and it has to do with the beginning of my dream last night." I pulled away from Shawn and got to my feet. I didn't know if he would believe me when I told him about Kristina and Stalker, but I had to tell someone.

"What happened?" Shawn leaned forward in his seat and waited for me to talk.

"Why were you working with Stacy last night and not Kristina?"

"She called in sick."

"Why would she need to call in sick from her dreams?"

"If she had a fever for one, or if something won't let you to sleep straight through. Kristina is claiming to have a cold and can't stop sneezing."

"Okay, I never thought of it like that."

"I wanted to work with Stacy. I needed a break from Kristina." Shawn leaned his head against the wall and stared at the ceiling. "Why?"

"Because I was in Kristina's dream last night. She wasn't sick, she was meeting with Stalker."

"What do you mean? Was she fighting him?"

"No." The idea of Kristina fighting him made me laugh. "You probably aren't going to believe me but, she is working with him to try to kill me."

"You can't be serious." He leaned back in his seat and crossed his arms over his chest.

"She's planning to break into my house, while I'm sleeping, and take down my dreamcatcher." I wrung my hands. *What would I do if he didn't believe me?*

"And you think she followed you and tried to push you into the shaft?" He rolled his eyes. "She can be a pain in the butt, but I don't think she would try to kill anyone."

"I didn't see her, but I saw a car that could have been hers and I know what I saw in my dream." I crossed my arms over my chest.

He ran his hand through his hair and stared at the ceiling. "It's not that I don't believe you it's just hard for me to wrap my head around her doing something like this. What are you going to do?"

"Keep the house locked up tight. I don't have any proof."

"I'll talk to her. I'm sure I can get her to back off."

"That's not going to help or stop her and we both know it. I'll just wait until she does something I can prove to the cops or your dad."

"You're right. I'll keep an eye on her too." Shawn stood up and pulled me into him. "What are we going to do about the mineshaft?"

"I don't know but I think we need to check it out. We've both dreamt of the place and never been there. It must mean something. The mare called the shaft his home, and all those voices down there wanted our help."

"I agree, we need to check it out, but I don't know when we will be able to, between the funeral, work and training it seems like we barely have enough time to meet in our dreams let alone in real life."

"I know, we'll make time." I rested my head against his shoulder. He was hurting, but I selfishly relished being in his arms.

"Liz, I'm falling…"

My alarm went off, and I glared at him confused for a second. "You're falling?" but it was too late. I blinked and stared at the ceiling of my room.

Chapter 21

The next morning, I ran my brush through my hair thinking about Shawn. He worried me, was he falling apart? I wasn't far behind him. With Stacy's death, Kristina siding with Stalker and Jon trying to get me to quit, it felt like everyone was against me. I left my bathroom, grabbed my bag from the back of my desk chair and went downstairs.

Mom and Dad had already left for work, and I was glad to have the house to myself after their freak out the night before. After I grabbed breakfast and texted them both that I was going to work, I left. For the first time since I started, I dreaded it. I had to be strong for Shawn but dealing with everyone's anger would be hard. I parked near the main entrance, glad the lot was almost empty. I sent my parents a text that I made it safely then went inside, wondering where Shawn was.

"Morning Marcy," I said as I stopped in front of the door leading to the offices. When she didn't answer, I glanced over at her. She didn't look up from her monitor, and I wondered if she heard me until she swiveled her chair around giving me her back. I tapped my badge on the lock, and the door clicked open. "Have a nice day then," I said and went through the door. I had to be strong for Shawn. Everyone would hate me, but it was better than Shawn being shipped off to Mexico. I made it to Tom's office without running into anyone else and knocked on his closed door.

"Come in," he said, and I went in, surprised to find Jo sitting in one of the visitor chairs.

"Hi." I took the other seat, trying to make myself as small as possible. The last thing I wanted to do was hang out with Jo after what she said and did the night before.

"Good morning." Tom gave me a smile until he saw the frown on my face and glanced at Jo who had said nothing. "Jo, why don't you go find a gi that will fit Liz, and we'll meet you in the training room in a few minutes."

"Sure, whatever Liz needs," Jo said under her breath, as she got up and went for the door.

"Did you and Jo get in a fight?" Tom asked as I rubbed my eyes to hide the tears trying to leak out.

"Yeah, kind of. She's mad about Stacy." I gave him a tight smile, wishing I could tell him what Shawn told me.

"This isn't the first time something like this has happened, and it won't be the last. Give everyone some time and it will get better." Tom turned his computer off and got to his feet.

"Really? You think Jo will get over it?"

"Yes, she needs time. Come on, we're going to do some martial arts training that's why Jo is here, she will be your partner."

"Are you sure that's a good idea? I think she hates me."

"Don't worry I won't let her hurt you."

Two hours later I winced as I pulled the shirt I'd been wearing before training down over my chest. Tom had been right about Jo not hurting me, but he hadn't told me about how sore I would be from the millions of punches and kicks he made me do. We didn't even spar, just practiced moves. I didn't know how it would make me better, but Tom was the boss.

I slid my shoes on and shuffled out of the locker room dropping my sweaty gi in the hamper. When I exited the locker room Jo was standing next to Tom with her arms crossed over her chest and her body turned away from him, she was mad about something.

"So, we are done until Monday," Tom said as we walked back to his office. "But I'm stuck here for a while and I was wondering if you would give Jo a ride home?"

I snuck a peek at her in time for her to roll her eyes. I really didn't think it was a good idea, but Tom was the boss. "Yeah, I guess."

"Great, thanks, I'll see you tomorrow." Tom ducked into his office and closed the door behind him before Jo could say anything.

"Jo," I started as she walked past me practically running for the door. I let her go, walking at an easy pace.

If she wanted to go home bad enough, she could wait for me. I didn't know if Shawn talking to her would make a difference or not; she said some pretty mean things that had nothing to do with Stacy.

When I got outside Jo and Shawn were waiting by my Jeep. Seeing Shawn made my heart speed up, and I wished we could run off and spend the day together away from Knights Inc.

"Hey," I said when I reached him and took his hand. "How are you?"

"I've been better, listen I wanted to see if you wanted to go to lunch but Jo just asked me to give her a ride home. Can I come over after?" Shawn was pale, and he had bags under his eyes. I wished there was something I could do to make his grief easier to bear.

"Yeah, sure."

He leaned in and kissed me on the cheek. "Okay, I'll see you later." They took off across the lot and got in his Rubicon.

I got in my Jeep and took out my phone. I sent a text to my parents telling them I was going home. As I drove, I thought about the conversation Shawn and Jo were probably having, I hoped she would forgive me. When I pulled in the driveway, I was surprised to find Heather's Subaru parked in the driveway. *Great now what?* I thought getting out.

"Hey, listen, Shawn told me what really went down with Stacy. I'm sorry I was such a bitch last night," she said after I got out of my Jeep and started toward her.

"No, I deserved it. Even if Stacy dying wasn't my fault, I still should have remembered to wake myself up and not run to Shawn." I crossed my arms over my chest. "Come on let's go inside." I unlocked the door, leaving it open for her to follow and went into the dining room.

"Still, I was a bitch and I'm sorry." Heather finally met my eyes. "Will you forgive me?"

I nodded my head. "Only if you forgive me for being an

idiot in my dreams.'

"Deal." She smiled then gave me a hug. "Moving on, I did some research on the location of the mare attacks in Trinidad." She sat down in the chair next to me. "It's like a trail. The first night there was one death, the next there were two about a mile away then three, all less than a mile from each other, but if you look at it on a map it almost goes in a straight line.

"You're kidding?" I looked at the table and tapped my foot. "Where did the first death occur?"

"I have a map." Heather took a folded piece of paper out of her pocket, unfolded it and laid it on the table between us. "Here, in the national forest." She pointed to a dot on the map. "Each dot represents a death."

"Was this guy in a tent or camper?"

"He was in a tent outside a cave. His wife told me he went spelunking in the cave the day before he died."

"This is a clue, Heather. Now we have to figure out what it means." I got up and went into the kitchen. "I'm going to make a sandwich, do you want one?"

"No thanks, I already ate." Heather followed me and took a seat at the bar while I made a turkey sandwich. "What do you think?"

The first person to die was in the middle of nowhere, then it was like the mares moved closer and closer to more populated areas. Has it been in front of us this whole time? "Bear with me," I said, taking a bite of my lunch while I organized my thoughts. "So, the first person to die in Trinidad was exploring a cave before he died." What did it mean? "The first people who died here were the Freeman kids, which means..." I took another bite of my sandwich.

"Means what?" Heather ran her hand through her hair.

"It means…" I paced around the room eating. There had to be a connection between the two. I went to the cabinet and got a glass out then filled it with water. "If the camper opened a gate in the cave…" I trailed off as I chugged the water. "What if Freeman opened the gate in the mansion?"

Heather slapped the table. "In the mansion? You've got to be kidding me." She stared past me like she was doing a complicated math problem in her head.

"I don't know, does it make sense to you?"

"Following your logic, it does. How ironic will it be if we are living in the house with the gate?" Heather glanced at her phone and read a message. "Crap, I have to go. The Council is arriving soon, and Dad wants us all there."

"Like the high council?" I gulped when Heather nodded. "Do they come whenever a knight dies?"

"No, but they would have come at some point this summer to see the new headquarters." I followed Heather to the front door. "I'll tell Shawn about the gate and we'll look for it when we have time."

"Sounds good. I guess I'll see you tomorrow then." I held the door open for her.

"Yeah, it will be a shitty day. I'm going to miss Stacy, she was fun." Heather hung her head and hurried to her car.

I closed the door and took the map to my room. We had a lead which was great but there wasn't anything I could do about it and that sucked. I didn't even have anyone to call. Jo might want to know, but I was going to the leave the ball in her court. I would be ready to talk to her when she was ready. My phone vibrated, and I dug it out of my pocket.

Hey sorry, I can't stop by. My talk with Jo took longer than I thought, and my dad needs me home. If I don't see you tonight, I'll pick you up tomorrow at nine.

I texted Shawn back telling him everything was fine, and he needed to talk to Heather. Having an evening to myself I opened my computer and researched weapons until I couldn't keep my eyes open any longer.

Chapter 22

I couldn't remember being in the room I found myself in before, but it felt familiar. I spun in a circle, trying to place it. It had a darkly stained hardwood floor with wide planks. The door matched the floor, and the sidelights were a rainbow of stained glass. A set of twin staircases along each wall curved in where they met the ground floor. The stain on the wood matched the floors and the newel posts were thick and shined with oil. The wood paneling on the walls gave the room a dark monochromatic feeling, where the massive gold-leaf, gas lit, chandelier hanging from the ceiling brightened the cavernous space.

I opened the door, wanting to figure out where I was. It was Twisted Pines, but it was smaller, somehow shabbier than what it normally was. Smoke billowed out of almost every chimney, odd for June, and something about the lake was missing, but couldn't put my finger on what. I snapped my fingers, there weren't any boats on the lake and the marina was missing. There were always boats on the lake in June.

I closed the door, I was in the Freeman Mansion, but many years before Knights Inc. had moved in. I remembered the foyer from when I was little, but it was dilapidated and dusty then. The room in my dream was new.

"Where are we?" A voice from behind me asked.

I jumped and spun while still in the air, ready to fight whoever was waiting for me. "You scared the crap out of me," I said to Jo while holding my hand to my heart. "What are you doing here?" If she had come to yell at me again, I didn't know if I could handle it.

"Shawn told me what really happened with Stacy. I'm sorry I was such a bitch to you." She laced her hands together and let them hang loosely in front of her refusing to meet my eyes.

"Jo, it's like I told Heather. Even if it wasn't my fault Stacy died, I still should have known better than to bug Shawn while he was working. And maybe I have been a little self-absorbed lately. I'm sorry." I was so happy Jo was talking to me.

"I don't want to be mad at you anymore. Can we forget about the past two days?" Jo peered up at me.

"Yeah, I would love that." I opened my arms, and she moved in, giving me a hug.

"Where are we?" She asked pulling away.

"The Freeman Mansion, only I think this is how it looked when it was first built." I glanced up the stairs. *If I opened a gateway to another dimension where would I do it?*

"Oh, cool. This is where you think the gate is, right? Shawn sent me a text."

"Yeah, but where? This place is huge. Somewhere no one would notice?" I moved away from the staircase and walked down the hall instead.

"Maybe his office or something?" Jo offered catching up. When we reached the first door, I opened it. Inside was a sitting room, with wooden chairs and couches with upholstered seats that appeared to be brand new but in the style of the eighteen-hundreds. There was a large fireplace with a fire roaring against one wall. We walked around the room, knocking on wallpapered walls, looking for something that didn't fit but, finding nothing, we moved to the next room, the office, and we did the same thing, knocked on the walls, moved pictures out of the way. We found a safe behind a picture, but it was open and empty. We went through the kitchen and breakfast room, but didn't find the gate. We ended up back in the foyer and stared at the stairs leading to the second floor.

"Do you think it would be upstairs?" Jo asked.

"I don't know but it doesn't feel right." I walked the perimeter of the room, stopping when I found a door under one set of stairs that I didn't remember seeing in the real-world mansion. I opened it to a room so dark I couldn't tell if there was a floor or if it dropped off into nothing.

"What do you think it is?" Jo glanced over my shoulder.

"I don't know." I manifested a flashlight and clicked it on before shining it into the room. It was small, four feet by four feet, with rock walls. Instead of a floor it had an iron spiral staircase leading down into darkness.

"If I was going to open a gate to hell, I think I would do it in the basement." I said, twisting my head to see Jo.

"Yeah, me too," she swallowed hard and tried to smile at me. "Are we going down there?"

"I think it's the only way," I said, trying to find the courage to take the first step.

"This is just a dream, and we're protected, nothing will hurt us," Jo said, her voice coming out stronger than before.

"Let's do this," I stepped onto the first step and grabbed the railing, afraid the stairs wouldn't hold my weight and would collapse leaving me broken and bleeding at the bottom. But the stairs held, and I let out a breath. I shook the railing and bounced around. It was solid. "I think we're good," I whispered, afraid I might wake up a monster below us.

"This is creepy." Jo said as we tiptoed down the steps making as little noise as possible.

At the bottom of the staircase I stepped onto a stone floor and swung my flashlight around. We were in a long dark hallway made of stone. It was humid, and I could hear water dripping somewhere ahead of us.

"I wonder if Shawn and Heather know there's a basement under their house." I walked down the hall.

"I don't know, I've spent a lot of time there, but I've never seen the stairs we came down or anything like this." Jo was standing so close I could feel her breath on my neck, and I shivered.

"Maybe this is all just my imagination." We stopped at the first door we came across and I tried the handle. "Locked."

"Bummer, let's keep going." Jo sounded like she didn't want us to find anything.

"No, we need to know what's behind the door." I pulled a skeleton key out of the pocket of my jeans and unlocked the door.

"How did you know what kind of key we needed?"

"I don't know. I just thought of a key that would open the door."

"I hope I'm as good as you are at manipulating your dreamscape someday."

"Well, I hope I can fight as well as you someday." I pushed the door open and was immediately hit by the smell of rotten road kill, defrosted after being buried under a pile of snow for months. I wanted to vomit but I forced the bile down and shined the flashlight around the room then gasped. The room was probably as long and as wide as my high school gym, but with a ten-foot ceiling. It was half-full of bodies. Men, women, and children were stacked lengthwise from floor to ceiling. I ran backwards, running into someone and screamed, forgetting Jo was behind me.

"Go" I yelled, pushing her back into the hallway. I slammed the door behind me and locked it.

"I think I'm going to puke," Jo said, walking away from the door, putting her hands on her knees, and taking deep breaths.

"I'm right there with you." I bent over and breathed through my mouth. "What do you think that was about?"

"I have no idea, and I don't think I want to know." She stopped at the next door. She tried the knob and it opened. She manifested a flashlight, shined it around the room, and let out a breath. I followed the beam of light. The room appeared to be empty, but I heard pounding footsteps coming our way. "Close the door." I pushed Jo away from the door when she didn't move.

Jo quickly swung the door closed. "What?"

"It wasn't empty, didn't you hear the footsteps?" I locked the door with the skeleton key then continued down the hall.

When we reached the next room, we could hear moaning and wailing. It could have been out of ecstasy or from pain, but I didn't want to find out which. "The gate isn't in there," I said when Jo stopped outside the door.

"They might need help," Jo said, putting her hand on the knob.

"I don't think we'll be able to help them until we close the gate. Let's keep going."

I went ahead of Jo to the next door. Light was leaking through the bottom, and I pushed my ear against it to listen. Someone was talking. I didn't know if it was friend or foe, but something told me I needed to see what was on the other side. I put my hand on the knob ready to open it when a voice stopped me.

"I see you brought a friend with you tonight." Stalker's scratchy voice made me jerk around.

"Jo, leave, it's Stalker."

"No, you can't fight him on your own." She stepped in front of me and dropped into a fighting stance.

"Jo, I'll be fine, he can't hurt me. But you need to leave." I yanked her arm, pulling her next to me.

"You're sure?" She gave me a sidelong glance.

"Yes, go." She nodded and disappeared.

"Go away," I said to Stalker, before I went through the door, and slammed it behind me. I stared at it and watched the handle begin to turn. I pulled the key out of my pocket and locked it, then took in my new surroundings. I was in a library, and looking around I forgot all about Stalker waiting for me on the other side of the door. The walls were impossibly tall with shelves and shelves of books at least three stories high. A fire was burning in a massive fireplace, there was an old-fashioned couch and two chairs arranged in front of it. Near the window there was a desk, stacked high with paper.

"Who's there?" A tired, gruff voice asked from behind the desk.

"Hi, I'm Liz." I moved around the desk finding the man the voice came from.

He pushed his chair back and stood. He was probably five-foot-seven, with thinning, curly, silver and brown hair. He wore round, wire rimmed glasses over his watery, beady, brown eyes. His sideburns came halfway down his cheeks, but he had no other facial hair. He had on a dingy long shelve shirt with an army green pinstriped vest. The top button of his shirt was undone, and his pocket watch dangled from its chain. His pants matched his vest and his scuffed and bruised, tightly laced boots seemed out of place with the rest of him.

"What are you doing here?" he whispered, leading me to the window and adjusting his glasses to get a better look at me.

"Trying to find the gate," I whispered back. "I want to close it."

"What a mistake, what a mistake," he mumbled, taking a handkerchief from his pocket, and wiping his eyes.

"What do you mean?"

"It was all my wife's fault, if her greed had not gotten the better of her none of this would have happened. Now look what I've done." He pointed out the window. I expected to see the same view of the town and the lake I saw from the front door but instead, I saw a line of people carrying buckets of dirt, shuffling along, staring at nothing with their mouths half open like they were in a trance.

"Who are they?" I glanced back that man.

"People who died in their dreams." He took his glasses off and cleaned them with the hem of his shirt.

"You mean the souls the goblins sucked out?"

"No, I mean the ones who died, before the mares could take their souls."

"They don't go to heaven?"

"No, the mares turned them into slaves. Maybe they will go to heaven when the gate is closed."

I was about to ask the man where the dirt came from when a man walking past the window looked familiar. "Victor?" I tapped on the window. The man peered at me confused for a second then dropped his bucket and ran to the window.

"Elizabeth? What are you doing here?" The window muffled his voice, but I understood him.

"I'm trying to help you. I'm going to close the gate." I put my hand on the glass as tears of joy and sorrow ran down my cheeks, it was my dad.

"Liz, no run away. Get out here. It's too dangerous." He beat on the window until two mares grabbed him and yanked him back, forced him to his knees then began beating him with two-by-fours.

"Dad, no," I yelled, beating on the window, trying to break it. He needed help.

"There is nothing you can do," the old man said, putting a hand on my shoulder. "Come away. Watching will not save them."

I jerked away rubbing my arms and glancing over my shoulder out the window. "Who are you?" I wiped my nose with the bottom of my T-shirt.

"Oh, I thought you knew. I'm Thomas Freeman. The man who built this house and who is responsible for destroying Twisted Pines."

"It was you?" I'd been right, Freeman opened the gate. Now if he could tell me where it was and how to close it. "Do you know where the gate is Mr. Freeman?"

"Yes," he ran over to his desk and picked up a piece of paper, "here's a map."

I took the paper from him. It was covered with random, intersecting lines that meant nothing. There were no reference points or an 'X' to mark the spot. "This isn't a map. Please, tell me, where is the gate? I'm trying to close it."

"It's right there." He took the paper from me and stared at it. His face fell. "I thought it was right here." He dropped the paper and put his head in his hands.

"Do you know how to close the gate?"

"That I know I have." He ran to his desk, pulled a paper from the pile, and gave it to me.

I read it and my heart deflated. It said the same thing over and over again. *Save yourself, save yourself.* I gave the paper back to him. "This doesn't say how to close the gate. How do you close it?" I wanted to take him by the shoulders and shake him.

"I know I have it written down somewhere." He shuffled the

papers on his desk around as he frantically searched for the answer. "Here it is." He held up a small journal. "This one is empty because he doesn't want me to remember how to close it, but if you find the real journal, the answer is inside."

My alarm clock beeped, and I fought not to wake up. "Where is the book Mr. Freeman?"

"They hid it from me. Find the book and close the gate, or we're all lost."

I wanted to ask him again, but I was back in my room with my alarm blaring. I reached over and pushed the button to silence it. I was so close to getting the answers I needed but I didn't have time to go back to sleep. I had a funeral to get ready for.

Chapter 23

I picked up my phone and sent a message to Jo praying Stalker hadn't followed her. I put my phone on my nightstand and got out of bed. Too much happened in my dream last night. Was it real or was my imagination giving me the lead I needed?

I was about to get in the shower when my phone buzzed; it was Jo. I let out a breath as I read her message.

I'm good, see you in a while. We have a lot to talk about.

Relieved she was ok, I text her back. **No kidding. See you there.**

An hour later I was standing in front of my closet trying to figure out what to wear when there was a soft knock at my door.

"Who's there?" I called, pulling my towel tighter around me.

"Mom, can I come in?"

"Yeah," I said, still staring at all the jeans and T-shirts hanging there.

"I bought you this, I figured you didn't have anything to wear today." She held out a pair of black slacks and charcoal gray jersey top.

"That's perfect, thanks. I didn't think I would need clothes like this until I was older." I hadn't spoken to my parents other than text messages since they made me tell them everywhere I went. I was still mad at the restrictions they put on me, but it was nice of Mom to get me something to wear. I put the clothes on the bed and picked up the charm bracelet Shawn gave me for my birthday. I took it to Mom and held it up saying nothing. She helped me attach the clasp, then I went back to the bathroom to comb out my hair.

"I'm sorry you have to go to a funeral." Mom was sitting on my bed when I came out with my wide-tooth comb in my hand.

"Me too, it's hard, she knew Victor, she was going to tell me about him." I flung my hair to one side of my head and leaned over while I worked the comb through it.

"I know you want to know more about Victor. I wish there was more to tell."

"It's not your fault, Mom, he left that world behind before he met you. I wish you would have been able to keep his things though. I feel like I could have learned a lot about him from his stuff." I flipped my head back over and went to get my brush.

"I know but I don't want you to go down the same path he did and end up dead." Mom stood in the doorway of the bathroom and watched me brush out my hair.

"Mom, that's the difference between him and me, I'm not doing this on my own. I have three other people helping me and watching my back." I sectioned out my hair and started a braid. I had been leaving it loose more than I had ever before, but it felt like I needed to have it up for a funeral.

"A bunch of kids taking on a century old goblin? You're right, I have nothing to worry about." She sniffled, and I peered over to see tears in her eyes. I rubber-banded the end of my braid and wrapped my arms around her.

"We're being careful, everything is going to be all right, Mom, I promise." She wrapped her arms around me and squeezed me so tight I thought I would pass out from oxygen deprivation before she let go.

"Be careful, sweetie," she said, before hurrying out of the room. I let her go. Talking to her about Victor always upset her.

I finished getting ready then went downstairs to grab something for breakfast. I had just finished eating when someone rang the doorbell. "I got it," I yelled through the house. It was probably Shawn coming to pick me up. I opened the door. "Hi."

"Hi, you look perfect." Shawn backed up a step, and I followed him out, shutting the door behind me. He looked good, dressed in a black three-piece suit with a white starched dress shirt and a thin, black tie.

"Thanks, where did you get the suit?" He took my hand as we walked to the car.

"We did move here from New York and my mom has an eye for fashion." He opened my door for me, and I climbed in.

"You remind me of a young stockbroker on Wall Street, very GQ." I put on my seatbelt as he got in the driver's side.

"Thanks." He pulled out of the driveway and headed down the road.

"Are you all right?" I asked.

"It feels weird talking about normal stuff when we are on our way to a funeral."

"Oh, I'm sorry. I have no idea what I'm doing. I've never been to a funeral." I laced my fingers together and rested them in my lap, determined not to say anything else.

"It's okay, it's been a while since I went to one too. It's going to be a rough day."

We drove the rest of the way in silence each lost in our own thoughts. When we reached the mansion, we parked and went in using the business entrance. The memorial was on the training room floor since it was the only place big enough to hold everyone attending.

When we entered the training room, I glanced around, not recognizing most of the people waiting for the ceremony to start. Shawn pulled me through the crowd, nodding at a few people until we reached Ivan and the knights I'd met earlier in the week.

"Shawn, I'm sorry," Ivan said, refusing to meet my eyes. "These things happen." He offered his hand as the knights with him nodded their heads.

"Thanks." Shawn shook his hand then put his hands in his pockets and stared at the floor. Ivan and the other knights turned as one and gave me their backs without a word. "What?" Shawn looked at their backs confused.

"We lost a knight because of her." Ivan glanced over his shoulder at Shawn. "You were doing your job. She should have known better."

I opened my mouth ready to say something but then

closed it. I was taking the hit for this. It was the least I could do for Shawn after everything he'd been through.

"Wait, it wasn't," Shawn started before I pulled him away.

"Shawn, it's fine," I said, trying not to let the hurt I was feeling into my voice.

"No, it isn't." Shawn squeezed my hand and led me through the crowd until we found Tom, Tina, and Jo.

"Hi," I whispered, trying to ignore the backs of knights around me.

"Hey." Jo scanned the room behind me, and I followed her gaze. Everyone in the room had stopped talking and turned their backs to us. She cringed and glared at Shawn. "Are you sure this is what you want?"

"No, not anymore," Shawn said, shuffling his feet.

"Shawn, don't, it's okay," I whispered.

"They'll move on. Give them time." Tina put a hand on my shoulder and squeezed.

My eyes filled with tears. *Maybe it would be better if I wasn't here*, I thought but then remembered that I didn't have a car to leave if I wanted to.

"This is ridiculous," Shawn said.

"Shawn," Tom said, putting his hand on Shawn's shoulder. "I agree with you, but is now the time?"

Shawn huffed and let out a breath. "You're right." He hugged me. "I'm going to make this right." I didn't know what to say so I just nodded.

"If everyone will please take their seats, we will begin," Jon said through a microphone at the pulpit set up at the far end of the room.

"I have to go sit with my family." Shawn took both of my hands in his. "Will you be okay?"

"Yeah, I'll sit with Jo." I didn't like the look in his eyes. "Don't do anything you'll regret."

"I won't." He gave me a tight smile, kissed my cheek, and left to join Heather.

"Let's find seats," Tom said, leading the way to the chairs. I followed behind them with my eyes glued to the floor, watching Tom's legs, so I didn't run into anything.

"Do you get the feeling Shawn is going to do something stupid?" Jo whispered once we were seated near the back.

"Yes." I looked up at Jon who was standing behind the podium. "I hope he knows what he's doing."

"We come here today to honor a knight who perished while saving a civilian." Jon started, and all the murmuring in the room stopped. "We live in perilous times, filled with acts of terrorism, shootings in schools, and vigilantes who wish to destroy our way of life."

I glanced at Jo with raised eyebrows *where was he going with this?* I wondered, she shrugged her shoulders and looked back to Jon. "With the all the perils the world is facing, it is a challenge to stay on course. We all want to save the world, but we were put here to save humans from their dreams, no more.

"We must put our squabbles aside and be the team that Twisted Pines needs us to be. We must hold ourselves to a higher level of ethics if we are to protect the world. We must be honest with each other and ourselves about our actions and how they affect others, for trust is the highest compliment we give each other.

"I will continue to lead us by nourishing our knights and squires with the knowledge they need to conquer the mares. Our research and development department is close to giving us real time play-by-play of dreams that will help us train and keep each other safe. I will continue to do everything in my power to help you and keep you safe from our enemies.

"Stacy, God bless her soul, was one of the most honest women I have ever had the pleasure of knowing. She would want us to continue in our quest to defeat the mares, not only to avenge her but to save the humans. I will always think fondly of Stacy and now I ask for anyone who wishes to speak about her to come forward and share your story with us."

Jon went back to his seat and bowed his head. I didn't understand the point he was trying to make. That we should be honest and avenge Stacy? But why did it feel like he was turning it into a political campaign? Shawn went to the podium and I held my breath while he adjusted the microphone. His eyes searched the crowd until he found me and grinned.

"Knights, family, friends, we gather here to celebrate the life of my aunt, Stacy. She was one of my favorite people and was one of the biggest influences on my life. When I was fourteen, I was failing as a squire and she sat me down and asked me why I wanted to be a knight. Of course, at fourteen I wanted be cool and get all the girls." Everyone laughed quietly.

"Stacy told me that wasn't enough. I would never be a knight if the only reason I wanted it was for the girls. She told me if I didn't believe in the good we were doing, then I should leave because there was no place for someone who didn't want to fight to save people. She was stern with me and at fourteen it was exactly what I needed. After that conversation I saw my future in a different light and got serious about becoming a knight.

"My father was right when he talked about the truthfulness of Stacy. She would give you the harsh truth if she thought you needed to hear it and in following in her footsteps, I cannot allow the deception that has taken root in our clan to continue."

Shawn paused as Jon get to his feet. I gave Jo a worried look. *What was he doing?* Was he going to tell everyone what really happened the night Stacy died? What would happen if he did? Would they shun him when they found out it was his fault Stacy died? I wanted to jump to my feet and tell him to stop but Tom put his hand on my leg. "Let him do this."

"The night Stacy died, I was her partner and as most of you know Liz Lawson-Robinson showed up. She was in bad shape and needed help, Stacy ordered me to help her. After Liz left, Stacy and I got back to work. The mare was strong, and I threw a grenade at him thinking Stacy was a safe distance away, but I was wrong. Stacy was behind him trying to cut his spinal cord."

"That's enough son," Jon said, trying to push Shawn way from the microphone.

"Dad, no, let him talk." Heather stood and put her hands on her hips.

"The tragic death of Stacy was not Liz's fault but mine. Dad wanted me to let her take the blame because he wants me to follow in his footsteps." There were gasps from the audience and I felt a tear track down my cheek. I didn't want Shawn to be ostracized as I had been. "Liz does not deserve your disdain, she had nothing to do with the loss of Stacy. Stacy would never forgive me if I didn't make this right and tell you all what really happened. All this talk of truth and honesty needs to be followed by everyone." Shawn glared at Jon whose hands were balled into fists and his face had turned as red as a tomato.

I was proud of Shawn for calling his dad out. It might not have been the best place for it, but he did what was right.

"It is amazing the stories a boy will tell to keep his girl close," Jon said, trying to laugh at Shawn's speech.

"Oh, no," I whispered as Shawn turned to his dad, brought his fist back, and punched him in the jaw. There was a collective gasp from the mourners and Shawn walked out of the training room without looking back. I moved to follow him, but Tom kept me where I was. Jon stumbled off the stage, holding a hand to his face and took his seat.

Jenny stood and marched to the podium. "I'm sorry everyone. Grief affects us all in different ways, for the Ericson men I guess that means making fools of themselves." There were a few tight laughs in the room.

"This is not what Stacy would have wanted for her funeral. She was the best sister anyone could ask for. She always had the back of any knight who needed her. She was a shining example of what it meant to bear the curse that was thrust upon us. She stood for what was right, and she didn't have a political agenda. She was born to hunt and kill mares and she was good at her job.

"If Stacy were here, she would tell us to stop bickering and placing blame. She would tell us to continue on and fight the good fight. Encourage the squires. Teach them what they need to know to keep them alive and killing mares. Without the squires we have no future and neither does the human race. She would also say stop trying to blame someone for what happened, what is done is done. Let's move on but never forget." Jenny was crying so hard by the end it was hard to understand what she was saying. I wiped the tears from my eyes and looked at Jo, who had been crying too. We gave each other tight smiles then returned our attention back to the podium.

We sat there for another hour listening as people told stories about Stacy and her life. It was one of the hardest days of my life. I barely knew the woman, but by the end I felt like I had known her my whole life and the thought of never getting to talk to her about all the stories that were told broke my heart. We needed to close the gate, there was no reason why anyone else should lose their life fighting the mares.

Chapter 24

After the formal ceremony ended Jenny invited everyone to stay for lunch but I skipped it to find Shawn. I glanced at Jo and she nodded. "Go find him. Let me know how he's doing."

"Thanks." I pulled my phone out and sent Shawn a text, asking where he was. I started toward the main entrance, checking my phone every five seconds for word from Shawn, but he wasn't replying. I walked as quickly as I could, ignoring everything in my path. Shawn's Jeep was still in the parking lot and I was about to head to the residential entrance when I heard someone call my name.

I spun and watched Kristina stomp across the parking lot toward me. I rolled my eyes; she was the last person I wanted to talk to. "What do you want?" I asked when she was a few feet from me.

"Why did you let Shawn do that?" She stopped and crossed her arms over her chest.

"Do what?"

"Tell everyone it was his fault not yours. It's political suicide."

"I had no idea he would get up there and tell the truth, but I'm proud of him."

"Don't you understand what it will mean for his future? He will never be more than a knight now."

"I didn't ask him to tell the truth, he did that all on his own." I crossed my arms over my chest, I wanted to ask her what she was doing with the goblin, but I didn't want her to know I knew yet. If I told her she might try something else.

"You play up the 'no one likes me,' bit pretty well, why wouldn't he want to make you happy?" She flipped her hair over her shoulder.

"Kristina, for someone who wants Shawn back, you don't understand who he is or what he stands for. All you want him for is to look good on your arm and to help you move up in the company."

"We are meant to be together." She stomped her foot and crossed her arms.

"But he doesn't love you and I bet you don't love him either."

"I could learn to love him."

"Only if doing so got you where you wanted to go." I needed to get rid of her and find Shawn, but she wasn't done yet.

"Why can't you just leave him alone? If it wasn't for you, we would already be back together." She stomped her foot again.

"Because I care about him, not what he can do for me." I walked to the residence door, leaving her standing in the parking lot.

"I would watch yourself around abandoned mineshafts if I were you."

My eyes widened, so it had been her. I spun around, ready to take off after her, but she was already at the main entrance and I didn't want to confront her in room full of mourning people. I would let it go for now, but Kristina would get what was coming to her.

Once I was inside, I checked the window, making sure she didn't change her mind and follow me.

"Hey, what are you doing?" Shawn asked and I gave him a tight smile. He was coming down the stairs with a duffle bag over his shoulder.

"Kristina…"

"God, she's just like my dad and I'm so tired of playing their games. I have to get out of here." He took my hand when he reached me and pulled me toward the door.

"Okay, let's go." I let him lead me to his Jeep. "Where do you want to go?"

"Just away from here. Can we go to your house?"

"Yeah, of course."

"Thanks, I need to distance myself from this place for a while."

"Don't worry I get it." I squeezed his hand then let go. "Are you all right driving?" I asked, going to the passenger door.

"Yeah, I'll be fine." He got in and threw his bag in the back seat.

I put my seat belt on and texted my parents as he started the car. "Thank you for what you did back there."

He pulled out of the parking lot, glanced at me, and gave me half a smile. "I couldn't let everyone think Stacy died because of you. I've learned a lot about my dad since we moved here and to tell you the truth, I don't like what I'm learning."

"Shawn I'm sorry, I think he has the best intentions, at least for his family."

"That's the problem, and the more I think about it the more it has always been the problem: he wants the best for him and his family but cares nothing about everyone else." Shawn slammed his hand against the steering wheel before turning onto my road. I didn't know what to say, so I kept my mouth closed and stared out the window as we drove up the hill. Shawn parked in the drive way when we reached the house. We had it to ourselves since my parents were at the lake.

I went upstairs to change while Shawn changed in the downstairs bathroom. I put on a pair of cotton shorts and a T-shirt, then I went downstairs and found Shawn in the kitchen wearing a T-shirt and a pair of kaki cargo shorts drinking a glass of water. "What do you want to do?" I asked sitting down at the bar.

"God, it feels like it has been forever since we got to hang out in real time. Do you want to go for a hike or something?"

I thought about the mineshaft and the clearing; I wanted to take Shawn there, but I didn't think it would be a good idea in his current state of mind. We could do the short loop though. "Yeah, let me get my shoes and we can go."

I put my shoes on and we made our way to the trailhead after I texted my parents. It was a beautiful day for a hike. The sun was out and there wasn't a cloud in the sky.

"Is this the same trail you took the other day?"

"Yeah, but we aren't going to the mineshaft, it's too late in the day."

"Is it this steep the whole way?" Shawn asked, breathing hard halfway up the first hill.

"No, once we get to the top, it levels out for the most part. Come on, do you need to work out more?" I giggled as I reached the top of the hill and stopped to wait for him.

"No, I just wasn't expecting it to be so steep." He met me at the top, and we waited while he caught his breath.

The trail was lined with twisted pines on each side as we made our way down the hill. "I get why the town is named Twisted Pines now," Shawn said from behind me. "They're kind of creepy and you can't see beyond them. It's almost like a fence."

"Yeah, they take a while to get used to, when I was little, they scared the crap out of me. I thought they would grab me and turn me into one."

"They would've scared me too. Why do they grow like this?"

"The Native Americans who settled here first had a few different stories, but a forest ranger told me it's because of all the snow and blizzards we get. It shapes them into what they are when they're young and their trunks are soft. They try to grow straight but they grow so slowly, and the snow bends them so much they end up twisted."

We came out of the forest into the meadow covered in early blooming spring flowers. I stopped and got my camera out of my bag.

"Wow." Shawn found a rock to lean against. "All that dark forest, then boom, I'm in the prettiest meadow I've ever seen."

I took a picture then put the camera back. "I know, not very many people know about it, so we shouldn't run into anyone." We continued on the trail, skirting the meadow until we came to the two-track that lead to the mineshaft.

"Is that it?" Shawn stopped to study the trail like it would disappear at any second.

"Yeah, I swear I've never seen it before last week." A chill shook me, and I closed my eyes, remembering I was safe.

"I think we should plan on checking it out with everyone soon." Shawn walked down the main trail again. "Hey, what did you and Jo get up to in your dreams last night? Heather told me you think the gate is in the mansion."

I told him about the dream with Freeman and my dad as we continued our hike. "I don't know if it was my imagination trying to solve the problem for me or if it was pointing me in the right direction."

"Good question, why don't you send them a text and see if they can come over now, if that's all right." We were coming to the end of the trail, and I pulled my phone out and sent them a text message. "Are you going home tonight?" I asked, remembering his duffle bag.

"No, I sent a text to Billy while you were changing. I'm going to stay with him for at least tonight." Shawn took my hand as we walked down the road.

"Good, I don't think my parents would have let you stay with us." I half laughed.

"I wasn't even going to ask; your dad probably would have gotten his gun out again."

"I wouldn't put it past him."

When we came around the last corner, I saw my parents

unloading Dad's truck. "I hope it will be okay with them if everyone comes over."

"Me too, your house is the safest place to meet." Shawn watched my dad struggling with a cooler. "Dr. Lawson, here let me help." He ran to help Dad.

I let them do their thing and went inside to find Mom. She was in the kitchen putting the leftovers of their lunch away. "Hi." I got a glass of water and sat down at the bar.

"Hi, did you have a good hike? How was the funeral?" She twisted her head to glance at me from the open fridge.

"The hike was good, the funeral was..." I wasn't sure how to answer her question. "Shawn punched his dad in the middle of the eulogy."

"Oh no, really?" Mom closed the door giving me a sad smile. "I told you I didn't like that man."

"I know, me neither, but he's Shawn's dad."

"Where's Shawn?"

"Helping Dad. Is it okay if Heather and Jo come over to hang out for a while?" I looked at the clock, wondering if the lunch was over yet. "We didn't really get to talk after the service was over."

"I don't see why not. I'll make burgers and potato salad." Mom went to the pantry and pulled out a bag of potatoes.

"Thanks Mom."

"Is Shawn going home tonight?"

"No, he's staying with Billy." I wondered how I would explain all this to Billy.

"Are you inviting him over too?" Mom raised her eyebrows at

me.

"I would but we need to talk about knight stuff."

"Elizabeth Lawson, call him, or I will. You'll find time to talk about work soon enough."

"Fine." I shrugged and went out on the deck text Billy.

Hey, we're grilling burgers do you want to come over? Jo, Heather, and Shawn are coming.

I hoped Billy was busy, but he responded almost instantly.

Sweet, I'll be over in a few.

I sighed and was about to go back inside when Shawn stepped out. "What's wrong?"

"My mom is making me invite Billy over." I leaned my head against Shawn's chest.

"We'll figure it out." He wrapped his arms around me and gave me a squeeze.

"Liz, Shawn, can you give me a hand?" Mom called.

Shawn let me go, and we went inside to help my mom.

Chapter 25

Heather wasn't thrilled to see Billy when she and Jo joined us on the deck. Jo, jumped into his arms, wrapped her legs around his waist and kissed him while my parents watched. My dad finally cleared his throat, and they broke apart.

"Sorry, Burt," Billy said, turning red, and taking Jo by the hand.

"I know what happens behind closed doors and in the front seat of your pickup but that doesn't mean I want to see it," Dad said from the grill as he flipped burgers.

"Amen, to that," I said, pouring water into the glasses sitting on the table.

Billy turned a shade redder then took a seat at the table across from Shawn. "Rough day, huh?"

"Yeah, I got into a huge fight with my dad." Shawn glanced over at my dad as I went inside to help Mom with the salad.

"What else Mom?" I leaned against the counter and watched her mix the potato salad.

"Did you take the condiments out yet?"

"I knew I was forgetting something." I took the catsup, mustard, and anything else I thought people might like on their burgers outside and put them on the table.

"Thanks for letting me crash at your place tonight," Shawn was saying when I got back outside.

"Yeah, no problem. My parents are cool with it."

"Let's eat," Mom said, bringing out the potato salad as Dad put a plate full of burgers on the table.

We sat and ate, talking about mundane things that Billy and Dad would understand. When we finished eating, Billy offered to help with the dishes and Dad went inside to watch the Rockies game.

"Did Jo tell you about the dream last night?" I asked Heather.

"Yes, but only her side. What happened when you went through the door?"

"I was in a huge library and the guy who built the mansion was in there. It was almost like he was being kept a prisoner or something. I asked him where the gate was since everything started when his wife and kids died."

"What did he say?" Heather learned forward, her eyes going huge.

"He rambled on about a journal, that everything we needed to know was in it and he left it in the house somewhere."

"What are the chances that a journal from the eighteen-hundreds is still there?" Jo asked.

"I don't know but I'll bet it's in the basement."

"But we don't have a basement," Heather said. "At least

I've never seen any stairs or access to one."

"The stairs we went down were behind the stairs you use in the residence, so maybe they were covered when they renovated the house," Jo offered.

"Hey what are you guys whispering about out here?" Billy asked sitting next to Jo.

"Just work stuff." Jo gave me a panicked look. I hated keeping this from Billy, but did we want him involved with this? He was more vulnerable than any of us.

"You guys are always talking about work stuff," Billy's eyes flared. "I don't even know what you do. Clue me in, I'm begging you."

I knew this day would come; it was impossible for me to keep a secret this big from Billy. I looked around the group, Jo was giving me pleading eyes, Heather looked like she would kill me if I breathed a word about Knights Inc. and Shawn shrugged like it didn't matter to him. "Fine, we are trying to close a gate to another dimension that allows goblins to enter our dreams and kill us."

Billy stared at me for a second then laughed. "Wow Liz, I didn't know you had such a big imagination." Billy waited for me to laugh with him when I didn't his mouth hung open. "You mean the sleeping death, right?"

"Yup, we're going to stop it." Shawn leaned back in his chair and put his arms around me.

"Right, the next thing you will tell me is that you are part of some secret government program where you can spy on people in their dreams."

I looked anywhere but at Billy. Jo's mouth was hanging open and

Shawn squeezed my hand in warning. "We don't spy on people. We just protect them. Well, Shawn and Heather do; Jo and I are still training."

"Prove it," Billy huffed, folding his arms over his chest.

I glanced around the table then back at Billy. "I wish I could, but I don't know how."

"Then let me help?" Billy asked leaning forward in his chair.

"Billy, sweetie, I don't know if you can. We all have special powers allowing us to fight the mares and manipulate our dreams. I can even jump in yours, but you won't remember." Jo ran a hand up and down his back.

"What?" Billy pushed back from the table. "You've been invading my dreams?"

"No," Jo said then glanced away. "Maybe once, just to see what you were dreaming about."

"This is so messed up. Why should I believe you?"

"Billy, you wanted to know what we were talking about and now you do. You can take or leave the information, but you can't tell anyone." I got up and closed the sliding door. It was bad enough we were telling Billy, I didn't want to try to explain it to Dad.

"Like anyone would believe me." Billy crossed his arms over his chest. "How did you get involved with this, Liz?"

"Victor, my bio-dad was one of them," I said, ducking my head.

"When did you find out? Why are you just now telling

me? I thought we told each other everything."

"After I hit the moose. Would you have believed me?" I arched an eyebrow at him.

He stared at the table and frowned, thinking. "No, I probably would've thought you had a brain injury. Wait, so you're trying to get rid of the mares, so we won't have to sleep under dreamcatchers anymore?"

"That's the plan." Heather flipped her hair over her shoulder like she would rather be anywhere but with us.

"Is that what you guys do? Close the gates that let them into our dreams? Is that why you move around so much?"

"No, normally we just keep them in check, no one knows where the gates are or how to close them. Victor thought he could figure it out though. We are going to succeed where he failed, then maybe we can live a normal life." Jo rested her head on his shoulder.

"So how can I help?" Billy asked. "There has to be something I can do."

I glanced around the table as everyone shook their heads. "We will figure something out. In the meantime, Heather do you think you can see if you can find the basement?" I asked as she pushed her chair back and stood.

"Yeah, I'll see what I can do. What are you guys going to do?" She took a step toward the door but stopped.

"We're going to find the gate in our dreams. I'm pretty sure it's somewhere in the mansion."

"Why do you think you will find it in your dream?" Heather asked.

"If it goes from the dream dimension to the mare dimension our dreams might be the only way to find it." I squeezed Shawn's hand.

"Okay, we find the gate, then what?" she asked.

"We find the journal Freeman was talking about. He said it contained the information on how to close it."

"Okay." Heather checked her phone. "Is there anything else? I'm on duty tonight since my brother ran away from home."

"No, that's it for now." I shrugged.

"Okay, Dad's on the warpath. If I'm late for my shift, there will be hell to pay." Heather turned to leave but spun back around and looked at Jo. "Do you need a ride or is lover-boy going to give you one?"

"I'll give her a ride." Billy rolled his eyes at the moniker.

"Why don't we meet for breakfast at the café tomorrow at eight?" Shawn asked.

"Sounds good little brother. I'll tell Mom where you're staying and that you're all right."

"Thanks." Shawn got to his feet and gave Heather a hug. When they broke apart Heather went to the door, and we all said bye.

"So, you're not working tonight?" I asked Shawn.

"No, I want to stay away from Dad for the time being." He sat and took my hand.

"Do you want to help me, and Jo look for the gate in the mansion?"

"Yeah, I want to see the basement too."

"Can I come?" Billy asked.

"You can, but you won't remember it, and you still have to sleep under a dreamcatcher," Jo said, giving him a pitiful look.

"That's okay you can tell me about it tomorrow."

Jo and Billy left after we decided to meet in Shawn's padded room. Shawn and I sat on the deck and watched the sunset before my dad chased him out.

"How are you doing?" I asked as I walked him to his Rubicon. It had been a heck of a day for all of us, but Shawn won first place in the crappiest day race.

"I feel free for the first time in my life. I've wanted to punch my dad for a long time and finally doing it was freeing. I have no idea what kind of punishment I will be in for when I get back, but he asked for it."

"I don't think I said thank you for defending me." I wrapped my arms around his neck.

"No, you didn't." He moved closer so our lips almost touched.

"Thank you, he hasn't been very nice to me. I haven't told you everything he's done but thank you for today." I moved to kiss him, but he pulled back.

"What do you mean? What else did he do?" Shawn pushed me away forcing me to let go of him.

I kicked myself mentally for bringing it up. I didn't want to tell Shawn all the horrible things Jon had said and done to me, but it was too late now. "When your sister was hurt on prom night, and you went to get help? I was fighting Stalker? He watched me but didn't do anything to help."

"What?" Shawn's hands balled into fists.

"Then the next day he bribed me to stay away from you... said I was a distraction. I had to threaten him so he would let me train. He tried to steal my rune that day too." Once I started talking I couldn't seem to stop. I needed to tell Shawn everything. "He also told me you and Kristina are all but engaged."

"Why didn't you tell me about this?"

"Because he's your dad. I won't whine to you every time he does something underhanded. You only get one dad, and I didn't want to drive the wedge between you any deeper." I shook my head. Me and my big mouth.

Shawn pulled me closer. "I'm so sorry, I knew he didn't like you, but I didn't know he did all those things to you. Why are you still doing this? Wouldn't it be easier if you didn't become a knight and went to the Air Force Academy?"

"Yes, it would be easier, but becoming a knight is so much bigger than the Air Force Academy. Don't you see, Shawn, if I don't become a knight, your dad will drive us apart, figure out a way to split us up. I can deal with a lot of crap but being away from you would tear me apart."

"I love you," Shawn whispered before pressing his lips against mine.

My eyes widened as his words registered. I pulled him in closer as our tongues tangled together. Did I love him? I wouldn't say it unless I really felt it. I had been thinking about it a lot lately. I had to be honest with him. I pulled away from him; I had to tell him. "I love you too," I whispered, gazing into his eyes.

He smiled, picked me, and swung me around in a circle. "I better go, but I'll see you later okay?"

"Yeah, make sure Billy gets to bed on time, I don't want to be waiting on his ass all night." I laughed as he put me down.

Chapter 26

After Shawn left, I helped Mom with the dishes. "That was quite the kiss," she said, bumping her shoulder with mine.

"You were spying on me?" I felt my cheeks burn as I stacked plates in the dishwasher.

"Hey, I'm the mom, I get to do what I want." She squeezed my shoulder. "It looks like you two are getting pretty serious."

"I guess. We barely get to see each other though; we make the most of what we can." I wasn't going to tell her we just confessed our love to each other. It felt very private; it wasn't something I wanted to share with anyone yet.

"Are you having sex?" Mom blurted, and I dropped the pot she used to boil the potatoes in on the floor. I jumped and gaped at her.

"Mom! No." It felt like my face was going to spontaneously combust.

"I'm sorry, sweetie, but it is my job to ask." She handed me the pot to put in the dishwasher. "Do you think it will? It's okay if the answer is yes, I just want you to be safe and happy."

My parents had put up with a lot since I met Shawn, it wouldn't kill me to be honest with them. "Maybe, I don't know. We haven't really talked about it."

"Well, if you think you might, I think you should talk to your father about getting on birth control."

"Please, don't make me talk to him." It was bad enough I was talking to my mom about it. I thought I would die of embarrassment if I had to talk to him about it too.

"There is no other option." Mom pulled the plunger out of the sink and dried her hands on a towel. "Look at it this way. He wanted to put you on birth control when you started dating Shawn. I don't think it will be too bad, dear."

"Fine, but will you talk to him about it? I can't do it without dying." I took the towel from her and dried my hands.

"Yes, but you know he will sit you down and talk to you about how to use it and the whole sex-talk thing again right?"

"Yeah, I'll figure out a way to deal with it I guess." I yawned. "I'm going to head to bed. It's been a long day."

"Okay dear. Sleep well." Mom kissed me on the cheek. I went upstairs, changed into a pair of sleep shorts and a T-shirt, then climbed into bed.

My dream started in Shawn's padded room. He was sitting on the couch waiting for me when I arrived. "Hi." I was being shy, still mortified from the conversation I had with my mom.

"Hey, what's wrong?" He pulled me into a hug.

"You don't want to know." I felt my cheeks heat up again.

"Your mom talked to you about the kiss?" He pulled away

and rubbed his thumbs over my hot cheeks.

"Is it that obvious?" I hid my face in my hands.

"No, I saw her watching us. Why is it making you blush?"

"Because I got the mother-daughter safe sex talk." I wasn't sure I was ready to talk to him about it, but the words were out of my mouth before I could stop myself.

"Really?" He stared at the floor as his ears turned red.

"Yeah, I'm glad I'm not the only one who blushes about it." I sat down on the couch.

"I guess we should talk about it at some point." He moved to the other side of the couch and sat down leaving enough space for someone to sit between us.

"Yeah, I guess it would be responsible of us." I couldn't seem to take my eyes off my hands. "I, you know I've never…"

"Me neither." He cut me off

"Oh, good." I wasn't sure why but if he had done it, it might have changed things for me. "Do you want to?" Was I really asking a seventeen-year-old boy if he wanted to have sex?

"Well, yeah, but not until we're both ready."

"Let's get this show on the road," Jo said, popping in with Billy holding her hand.

I made a strangled sound in my throat wishing I could hide as my face felt like it would combust at any second. I glanced at Shawn; I couldn't tell whose face was redder

"What did we walk in on?" Jo asked with a sly grin on her face.

"Nothing," Shawn said, scrambling to his feet. "Why would you think you walked in on anything?"

"Well, you are both blushing like you just took your first health class, and you were sitting on the opposite sides of the couch. Something good was happening."

"Whatever, just drop it." Shawn offered me his hand.

"I'm really not going to remember this?" Billy asked, taking in the room.

"Doubt it," I said, taking Shawn's hand, and letting him pull me up. "You have your dreamcatcher up, right?"

"Yes, I'm not stupid." He rolled his eyes.

"Should we go?" Shawn asked, still trying to avoid making eye contact with Jo.

"Yeah, let's see what we can find." I took his hand, relieved that he changed the subject.

Shawn took one of Jo's hands, she took Billy's with the other and the padded room dissolved around us, leaving us in the sitting room from the night before. Nothing had changed and I let out a relieved breath, maybe it wasn't just my imagination.

"Where are we?" Shawn asked going over to check out the unlit fire place.

"In the sitting room of the mansion." I began checking the books on the end tables. "I don't know what part of the mansion this is now, but it's a place to start."

"Did you find anything?" Jo asked as I checked the last of the books.

"No, they are all fiction books. There is nothing about the gate. Let's show Shawn the basement." I went to the door.

We left the sitting room and went down the hall to where

the foyer should have been, but instead of ending there, we found a staircase that only went up. "I don't remember this being here," I said, turning to Jo.

"Me neither, did we go the wrong way out of the room?" Jo glanced behind her.

"I don't think so and it's too dark to see what's at the other end. Should we check it out?"

"Let's do this." Shawn sounded excited at the prospect of exploring. He took my hand and led me to the other end of the hallway. "What the hell?" We stopped a few feet from another staircase going up. "Are you sure we're in the right place?"

"I thought we were." I looked up the stairwell, the stairs were swallowed by darkness after the first landing.

"This was not part of the tour last night," Jo said, following my gaze. "What do we do?"

"Well, we could concentrate on the foyer, and see if we ended up there, or we could see where the stairs lead." I didn't know what the best option was, something about this place was giving me the creeps.

"Let's see where the stairs lead. It's a dream, so maybe it will lead us where we want to go." Shawn started up them.

"Okay, but let's stick together, it almost feels like someone is playing a trick on us." We started up the steps, stopping when we reached the first landing. There was a doorway at the top of the next flight, but we couldn't see what was beyond it. "I guess there's nowhere to go but up."

We reached the top of the stairs and went through the door and into a hallway, but it felt like we were in a different house all together, a house that no one had lived in for decades. A dim light came through a dirty window at the end of the hall. Cobwebs clung to the ceiling and the walls. The wood plank floor was covered in a thick layer of dust and creaked with every step.

Shawn took my hand as we came to the first closed door. He tried the handle, and it creaked open. It was Shawn's room. It was just like the last time I was there. A bookshelf was crammed with books, the green comforter and matching area rugs on top of the gleaming hardwood floor. His desk was clear except for a piece of paper. "What's going on?" He stepped into the room and spun in a circle.

"I wish I knew," Jo said, rubbing her arms, and looking around. "Whose dream do you think we are in anyway?"

"What do you mean?" Billy asked.

"I mean, we have to be in one of our dreams. The four of us can't create our own dream. It has to be based on one of ours."

"Who knows," Shawn said, spinning around. "There's no way to find out. Let's keep moving, maybe there's another set of stairs that will take us back to the ground floor."

The hallway was the same as it had been before we entered Shawn's room and even though it was creepy, I relaxed a tiny bit; it hadn't changed on us. We checked the next door which was Heather's room. It was set up similar to Shawn's only it was done in white. We moved down the hall to the next room. "This is the master bedroom," Shawn whispered before opening the door.

This room was the same as the hallway. The floor to

ceiling windows overlooking the lake were brown with dust, a tarnished brass bed set against one wall, the mattress was sitting half on the floor and half on the frame. Cobwebs hung to the walls, ceiling and the wood night stands and dressers. The fireplace in the corner had nothing but cold gray ash sitting in the bottom of it.

I walked to the window, wondering if I would see the lake or slaves. I pulled the hem of my shirt up and wiped the dust away. Peering through the window, I saw town and the lake.

"What's out there?" Shawn asked, coming to my side.

"Just town, I can't tell if it's present day or not." I stepped away, feeling frustrated. "This isn't working. How are we going to get back to where we were last night?" I stared at Jo, expecting her to have the answer.

"I don't know. Let's keep moving though." Jo led the way out of the room, and down the hall to the last door. She opened it and let out a sigh of relief. "Stairs."

They were just like the stairs leading to the basement: metal and spiraling down. I shrugged and led the way down. It felt like we had descended four floors by the time we reached the bottom.

"Thank God. I didn't think we would ever reach the bottom," Shawn said. "Wait, where are we?"

I spun in a circle. There was a high ceiling with a mezzanine bordering the room. The floor was a beautiful hard wood, shining with varnish. A crystal chandelier hung above our heads and oil sconces hung from the walls every few feet. "The ballroom," I said.

"Wow, this place was cool, but why do you think we're here?" Shawn walked toward the double doors at the end of the hall.

"I don't know." I followed Shawn with Jo at my side and Billy on her other until we came to the doors. Shawn tried to pull them open, but they wouldn't budge.

"Locked." Shawn ran a hand through his hair.

Jo stared at me, and I rolled my eyes then pulled a skeleton key out of my pocket. "Here try this." I handed it to Shawn.

"That's why I love you, you always have the best ideas." He put the key in the lock and turned it. The door opened to the offices at Knights Inc. "You've got to be kidding me."

"Did he say he loved you?" Jo whispered in my ear.

"Yeah." I grinned loving hearing him say it. "It's kind of new."

"And you feel the same?"

"Yes, how could I not?"

"Good, otherwise I might have to kick your ass." We stopped inside the doors. "This is just messed up."

"No kidding." I followed her down the hallway. We checked the offices as we came to them, they were all empty and looked the same as it did in real life. When we reached the door to the lobby Shawn pulled on the handle, but it was locked.

"Let's see if I learned something tonight." Shawn pulled a keycard from his back pocket. He held it in front of the panel, the door clicked open and Shawn held it for us.

I was almost through the door when Shawn lost his grip on the handle and it slammed in my face so hard the wall shook. I jumped back then tried the handle; it was locked. I pulled a key card out of my pocket but before I could use it Stalker joined me.

"Finally, alone, little lamb chop," Stalker said from behind me. I spun to face him, my hands shaking. Even though I fell asleep with my dreamcatcher, Jo and Shawn didn't have the same protection as I did.

"Why won't you leave me alone?" I asked listening as Jo, Shawn, and Billy pounded on the other side of the door.

"Go you guys, I will meet you at Shawn's, just run," I called, blocking the door.

"Don't make them leave. I want to play." Stalker ran at me and even though I knew he wouldn't be able to touch me, I braced for impact. I would not let him near my friends. He bounced off my bubble, flew through the air, and landed sprawled on the floor.

"Why won't you give up?" I leaned over and shook my finger at him.

"Why won't you give up and face your fate?" He got to his feet and rubbed his hands together. "Why are you here? Are you looking for something?" He walked around me, pushing on my shield as if trying to find a weak spot.

"Lots of people dream about work. I could ask the same of you. How did you know about Shawn's padded room and that he and Kristina used to date?"

He waved his hand. "How I know, what I know, is no concern of yours and I don't believe you. I've been following you. I think you are looking for something. But why would you be searching here?" The office morphed into the basement we'd been trying to find all night.

Great, I was finally where I wanted to be, but I couldn't do what I wanted thanks to Stalker. "Why would I tell you?"

"Hmm," he walked down the stone hallway, opening doors. "Maybe I can figure it out for myself." The stench from the corpses reached me and my stomach rolled. "These souls have already been taken. You can't save them." He closed the door and moved to the next one.

"Why are you keeping them? Can't you at least bury them?" I held my hand over my nose, hoping the stench would leave before I threw up.

"Because they're mine, and I will need them before too long." He stopped and smiled, showing me his sharp teeth and I took an involuntary step back.

"What do you need them for? You already ate their souls."

"You have your secrets, I have mine." He stopped at the door where I heard the footsteps but didn't want to know what was inside the last time I'd been there. He opened it and a monster stuck his nose out. It was half-wolf, half-bear. It had long pointed ears of a wolf, the deep brown eyes of a bear, and a snout as black as night. There was a long string of drool hanging from its mouth. His fur was a long, saggy, sorrel, and he stood on the hind legs of a bear. He roared at Stalker and batted him aside.

"Oh, look what I let out," Stalker sang, picking himself up off the floor as the beast sniffed the air then set his eyes on me. He roared again, fell onto his front legs, then ran at me.

I had no idea if my dreamcatcher would work against him, but I wasn't going to wait around to find out. I thought of Shawn and the room disintegrated just as the monster's paw came up to swipe at me. I fell to the floor and looked around; I was in Shawn's padded room with him, Billy, and Jo hovering over me.

"Are you all right?" Jo asked.

"We tried to jump to you, but we couldn't. What happened?" Shawn asked, offering me a hand up.

"Yeah, I'm fine. Stalker showed up once you guys were out of the room." I was out of breath and shaking; the monster had scared me more than Stalker for a change.

"Come sit, you're shaking." Shawn led me over to the couch and sat me down. "Now tell us what happened."

I told them everything, worried that the mare would harass them now. When I was done, I asked. "When did you try to jump to me?"

"After we got back through the door to the office and you weren't there." Jo sat in a chair across from the couch.

"You couldn't jump to the basement then," I said to myself as I processed the information. "There must be something special about it if you couldn't jump there. Are there any other places you can't jump to?"

They glanced at each other then shook their heads. "I can't think of anywhere I haven't been able to jump to if I have been there before or if someone needs help." Shawn ran his fingers through his hair.

"But you've never been there." I pointed out.

"Yeah, but I have." Jo crossed her arms over her chest. "I should have been able to jump there without a problem."

"Something is hiding down there, and someone doesn't want us to know what it is."

"You think so?" Shawn asked taking my hand.

"Why else would you not be able to jump there? Jo and I have both been there before. I wonder why the mare was able to take me there, but you guys couldn't follow."

"Are you thinking what I'm thinking?" Shawn asked, glancing from me to Jo then back again.

"I don't know. What are you thinking?" Jo asked.

"That the gate is in the basement. We have to find a way to get down there."

Chapter 27

The next morning, I got up early, ready to meet the gang and talk in real time about finding the gate. After our dream the night before I was convinced the gate was in the mansion. It was the only place that made sense. I took a shower and dressed in a pair of capris and a Green Day T-shirt then went downstairs to find Mom and Dad eating breakfast at the bar.

"You're up early for a Sunday," Dad said, taking a sip of his coffee, and grinning like he knew something I didn't.

Crap, I forgot about my conversation with Mom. She probably ran to my dad to tell him I wanted to get on the pill. "Yeah, we're meeting at the cafe for breakfast." I ignored the elephant in the room.

"Then what are you going to do?" Mom asked, taking a bite of her eggs.

"I don't know, it is one of my only days off so probably hang out, but it depends on what everyone else has planned."

"Text us when you leave the café," Mom said, glancing between me and Dad.

"Fine." I still wasn't okay with the new rules about telling them where I was.

"Liz, don't complain. You did this to yourself." Dad glanced up from the Denver Post for a second.

"I know, but how long am I going to have to do this?"

"Until your wedding day." Dad winked at me before going back to the paper.

My eyes widened. "You've got to be kidding me." I put my Chucks on and grabbed my bag. "I'll see you guys later."

"Have a good time, sweetie," Mom called as I closed the door and went to my Jeep. It was a crisp morning, but the sun was out and there were only a few white, puffy clouds floating in the sky. It would be a beautiful day. I drove to town with the heat on since I didn't have a top on the Jeep, and I was thankful I put my hair in a braid before I left.

Shawn's Jeep was parked outside Twisted Café when I got there, and I parallel parked like a champ then went inside. I found Shawn sitting at a long table by the window with a cup of coffee in front of him. He was grinning like a madman and I wondered what he was so happy about.

"Hi," I said, leaning over to give him a kiss. "Where's Billy?"

"He still had to shower, and I wanted to make sure we got a table since it's the busy season," Shawn said as I sat next to him. "He will meet us here."

"Good. Last night was messed up," I said as the waitress came over and I ordered a cup of coffee.

"No kidding, I don't think I've had a dream like that since

I was a kid. It was almost like we had no control over it."

"Yeah, now I know how regular people must feel when they dream." I thanked the waitress as she set my coffee on the table.

"I never thought of it that way, I guess you're right." Shawn looked up at the ceiling.

"Right about what?" Heather asked as she sat across from me and Jo took the seat across from Shawn.

"Our dream last night, we couldn't control it." Shawn glanced across the table at his sister.

"We can't control what happens when we're fighting mares," Heather said, rolling her eyes at him.

"No, this wasn't like fighting mares," Jo said. "Not that I've ever fought one, but we couldn't control the environment."

"What do you mean?" Heather asked as Billy came in and kissed Jo on the cheek before sitting at the end of the table.

"Hey, I thought you guys were going to take me with you last night," Billy said, giving me a death stare.

I gave him a sad smile before taking a sip of my coffee.

"Sweetie, you were with us last night." Jo took his hand and patted it. "You don't remember."

"Oh." Billy sat up straighter and blinked quickly like he was trying not to cry. "Guess you were right."

"Hey, it's okay." Jo put a hand on his shoulder. "It doesn't change the way I feel about you."

"Are you sure?" he asked, glancing at her from the corner of his eye.

I looked everywhere but at Jo and Billy, feeling like I was intruding on a private moment.

"Yeah, don't worry."

"Can we get back to what happened last night?" Heather asked, rolling her eyes at the lovebirds.

"We couldn't control where we went inside the mansion. It was like something was setting us on a path and there was no way around it," Jo said, turning way from Billy to face Heather.

Heather thought about it for a minute. "I don't know what that would be like. Did you find anything?"

"No, all we did was walk through different eras of the mansion," Shawn said, running a hand through his hair.

"What do you mean?" Billy asked, raising an eyebrow at Jo.

We explained what happened the night before, then ordered our food.

"It sounds like a normal dream to me," Billy said.

"You don't get it, we don't have normal dreams. We can control them for the most part," Heather said, rolling her eyes. I didn't think she liked him being part of this, but it was too late now.

"Oh." He stared at the table and rubbed the back of his neck.

"Moving on," Shawn started, "Heather, were you able to find anything?"

"Yes, and no." She took a sip of coffee. "I think I found the stairway to the basement."

"You did?" Shawn asked, grinning with brotherly pride.

"But, it's behind a wall and I don't know how to access it without tearing the wall down."

"Where is it?" I asked.

"Let's tear the wall out," Shawn said, and Jo nodded at him.

"First, how would we explain it to Mom and Dad? They just spent a boat load having the place refurbished. Two, its right where you said it would be Liz, behind the main stairs."

"What do we do now?" Billy asked with wide eyes.

"Wait," Shawn said, glancing at Billy. "What if we staged a fight and one of us got pushed through the wall and wow, what are a set of stairs doing here? I wonder where they go."

Jo rolled her eyes at me. "Leave it to the boys to solve the problem with violence."

"What if it's a secret passage and we just have to find the latch to open the door?" I was grasping at straws but, it sounded better than the boys fighting.

"I don't know, Heather you know where the stairs are, does it look like it opens or could open?" Shawn asked.

"Let me think," Heather said, closing her eyes. "Liz might be right. There is wood paneling on the wall, and it has natural breaks that could hide the seams of a door."

The waitress brought our food then, and we were all silent for a few minutes as we thought about it and chewed our food.

"If you created a secret passage, how would you open it?" Heather finally asked.

"My only reference is movies so who knows," I said. There had to be a way to find out what was behind the wall.

"Are there any lights on the walls or a bookshelf where one of the books could open the door?" Billy asked.

"No, the lights are all recessed canned lights and there isn't anything that isn't new. Heck, we might be going about this all wrong, maybe you're right, Shawn. You and Billy could get into a fight and bust through it." Heather looked tired and defeated for the first time since I met her, with dark circles under her eyes. She wanted to close the gate just as badly as I did.

"Are you okay?" I asked.

She gave me a sad smile. "Yesterday was hard, Mom was freaking out because Shawn didn't come home, even though I told her he was staying with Billy. Then work last night sucked. I was stuck with Kristina and she wouldn't shut up about Shawn."

"Mom was mad, huh?" Shawn slumped and stared at his plate.

"She isn't mad, she's worried. She hates it when you and Dad fight and yesterday was a big one. I think she's embarrassed too. You hit your father, the man in charge of this territory in front of everyone. Dad spent the rest of yesterday in meetings with the council and he wasn't talking to anyone when he came out."

"Crap," Shawn ran his hand through his hair. "I guess I should come home then?"

"It would be helpful, although I don't know what Dad will do to you." She pushed her plate away. "But I could use your help with the secret passage."

Shawn looked at me. "I was hoping we could spend the

day together, but …" he trailed off.

"Go home, take care of your family. You need them, and they need you." I cupped his face with my hand. "There will be other times for us to hang out."

"Thanks, how did I end up with such a great girlfriend?" He leaned in to kiss me.

Puke noises brought us out of our moment as we broke apart and glanced at Bill and Jo who were pretending to throw up.

"Get over it. Do you want me and Shawn to mock you when you kiss?" I gave Billy an evil eye.

"Whatever, we look like a couple in the movies when we kiss, everyone loves it." Billy moved to kiss Jo, but she pushed him away.

"They're right, let's try to keep the kissing to a minimum when we are around each other," Jo said.

"Deal," everyone, including Heather, said.

We were dividing up the bill when I realized I had nothing to do. "Billy, what are you doing when we're done?"

He gave me his I'm sorry smile. "Jo and I are going out on the boat. You can come if you want."

It was nice of Billy to offer, but it was obvious he didn't want me to join them. "That's okay, I wouldn't want to intrude on your make out time."

After we paid the bill, Shawn walked me to my Jeep. "What are you doing today?"

"Nothing major, probably just hang out with my parents. I haven't seen much of them lately." I put my bag in the Jeep. "Do you think you will have to work tonight?"

"I shouldn't, but who knows with my dad in charge." He pulled me in close. "Will you be all right?"

"Yeah, dreamcatcher remember?" I gave him a bright smile and wondered if we would ever get time to just be together.

"Okay, I'll see you tomorrow." He brought his lips to mine, and I kissed him like I wasn't going to see him for a month. With our luck, we would be lucky if it was a month. "Love you."

"Love you too," I murmured as I watched him walk back to his Jeep.

I got into mine and started it up. I knew where I wanted to go; I hadn't been there in a long time but after everything I'd been through since I met Shawn, it was long overdue, and I wasn't going to tell my parents.

Chapter 28

The Twisted Pines Cemetery sat on the side of a mountain overlooking the lake. It was small, maybe only twenty acres and barely half full. I parked as close to Victor's grave as I could then got out of my Jeep, leaving my bag and phone in the passenger seat. I had been a long time since I visited the grave of the man I'd never met, but who I would always thing of as my father.

I came around a blue spruce and gave a start when I found a man standing at Victor's grave. I recognized him almost immediately, Jon. Great. Just who I wanted to run into. I thought about leaving but it was my father's grave, Jon would have to deal with it. I stood next him and stared at the tombstone.

Victor Robinson

The man who never stopped chasing his dreams

Rest in Peace

"He was my best friend," Jon said in a low voice, and I swear I heard it crack.

"I know." I was not in the mood to deal with Jon, but as long as he was civil, I could be too. "I read his journal; I have pictures of the two of you."

He turned to me. "You knew? Why didn't you say anything?"

"Because I didn't think it ended well between you and with the way you've treated me. I didn't think you would want to know."

"I didn't know Sven gave him the rune. Then he left because he didn't like the way I was doing things. All I was trying to do was give us a future."

"A future where you are only putting a Band-Aid on a cut not finding an antibiotic to kill the bacteria."

"You know about his theory on the gates?"

"It was in his journal, his last entry said he knew where the gate was, and he thought he knew how to close it. He was wrong."

"So, he died trying to close the gate?"

"Yes, and Stalker, the mare who won't leave me alone, told me he's the one who killed him." I wiped a tear from my eye.

"Is that why you wanted to join us so you close the gate?"

I wanted to tell him the truth, but if I did what would he do with the information? Could I trust the man who had made everything harder than it needed to be? "Heather thinks if we close the gate, then kill the mares on this side, I won't have to worry about being marked anymore."

"It's a good theory," Jon put his hands in his pockets and turned to gaze at the lake, "but if Victor's theory is correct, there are gates everywhere. Are you going to close them all?"

"I haven't thought that far. First I have to close the one here, then we'll see."

"God, you are just like him. Every time I see you all I see is him." Jon's voice became hard. "He left me in the middle of the night to chase this dream of closing the gates. It got him killed, it will kill you, and you're dragging my children into this."

"I didn't drag them into it, they wanted to help. They don't want to waste their life doing the same thing over and over again with no end in sight."

"But it's our way, and it has been our way for thousands of years."

"Change is hard, but it's good. Don't you want something better for them? Do you think Jenny wants to spend the rest of her life worrying if Shawn or Heather won't wake up?"

"She understands our calling. You don't understand what it's like growing up and living with mares."

"I know, and I'm thankful for it. I could never stand aside while people were dying if there was something I could do to help them. Why don't you want to close the gate?"

He was silent while he thought of his answer. "I don't know any other life. What would I do? I'm not in the position or old enough to retire. I would have to get a real job, but what skills do I have?"

"Do you want Shawn and Heather to end up like you?"

He grimaced and glanced at me. "I never want them to fear anything. They are the most important part of my life and they are barely speaking to me."

"Well, if you stopped blaming me for everything going wrong and keeping me and Shawn apart, it might go a long way to making things better."

"I'm sorry I've treated you badly. Whenever I see you, I think of Victor and how he left us. I hate him for it. I'm taking it out on you. I have a feeling you will run out on us like he did."

"Give me a chance, I'll see this through. I'm not my father, I never even met the man. I think he did what he thought was right. It doesn't mean it was though. If you don't want me, or anyone else to leave, think about how you treat other people, especially your kids. They want to love you, but you need to let them."

"Can I convince you to stop searching for the gate?"

"No."

"Will you stop Heather and Shawn from helping you?"

"No, I'm not forcing them. Like I said they don't want to do this for the rest of their lives."

"Can you please not do anything stupid until the council leaves at the end of the week?"

"Why are you worried about them?"

"After what Shawn pulled at the funeral, and what I tried to do to you, they aren't sure that leading a territory is the best fit for me."

"You did that to yourself."

"Please, if I lose this position, they will send me and the family to Alaska."

I balked; Alaska was so far away. Would Shawn and I be able to handle a long-distance relationship? How would I find and close the gate without his help? "I don't want you to lose your job, and I'll try not to make any more waves, but you need to be on your best behavior too. If you take Shawn to Alaska, or exile him to Mexico, I will make you suffer."

"Deal, just be careful with my kids, don't get them killed." Jon made a fist and rubbed his eyes like he had dirt in them.

"I'll do everything in my power not to."

"Can you send Shawn home? Jenny is having a hard enough time losing her sister, Shawn running away isn't making it any better."

"He should already be there."

"Thank you, I'll leave you with your father then," Jon said, before leaving me.

I stood there in stunned silence for a minute. Was Jon actually going to stop treating me like I dirt? It would make my life a heck of a lot easier if he treated me like a human for a change.

"Hi, Dad," I whispered staring at Victor's headstone. "Guess you saw all that, right? Well, I came to see you because Stacy was killed the other night and I'm scared. Closing the gate is the only way I will survive, but we can't find it and we have no idea what we're doing.

"I know if you were here you would tell me to leave it alone, it's too dangerous, but I can't live my life running from mares and with my mark it's all I will do until we find a way to get rid of them for good.

"I'm dating Jon's son, Shawn. Don't worry he isn't anything like his dad. I love him, Dad, and I wish you were here so we could all meet. I think you'd like him.

"I saw you the other night in a dream, you told me to run. I don't know if you're a prisoner or a slave but if it wasn't just a dream, I will free you.”

I stood staring at his grave letting my words soak in, hopefully they would find their way to him. I went back to my Jeep when I was done; I didn't know if Victor heard me, but it felt good to talk to him. I sat in my Jeep for a few minutes, dreading going home. I didn't want to face what was waiting for me there, but sometimes it's just better to get things over with than to think about them for too long.

Chapter 29

Later that night, while I was getting ready for bed, I was trying not to think about what happened after I left the cemetery. Just thinking about the conversation, I had with my mom and dad, then the trip to the clinic made me blush. Shawn sent me a text; he and Heather would be working that night so I would be on my own. I asked Shawn about seeing the shrink, but his dad overruled the requirement since they were shorthanded. I thought about finding Jo, but after what happened in the basement last time we were together, I thought it would be safer for her if she wasn't with me.

My dream started with me in the foyer of the mansion. *How come I didn't start here when Shawn was with me?* I wondered as I walked to the door under the stairs. Before I opened it, I studied it. It was just a normal door with a brass door handle, nothing told me how to open it from the real-world side. I glanced around, trying to memorize the room, there had to be a way to open it on the real-world side. What was the same in my dreamscape and in real life? The stair railing, the walls, and the floors were the only things I could remember being the same in both places.

Giving up, I materialized a flashlight and went downstairs. When I hit the bottom step, I froze, remembering the monster Stalker released the night before. I turned the flashlight off and stood silently, listening for the monster, but everything was eerily quiet. I dashed out of the stairwell and ran as fast as I could to the library. The door was unlocked, and after I was in, I slammed it then locked it.

I bent over and took a few deep breaths to catch my breath then I stood up and took in the room. It looked the same as it had last time, but there was no sign of Freeman. I ran to the window and saw downtown Twisted Pines as it was now, not the eighteen-hundred version. I was expecting to see the people from last time, but they were gone too. It was like they'd never been there.

I went to the bookcase and began reading the titles; they were all classics from the beginning of the written word through the twenty-first century. Nothing said, 'Thomas Freeman's Journal' though. I pulled a book off the shelf and read the spine, <u>A Tale of Two Cities</u>, I opened it to the first page. It was blank, I thumbed through the rest of the book and found nothing but blank pages. I pulled another book down, the inside was blank. I moved to the other side of the room and pulled out a Bible. It too was blank. I put the book down and walked to the center of the room.

What was the point in having all these books if they were blank on the inside? I wandered around the room, tapping my finger against my lips. It was almost like a set in a movie or a play.

It was all fake, this was a dream and things could be fake, but I would've at least put words in the books. It was almost like the books were a decoy, but for what?

I tightened my ponytail thinking, *for a gate!* I ran over to the closest bookshelf and swept my arm along it, sending the books crashing to the floor. I shrugged when I found nothing but a smooth stone wall where the books had been. I did the same to the next shelf and the next, but there was nothing but wall behind them. I went to a chest sitting next to a chair and opened it, hoping to find something, but it was empty. Then I went to the desk and pulled out all the drawers only to find them empty. The room was a complete mess by the time was I done, and I had nothing to show for it.

I stood in the middle of the room and turned in a circle, wondering what the point was when I stopped and stared at the only window in the room. *What if the window was the gate?* I picked up a lamp that had fallen to the floor. I brought my arm back and swung the lamp like a baseball bat. It hit the window but instead of the glass shattering it bounced off.

I brought it back again, ready to give my swing everything I had when the monster from the night before slammed into the window. His canine teeth were slick with drool, and his tongue hung out like he was a puppy who wanted to play, but his red eyes told me I wouldn't like the way he played. I jumped back, dropping the lamp.

The monster roared and rammed the glass with his shoulder, causing the wall to shake. I ran for the door. I sprinted back down the hall and ran upstairs. I wanted to get as far away from the monster as possible. I went through the front door and was about to close it when I heard the monster roar from close by. I went back into the mansion and slammed the door behind me. I needed a place to hide. I wanted to stay on the ground floor but the hallway I had explored before was gone, replaced with solid wood paneling. I only had two ways I could go, up or down.

I ran up the stairs, figuring I was just boxing myself in, but it was better than the basement. When I got to the top of the stairs, I saw someone go into the master bedroom. I ran down the hall after him, hoping it was Freeman. I went through the door and closed it behind me. The man was standing with his back to me studying the fireplace.

"Hello?" I asked tentatively, keeping one hand on the door in case I needed a quick escape.

"Elizabeth." The man faced me, and I almost fell to the floor. It was Victor.

"Dad, is it really you?" I asked, even though it felt strange to call him Dad when Burt was the only other person I had called that name. He was taller than I thought he would be, well over six feet. His blond hair was shaggy, like he hadn't been to a barber in years instead of months, he eyes were how I recognized him though, they were the same blue I saw when I looked in the mirror,

"Liz, you must stop this. You can't win." He put his hands on my shoulders. "This is bigger than all of us."

"I'm not giving up." I pulled away from him. "Don't you see it's the only way to end it?"

"I know, and I tried, but look what happened to me." He

gestured at his body. "I've been stuck working for that goblin for over seventeen years. I don't want the same thing to happen to you."

"It's not going to. I have friends helping me and I think I convinced Jon that closing the gate is a good idea."

His eye widened when I mentioned Jon, but he shook his head and stared at the floor, defeated. "Don't trust Jon, he'll say one thing then do the opposite when you aren't paying attention. Are you prepared to sacrifice your friends to close the gate?"

"No, but I'll sacrifice myself." I held up my wrist with the mark on it. "What do I have to lose? With this mark I won't have peace until I send them all back where they came from or die."

He took my arm and stared at the mark. "Damn it! This is not the life I wanted for you."

"It's not what I wanted either, but what choice do I have? No matter where I go, they'll find me."

He pulled me into a hug. "I'm sorry, sorry for so many things." He jerked his head up. "I have to go. The mare is coming, and if he finds me with you, we'll both suffer." He pulled away from me and disappeared.

I faced the door readying myself to deal with the mare when my alarm sounded. I rolled over in bed to turn it off, then I laid there and thought about what Victor had said before I pulled myself out for bed and ready for the day.

Chapter 30

"Again," Tom said as I landed on my butt.

I rolled to my feet, took my fighting stance, and waited for Jo to come at me again. Everyone from my dream training class was in the training room this morning and I think their favorite thing to do was watch me land on my butt. Every time it happened there would be a few laughs from the crowd. They could suck it, the only training I had before I started at Knights Inc. was wrestling with Billy and we hadn't done that in a few years. Jo came at me with a plastic knife in her hand raised high above her head like she planned to cut me from chest to navel. When she was within reach, I dropped my center of gravity and threw a roundhouse kick aimed for her middle. I didn't think it would connect but when I felt her body meet my leg, I brought it back trying to lessen the blow, but it was too late. Jo fell backwards, landed on her butt and grabbed her middle.

"Jo, I'm so sorry I didn't think I'd hit you." I rushed over and offered her a hand.

"Nice kick," she wheezed, trying to catch the breath I knocked out of her. She took my hand, and I pulled her to her feet.

"Good job, Liz," Tom said, facing the rest of the group. "Let's call it a day, nice work. I'll see you all tomorrow night."

I walked over to my bag and grabbed my water bottle. The day hadn't gone as badly as I thought it would. No one was shunning me, and Jeff apologized for giving me the cold shoulder at the funeral. I didn't need an apology I was happy everything was back to normal, well as normal as it could be when I was training to kill mares.

I put my bottle back in my bag and walked over to Jo. "Hey, do you need a ride home or are you going to catch one with your dad?" I asked as she picked her bag up off the floor.

"I'll ride with you if you don't mind, Dad's going to be here for a while, and I would rather spend my day somewhere else."

"I'm ready when you are." I waited for her to sling her bag over her shoulder.

"Okay, let's swing by my dad's office so he knows I'm leaving."

We walked down the hall until we reached Tom's office and Jo stuck her head in. "Hey, Liz is giving me a ride home."

"Okay, enjoy the rest of your day," Tom said.

We were almost to my Jeep when I noticed Shawn sitting in the passenger seat. "I wonder what he thinks he's doing." I asked Jo as we drew closer.

"I don't know, but I would say he's making sure you don't leave without seeing him." She laughed as she went around and smacked him lovingly on the back of the head.

"Hey what did I ever do to you?" He straightened in his seat. "How was class?"

"Jo gave me a few new bruises, but I finally knocked her on her ass." I got into the driver's seat.

"What are you guys doing now?" Shawn asked, giving no indication that he planned to move and forced Jo to climb over the back to get in.

"I was going to give Jo a ride home. Why? What did you have in mind?" I started the car and turned the volume on the radio down.

"Lunch, Heather and Billy are meeting us at the diner."

"How did you know we would be done in time for lunch?" Jo leaned between the front seats.

"I talked to Tom before you showed up this morning." Shawn winked at me.

"Jo, you up for lunch?" I put the car in gear as they put their seat belts on.

"Yeah, I'm starving after this morning. Plus, I want to hear where everyone is at with the search for the gate."

"Cool." I sent a quick text to my parents, turned the radio up, and drove toward downtown. We didn't talk as we drove to the diner, the wind noise was too loud to hear each other, or it could have been the music, it didn't matter we would talk soon enough.

Heather and Billy were both waiting for us when we walked in. They had one of the larger booths with water waiting for us.

"Hey." I slid in next to Heather, and Shawn sat next to me. "Thanks for getting a table."

"No problem, I'm starving." Heather pulled the menu out of the holder behind the mini jukebox.

"Do you guys want something to drink besides water?" Tiffany asked, staring at the table, refusing to make eye contact with us. Our little prank after prom had worked. Every time I saw her in the hall or around town, she would turn the other way. Shawn said she did the same thing to him.

"Can I get a Mountain Dew?" Billy asked.

"I'll have an iced tea," Heather said.

"I'm good with water," I said.

"Me too," Shawn and Jo said at the same time.

Once Tiffany left to get our drinks, I got the meeting started. "Did you guys have any luck figuring out how to open the door to the basement?"

"No." Heather laced her fingers together and rested them on the table. "I don't know how long we knocked on walls and pulled on the newel posts on the stairs. I don't think there's a door."

"That sucks." Billy took a sip of his water.

"I searched for a latch in my dream last night, but it was just a regular door."

"You dreamed of the mansion last night?" Shawn pulled his eyebrows together.

"Yeah, but not on purpose. It started in the foyer and I went back to the basement library. I paged through all the books. They had titles, but the insides were blank. I thought maybe they were trying to cover something up, so I ripped them all off the shelves."

"Did you find anything?" Jo asked as Tiffany brought the drinks over and took our food order.

"No, it was just a stone wall, but I think the window is the gate." I continued after Tiffany left.

"Why the window?" Shawn rested his arm behind my shoulders.

"I don't know, it seems like the only thing that doesn't fit in the room."

"Your mare didn't show up?" Jo asked.

"No, but Victor did."

"What do you mean Victor did?" Billy asked.

"What did he say?" Heather asked.

"He told me to stop, that I won't be able to close the gate." I stared at the table, rubbing a spot that would never come off.

"Did you ask him where it was?" Shawn asked.

I hit my hand to my forehead. "I didn't even think of asking him. I was so caught up because he was there, and I was talking to him, it never crossed my mind." I thought about our conversation. "I don't think he would have told me though."

"Do you want to quit?" Jo asked, glancing at Billy then at me. "I would be fine if you did. I think we would all understand."

"I can't believe you said that." I shook my head. "The last thing I want to do is quit. I want to live my life without my dreams being a nightmare."

"Okay, then," Shawn offered. "Maybe I should ask if you guys are still in. If you want out, it's not a big deal we can continue without you."

Everyone stared at him like he had lost his mind. "I'll take that as a yes." Tiffany brought our food out at that moment and all talk of the gates stopped while ate our lunch.

"I told Jon what we were doing yesterday," I said, refusing to meet their eyes as I spoke.

"What?" Shawn asked almost spitting his food across the table. "When did you see him?"

"After breakfast." I hadn't planned on telling them, but since I had already opened my mouth. "I think he understands why we want to do this."

"Do you think he will help?" Heather asked.

"No, but I don't think he will try to stop us either. He has too many people watching him."

"What do we do now?" Shawn asked, picking up his last fry.

"I want to go back to the library and try to break the window."

"Why would you need to break it if it was the gate?" Billy asked. "If it was the gate wouldn't it be broken or open?"

I opened my mouth to argue, but then closed it. He made a good point.

"But, in her dreams the mare could make it appear to be closed, when it's open in real life," Heather said, crossing her arms over her chest.

"Besides where else would the gate be?" Jo asked, twisting to glance at Billy.

"I don't know." He held his arms up in surrender. "It was just an idea."

"It was a good one, Billy." I tightened my ponytail. "And

you might be right. Until we can access the basement, we have no way of proving or disproving if the window is the gate." Tiffany brought us our bill and Shawn snatched it before anyone else could. "We will have to keep to searching until we know for sure."

"I got lunch today, you guys can get it next time." Shawn threw some money on the table and changed the subject. "Is there anything else you guys want to talk about?" We all looked at each other and shook our heads. "Then I say we are done for the day. Heather can you give Jo a ride? I need to talk to Liz."

I stared at Shawn confused as I scooted out of the booth after him.

"Yeah, I can unless Billy wants to." Heather moved out after I did.

"Yeah, I can. I'm off for the rest of the day. Do you want to do something?" Billy asked, moving out of the booth.

"Sure, but I need to go home and shower first. Dad had us working hard." Jo took Billy's hand as we walked to the exit.

"Great, I'm going to go home to sleep." Heather waved at us as she went to her car.

I hadn't thought about how I smelled until Jo said something. I wanted to check my pits, but I didn't want to look like an idiot, so I left my arms at my sides hoping to lock in any odors.

"I'll see you later," Jo said as they took off for Billy's truck.

"Okay sounds good," I called, realizing that she must mean in our dreams.

Shawn took my hand and led me across the street instead of to my Jeep. "What did you want to talk about?" I asked feeling the food I ate flip in my stomach.

"Nothing bad. I wanted to get rid of everyone because we haven't had much us time." He took us down the street leading to the lake.

"Oh, yeah, you're right. I kind of miss you." I squeezed his hand.

"I've missed you too." Once we hit the sand, I stopped and took my running shoes off. I needed the sand between my toes. Shawn did likewise, and we walked to the edge of the water. "How was going home yesterday?"

"Drama, my mom hugged me like she hadn't seen me in a year. I think she really thought I was running away." Shawn went silent after that like he didn't want to tell me what happened with his dad. It had to be hard for him. I figured he would tell me when he was ready. We walked along the water until we reached the end of the short beach. "When my dad got home, it was another story."

"You don't have to talk about it if you don't want to." I bumped into him, causing him to stumble into the lake a few steps.

"Damn, that's cold water." He jumped out, and I laughed.

"I'll get you for that. Maybe not today, maybe not tomorrow, but I'll get you." He grabbed my arms and pushed me toward the water but stopped before he forced me in.

"Oh, it's just water. It won't hurt you," I said, still laughing at him.

He led me over to an empty picnic table, sat down on the end, then pulled me between his legs. I wanted to wrap my arms around him, but I didn't want him to smell the stink from my workout. I kept my arms at my side and leaned in to kiss him. His lips tasted salty from his fries, and I still couldn't get over how soft they were, I needed to ask him what brand of lip balm he used. When we finally broke apart, he stared at me.

"Are you okay?" I asked, he was acting strange like this might the last time we would be together.

"My dad was pissed when he got home. He took me into his office and yelled at me for over an hour about how upset my mom was about the funeral."

"Shawn, I'm sorry. I hoped that after we talked, he wouldn't take it out on you." I rested my forehead on his shoulder. Maybe I shouldn't have talked to Jon the way I had.

"No listen," Shawn pushed my shoulders back, forcing me meet his eyes, "when he was done yelling at me, he apologized for everything. For treating you so horribly and setting you up to take the fall for Stacy's death. He begged me not to leave."

"Really?" I thought Jon and I abolished our mutual hate for each other, but he didn't seem like the kind of guy who would apologize for being a dick.

"Yeah, all he wants is for me and Heather to be happy. He even offered to change my schedule so I can spend more time with you."

"Okay, something's wrong." I shook my head it was too good to be true. "Are you sure we're talking about your dad? Maybe he was kidnapped, and they sent someone else who looked like him back in his place."

"Nope, it's really him. I don't know what you said to him but thank you." He leaned in and kissed me quickly. "Hey, how come you haven't hugged me today?"

I felt my face heat. "Well, you know how Jo said she needed to go home and take a shower?"

Confusion crossed Shawn's face. "Oh, I get it." He laughed and forced his arms under mine and pulled me in for a hug. I had no choice but to hug him back. "I don't care what you smell like."

I let out a laugh. "Yeah, but I do." I pulled out of his arms and smiled at him. "Do you have to get back to the mansion?"

"No, I'm yours, if you want me."

"Okay, well do you mind if we go to my house so I can shower?" I asked, still feeling weird about it.

"Let's do it." Shawn jumped off the table, grabbed my hand, and dragged me to the Jeep.

Chapter 31

After I went home to shower and change, I took Shawn to the national park. He hadn't been yet, so we drove around while I gave him the highlights. When we were on our way back his mom called and invited me to dinner. I sent my mom a text letting her know I was eating at Shawn's and would be home later.

I parked my Jeep next to Shawn's when we arrived, and I stared at the mansion, wondering if I was ready to see Jon again so soon after our talk.

"Are you remembering your dream?"

"No, actually I'm wondering if your dad will be cool to me like he was yesterday." I gave Shawn a sad smile.

"It doesn't matter, he isn't here. He is busy with the council. Mom said he wouldn't be home for dinner." He got out and waited for me to follow.

Relieved I wouldn't have to deal with Jon, I followed Shawn inside and we went straight to the kitchen. I wanted to search the foyer, but it could wait until after dinner.

"Liz," Jenny cooed when we reached the kitchen. She came over to me with wet hands from the sink and hugged me. "I'm so glad you're here. I've been meaning to have you over for ages, but things never seem to slow down long enough for me to put something together."

"Thanks for having me," I said as she pulled away.

"Shawn, go get Heather, I want to talk to Liz." She shooed Shawn out of the kitchen then motioned for me to take a seat at the four-person table in the corner of the room. "Please sit down."

I took a seat. "I'm sorry about Stacy." I hadn't had a chance to talk to her at the funeral.

"I am too, but she will live on in all of us." Jenny sat down in the chair next to me. "Thank you for dealing with Jon. When I found out he framed you to save Shawn, I almost hit him with my cast-iron skillet."

"Yeah, well, I should've remembered to wake myself up."

"I'm glad Shawn stuck up for you. Jon can be very cruel when he chooses."

I wanted to ask her why she puts up with him if she knew how cruel he could be, but this was my boyfriend's mother—it was none of my business. "Yeah, I've seen a bit of that."

"Well, I think everything will be better now. Jon told me you talked yesterday. It sounded like you two worked things out." Jenny got up to check the oven.

"I hope so, it will make working here a lot better."

"Are you enjoying your training so far?"

"Yes, I'm learning a ton, but I'm years behind everyone

else my age. I hope I pick everything up quickly." I watched her pull plates and silverware out of various cabinets and drawers.

"You are your father's daughter." She gave me a wink. "From what Shawn and Tom have told me you're leaps and bounds ahead of where you should be."

"That's what they keep telling me but..." I trailed off.

"But you want to be out there in the field, hunting them already, right?" She pulled a roast chicken out of the oven and set it on the stove.

"Yes, I want to help people."

"You will soon enough, and you won't be practicing, it'll be the real thing. Things change when you're fighting for your life or the life of someone else. Enjoy this time while you still have it." She gave me a sad smile.

I smiled back, thinking about what she said. Shawn became a Knight shortly before I met him, and it made me wonder what he was like before they knighted him. "Hi Liz," Heather said, joining me at the table. "Are we eating in here, Mom, or the dining room?"

"Hi," I said, smiling at her.

"Since it's just the four of us why don't we eat in here?" Jenny brought the pile of plates and silverware to Heather.

"Here, I can help," I said, getting up.

"You're company and will do no such thing." Jenny pointed a wooden spoon at me. "Shawn, will you get everyone drinks?"

"Sure, what do you want?" he asked, coming through the door and putting a hand on my shoulder.

"Do you have a coke?" I asked.

"Sure, Heather?"

"Same." She sat the plates on the table followed by the forks and knives.

"Mom?"

"I'll have a glass of wine. The bottle's in the fridge."

Shawn moved around his mom getting us all drinks and Heather sat down across from me. "You guys do anything fun this afternoon?"

"We went up to the national park. Shawn finally got to see a moose. Have you ever seen one?"

"No, but it sounds like I will before the summer is over." Heather gave me a bright smile.

"They're huge." Shawn put glasses filled with ice on the table. "Seriously, I can't believe Liz survived hitting one with her Jeep."

"It sounds like you were very lucky." Jenny put the chicken on the table. "Heather, will you grab the salad and Shawn will you grab the beans?" They both jumped up and gathered the rest of dinner then returned to their seats. "Let's eat."

We talked about the other wildlife they should keep their eyes out for: bears, mountain lions, elk, deer, and badgers. Heather and Jenny made plans to visit the park the next day. It was nice to sit with another family and have a normal dinner, not talk about goblins, or dreams, just everyday life.

When we finished eating, Heather and Shawn took all the dishes to the sink and rinsed them off to put in the dishwasher. Jenny took a sip of her wine and stared out the window like she forgot I was sitting there. Uncomfortable, I was about to get up and offer to help with the dishes when she spoke. "Did you know Stacy and your dad were high school sweethearts? Just like you and Shawn?"

"Really?" I smirked at the idea. It was odd to think of Victor my age. He was frozen in my mind at twenty-five, the age he was when he died. "What was he like?"

She smiled. "He was a troublemaker, and Jon was his sidekick. Throughout school, no matter where we were, both of them would get suspended during our first week."

"Dad got suspended?" Heather turned off the sink and picked up a dishtowel to dry her hands.

"Don't you dare tell him I told you, and Shawn, don't get any ideas." Jenny leaned back in her chair and took another sip of her wine.

"We won't." Shawn came back to the table. "What did they do to get suspended?"

"Which time? Those two did everything from bringing firecrackers to school to pulling the fire alarm," Jenny laughed. "Our family joined the clan right before Victor passed his final test and became a knight. He and Stacy hit it off from the beginning. Your grandfather was hard on us, always pushing us to be better and marry a strong knight. I think Stacy loved how carefree Victor was. They both gave us an escape from the strictness of our father."

"Why did they break up?" It sounded like they were perfect for each other.

"Your dad became obsessed with something. Stacy never told me what, only that it was dangerous, and she didn't want to be there when he failed." Jenny's eyes went wide. "Oh Liz, I'm sorry, I should have found a better way to say that."

I blinked, Stacy knew what Victor was trying to do? I glanced at Shawn and Heather. "And she never told you what he was doing?"

"No, by that time Jon and I were engaged, and Jon and Victor weren't getting along. I don't think she trusted me." She chugged the rest of her wine. "It broke her heart to end it with him though. She never dated anyone else. When she found out he died, she cried. I wondered over the years if she was waiting for him to come back." A tear slipped down her cheek. She blinked and wiped it away quickly. "If you will excuse me." She left us staring at each other.

"Do you think she knew what he was trying to do?" Heather asked, taking the empty wineglass to the sink.

"Yeah." I rubbed my face, why did she have to die? "Sucks, we'll never find out what she knew."

Shawn banged his hand on the table. "Can we please talk about something else?"

"Oh, Shawn, I'm sorry." I rested my hand on his arm. How could we be so thoughtless? He already felt bad enough, so talking about her was just rubbing salt on the wound.

"Sorry, little brother." Heather gave him a shove. "Let's go check out the foyer."

I looked around the space, trying to figure out where the door should have been in relation to my dreams. Heather came in and smiled. "Should I get a sledgehammer?"

"Not yet, I'm just checking it out." The wood paneling

covering the walls was the same as it had been in my dream. I walked along the wall, running my fingers over the wood. I wasn't looking for anything specifically, just trying to get a feel for the space and compare it to my dreams. When I reached the back wall where the door should have been, I noticed a difference in the wood grain. It looked like the same wood, but it felt different. I ran my fingers around the edge of the paneling. The gap was wider than where the other panels met by the smallest amount, but it was enough to confirm my thoughts. "This is the door, right?" I asked, turning to them.

"Yeah, well, it's where we think it is," Shawn said as I stared at the wall and the surrounding area, searching for a way to open it.

"This panel is different than the other panels." I pointed to the adjoining wall. "Do you know which one is original?" I asked without taking my eyes from the wall.

"I have no idea," Heather said, stepping to my other side. "Do you think it means something?"

"No, maybe. If this one, the one with the door, is original then I would say there has to be a way to open it. If it's not, then we'll need that hammer and your mom won't be happy." I leaned against the paneling. *Where would I put the latch to open a secret passage?*

"Yeah, Mom won't be thrilled if we tear apart the foyer," Shawn said.

Everything was decorated minimally. The only furniture in the room was a side table. There was a coat closet to the left of the exterior door. The floor was the original wood, with a fresh coat of varnish, and an area rug covered most of it. When someone came in the front door, they could go up the stairs, take the hallway to the left, or to the right.

The area where we thought the door to the basement was about ten feet long and five feet wide. The walls under the stairs were covered in the same inlaid wood paneling as the walls.

"I think you guys are right." I went over to the front door and leaned against it. "We're going to have to punch through the wall to get down there. Unless you think a crowbar could fit between the paneling?"

Shawn ran his hand down the crease. "I don't know. It would have to be really thin."

"We could try, though," Heather said, running her hand over the seam. "I'll go to the hardware store tomorrow and see if they have anything that will work."

"Sounds good." Shawn put his arm around my shoulder. "Do you want to watch a movie or something?"

I glanced at my phone; it was already past eight. "I would but it's getting late and I better get home since I have work tomorrow."

Shawn looked bummed but after he checked the time he nodded. "I guess I didn't realize how late it is. I have to be ready for work in an hour. Come on, I'll walk you to your car."

"Bye, Heather, see you later," I said as Shawn opened the door for me.

Shawn walked me to my Jeep and gave me a proper goodnight kiss. As soon as I pulled out of the parking lot, I noticed a red car behind me. I was sure no one was coming when I pulled out. Maybe I was more tired than I realized. I shook my head and turned up the radio, whoever it was would get over it. I forgot about the car, thinking about the crowbar Heather planned to buy and if we could pry the door open.

When I turned off the highway, the car, I wasn't sure but I thought it was a Subaru, behind me did the same. *Were they following me?* I sped up a little, wanting to put some distance between me and them, but if it was a cop, I didn't want to get a speeding ticket. I kept one eye on the road and the other on my rearview mirror as the car behind me kept up.

I let out a relieved breath when my house came into view. All I had to do was grab my bag and run for the mudroom door. If they followed me, I would call the cops.

I turned in to the driveway, slammed on the brakes, ripped my keys out of the ignition, and ran for the door. I glanced over my shoulder before I went inside to see what the car was doing. It sped past and I slumped in relief. It was probably a neighbor, but I didn't remember any of them having a red Subaru. I turned the handle, but it was locked. *Damn my parents for doing as I asked*, I thought, unlocking the door.

Chapter 32

I glanced around and sighed. I was in the clearing, not in the mansion. I had been planning on breaking the window in the library. I didn't know why I hadn't thought about it before, but I was going to manifest one of those glass breakers people keep in their cars to break tempered glass.

I thought of the mansion. I thought about the foyer and how it looked a few hours before when I was there. When I opened my eyes, I shrugged. I was still in the clearing with the mineshaft. *I'm not finding the gate tonight.*

"Hey, what are we doing here?" Jo asked, appearing at my side.

"This is the clearing I always dream about. This is where I went when you guys thought I was lost in the woods." Keeping my eyes on the ground I walked toward the mine, searching for any evidence that someone had been there.

"Really? This place is kind of creepy, it doesn't seem like it should be in real life." Jo walked beside me. "What are we looking for?"

"Any sign that someone has been here. Footprints, animal poop, trash, anything." I looked up to gauge my bearings, we were still a hundred feet from the mine.

"Okay, but this is a dream, why would there be any?"

"Because when I was here in real time there was no evidence that anything had been through here. I'm talking no birds, chipmunks, even bugs, it was completely barren except for the dead grass and the freshly mined earth."

"What do you mean freshly mined earth?"

I pointed at the pile of dirt near the opening of the mine. "Come on, I'll show you." When we reached the pile of dirt, I knelt and picked up a handful. "See this dirt. It's dark and loose. Something had to put it here, and it's new."

"How do you know?" Jo picked up a handful before letting it slide through her fingers.

"If it had been sitting for a while it would be dull, almost gray and the sun would have hardened and compacted it. I think something or someone is bringing it out of the mine." I picked up another handful and studied it. It was clean. There weren't any roots, or debris, only dirt. There weren't even any worms.

"Yeah, I think we should get out of here." Jo got to her feet and yelped.

Startled I stood up and scanned the clearing finding Stalker and the monster from the basement on the far side of the clearing.

"Ah, I see you brought your friend with you tonight," Stalker said, pulling on a chain attached to the monster. The wolf-bear thrashed his head back and forth sending drool flying before lunging at us. He stopped when he reached the end of his chain and howled up at the sky, as if he was begging to be released, then lunged at us again. Stalker's arm jerked, and the monster winced as the chain tightened around his neck.

Jo took a step back, and I grabbed her to keep her from falling down the shaft. "Jo, go, either jump out of here or wake up," I whispered to her.

"Go get them, boy," Stalker said, releasing the beast. The wolf-bear stood still for a moment, staring at the chain no longer attached to his collar, then threw his head back and howled at the night before charging us.

"No, I got this." Jo materialized a sword and stepped in front of me as time seemed to slow down.

I wanted to take Jo and run, but there was nowhere to go. The mineshaft was behind us and the closest trees were too far away to reach then climb before the monster caught us, and I couldn't jump somewhere else. I had no idea if my dreamcatcher would protect me from the beast since it wasn't a mare, but I wasn't going to wait and see. I thought of my dad's 30.06 and brought it to my shoulder. I aimed but Jo was in the way.

The wolf-bear loped toward us with his upper lip pulled back in a snarl. Jo waited until he was in range then brought the sword up, aiming for his neck but he moved at the last moment. She made contact with his neck, but it wasn't deep enough to do any real damage. The monster reared onto his hind legs and swiped at Jo with his bear-like paws. Jo tried to jump out of the way, but she wasn't fast enough and fell to the side, giving me the shot. I rested my crosshairs between the wolf-bear's eyes and squeezed the trigger. He yelped in pain, the force of the bullet driving him onto his back. He clawed at the sky until he stopped moving completely.

I let go of the gun, letting it disappear and fell to my knees at Jo's side. "Are you all right?" I winced at the blood covering her shoulder.

"Yeah, it's not deep. I might have broken my leg though." She sat halfway up, bracing herself on her forearms and peered at her leg. I followed her eyes and had to swallow back bile. Her right shin bone was sticking out of her skin. The sticky white bone didn't look like a bone, but an accessory of her jeans which were changing from blue to dark purple as blood soaked them.

"Crap," I said, glancing around. Stalker was walking toward us like he had all the time in the world, and we were just going to sit and wait for him. "Jo, you have to wake up. He is coming over."

"No, what about you?" Her body shook with the beginnings of shock.

"I have my dreamcatcher, now go." I was beginning to worry. We just had a funeral for a knight. The last thing I wanted was to be the cause of another one. "Go now."

I stood and turned my back on her, hoping she would wake herself up, it was the only way she would make it. The scratch wasn't that bad but the blood pouring out from her leg was. "What are you going to do now?" I asked Stalker while I thought of my holster and 1911 Colt.

"I am performing an experiment of sorts," he said, coming closer. "You either messed up and went to sleep without your protection, or the monsters in your dreams can hurt you even with it." He was only a few feet from me when he jumped. I crouched, always expecting him to land on top of me, but he bounced off my bubble and fell to the ground.

Great, I thought, *he can't hurt me, but monsters can. What was he going to throw my way now*? Would my rune work against something other than mares?

"Just as I thought. I'll get you one way or the other." He waved his hands in the air. I glanced behind me relieved Jo was gone as the howling of first one then another coyote echoed off the mountains.

"But if something else kills me, you won't get to suck out my soul." I searched for a way to escape, but there wasn't even a rock to hide behind. I could run down the trail but, coyotes loved a good chase.

"I don't really need you anymore. With all of your friends, I will get the power I need. Getting you out of the way is all I really want to do." He laughed and took a step back as the coyotes came out of the trees and into the clearing.

I was done. I needed to get away from the clearing before the coyotes came any closer. I closed my eyes and thought of my room. The mare laughed again, and I opened my eyes. I was still standing in the clearing. What was I going to do? I spun, ready to run, but the predators were less than fifty feet from me. I had to do something and fast. I thought of my Jeep with every important detail I could muster, from the engine to the brakes, the seat, and seat belt. One second I was standing in the middle of the clearing, and the next I was sitting in the driver's seat. I stared at the ignition, of course I forgot the keys. I dug in the pocket of my jeans and pulled them out. I shoved them in the ignition and turned it. The Jeep started, and I slumped in relief. I put it in gear but before I could move one of the coyotes jumped over the door through the open window at me. I punched it in the jaw reflexively, and it fell to the ground, yelping. I put my foot on the gas and released the clutch, and drove over the bumpy ground toward the trail as fast as I dared.

The trail was about two hundred yards away and as I bounced along, shifting from first to second, then to third gear, the trail disappeared. The twisted pines moved and grew together, blocking my escape. I thought about ramming through the trees, they couldn't be that tough, but I lost my courage at the last second. I slammed on the brakes, and turned the Jeep hard to the left, so I came to a sliding stop parallel to the trees.

I glanced back at Stalker; he was standing undisturbed in the middle of the clearing, smiling. The coyotes were racing toward me; I was trapped. I stood and pulled my 1911 out of its holster. Using my roll bar for a rest I took aim at the closest coyote, I tried to line up my sights on him, but my hands shook with fear. I didn't understand how Stalker had been able to trap me. The first coyote was ten feet away when I pulled the trigger, hitting him behind the front shoulder, killing him. The next one was almost on me when an air horn blew and echoed around the clearing, making the coyotes cower and Stalker scream in frustration. I smiled, it was time to wake up.

Chapter 33

As soon as I realized I was awake, I grabbed my phone off the nightstand and sent a text to Jo.

Are you OK?

After seeing her shin bone sticking out of her skin it was hard to imagine that she would wake up feeling fine. I got out of bed and took my phone with me into the bathroom. As I was brushing my teeth, my phone beeped with an incoming message. I picked it up with my free hand and pushed the button to light up the screen. There was a text from Jo:

Right as rain, see you at work.

I sighed and relaxed. She was fine. I finished getting ready then ran out the door, realizing that I would be late if I didn't move it. Shawn met me in the parking lot, surprising me. "Hey, I figured you would be debriefing now." I got out of my Jeep and gave him a hug.

"I'm due in about fifteen minutes so I thought I would walk you in." He moved closer to me to kiss me for too brief a moment. "Are you all right?"

"Just what a girl wants to hear first thing in the morning." I rolled my eyes. "I had a pretty rough night with Jo and Stalker." I took his hand as we walked.

"Are you okay? Is Jo okay?" Shawn watched my face as we walked.

"Yeah, I checked on her first thing this morning. She broke her leg really bad in the dream last night and got cut pretty badly." I clenched my jaw, I couldn't believe Stalker figured out how to hurt me.

"What happened?" Shawn stopped but didn't let go of my hand, forcing me to stop and face him.

"Stalker figured out that other things in dreams can hurt me, even if he can't." I let my hair fall between us, creating a curtain for me to hide behind. "Jo saved me from a monster, then he called a bunch of coyotes. They were just about to attack when my alarm went off. It was a fight all night long."

"I'm sorry, why didn't you leave?"

"I tried, I was stuck there." I pinched my lips together. "I'm getting scared, Shawn, Stalker said he doesn't care if he gets my soul now. There are enough knights around that he doesn't need mine. He wants me out of the way."

Shawn pulled me into a hug. "We'll find a way don't worry." He pulled away and stared into my eyes. "We'll figure this out."

"I hope so and soon. I don't want anyone else to die." I pulled away and kept walking.

"Yeah, we'll talk about it more after work, okay?" He held the door for me.

"Okay." I walked through then dug my keycard out. "Morning, Marcy."

"Good morning, Liz, Shawn," she replied, glancing up from her computer for a second.

I tapped my card and opened the door. We walked down the hall hand in hand but said nothing. I hated making him worry, but he needed to know what Stalker said. When we reached the door to Tom's office we stopped.

"Call me when you're done?"

"Yeah, I want to go home and shower before we do anything though."

"Okay, then call me when you are ready."

"Will do."

"See you later." Shawn squeezed my hand, and I watched him walk down the hall before I went into Tom's office.

"Morning," I said, smiling, hoping I didn't look too tired.

"Long night?" he asked, looking up from his computer.

"Yeah, the mare wouldn't leave me alone." I didn't know if he knew Jo was with me in my dream or not, but I wasn't about to tell him.

"I'm sorry, but after what happened last time, I think it's best if you continue to sleep with your dreamcatcher." He grimaced, before leaning back in his chair.

"It doesn't matter. He doesn't care about my soul anymore. He wants me dead. Last night I found out my dreamcatcher doesn't work with dream-manifested monsters." I sat down and shrugged my bag off my shoulders. "What are we working on today?" I wanted to get training over with. It wasn't like Tom could help me solve my problem with the mare.

"Liz, crap, I'm sorry. Is there anything I can do?" Tom ignored my question.

"No, I can fight them too, so it's not like I'm helpless, but I don't think the rune will save me."

"Why not?"

"Because I think it's only designed to keep mares from sucking my soul out, not from getting hurt. At least that was what happened on prom and when I fought Stalker the night Stacy died."

"I wish there was something I could do to help you."

"Just think of it as extra training." I didn't want to talk about it anymore. There wasn't anything he or anyone else could do about it until we closed the gate. "So, what are we doing today?"

"First you're going to work on hand to hand with Jo—she's warming up right now—then we will put you in the simulator." Tom pushed away from his desk and got to his feet.

"Let's get started then." I followed him to the training room. I was glad it was just Jo, I wasn't in the mood to deal with anyone else after the night I had. Tom pushed open the door and held it for me. Once I was inside, I glanced around and found Jo on the mats, stretching. I smiled, I was so happy to see her alive and healthy.

I waved at her, then ran into the locker room, changed into a gi, then joined her on the mats and stretched with her while Tom watched. "You scared the crap out of me last night."

"I know, I kind of scared me too. Thanks for making me wake up." She glanced over her shoulder at her dad, who was starting up the simulator. "Did you tell Shawn what happened?"

"Yeah, he wants to talk about it when we are done." We both stood and pulled our arms over our heads to stretch our backs.

"Don't worry, we'll figure it out," Jo said as Tom joined us.

"Let's get started," he said, clasping his hands together. "Today you will practice with swords." He motioned to a table where two wooden practice swords waited.

Two hours and a dozen bruises later, I chugged the contents of my water bottle, then wiped the sweat from my face.

"You're getting better," Jo said between sips of her own water.

"Right." I didn't believe her for a second. I wanted a few bags of ice and my couch.

"You're tired," Tom said, joining us along the wall. "Your technique is getting better, but I could see the fatigue in your body. You need to get a good night's sleep." I rolled my eyes, *like that would happen.* "Let's move to the simulator." Tom motioned to the computer and bed. "Jo you can head out."

"Where would I go? I don't have a car and it would take me an hour to walk home." She slammed her water bottle down and stared at her dad.

"Go find Shawn, he'll give you a ride or you can find something to keep yourself busy until I'm done with Liz."

I wanted to offer Jo some help, but this sounded like an ongoing fight and I didn't want to get in the middle. Instead, I walked over to the bed and sat down. I tried not to watch as father and daughter got into a heated debate about her not having a car. A few minutes later, she stomped out of the training room and Tom ran a hand through his hair before coming over to hook me up to the machine.

"Sorry about that. Jo wants a car, and I want her to have one, but she is going to have to wait." He attached the probes then signaled me to lie back. "The truth is, we're getting her one for her birthday next month, and it's taking everything I have to keep it from her."

I laughed as he put the goggles over my eyes. "Really? She'll be so excited." Living in Twisted Pines without a car sucked.

"Yes, please don't tell her. We want it to be a surprise." Tom moved away. "I am going to run you through a program where close combat will be your only course of action. You can use whatever you want, but a gun won't stop your enemy."

"Good, it's what I need the most help with." The darkness receded and changed into lush green grass with tall oak trees scattered around. It reminded me of a park in a big city. I searched for a threat and not seeing any, I ran to the nearest tree and put my back to it to protect my blind side.

I still didn't see anything out of the ordinary. "Tom? Where are the bad guys?" I asked just as one materialized five feet from me. She looked human mostly. She was tall, had at least six inches on me. Her hair was black as night and her Asian features made me think of the ninja marathon Billy and I had watched over winter break. I was going to get my ass kicked for the second time today.

I dropped into a fighting stance as she glided toward me. She was only walking but her movement was so fluid it was hard to believe her feet were touching the ground. Lost in watching her move, she was on me before I had time to think about how to stop her. She threw a punch at my face, and I easily blocked it, but it was a fake, as soon as I threw up my arm to block her, she swept her leg out, hitting my shin and causing me to lose my balance. I tried to recover, but her other arm shot out and pain exploded in my chest. I was on the ground with her above me before I knew what was happening. I braced my arms above my face to protect it and kicked up hard, catching her in the thigh; she fell back a step and I jumped to my feet.

A tight-lipped smile crossed her face as a knife appeared in her hand. I thought of my hunting knife and held it up, ready to battle with her again. She charged this time, pumping her arms so fast I couldn't keep track of where the knife was. When she reached me, I dropped to the ground and rolled to the other side of her cutting her Achilles tendon as I passed by. She let out a scream as I rolled to my feet ready for more.

She ran at me like I didn't just make it impossible for her to walk, *damn dreams, if this was real life she would be done*. I would have to stab her in a vital organ or cut her throat to stop her. She attacked me again, but she was too close, I couldn't get my knife up to block her. She took a swipe at me and I blocked it with my arm, but in the meantime, she punched me in the kidneys, and I doubled over in pain. I forced myself to straighten and prepared for her next attack.

She brought her arm up to stab me in the gut and I brought mine across her throat. As her knife separated the skin of my belly and slid through my tissue and guts, blood gushed out of the slice I made in her throat, covering my hands. Pain blossomed in my belly and my legs became slick with blood.

We both fell backwards, and I smiled as I closed my eyes. I didn't beat her, but she didn't win either. It was progress.

Tom ripped the goggles off my face along with the headphones. "What in the hell was that?" He was standing above me with sweat beading on his face.

"What? I killed the bad guy." I sat up, forcing him to take a step back.

"By sacrificing yourself?" his voice was sterner than I had ever heard it. I guess I hadn't handled the situation like he wanted me to.

"She was too good, and I knew I could wake myself up. She wasn't going for an instant kill she was trying to maim me, so I couldn't get away." I crossed my arms over my chest.

"But what if you couldn't wake up? Self-sacrifice isn't something we teach or encourage. You need to beat them not let them kill you."

"How would you have killed her?" I narrowed my eyes at him. I liked having Tom as my trainer and my boss, but couldn't he see that what I did was the only way to kill the mare?

"I would have faked a leg sweep, stepped around her, and driven the knife into the base of her neck."

I thought about it, visualizing how it would work in my head. He was right, there was a better way to beat the woman. "Can I go again?"

"Yes, but if you sacrifice yourself again, you're done for the day." He gave me back the earphones and the goggles then went to the computer.

Three hours and six simulations later I took off the sensors and stood up to stretch.

"You did a great job with the last one." Tom stood and stretched with me. After I re-did the first simulation and I killed my opponent in the first two minutes, Tom made them harder, forcing me to fight dirty. The rules in dreams weren't the same as in reality, I would always be weaker, would always have to think faster and smarter. Not following the unsaid rules of fighting would be how I beat the mares who came after me. "What changed?"

"I changed. When you gave me the idea to stab them in the back, I realized you were right. Mares will always be faster, stronger, and tougher than me. I need to fight dirty if I'm going to win." I put my hands on my hips. I glanced at the clock on the wall. It was past noon, and I was ready for lunch.

"Good, let's call it a day then." Tom went back to the simulator and began shutting it down.

"Okay, see you tomorrow." I went to the locker room and changed quickly, but I wished I had brought stuff to shower with.

"Hey, what are you doing?" I asked Shawn when I entered the lobby.

"Waiting for you. See you, Marcy." Shawn pushed away from her desk, grabbed my hand and led me to the parking lot.

"Shawn, what's going on?" I asked, running to keep up with him.

"Heather bought the wrong size crowbar and is getting a new one now. I thought we could go to lunch while we waited for her to come back."

"Sounds good, but I've got to take a shower first." I pulled my hand out of his and started for my Jeep.

"You should have brought stuff and showered here." He pouted.

"I was going to, but I spaced it." I shrugged my shoulders and threw my bag into the passenger seat "I'll run home, shower, and then we can do whatever you want."

"Okay, but hurry." He put his hands on my hips and pulled me in. "I want to hang out."

"Me too." I leaned in and he captured my lips with his. I wanted to run my hands through his hair, but I was sweaty and smelly. I pulled away. "But the quicker you let me leave the sooner we can meet up." I pressed my forehead to his.

He pushed back. "Fine, just hurry."

"I will." I got in and took off, excited to spend time with Shawn. I stopped at the end of the driveway and had to wait for traffic. I glanced in my rearview mirror, expecting no one to be behind me and jumped when I saw Kristina in her Subaru. It was strange that Shawn and I hadn't noticed her in the parking lot, but then again, we had been caught up with each other.

I shook my head and pulled onto the highway ready to go home. Kristina pulled in behind me, but that wasn't anything strange. Most people lived in that direction.

Everything was fine until I turned onto my road and

Kristina followed me. I knew everyone who lived on my road; no one had sold their house or moved in the past three years. Kristina wasn't going home. She could have been visiting someone, but I wasn't buying it. She was following me, and I didn't know what to do. My phone was buried in my bag and even if I could get it out without wrecking, I probably wouldn't have any service.

I had three options. I could go home, see if she stopped, and find out what she wanted. I could pull over on the side of the road and wave her around me. Or turn around and go back to Shawn's.

Screw it, I thought. I wasn't afraid of her. If she tried anything, I would just run inside. I didn't want to fight her, she would kick my ass, but I wanted her to stop following me.

I pulled in my driveway, parked the Jeep, and pulled my bag into my lap. I wanted my cell phone. I wanted to document what happened.

I unlocked my phone, opened the video app, and hit the record button before I got out. She pulled in the driveway but didn't turn her car off. I held my phone up like I was talking on it with the camera facing Kristina.

"Okay, bye, Mom," I said, louder than I needed to, and brought my phone down. "Kristina?" I asked, acting like I didn't know she'd been following me. "What are you doing here?" I walked over to her car.

"I can't believe you would do this," she said, staring at me over the top of her sunglasses.

"What do you mean?" How did she know we were doing something?

"You are trying to get them to quit Knights Inc."

"I have no idea what you're talking about. I just started, why would I want them to quit?"

"I don't know, but I know what I heard, plus you four are always sneaking around, whispering. I tried to find Shawn in my dreams the other night, but I couldn't find him. Where was he?"

"Again, I have no idea. He is my boyfriend, but I don't know where he is every hour of the day."

"If you don't tell me what you're doing I have ways of making your life hell." She grinned and pushed her sunglasses up her nose.

"Are you threatening me?" I was getting a headache, trying to figure out what she wanted.

"Just watch your back, bitch." She threw her car in reverse and backed out of the driveway. I pulled my phone up and stopped the recording then went inside to call Shawn.

"That was a quick shower," Shawn said, answering on the first ring.

"I haven't showered yet. Kristina followed me home, wanted to know what we were doing and threatened me if I didn't tell her."

"You're kidding? Why would she do that and how would she know if we were up to something?"

"I don't know, but I think we need to meet with everyone and talk about it."

"Okay, where and when? I'll see if everyone can meet us."

I thought about it for a second; I didn't want to meet at the house, Kristina might be watching the road and we didn't need her telling Jon or her dad we were meeting. "Let's meet on my parents' boat." She probably didn't know we had one.

"Okay, I'll call everyone."

"I'll take a quick shower then I'll be on my way. Just keep an eye out for her." I told him which slip the boat was in then ran upstairs to shower.

Chapter 34

I had just finished opening up the twenty-nine-foot sailboat up when Shawn walked up the dock. "Permission to come aboard?" He smiled at me with his hands on his hips.

"Yes, but take your shoes off," I said, seeing the black soles of his flip-flops. "If we get black marks all over the deck, my dad will kill me."

Shawn toed his shoes off then climbed aboard. "This is cool, are you going to take me out on it sometime?"

"Yeah, I have to ask my dad but I'm sure he'll let us." I moved to the small cooler I brought, filled with water and soda. "Do you want something to drink?" I opened it and grabbed a water for myself.

"No, thanks I'm good." He sat down, facing the dock. "So, tell me more about what happened with Kristina."

"Let's wait for everyone. There's not a lot to tell but it will be easier to only tell it once." I took the lid off the water and took a sip.

"Okay, but I'm worried about you." He put his arm around me, and I leaned against his chest. "It's bad enough you have to deal with Stalker in your dreams. You shouldn't have to deal with one while you're awake too."

"It'll be okay. We just need a plan." I closed my eyes.

"I wish I wasn't working tonight but since you have training, you should be alright." He kissed the top of my head. "Heather and I are on opposite shifts now, maybe you can hang out with her after training."

"I hate being a nuisance, but this week has killed me with the dreams." I opened my eyes when I heard someone on the dock. Heather waved when she spotted us.

"I know, we'll work it out. Hey, what shoes do you have on?"

Heather lifted her feet up to show us her white-soled Keds. "I've been on a boat before. I know what shoes to wear. May I?" she asked motioning to the boat.

"Sure," I said as she climbed aboard and sat across from me.

"Are you okay?" she asked, cocking an eyebrow.

"Yeah, just a long night and a long day. Did you find a crowbar?"

"I think so. It's in my car. Shawn called me while I was at the hardware store. I haven't had time to try it yet."

"Can you hang out with Liz when she's done with training tonight? She needs a break from Stalker." Shawn asked while pulling me closer to his side.

"Yeah, I'm sorry you're having so much trouble."

"Not your fault and thanks. The dreams are wearing me out, then I have training for most of the day. I feel like I will never catch up on my sleep."

"Don't give up. We'll close the gate and get rid of the mare." Heather patted my knee.

"Ahoy," Billy said as he and Jo came up the dock.

"Do I need to take my shoes off?" Jo asked seeing Shawn's sitting on the dock.

"Only if you have black soles," Billy said, checking her shoes.

"Okay, sorry, I didn't know," Jo slid out of her shoes then accepted Billy's hand to climb aboard.

"It's alright, my dad is just anal about black marks on the deck. I take it you found a ride home," I asked as she and Billy settled in on the bench across from us.

"Yeah, thanks to Heather," Jo gave her a smile. "I'm so tired of not having a car. It's not like there's a bus I can take."

"Major bummer." I agreed, making sure my face didn't give away the surprise. "Now that we are all here. I want to show you something." I pulled my phone out and played the video of Kristina at my house.

"How does she know we are doing anything?" Shawn asked when the video was over.

"I don't know, it's not like we talk about it anywhere she could overhear us. Could she be spying on us in our dreams?" I pulled my eyebrows together.

"Well," Heather said and glanced at Jo. "She might have overheard me and Jo talking at the funeral."

"What?" Shawn's eyes went wide. "What were you talking about?"

"She may have heard me say with Liz's help I am going to leave the knights and go to college." Jo wrung her hands, not making eye contact with anyone.

"We were barely talking above a whisper. What's the big deal? I'm going to college." Heather straightened.

"Are you sure she didn't hear you? She accused me of talking you guys into quitting Knights Inc."

"Now that I think about it," Jo cocked her head to the side. "I think I remember Kristina standing nearby. Damn, I'm sorry, guys."

"That's not all. I told Shawn about this already, but the night Stacy died, I ended up in Kristina's dream on accident. She was meeting with Stalker. They are working together to kill me."

"What?" Jo jerked in her seat. "Are you sure it wasn't a dream of your own making?"

"Yeah, that was the first thing I checked. I know it's hard to believe, and I won't blame you if you don't, but I needed you all to know what's been going on with her."

"I believe you." Heather rolled her eyes. "I never trusted that girl. All she wants is money and power and she doesn't care who she steps on to reach the top."

Shawn rolled his eyes, and I elbowed him in the gut. "Hey, it's okay, we just need to be more careful about what we say when we aren't sure who is listening." As I spoke, I watched a black Audi pull into the marina parking lot. "Wow, nice ride."

Everyone turned to look, and Shawn cursed under his breath. "I think that's Magnus's car. What's he doing here?"

A second later a girl with long blonde hair got out of the passenger seat. She moved to the trunk of the car then adjusted her sunglasses as the driver side door opened and Magnus got out.

"Maybe they're renting a boat for the afternoon." I shrank lower into the cockpit.

"How would she know where we were?" Jo asked.

"Do you think she's trying to get us in trouble?" I glanced at Shawn then Heather.

"I have no idea. What is she hoping to prove?" Heather narrowed her eyes.

"What do we do?" Billy asked.

"We aren't doing anything wrong." Shawn squeezed my hand. "We shouldn't have to do anything."

"Agreed." Heather crossed her arms over her chest. "Is there anything else we need to talk about?"

"Oh, my dreamcatcher doesn't protect me from dream manifested enemies, I found out last night."

"Great," Heather shook her head. "Can you fight them?"

"Yes, thank God." I shrugged. "So not a huge deal," I said, not taking my eyes off Kristina and Magnus. They had found one of the marina attendants and were pointing and waving their arms around, obviously not getting their way.

"Have you tried manifesting a monster to attack him?" Billy asked, and I pulled my eyes away from Kristina to stare at him with my mouth hanging open.

"That's a great idea, Billy," Jo said, nudging him with her elbow. "You should try it."

"But how? It's one thing to manifest a working gun, but a living monster, that would take work. Do you think it would be part of my bubble?"

"I don't know, but I think it's worth a try." Shawn put his arm around my shoulders and gave me a squeeze.

"I'll try it next time a mare shows up. Thanks, Billy." Kristina and Magnus must have gotten the code for the gate because they were headed straight for us. "Incoming." I nodded my head toward them.

"We aren't doing anything wrong." Shawn said out of the side of his mouth. "Liz, get everyone a drink."

I opened the cooler, blindly reached in, and gave everyone something to drink.

"So, there I was," Billy said, opening his pop. "Ten feet away from this bull elk. He had his head down and was pawing the ground."

"Magnus, Kristina," Shawn said, interrupting Billy. "What brings you out here today?" He didn't move from his seat but pulled me closer to his side.

"Kristina said you were supposed to pick her up for a date at one and you never showed. She thought you would be down here, so I gave her a ride to make sure you two were okay."

I was about to launch myself at Kristina and punch her in the face, but Shawn held me back with the hand on my shoulder.

"That's quite a story, since I'm dating Liz, not her and wasn't Kristina threatening you at your house around one Liz?" Shawn gave me a squeeze.

"Yeah, she was." I kept my voice calm somehow and wondered who she had followed. There was no to her way for her to know where we were.

"You lying brat," Kristina hissed.

"I have it on video, Kristina." I held up my phone. "Who's the one lying?"

"May I see that?" Magnus asked holding his hand out. I glanced at Shawn, not trusting Magnus. He nodded his head, and I handed the phone over.

Magnus watched the video then passed the phone back without a word. I thought he would leave but instead he took his glasses off. "I don't know what you kids are up to, but you'd better stop rocking the boat or you won't like the outcome."

"What are you talking about?" Heather asked, cocking an eyebrow at him.

Magnus glanced at Billy then Heather. "You know what I mean. The board of directors aren't thrilled with how your father is handling things so far. If there is more unrest between him and the clan, they will replace him and who knows where you'll all end up. I heard talk of Alaska."

Shawn's grip on my shoulder tightened and Heather gulped. "We aren't doing anything but hanging out on a boat, Magnus. I hardly think it counts as a coup." Heather took a sip of her water.

"Then you won't mind if Kristina joins you." Magnus's eyes shot to Kristina and he nodded. "You all used to hang out together."

"That was before she turned into a b..." Jo stopped herself before she finished.

"Actually, yes, I mind, and since it's my parents' boat, I have a say." I pulled away from Shawn, who was still trying to hold me back and got to my feet then I put my hands on my hips.

"What?" Magnus copied my stance. "How dare you?"

"How dare I?" I pointed at my chest then at his. "How dare you presume that I will just roll over and do your bidding? Your daughter is not my friend, she has done nothing to try to be my friend. From the moment she arrived she has tried to break me and Shawn up, followed me around, threatened me, and I'm pretty sure she tried to push me down a mineshaft. She isn't welcome on my boat or at my house." I left out her meeting with Stalker, I had no proof, and I didn't think it would help my case.

"You aren't making any friends acting like this." Magnus's gaze went from me to his daughter, pressing his lips together.

"I try not to make friends with psychopaths." I narrowed my eyes at Kristina.

"Let's go, Kristina." Magnus started down the dock.

I looked at my friends and flexed my hand. I was shaking with anger. "What do we do now?" We were going to have to be more careful about the gate now.

"I can't believe she had Magnus come down here." Shawn put his elbows on his thighs and ran his hands through his hair. "She isn't the person I thought she was."

"I'm sorry, little brother," Heather sat down next to him and rubbed his back, "I tried to warn you years ago about her. She will always have her own best interest at heart."

"But she told me we were all good, that she was fine with me and Liz dating." He shook his head. "What are we going to do if she moves here?"

"We have to be more careful than ever from here on out. She knows we're up to something, but we can't let her know what. If Magnus finds out, we'll be shipped off to who knows where." Heather crossed her arms over her chest.

"Why do you say that?" I asked, confused.

"Magnus works for the council. He makes sure every clan works well. If there are any issues, he solves them. With something like this, he would probably separate us." Heather ran her hands through her hair.

"But none of us are over eighteen, except for you. I don't want you to leave, but could he take us away from our families?" I didn't want to lose these people. I'd only known them for a few months, but they were the most important people in the world to me.

"He will if there's no other way to solve the problem and our parents will let him. I've seen it happen before," Heather said and stared at her hands. "When I was sixteen there was this group of kids who didn't want to work for Knights Inc., but their parents were making them until they turned eighteen. They were causing all kinds of trouble. Magnus came in, saw what was going on and recommended separating them. He thought they would all fall back in line if they weren't together. He placed the kids with extended family all over the states since they couldn't transfer the families to other clans."

"What happened to the kids?" I asked. "Did they fall in line and become knights?"

"All but one." Heather met my eyes, and she squinted. "He ran off as soon as he turned eighteen and no one's heard from him since."

"How are we going to keep this from happening?" I peered at Shawn. I didn't know what I would do if we were all separated.

"No more texting or messaging about anything gate related. We fall in line and don't give them a reason to think we are doing anything but our jobs." Shawn got up and paced back and forth in the small cockpit. "We meet in secret and keep our eyes open for Kristina and Magnus. We were in stealth mode before, now we need to be in double super-secret stealth mode."

"Sounds good," Jo said and gazed at the thunder heads building. "We'd better go."

"Yeah, you have work tonight right, Shawn?"

"Yeah, and you two have training." He glanced at me and Jo.

I closed up the boat then Shawn walked me to my Jeep as everyone else left. "Did I really mess up with the way I stood up to Magnus?"

"No, I don't think there is much he can do to you." He pressed his forehead to mine and closed his eyes as thunder bounced off the mountains. "Thank you for being so great about all this."

"Thank you for not giving up on me when I woke up with this," I said, showing him my mark. He leaned in and kissed me.

"I love you."

"I love you too. See you tomorrow okay?"

"Yeah, tomorrow."

I made it home before it started raining, had dinner with my parents, then went up to my room, trying not to think about how mad I was at Magnus and Kristina. I was so tired. I all I wanted was a dreamless sleep, but I had training, at least Stalker wouldn't be there, and Heather would keep me company after. It would

be all right.

307

Chapter 35

As soon as I realized I was dreaming, I jumped to Tom. I didn't want to risk getting trapped in the clearing or the mansion again. I was the first to show up and found Tom sitting on a park bench in a lush green park with short green grass, thick enough to cushion a fall. I had a feeling it was going to be a long night.

"Hi," I said, sitting on the ground in front of him. I wanted to save my energy for training.

"Hi Liz, how was the rest of your day?"

"You don't want to know. What are we working on tonight?"

"I'll go over it after the rest of the class arrives." He wouldn't meet my eyes and I noticed his foot tapping the ground to a beat only he could hear.

"Hey," Jo said, sitting down next to me. "What are we doing in a park?"

"I have no idea." I glanced at Tom as he counted heads, confirming everyone had made it. "But I don't think your dad is happy about it."

Jo glanced at him then nodded her head. "Yeah, you're right we must be doing one of the required classes the council thinks we need."

"Are they that bad?"

"Some of them are. They want everyone to have the same skill set. Then if you get transferred, everyone will know the basics." Jo shrugged as Tom cleared his throat.

"Alright settle down now." Tom motioned with his hands for us to be quiet and everyone stopped talking. "First of all, Steven will not be joining us tonight, his mom told me he had a stomach bug. Let's hope no one else gets it. Second, tonight we have a few special guests joining us." He paused for a moment and rolled his eyes. "Magnus will be doing his evaluation and he is bringing his daughter so let's bring our A game." As if on cue Magnus and Kristina popped in next to Tom.

Kristina's eyes locked on me as soon as she found me, and her face went from a fake smile to a frown. I rolled my eyes and watched Tom. *So much for an easy night of training. She would make my life hell.*

"Good evening Squires, I hope you won't mind the brief interruption of your training." Magnus glanced around, his eyes stopping at me and Jo, the only ones sitting on the grass. He sounded like a nice guy. His voice was completely the opposite of what it had been at the marina. "Let's begin, shall we? Form a line, please. This will require you ladies to stand."

Jo and I looked at each other for a moment, *was this guy for real?* We got to our feet then joined the line and waited for his instructions.

"To start with, I will give you a list of weapons to manifest. You will be judged on how long it takes you to manifest them." Magnus went to the front of the line with Kristina trailing behind him holding a stopwatch.

"What is your name?" Magnus asked Jeff. I felt for him. He didn't deserve to go first. They should have started with Mary, she needed to be taken down a few pegs.

"Jeff," he answered as his voice broke.

"Very well, let's get started. Kristina are you ready?"

"Whenever you are." She brought the watch up, ready to hit the button.

"You'll be timed through the whole sequence, not each weapon," Magnus said with a deviant smile. "No one will have the same sequence, Jeff, so don't worry about everyone else getting a sneak peek."

"Okay," Jeff said, sounding a little stronger now. He was good, I knew he'd do well.

"Go," Magnus said, before barking, "Pocket knife."

We all watched as Jeff held one in his hands almost immediately. "Bowie knife." Again, Jeff replaced the small knife with the larger one effortlessly. Magnus continued running through weapons and Jeff kept manifesting them until he came to the gun. He slowed down then, but he still produced a weapon. Finally, Magnus called an end to it. Jeff wiped the sweat from his forehead and gave us a weak smile as we all clapped. I thought he did a good job.

"What was his time?" Magnus asked Kristina.

She glanced at the stopwatch then up at her dad. "Five minutes, forty-five seconds."

"What are you clapping for? That is one of the worst times I've seen since I became the superintendent of training. How long have you been training?"

"Five years, sir."

"You have a lot of work to do before you will be ready to take the final test." Magnus shook his head then moved to Mary.

Mary did better but not by much. Jo went next and was quicker than Mary and Jeff. Magnus gave her a nod before moving to me.

"Elizabeth, correct?" he asked like I hadn't told him his daughter wasn't welcome on my boat hours before.

"Yes." I was proud my voice didn't reflect the anxiety making my stomach churn.

"Are you as good as your father was?" He cocked his head to one side.

"I don't know. I haven't been training long." I had a feeling he would fail me no matter how well I did.

"Very well." He nodded to Kristina. "Begin. Kershaw."

I gave him a blank expression, *what the heck was a Kershaw?* "I would be happy to manifest it, but I don't know what it is."

"Then say pass."

"Pass," I said and glanced at Tom, standing behind Magnus. He nodded. He thought I could do it.

"Clauberg Sawback."

I pursed my lips and narrowed my eyes, he found a way for me to fail. "Pass." I was sweating. If I got kicked out because of this I would be pissed.

"Do you know anything? How about a Buck knife?"

My hunting knife appeared in my hand and I let out a breath, he finally asked for something I knew.

"Machete."

The Buck knife transformed into a machete.

"Katana."

It was a little harder for me, but I imagined the sword from the Kill Bill movies.

"Flyssa."

"Pass." I let out a frustrated breath while he shook his head.

"9 mm Glock."

Thank God an easy one. It was in my hand faster than the Buck knife.

"Sixteen-gauge, side by side, stagecoach shotgun."

I didn't know what stagecoach meant, but I had a shotgun with a short barrel in my hand in seconds.

"300 Winchester sniper rifle with a scope and tripod."

I almost lost my balance when the gun appeared in my hands, it was heavy.

"Time," Kristina said with a grin.

I let the gun disappear and stepped back in line. I didn't want to know what my time was.

"What was her time?" Magnus asked.

"With deductions for her passes. Seven minutes fifty-nine seconds."

"I would like it noted in her file that our armory carries none of the weapons she passed on," Tom said, stepping into Magnus's personal space.

"Then it sounds as if the head trainer isn't doing his job. They are common weapons, many of our clans use them nightly." Magnus narrowed his eyes at Tom as if asking him who he wanted to throw under the bus, me, or him.

"Maybe the training superintendent should send his trainers a list of weapons our squires will be tested on."

I glanced at Jo and saw her mouth hanging open. I was in awe too, I couldn't believe Tom was sticking up for me. Magnus huffed out a breath and shifted his gaze back and forth. "You're right I'll send you a list. Then you can acquire them for your squires. Moving on," he moved to the next person in line. Tom shook his head when I was about to say something, and Jo put her arm around my shoulder.

"What a dick," she whispered in my ear, and I nodded.

We watched Magnus perform the test on Brent with slack jaws. He had the easiest things to manifest. Things like kitchen knife, flay knife, broadsword, and .22 rifle. I wanted to lodge a complaint, but Tom told me with his eyes to keep my mouth shut.

After they finished with Brent, I really hoped they would leave, instead the stopwatch in Kristina's hand disappeared and her short skirt and midriff top morphed into a white karate gi. "Now for the sparring observation," Magnus said manifesting a whistle. "You will each fight one opponent to submission, since there is an odd number of you, Kristina will join this portion of the evaluation.”

Well, I knew who I would spar with. I rolled my neck while everyone morphed into their sparring clothes. I followed suit then waited as Magnus paired everyone off. The boys with the boys; Mary with Jo and what do you know? Me and Kristina.

“Magnus, I think it would be better and more balanced if you had Jo spar with Kristina,” Tom said, his eyebrows pulling toward each other so close they almost touched.

“Are you trying to play favorites? You want your daughter to be evaluated sparring with a knight instead of another squire?” Magnus cocked an eyebrow.

“No, but Liz doesn’t have very much experience.”

“Then I’ll get a good idea of where she needs improvement.” Magnus glanced over Tom’s shoulder at Kristina. “Why don’t you two go first?”

I blew out a breath and thought about earlier that day with Jo and the simulator, but without the killing part. I could do this, *just pretend she’s a mare and you’re fighting for your life*. While I was thinking, everyone spread out and made an impromptu ring around us. I moved into the center and Kristina moved to stand about four feet across from me with a half-smile on her face. She thought it would be easy. Was she right? I didn’t have a chance, but if I let those thoughts linger, I would fail before I started.

“Begin,” Magnus said, backing away from us.

I dropped into my fighting stance and waited for her to come to me. I didn’t have to wait long. She moved in, faking a punch to my face, and kicked me hard in the midsection. I flew backward and landed on my back. I tried to breathe but my lungs felt like they had collapsed. I panicked for a second then remembered it was a dream. I wasn't really hurt. I forced my lungs to work and sprung to my feet. Kristina's smile turned into a grimace as I moved around the circle. I could do this. I needed to think about Hulk or Captain America. I needed to be quick and powerful. She came at me again with a battery of punches and kicks. I blocked most of them luckily. She slowed down with fatigue giving me the opening I needed. I faked a kick; she took a step forward trying to grab my foot, but it wasn't a full kick and she missed. She moved in and I took advantage of her proximity and punched her in the face hard enough to send her flying backward and slamming her back into a tree. Blood exploded from her nose and mouth while she sat there stunned.

I moved to go after her, but Magnus blew a whistle. "Stop, I think that will do for tonight, Liz." He went over to the tree and spoke to Kristina in low tones. When he was done, he walked back to the group.

"Are you hurt? I guess I didn't know my own strength," I said, offering her my hand.

She glanced at my hand then at me. There was pure hate in her eyes, and I wasn't sure what to do. If I pulled my hand back, she might become more enraged, but if I left it, she might try to tear it off. Before I knew what was happening something slammed into my jaw and it was my turn to go airborne for a few seconds until my back hit the ground hard. There were screams and shouting, and while I lay there with my eyes closed, I felt my body out to see if anything was broken. My body hurt but more from blocking and taking Kristina's punches then from landing on my back. My jaw hurt from whatever hit me.

"Liz, are you all right?" Jo asked as my eyes fluttered open.

"Yeah, what happened?" I propped myself up on my elbows.

"Kristina sucker-punched you." Jo helped me to my feet as I looked around. Magnus and Tom were on either side of Kristina speaking in low voices while the rest of the class huddled around me.

"You kicked her ass," Jeff said, giving me a pat on the back.

"I was kind of impressed," Mary said, giving me the first real smile I had received from her.

"Thanks," I said, smiling, and keeping one eye on Magnus and Kristina. "What do you think they are talking about?"

"Probably Kristina, she crossed a line tonight. Knights should have more control than that." Jo crossed her arms over her chest.

I watched as they came to a decision. Kristina disappeared and Magnus and Tom came over to us. "After that we are going to call it a night. Thank you, everyone for your hard work. If Magnus has time, he will join us on another night to complete his evaluations you are all free to go but Liz, can you please stick around for a minute?"

"Sure." I turned to Jo with my eyebrow raised. "Guess I'll see you later."

"Yeah, I wouldn't worry. He doesn't look mad."

"Thanks." I winked at Jo and she disappeared along with everyone else including Magnus. I walked over to Tom and waited.

"Are you all right?" He put his hands on his hips and looked at me.

"Yeah, a little bruised but nothing I'll feel in the morning." I shrugged.

"Good, what Kristina did was completely out of line. We are all on the same team, we use these sessions to improve not take out our aggression on each other. Her father agreed that disciplinary action needs to be taken."

"What does that mean?" I tried not to smile, praying she would get kicked out.

"It will depend on what happens at the hearing. Magnus, Kristina, and I will meet with Jon tomorrow to talk about it. We may need you to shed light on things. Do you think you can work on your own for a few hours tomorrow?"

"Yeah, I need to spend more time in the armory, anyway."

"Good idea. I'm glad you're all right, and I'm glad you beat the crap out of her." Tom winked.

"Thanks, I couldn't have done it without you. See you tomorrow." I thought of Heather and in a blink, I was in her room.

"Hey, are you all right? It looks like you got the shit beat out of you. Was it the mare?" She jumped from her bed.

"No, it was Kristina. Magnus showed up for our evaluation and of course he made us spar each other." I went over to the bed and fell backwards on it.

"Do I want to know what Kristina looks like?" Heather sat next to me on the bed

"I kicked her ass, one punch, and she flew back, hit a tree, and bled everywhere. Then she sucker-punched me." I turned my head to watch her reaction

"What? Tell me everything." Her eyebrows climbed up her forehead.

I pushed myself up, leaned against the headboard, and told her what happened.

"You know he was trying to get back at you for earlier, right?" she asked after I told her.

"Yeah, I figured it out. Very childish." I sat up and hugged my knees to my chest.

"No kidding, it's not like you would've been kicked out for not knowing. If anything, it would have made Tom look bad. It makes me wonder what Magnus is really doing here." Heather stood and paced around her bed.

"You think he's after Tom's job?" I pulled my eyebrows together.

"No, that's beneath him, and believe me, he won't do anything he thinks is beneath him." Heather paused for a second before resuming her pacing.

"What do you think it is?"

"I don't know but I'm going to find out." She sat on the edge of the bed. "I can't believe the weapons he wanted you to manifest. When he did my group, we had nothing like that. I can't believe Kristina lost it in front of Tom and her dad. She will be in so much trouble."

"What will happen to her?" I asked, staring at the ceiling.

"I don't know, but they will probably put her on probation."

"Tomorrow should be interesting then." I wondered if Jon still wanted Shawn and Kristina to end up together. It might put an interesting spin on things. "Did you try the crowbar on the door yet?" I asked just remembering the door.

"I got one I could wedge between the panels, and I tried to pry it open, but it didn't budge. I was afraid of using too much pressure and breaking the panel. We have to find another way to open it."

"Dang, I was hoping it would just click open with a little pressure."

"That's what I thought too, looks like we need to go back to the drawing board."

Chapter 36

The next morning, I woke up feeling refreshed, which was strange, considering how my body felt when I was done fighting with Kristina, but it had been too long since I felt this good, I didn't want to overthink it. I got up and went to work, feeling lighter on my feet than I had in weeks. Maybe it was because Shawn didn't have to work that night and we would get to hang out, or maybe it was because Kristina was getting in trouble for her sucker punch.

I pulled into the parking lot at Knights Inc. and smiled at Shawn as he came out the doors of the residence and waved at me. I parked my Jeep, grabbed my bag, and got out. "Morning," I said as he pulled me into a hug and gave me a good morning kiss.

"Good morning, you look rested." He took my hand and led me to the main entrance.

"I am, but I'm not sure why, I had to spar with Kristina last night. Magnus was evaluating us. I'm sure I failed." We went through the door and I waved at Marcy, as she spoke quietly into the phone.

"I never went through an evaluation. What did he do?"

"He timed how fast we could manifest weapons then I think he planned to rate us on our fighting skills. But after I sparred with Kristina, we didn't get any further."

"What happened?" Shawn asked as we tapped our cards and went through the door leading to the offices. I walked by Tom's office, heading to the training room and the armory beyond. "Where's Tom?"

"Just wait until we get to the armory and I'll tell you. I don't want anyone to overhear." I picked up my pace as we went through the doors to the empty training room, and into the armory.

"Okay, tell me." He crossed his arms over his chest.

"I kind of beat the crap out of Kristina while we were sparring. When Magnus stopped the match, I went to help her to her feet and instead of accepting the help she punched me in the chin. They are having a disciplinary meeting this morning." I walked over to the knife section and picked up a knife I'd never seen. I read the label, *competition chopper*. I cut it through the air a couple of times testing its weight and feel before I put it back and picked up another one.

"Wait, so you're telling me you beat up a knight last night and she got mad and sucker-punched you?" Shawn grimaced and pulled me into a hug. "And now she's in a meeting with Dad, Tom, and Magnus? Are you alright?"

"Yeah, it was a dream, but I might have to give them a statement. That's why I'm here. Tom wanted me to be around in case they needed me. Do you think she'll get into a lot of trouble?" I pulled out of his arms.

"Getting mad and hitting a squire is bad, it makes the whole organization look bad. We might be rid of Kristina easier than I thought." Shawn crossed his arms over his chest and stared at the ceiling, thinking.

"It wasn't that easy, believe me," I said, thinking of the pain I had after the fight. I picked up a sword and cut the air with it.

"I'm sorry." Shawn watched me parry with it. "She shouldn't have been so hard on you."

"I was scared at first." I put the sword back and gave Shawn a smile. "But it was the best thing that could have happened. I kicked her ass, Shawn. I needed to know I could, and that I'm improving. I felt like I was so far behind everyone else when it came fighting. Beating a knight, especially Kristina, was what my confidence needed."

"Yeah, but then she sucker-punched you." Shawn pulled me in close and cupped my face with his hand.

"She did, and now she's paying for it." I rose onto my tiptoes and kissed him. He wanted to protect me and keep me safe. I was the luckiest girl alive.

A throat cleared, and we jumped away from each other. I stared at the floor as my cheeks burned. "Liz," Tom said, and I brought my head up. "Jon would like to talk to you about last night."

"Okay." I took a few steps toward him, but I stopped midway and glanced at Shawn. "Wait for me?"

"I'll be here." He gave me one of his bright smiles and I followed Tom out of the armory to the door at the far end of the training room that led to Jon's office. "Should I be worried? I mean, did I do anything I could get in trouble for?"

Tom laughed. "No, just answer his questions and everything will be fine. I didn't have time to tell you last night, but I'm proud of you and your dad would have been too." He patted my shoulder as we came to Jon's closed office door. Tom knocked, waited a beat, then opened it for me.

Jon was sitting behind his desk, reviewing a paper, Magnus was sitting next to the desk with a deep frown on his face, and Kristina was sitting in one of three chairs in front of the desk. Jon met my gaze after a moment and motioned for me to take the seat next to Kristina while Tom took the one next to me.

Once we were seated, I folded my hands together and rested them in my lap to keep myself from fidgeting. I didn't like the feeling of the room; it felt like I was the one on trial not Kristina. Jon glanced up from his desk at me with a neutral expression. The man who was mourning the loss of his best friend I saw in the cemetery was gone.

"Liz, it sounds like you had quite a training session last night. How are you feeling today?" Jon moved the papers he was reading to the side.

"Fine, sir."

"Good, now I want you tell me what happened." He picked up a pen and began writing.

I explained what happened while we were sparring and how I had beat Kristina then had offered her my hand in good sportsmanship and the next thing I knew I was on the ground with everyone standing around me.

"So, you didn't see the punch coming?" Jon asked.

"No, we had finished, I let my guard down."

"Very well, Magnus did you have anything that you wanted to ask Liz?" Jon made some notes on his paper.

"Yes, Kristina said you were trying to convince Jo, Heather, and Shawn to quit Knights Inc. Is this true?"

Jon's and Tom's eyes shot up to mine, and it took everything I had to keep my expression natural. "I have no idea what she is talking about. How would I be able to do that? And why would I want them to leave? They are my friends and boyfriend and I just started. Kristina is the one following me around, threatening me."

"Is this true?" Jon asked.

"I saw the video," Magnus said, leaning back in his chair.

"That is the biggest pile of bull sh…" Kristina started to say when a look from her father had her closing her mouth.

"Thank you, Liz. That will be all." Jon held his hand up toward the door.

"Wait," Magnus said when I moved to stand. "I heard you were marked. Can I see it?"

I gulped and glanced at Jon. He nodded his head, and I took off my watch and showed Magnus the mark. He inspected it without touching me like it might be contagious. "How are you still alive?"

"My dreamcatcher, and my training." I put my watch back on.

"Thank you, Liz," Jon said, and I left.

I'd never been good at lying but it was the only way to stay below the council's radar. I didn't know what they would do if they found out what we were doing but I wanted to ask for forgiveness instead of permission. I found my way back to the training room and found Shawn on the bench press.

"Hey." I sat on the bench next to him.

He turned his head, smiled, then put the bar back in its holder. "How did it go?"

"It was fine. I told Jon about last night and what happened with her following me home. I guess Kristina told Jon that I was trying to convince you, Heather and Jo to quit."

"What did you say?"

"That I had no idea what she was talking about. I just started. Why would I want you to quit?"

"Do you think they believed you?"

"Yeah, I think so." I lay back and wrapped my hands around the bar but didn't lift it.

"Do you want to pump iron with me?" he asked, giving me a wink.

"Shawn?" Tom called from the doorway. "Jon wants to see you. Liz, why don't we call it a day and I'll see you tomorrow."

"Okay," I said, trailing off. "This must be a bigger deal than I thought."

"Must be. Are you going home?" Shawn asked as I walked with him to the door.

"If I'm done working, I might as well."

"I'll call you when I'm done." He gave me a kiss on the cheek then followed Tom through the door.

I left, wondering what they wanted to talk to Shawn about. I wasn't worried. He wouldn't say anything he shouldn't. Plus, he was used to playing the politics game.

When I got home, I didn't know what to do with myself.

It had been so long since I had a day to myself at home I was stumped. I went up to my room, sat down at my computer, and did research on secret passageways and trap doors. There was a reason why they were called secret passages because nothing I found helped. I was about to give up when my phone beeped. I picked it up and opened a message from Shawn.

Done, can we all meet at your house to talk?

When he said all, I thought he meant Heather, Jo, and Billy.

Yeah, come on over.

OK, be there in a little while.

I closed my computer down and went down to the living room. I didn't know what Shawn wanted to talk about, but it must be important. We didn't really have time to talk about the gate and the journal the day before, but hopefully, today would be different.

Twenty minutes later we were all sitting around the table on the deck waiting for Shawn to tell us what happened with Jon and Magnus.

"So, what happened?" Heather asked Shawn who was sitting at the head of the table.

"I went in and Dad and Magnus were sitting there wearing frowns and being dicks as usual. Dad asked what we were up to, like he didn't already know. I said I had no idea what he was talking about. Magnus changed the subject then, and it got personal. He asked me why I was leading Kristina on. I was like, what are you talking about? She's known I have a girlfriend who's training to be a knight since they showed up in town. Then he asked why I was spending so much time with her, and I was like, you guys made us work together, you made me show her around. If anyone is leading her on it's them.

"Kristina burst into fake tears then, and Magnus called her out on it. He asked her point-blank why she punched Liz and she said because you stole me from her." Shawn stopped to take a sip of the Mountain Dew he brought with him.

"She really is delusional, isn't she?" Jo asked rolling her eyes.

"Yeah well, she's getting what's coming to her. They suspended her until she takes and passes an anger management course."

"That's great news," Heather said. "I was supposed to work with her tonight."

"Yeah, but I think we'd better watch our backs." Shawn ran a hand through his hair then met my eyes. "And she hates you, it's bad enough you have to deal with mares, but you need to watch out for Kristina too. She doesn't play fair. I think you are right about her plotting with Stalker."

"I'm glad you believe me." I put my head down and banged it on the table.

"So, what do we do now?" Jo glanced at us.

"We keep searching but make extra sure Kristina doesn't find out about it," Shawn said.

"Do you think we could talk to your dad about letting us break through the wall to access the basement?" I was positive we would find the gate in the basement.

"I think he's only on our side because he doesn't have to acknowledge what we're doing. If we ask him to knock a hole in the wall, he would have to admit he knows we are up to something. I don't think he would go for it. Plus, Mom would kill us." Heather stood and paced around.

"I did some research on secret passages," I said, watching Heather stop her pacing to stare at me.

"Did you find anything?" she asked.

"Not a lot, there's a reason they are called secret passageways, but it gave me a few ideas. I think we need to check the floor. It's the only place we haven't checked."

Shawn and Heather glanced at each other and shook their heads.

"What?" Billy asked. "You already checked the floor?"

"No, we're idiots for not thinking of it. We'll check when we get home." Heather looked like she was ready to leave. "Do we need to go over anything else?"

We all looked around at each other. "Guess not," Billy said, standing.

"Then I'm going home. Shawn, you're still off tonight, right?" Heather asked.

"Yeah, I'll have Liz covered."

"Good, then I'll see you guys later. Shawn let's check the floor after dinner," Heather said, before leaving.

"We are going to get out of here too," Jo said, joining Billy in the doorway.

"Ok, see you guys," I said as Shawn took my hand. "What do you want to do now?"

"See that hammock down there?" he asked, pointing to the one hanging in the backyard.

"Yeah," I said unable to stop the smile from crossing my lips.

"Let's go relax and enjoy the day."

Chapter 37

My dream started in the clearing. *Great*, I thought to myself and manifested my 1911. I scanned the area. The mare wasn't there yet, and I wanted it to stay that way. I thought of Shawn and waited to be transported to his padded room where we planned on spending our dreams, but the scenery didn't change. I couldn't shift out again.

"Hey, what are we doing here?" Shawn asked, searching for an enemy as a shotgun appeared in his hands.

"I tried to go to you, but I couldn't. I don't know what's going on." I glanced at the mineshaft and dirt surrounding it. *Was there more than the last time I dreamed of this place?* I walked to the opening.

"Stalker hasn't shown up yet?" Shawn asked, catching up with me and walking by my side. We probably would have held hands, but we needed to be ready in case Stalker or some other nasty thing showed up.

"No, nothing yet. Did you guys find the latch for the door to the basement?"

"No, it was the council's last night in town, and we had a dinner party for them. Heather and I were stuck listening to them talk all night."

"Bummer." I gave him a smile then stopped and crouched down.

"What is it?"

"I think there's more dirt than last time." I picked up a handful, and let it fall through my fingers; it was definitely fresh.

"Do you think someone or something is mining for gold?" Shawn asked, turning in a circle around us.

"What good would gold do them in a dream?" I straightened and wiped my hands on my jeans. "What if they aren't mining gold? What if they're digging out the gate?"

"Why would they be digging it out? It's already open and I thought it was in the mansion." Shawn grabbed my hand and I looked up to see confusion is his eyes.

"I don't know, but why else would we dream of this place over and over again. Why did it show up in the real world?" I traded my gun for a flashlight and shined it down the hole. It was too deep to see very far, but flat for the first hundred feet or so. "It has to mean something."

"You want to go check it out, don't you?" Shawn asked.

"Yes. With us together we will be okay." I imagined a hard hat with a light on the top and good hiking boots.

"I don't like it." He changed his outfit to match mine.

"Me neither but all we are coming up with are dead ends and I'm tired of waiting around." I took a step toward the mine.

"What are you doing?" A deep voice asked from behind us.

Shawn and I turned as one with our guns up. "Who are you?" Shawn asked.

"Shawn, it's Victor." I lowered my weapon.

"How do you know it's not the mare messing with you?"

"Look at his eyes, Mares can't change their eyes." I put my hand on the barrel of his shotgun and forced him to lower it.

"I told you to stop trying to close the gate, Liz." Victor stomped over to us, stopping a few feet away and putting his hands on his hips.

"Dad, if I don't close the gate the mare will win and kill me." I stared at him refusing to blink until he looked away. "Is the gate down there?"

"One of them," he said, refusing to meet my eyes.

"How do we close it?" Shawn asked taking a step toward him.

"If I knew I wouldn't be here, stuck in this purgatory. I would be alive and well watching my daughter grow up."

"What should we do? Where do we find out how to close the gate?" I put a hand to Shawn's chest to keep him from getting closer to my dad.

"Just leave it, sleep under your dreamcatcher, and you'll be fine." He turned his back on us. That would not work. I was done taking no for an answer.

"Dreamcatchers don't always work, and Stalker found a way around it."

"How?" Dad spun around with his fists clenched as his side.

"Dream animals and monsters can still hurt me. The dreamcatcher only protects me from the mares and the rune only keeps them from eating my soul."

"You need to find the gate in the real world but not…," Dad started before snapping his head behind him. "Go, he is coming." He disappeared and I glanced at Shawn.

"Damn it." Shawn grabbed my hand. "Let's see if I can get us out of here." Shawn closed his eyes, and the world melted around us into his padded room.

"How come you could get us out of there, but I couldn't?"

"I don't know, but we know where the gate is. We need to get everyone together and talk about it. Stay here I'll be right back."

Shawn left and I sat on the couch. I didn't understand how he could leave me in his room and not have it disappear on me. He would have to explain it someday. He was back a few seconds later with Jo and Billy.

"Hey," I said.

"Hey." Jo pulled Billy over to the couch and sat next to me. Shawn was back with Heather a moment later.

"This better be important. If anyone finds out I'm not at my post there will be hell to pay," Heather said, sitting down on a white leather chair that appeared.

"Liz found the gate," Shawn said, pacing back and forth in front of us.

"What?" Jo and Heather screamed at the same time. "You did? Where is it? Is it the window in the basement?"

"The window?" I looked at her confused for a second. "No, I was wrong about that. It's in the clearing."

"You're kidding?" Jo shook her head. "Are you sure? You seemed pretty convinced it was in the mansion last time I checked."

"Yeah, I'm sure." I met Shawn's eyes. "Victor showed up

and confirmed it."

"You mean Victor, your bio-dad?" Billy asked.

"Yeah, I saw him as a slave once and now he pops in whenever he wants."

"Does he know how to close it?" Heather asked.

"He was about to, but he had to leave because Stalker was coming. He did tell us that we had to find the gate in real time."

"So, what do we do now?" Jo asked.

"We hike up there and find the gate. There might be something there that will tell us what to do." Shawn stopped pacing and put his hands on his hips.

"We will need some major gear. Mineshafts are really dangerous." I glanced at Billy.

"I have rock climbing and rappelling gear. I don't know how much and if I won't remember this dream someone will have to call me in the morning to remind me."

"I will, sweetie." Jo put a hand on his thigh. I turned away not wanting to see them get all googly eyed at each other.

"We need to leave early like seven, can you guys be at my house by then?" I asked.

Jo and Billy nodded their heads, but Shawn and Heather were frozen in place staring at each other. "We have to go," Heather said, disappearing.

"What is it?" I asked.

"There's an emergency. Will you be alright on your own?" Shawn took both my hands in his.

"Go, I can deal with Stalker."

"No, I don't trust him. I'm taking you with me and if anyone bitches, I will deal with it." Shawn grabbed my hand and the padded room melted into a bedroom.

There were white curtains billowing from an open window, and the bed must have had a matching bedspread at some point, but it was covered in blood now.

Heather and Stalker had swords locked in heated contention while Jon stood in front of the open window grabbing his side. When Stalker saw me, he pushed Heather away and gave me a nod. "There's my lamb chop." He ducked under Heather's sword.

"Don't just stand there, Shawn," Jon growled. "Help your sister. I'm hurt."

Shawn jumped into the fray with Heather and hit Stalker in the midsection. "Hold him," Heather panted, taking aim with her sword.

I moved next to Jon, thinking my protection might keep him safe. "Jon you're hurt, wake up, they have this."

He gazed at me then gave me a sad smile. "I never get to watch them fight together. I love watching them."

I leaned against the wall next to him and watched. It was like watching a ballet. Heather the prima donna and Shawn her leading man. They knew what and how each other moved, knew what the other one would do next. I was in awe and wondered if I would ever be as good as they were.

Shawn finally got his arms around Stalker and Heather came forward with a knife ready to cut his head off when the goblin threw Shawn off his back, slamming him against the wall on the opposite side of the room. Shawn slid down the wall then shakily returned to his feet.

Heather and Stalker circled each other with their legs bent and their arms out at their sides.

"You Martröð Veiðimaður need to give up," Stalker croaked, searching the room. "You will not beat me."

"You're the one who needs to give up. It's three on one." Heather glanced at Shawn who was waiting for an opportunity to jump back into the fight.

"We can fix that." Stalker jumped at Jon, startling him backwards. Jon's legs hit the wall and his torso went through the open window. He lost his balance and fell headfirst. I made a grab for him, but it was too late.

"Dad!" Heather ran to the window, pushing me out of the way and jumped out after him.

I stood frozen. I didn't know what to do. I looked out the window, hoping we would be on the first floor of the house, but we were on the fourth floor and on the ground below Heather knelt over Jon.

"I will have you all." Stalker laughed "I don't care how long it takes." I turned ready to tell him it would be a cold day in hell, but the words got caught in my throat as Shawn came up behind him swinging his sword out and cutting Stalker's head off.

"This isn't the end, lamb chop. I'll be back for you and your little boyfriend too." I walked to where his head was lying separated from his body on the floor and tried to stomp on it, but my dream bubble only pushed it out from under my foot leaving a trail of blood as it rolled across the floor.

"I got it." Shawn stopped the head with the toe of his boot, then stomped on it making a sickening wet sucking and a crunching noise as he ground his foot into it.

"We need to go," Shawn said when he was done. He took my hand and we jumped from the bedroom to the ground outside where Jon lay. He let go of my hand and knelt next to Heather. I stood a few feet back; I didn't know if Jon was dead or just unconscious, but I thought they needed a moment together.

"I thought I could catch him, but I was too slow," Heather was saying between sobs. "He's not dead, right? I am seeing him breathe right?" She wiped her nose on the hem of her shirt.

"Yeah, he's breathing," Shawn whispered before getting to his feet and touching the radio in his ear. "Base, this is Shawn, we need someone to wake Jon up now."

"I don't care what he said, he's unconscious and needs to be woken before it's too late."

"Heather, wake up then go wake him up. Liz and I will stay with him." Shawn put a hand on her shoulder, and she stood.

"I'm sorry, Shawn, I should have been quicker." Heather gazed at me, her eyes full of unshed tears, then she was gone.

"What can I do?" I moved to Shawn's side.

"Let's give them a few minutes, see if he wakes up." He grabbed my hand and squeezed. His whole body was shaking uncontrollably. I let go of his hand and wrapped my arms around his torso, thinking if I held him tight enough, he would stop shaking.

"Should we try to talk to him?" I watched Jon lay there with his chest slowly moving up and down.

"Yeah, maybe." Shawn pulled away from me and knelt at Jon's side. "Dad, you have to wake up. You aren't dead and I killed the mare. Wake up, we need you. Heather, Mom, and me, hell everyone in Twisted Pines needs you. You can't just give up like this." Shawn stopped and stared at the surrounding night.

"Copy base," Shawn said, getting to his feet.

"What's going on?" I rubbed my arms as a chill gave me goose bumps.

"They're calling an ambulance. They can't wake him up." Shawn's voice broke on the last sentence and I stood up, not sure what to do.

"What do we do now? Do you need to go? I can stay with him."

"Yeah, but we need to move him first." Shawn took Jon's hand. "Grab onto me."

I put my hand on Shawn's shoulder and we moved from the ground outside the house to a room similar to Jon's bedroom in the mansion. Jon was lying on top of a white duvet with his hands resting at his side. Shawn squeezed his dad's hand then got to his feet. "Can you stay here until someone comes to relieve you?"

"Yeah, but what do I do if a mare shows up? I can't fight them."

"I don't know, try to distract them. Do whatever you can to keep him safe for me."

"I will." I gave him a hug. "It will be all right, he'll wake up."

"I know. Call me when you're up." He kissed the top of my head then was gone.

I went over to a winged-back chair sitting in front of a fireplace and dragged it over to the side of the bed. I sat down and watched Jon. "Please wake up, please. Shawn needs you, heck I need you. I know we haven't always gotten along, but I need you to help me be a better knight. We all need you." I closed my eyes and said a prayer that he would wake up and everything would go back to normal.

I didn't know how long I had been sitting there staring into space when Tammy, another knight showed up. "Liz?" she asked bringing me out of my stupor.

"Yeah," I said, getting to my feet.

"I'm here to relieve you," she said, standing by the bed, and staring at Jon. "God this sucks."

"No kidding. Are you going to be all right?"

"I'm a big girl," she said, giving me a grin. "Wake up, Shawn and Heather need you."

"Okay, take care of him."

Chapter 38

As soon as I opened my eyes, I grabbed my phone. There was a message from Shawn, he was at the hospital with his dad in Spruce. I jumped out of bed, took a quick shower, and dressed in the first things my hands landed on. I ran down the stairs, filled up my coffee to-go cup, and ran out of the house to my Jeep. I drove as fast as I could, thinking about the night before. Stalker had been playing with them. The more I thought about it the more it added up. I didn't know if he knew who Jon was, but based on the things he seems to know about reality, I wouldn't be surprised if Stalker knew Jon was the leader of the knights in Twisted Pines. Getting rid of him would cause an upheaval and power vacuum, which was probably what Stalker wanted. We needed Jon to wake up, if for nothing else than to keep us together.

I went to Jon's room and lightly knocked on the door. I heard Shawn call for me to come in. I went inside but froze when I saw the bed. When you see someone every day as a strong and intimidating person and then you see them in one of those big hospital beds with tubes and wires running everywhere, it's shocking. Jon looked small, almost shrunken with no color in his face.

Shawn was on his feet with his arms around me before I could defrost. I let him hold me for a long time rubbing his back trying to think of the right thing to say. What do you say when your boyfriend's dad fell into a coma fighting a nightmare? *Sorry* just didn't seem like enough. "How is everyone holding up?"

Shawn pulled away and went back to the chair pulled close to the bed. "Mom is staying strong. Heather took her home to change and sleep. Heather feels like it's her fault for not catching him."

"What about you?"

"I don't know. It's not my fault, it's not Heather's fault either, it's Stalker's fault, but I was there, and I should have done more. I wish we knew where the gate was, or we had already closed it. There are so many things I wish I would have said to him."

"Shawn, he's not dead. We'll find a way to wake him up. We all need to stay strong and positive."

Shawn was staring at his dad like he didn't hear a word I said, and I couldn't blame him. If it was my dad, Burt, lying there, I wouldn't listen to anything until he woke up either. "Do you need anything?"

He glanced at me. "Could you bring him a dreamcatcher?"

I smiled, "I'll get the one Billy gave me out of the Jeep. Be right back." I ran to my Jeep and took the dreamcatcher off my rearview mirror. I doubted Jon would need it in Spruce, but if it gave Shawn peace of mind it wouldn't hurt anything. When I came back, Shawn was asleep in the chair. I worried for a minute that he didn't have a dreamcatcher, but he was a knight, he could take care of himself. I moved to the other side of the bed and hung the dreamcatcher on a hook probably used for a hose or tube. It would work just as well for a dreamcatcher.

I found a blanket in the closet and covered Shawn up with it then went back to Jon's side. I leaned in and whispered. "You better wake up, old man. You're going to want to see the great things your son does. He will rock our world, and I know you don't want to miss it."

With nothing to do, I went back to my Jeep. My phone buzzed in my pocket as I walked across the parking lot and I pulled it out. Someone at the mansion was calling. "Hello?" I opened the door to my Jeep and got in.

"Liz, it's Tom, where are you?" He sounded concerned.

"I'm sorry I forgot to call you. I'm just leaving the hospital in Spruce."

"Can you stop by here on your way back?" He sounded distracted, and I hoped he wasn't mad that I didn't show up for work. I figured he would know where I was, but I should've called.

"Yeah, I'll be there in twenty."

I went straight to Tom's office when I reached the mansion. Ivan, Fredrick, Derick, and Morton were standing outside Tom's door whispering to each other. "Hi, is he in with someone?" I asked Fredrik.

"What? No, you just came from the hospital, right?"

"Yeah." They all stared at me like they hadn't eaten in a month and I was holding a Thanksgiving turkey.

"How does he look?" Ivan asked.

"Pale, but good." I didn't know what to tell them. How does anyone look when they're in a coma?

"He's alive?" Derick asked. "Someone said he died last night."

"What? No, he's not dead." I was shocked that a group this close would spread lies.

"Liz," Tom called from his office. "Can you please come in here?"

"Guess I better go." I ducked my head and slinked into the office.

"Why don't you close the door, we don't need any more rumors getting started," Tom said before I could sit.

I closed the door then sat. "Good idea."

"You were there last night?" Tom glanced at me with tears in his eyes.

"Yeah, there wasn't much I could do but watch." I shrugged, not wanting to meet his eyes.

"I know, but you can tell people what happened, and we don't have to stress Heather and Shawn out any more than they already are."

"Do you want me to make an announcement?" I really didn't want to, it didn't feel like it was my place.

"No, but Magnus might need a report from you."

"Great, just who I want to talk to." I rolled my eyes.

"Well, he'll be in charge at least for the time being. Maybe longer if Jon doesn't wake up."

"What will happen if he doesn't?"

"We have a home for knights who are injured beyond recovery in Florida. It's safe and they receive the best medical care around. Most of them have mental issues, but there are a few like Jon who went into a coma and never woke up."

"What will happen to everyone here? Will you move?"

"No, I doubt it, there are too many mares here, but I don't know what Jenny will want to do if they move Jon to Florida."

My heart rate doubled. With Jon in Florida it would only make sense for Jenny to want to move with Shawn and Heather to be close to him. I felt my eyes prick with tears when I thought of them leaving. "What if they stay?" I shouldn't get my hopes up, but I needed something to keep me going.

"They'll have to move out of the mansion so whoever takes over can move in. If it's not Magnus, then the council will bring someone in from another territory. Believe me none of us want it to happen. Jon can be a pain in the ass, but he's our pain in the ass."

I sniffled. "What did you want to see me about?" I tried not to blink so the tears wouldn't fall.

"Do you think you can help guard Jon in the dream dimension?" He pulled a piece of paper out of a folder with gridlines drawn on it.

"I want to." I rubbed the red welt of my mark peeking out from under my watch and looked at the names in the boxes. It must be the schedule for guard duty. "But, I'm a magnet for mares. I don't want to be the reason Jon loses his soul, and I would have to sleep without my dreamcatcher to fight them. Is it worth the risk?"

"I forgot about your mark." Tom ran a hand through his hair and squeezed his eyes shut. "Okay, well we might need you to help patrol or help in the communications room until we get this sorted out."

"Whatever you need I'll be here. I'm sorry I can't help with the guard duty."

"No, you're right. I can't believe I forgot." He glanced at the clock on the wall behind me. "I'm canceling training for the rest of the week, there is just too much going on, and I have to help take care of Jon's duties."

"Okay, let me know what I can do." I stood and started for the door.

"I will, but I think Shawn and Heather need you more than I do."

When I left, I checked the parking lot for Heather's car, but it was gone. She probably went back to the hospital. With nothing else to do, I went home which drove me crazy. All these terrible things were happening and there wasn't anything I could do but go home and wait for someone to call.

I had just turned off the highway onto my road when I noticed a red Subaru behind me. It was Kristina again, *great*. I didn't want to bug Shawn or Heather, so I fished my phone out of my bag and called Billy. After what had happened the last time, I wanted back up. I know, it's not safe to talk and drive, but I didn't trust her, and my parents wouldn't be home from work for hours.

"Hey, are you okay?" Billy asked answering the phone without a greeting.

"I'm not sure. Kristina is following me home again."

"Kristina? What do you want me to do?"

"Can you come over?" I slowed down, wanting to give Billy more time. "I don't trust her."

"Yeah, Jo and I were on our way to the hospital, but we haven't made it to your turn off yet. We will be there in a few."

"Thanks." I ended the call and sped up. I wanted to be out of the car before Kristina was out of hers.

I parked in the driveway, left my bag on the seat, fisted my keys in my hand, and waited for her. She jumped out of her car and stomped over me.

"What are you doing here?" I asked as she stopped a few feet from me.

"Why does Jo think she will be able to go to a regular college?" She crossed her arms over her chest.

"Even if I knew, it's none of your business."

"Please, you're trying to ruin Knights Inc. You're barely one of us. Your father was a traitor, and it looks like you are too."

"Excuse me, my father left because he didn't agree with how things were being handled, and he did nothing to hurt Knights Inc."

"I don't know where you heard that, but my dad tells a completely different story." She put her hands on her hips and pursed her lips.

"What do you want?" Arguing with her wasn't going to get me anywhere.

"I came to give you a warning." She glanced over her shoulder as Billy parked and jumped out. "Your other boyfriend came to save you from me?" She laughed and shook her head.

I rolled my eyes. "He isn't here to save me. He is here as a witness." I glanced over Kristina's shoulder and nodded to him as he pulled out his phone, hit the screen a few times then held it out to video us.

"Paranoid much?" She crossed her arms over she chest and cocked a hip.

"With you I have no reason not to be." I put my hands on my hips. "If there is nothing else, you can go."

"Fine, but with Jon out of the picture, my dad will be in charge and things are going to change. He won't let someone who's marked become a knight. It's out of the question, he's talking to the council about it right now."

"Is that all you came to tell me?" I tapped my foot on the ground. I wasn't ready to think about what would happen with Magnus in charge.

"No, stay away from Shawn, he doesn't need your kind of influence. He is going places." She flicked her hair over her shoulder.

"But only if he hooks back up with you, right? In case you haven't noticed he can't stand you." I narrowed my eyes at her.

"Just watch your back." Kristina marched back to her car, she flipped Billy off on her way, started it, and peeled out of the driveway pelting Billy's truck with gravel.

Jo got out of Billy's truck after she left. "What's her problem?"

"She thinks I'm the trying to get you to leave Knights Inc. Do you guys want to come in?"

"Yeah, what happened last night?" Billy took Jo's hand

and walked beside me to the front door.

"Have you talked to Shawn?" I unlocked the door and held it open for them.

"No, we only know what my dad told me when I got up this morning. Shawn and Heather have enough going on," Jo said as I led them into the kitchen.

I told them what happened while I poured myself a bowl of cereal and milk. I was starving since I ran out of the house without eating earlier. When I finished, they were both staring at me shocked. "What?"

"It's just, Jon has always been like a god to me. He got his ass kicked and he might never wake up. It's just, I don't know what to do with myself."

"Pray he wakes up, or it sounds like they will move him to Florida. It's bad enough Magnus is going to be in charge." I took my now empty bowl to the sink and ran water into it.

"Why would they have to move?" Billy asked, looking confused.

"There is a nursing home in Florida for knights who are hurt in dreams. Liz thinks if Jon doesn't wake up, Jenny will move them all down there." Jo's eyes stared past me into infinity. She hadn't thought of it yet. "I don't know what I would do if they moved. Shawn has been part of my life for as long as I can remember."

"It'll be okay," Billy said, rubbing her back. "I'm sure Jon will wake up before you know it."

"I don't know, this is bad." Jo looked up at me. "So, Shawn killed Stalker?"

"Yeah, but he'll be back. We've killed him three times since you guys moved here. He always comes back." I leaned against the counter not sure what to do.

"We need to close the gate." Jo sat up straight. "Let's hike up to the mineshaft now and see what it looks like."

"We can't now, we need to be smart about this and going up there with everything so fresh isn't smart. Let's see when Shawn and Heather can go, then we can do it with clear heads. I don't think Jon will wake up if we close the gate. His mind is broken, it needs to heal itself."

"You're right." Jo ran her hands through her hair. "I hate sitting here not being able to do anything."

"We all do." I gave her a tight smile. I wanted to call Shawn to see how he was doing but he had a lot on his plate. He would call me when he was ready.

"We are going to head to the hospital then." Billy moved toward the door and Jo followed. "We'll see you later."

"If you see Jenny and Heather tell them I'm sorry. They weren't there when I went by this morning." I walked them to the door.

"We will. Don't worry, Liz, everything will work out." Jo gave me a hug. "I'll see you tonight."

"Bye." I shut the door and leaned against it for a second then pushed off and walked through the house without a purpose, feeling like everything was lost. Jo was right, if we were searching for the gate at least we would be doing something.

I went to the garage and restocked my backpack. Going down the shaft was crazy and dangerous, but it would be better than doing nothing.

I had just finished zipping up my pack when I heard a car pull into the driveway. I went to the front door and looked through the sidelight. Shawn was standing on the other side, pulling his hand up to push the doorbell.

"Hi." I opened the door wide for him to come in before he reached the button. He looked tired; he was hunched over with bags under his eyes so dark it looked like he got punched in the face. "How are you holding up?" I took his hand, led him into the living room, and sat on the couch.

"I'm here. I was worried about you when you left without telling me at the hospital." He pulled me against him and brought his leg up on the couch, so I sat between his legs, my back to his front.

"You were sleeping. I didn't want to wake you. You needed the sleep."

"I wish you would have, all I dreamed about was saving my dad, getting to the mare quicker, but it didn't matter how many times I tried, he still ended up falling out the window."

"I wish there was something I could do." I ran my hand up and down the outside of his thigh while staring at nothing.

"All we can do is wait and pray he wakes up." Shawn sounded far away.

"What do we do in the meantime?" I closed my eyes, feeling his breath slow as he relaxed.

"Figure out how to close the gate." He was almost asleep, and I wondered if he would sleep better with me next to him.

I lay there for a while, waiting for him to fall into a deeper sleep. When he did, I untangled myself, pulled the dreamcatcher out of the drawer in the end table and hung it over his head. Then I got back in my spot and fell asleep, hoping we would both dream of nothing.

Chapter 39

Someone was shaking my foot, but I didn't want to wake up. I rolled instead and hit the floor face first. I yelped, then remembered where I fell asleep. I glanced at Shawn, he was still sleeping on the couch, *he must be exhausted to sleep through that*. I got to my feet and saw my mom standing above me with a horrified expression on her face.

I went into the kitchen, knowing I was going to get yelled at and got a glass out. "What were you doing?" Mom asked in a low voice while I filled the glass with water.

"What did it look like? Sleeping." I turned the faucet off and chugged the water.

"Why were you between his legs? If your father would've come home to that…"

"It's the new way kids are having sex, didn't you know? Back to front with all their clothes on." I rolled my eyes and put the glass in the sink. "It's been a really long, really crappy day Mom, we fell asleep on the couch. That's all."

"Why was it a bad day?"

"Shawn's dad is in a coma, I don't know how long Shawn has been up, but he needed to rest." I crossed my arms over my chest.

"Jon is? What happened?" Mom put her hand in front of her mouth and narrowed her eyes.

"He fell out of a window in his dream last night and hasn't woken up. He is in the hospital in Spruce, Shawn's been taking care of his mom and his sister since it happened."

"In his dream? How?"

"Have you ever had one of those dreams where you're falling?" I leaned against the counter.

"Yes." She crossed her arms over her chest.

"But you never hit the ground, right?"

"Well, no I guess not."

"Well, Jon hit the ground." I rubbed my eyes trying to get the sleep out.

"I'm so sorry for them." Mom turned away with her eyes downcast and I wondered if she was thinking of Victor not waking up from his sleep.

"Me too, that's why you found Shawn and I asleep when you came in. He slept a little at the hospital, but he kept having bad dreams." I put a hand on her shoulder, wanting to comfort her without talking about it.

"What will happen now?" She squeezed my hand then let go and turned her face into a neutral mask.

"I don't know, neither does Shawn." I peered around the corner of the kitchen, Shawn's face was scrunched up and his legs were twitching. "I better wake him up."

"Okay, ask him if he wants to stay for dinner."

I went back to the living room and knelt on the floor and shook his shoulder. "Shawn wake up, it's a dream."

He opened his eyes and looked at me. "Liz." He let out a breath and pulled me into a hug. "It was the worst dream, thank God you're all right."

"Do you want to talk about it?" I hugged him back, wishing there was more I could do.

"No, if it's okay with you. What time is it?" He pulled away and ran a hand through his hair.

"After five, Mom wants to know if you want to stay for dinner." I stood then sat next to him as he put his feet on the floor.

"Can I stay forever? I slept so well with you at my side. After you left, my dreams got scary." He laced our pinkies together like he had to keep touching me.

"I doubt they will allow that." I laughed, bumping my shoulder with his.

"Okay, let me see what's going on with Mom and Heather. Can I use your phone?"

"Yeah, I'll go grab it." I ran to the kitchen and pulled the cordless phone off the stand. Mom raised her eyebrows at me from the counter. "Shawn wants to stay, but he needs to check in with his mom and sister."

"Okay." Mom turned back to the sink, and I took Shawn the phone.

"Thanks." He got up and took it from me. "I'm going to go outside."

"Whatever you need." I waited for Shawn in the living room. I was glad he'd slept while we had been together, and maybe if we were together in our dreams, he would be okay too. I hadn't dreamed during my nap which was strange because I couldn't remember the last time I hadn't dreamed.

"I need to head home. Tell your mom, thanks, but I'll take a rain check. Mom wants us together tonight, but I'll see you later," he said, coming back with the phone in his hand. He pulled me into a hug. "I don't know how I would get through this without you."

"Everything will work out. Tell your mom and Heather I said hi."

"I will, and I'll see you later." He raised his eyebrows like he didn't want my mom to know that we met up in our dreams.

After Shawn left, I went back to the kitchen and told Mom he would not be joining us. She understood, if something like that was going on with us, she would want me with her to make sure I was safe. I spent the rest of the evening with my parents, thankful that what happened to Jon would never happen to them.

Even though I hadn't done much that day and took a nap, I went to bed early; the stress of the day had worn me out. When my dream began, I was in Shawn's padded room and he was waiting for me.

"Has there been any change?" I asked, sitting next to him on the couch.

"No, Mom is spending the night in the hospital and everyone is on rotating duty to guard Dad until he wakes up." Shawn put his arm around my shoulders, and I rested my head on his chest.

"I wish there was something I could do to help."

"Me too, I hate waiting. That's why everyone will be here soon." He leaned his head back and rested it on the back of the couch.

"What are you thinking?" I peered up at him.

"I'll tell you when everyone else gets here." He closed his eyes and pulled me in closer.

Heather materialized a few minutes later, looking exhausted, wearing sweatpants and a T-shirt. I didn't think I had ever seen her dressed down before. I pulled out of Shawn's arms and ran to hug her. "How are you holding up?"

"I'm okay, I wish he would wake up already." She pulled away and tightened her ponytail. "Where's Jo and Billy? I have guard duty in ten minutes."

"Right here," Jo said, pulling Billy by the hand. "What's going on, Shawn?"

"Let's hike up to the mineshaft tomorrow." Shawn stood and ran his fingers through his hair.

"Are you sure? Don't you want to stay close in case your dad wakes up?" I raised my eyebrows, surprised.

"Yeah, I'm tired of dealing with the monsters. I want to get rid of them once and for all. It's what dad would want us to do. Not sit around and feel sorry for him."

I glanced at Heather who nodded. "You're right, he may not want us to go down a mineshaft that's who knows how old, but he would want us to keep working."

"So, we'll meet at my house at seven tomorrow then?" I asked.

"I already set my alarm," Billy said.

"How did you know we would go tomorrow?" Jo asked.

"I know you guys, shit happens, but you won't put something this big on the back burner." He shrugged. "I got everything ready to go before I went to bed."

"Perfect." Shawn forced me to stop pacing and pulled me into him from behind.

"Then I'm out of here," Heather said, closing her eyes.

"Wait," I said before she could leave. "Kristina followed me home again."

"What?" Shawn asked. "Why didn't you tell me?"

"You had other things to worry about." I took his hand. "She isn't letting it go."

"What can we do?" Jo asked.

"I don't know, but we need to be careful." I jerked and looked around. "Did you guys hear that?" It sounded like something hit the wall.

"Hear what?" Shawn asked as a chill over took me and I shivered.

"Something's wrong." I pulled away from Shawn and woke myself up.

My room was cold, and I pulled my blankets up higher. I stilled when I heard something, and I strained, trying to make out the sound. There was a breeze blowing in from the window in front of my desk. Funny, I didn't remember leaving it open. Then I heard it: someone shuffling across the carpet. I cracked my eyelids and looked around. The half-full moon was shining in through the window, allowing me to see the outline of a human creeping towards me.

I wanted to call for help, to attack them, stop them, do something, but lying in my bed gave me the advantage I needed. I would wait until they were close enough to grab or until they turned their back on me.

They crept closer and I tensed my muscles, ready to tackle them when my phone vibrated on my nightstand. It was probably Shawn, I sprung from my bed, wrapped my arms around their waist and forced them to the floor.

"Mom, Dad, help!" I yelled at the top of my lungs while my would-be attacker tried to roll me off them. Thankful for all the training Tom and Jo gave me, I squeezed my attacker's side with my thighs and grabbed their arms pinning them to the floor.

"Let me go," the feminine voice hissed in a whisper. I felt like I should know who it was, but it was too dark to see her face.

"Mom, Dad," I yelled again before the door to my room burst open and the light came on, forcing me to blink until my eyes adjusted to the light.

"Liz?" Dad asked running to the far side of the bed. Finally, able to see, I looked down at my burglar. Kristina was under me still trying to get struggle free. "Sandy call 911, we have an intruder." Dad leveled his pistol on Kristina. "Colorado is a Make My Day state, sweetheart. I suggest you stop struggling and wait for the sheriff to get here before I decide you are trying to kill my daughter."

"Fine," Kristina breathed. I rolled off her and got shakily to my feet.

"What are you doing here?" I asked, standing behind my dad with my arms crossed over my chest.

"What Jon should have done when he found out you were marked. Give you to the mare."

"Why are you so hell bent on getting rid of me?" I sat on the edge of my bed as blood pounded in my ears.

"You are bad for Shawn, you are bad for everyone at Knights Inc." She sat up and crossed her legs like my dad wasn't pointing a gun at her head.

"You don't know anything about me. What gives you the right to make that call?" I pulled my hair out of my face.

"That is why. If you hadn't taken advantage of Shawn, your mark would've already killed you." She pointed at the mark on my wrist and I wished I would have worn a long sleeve shirt to bed.

"Liz, what is she talking about?" Dad asked a little louder, glancing at me from the corner of his eye. "Is that a tattoo?"

"Burt, the sheriff is on the way," Mom said from the doorway, wearing her favorite blue silk pajamas and matching robe.

"Dad, we'll talk about it later." I glanced at Mom then back at Kristina, narrowing my eyes at her.

She laughed, covering her hand with her mouth. "He doesn't know?" She shook her head. "That's just grand."

"Liz, what is she talking about?" Dad asked, his gun hand twitching.

"Burt, calm down. We'll tell you everything later." Mom

came up behind him and put a hand on his shoulder.

My phone vibrated again. If I didn't answer it, Shawn would probably come over and that was the last thing I needed. Giving Kristina a wide berth I snatched it off my nightstand and sent Shawn a text.

"Liz, who is calling you at this hour?" Dad was starting to sound mad, and I frowned. I hadn't done anything wrong.

"Shawn."

"Why don't you tell him why Shawn knows that something is wrong?" Kristina laughed as I narrowed my eye and squeezed my phone so hard I was surprised it didn't break.

"Liz, what's she talking about?"

"Later, dad." I took a step toward her. If I punched her now, I could claim I did it when she was sneaking in. Mom and Dad would back me up. The doorbell rang, stopping me from my thought, and Mom ran to let the sheriff's deputy in.

The deputy arrested Kristina for breaking and entering. She had used our ladder to come in through my bedroom window. She refused to tell the police why she broke in and wanted to call her dad, but they didn't let her. She was eighteen, they didn't have to. She would get her one phone call at the station after she was booked.

After they left, Mom, Dad, and I stood in the kitchen silently staring at each other. I didn't know how to explain to Dad that I had the power to dream walk or that I had been marked by a monster who wanted me dead.

"I don't know what's going on," he started. "But it's been a long night. Let's go to bed and talk about this tomorrow." Saying nothing else he left Mom and I in the kitchen.

I looked at Mom, pleading with her to make him forget. "We have to tell him, Liz. He's your father. He deserves to know." She turned and followed him upstairs.

I locked up the house and turned the lights off before I went back to my room. Then I locked the window and went back to bed. I thought it would be impossible to fall back to sleep but somehow, I managed. I found Shawn in my dreams and we spent what was left of the night in his padded room. I told him everything, and he held me as I worried about telling my Dad about the Knight Flyers.

Chapter 40

The next morning, I woke up smiling. It only lasted for a second, but it felt good to wake up not covered in sweat or worrying about who Stalker killed the night before. It was early, so early my parents were still home. I rolled out of bed and tried not to think about how I was going to tell my dad about Knights Inc.

I dressed in jeans and a T-shirt. I tied a flannel shirt around my waist and put my thick hiking socks on after I brushed my teeth and put my hair in a ponytail. I still had a half-hour before everyone would show up and if I didn't tell my parents where we were going, they would freak out later. After I told my dad about Knight Inc. I would probably be in enough trouble.

I went downstairs and straight to the coffee pot. "You're up early," Dad said, sitting at the bar with a cup of coffee and his tablet, acting like a deranged lunatic hadn't broken into my room the night before.

"Yeah, we're going on a hike and wanted to get an early start." I poured my coffee and took a sip.

"Where are you going?" Mom asked coming in from the patio.

"We're going to take the new trail I found. Do a little exploring."

"That will be fun who all is going?" Dad glanced up from his tablet.

"Well Shawn and me." I paused for a moment and watched his expression change from friendly to dark. I pushed him too hard sometimes. "And Billy, Jo and Heather."

"Liz, why do you torture him?" Mom laughed nervously while I got a bowl and the cereal out of the cabinet.

"Because it's too easy." I poured my cereal into the bowl then went to the fridge for the milk. I poured my milk in the bowl then got a spoon.

"I have to go, but you kids be careful out there," Dad said, getting up and heading toward the mudroom.

"We will." I was surprised he was acting so normal, maybe he thought last night had been a dream.

I heard the front door open. "Liz, are you up?" Billy called.

"In the kitchen." I watched Dad slip out the garage door.

"I have to go too. I know yesterday was hard." Mom pulled me into a hug. "Try to have some fun today but be careful."

"We will, thanks." She pulled away and hurried to the garage.

"Hey, where'd your parents go?" Billy asked, coming into the kitchen with Jo trailing behind him.

"They didn't want to see you." I laughed then drank the milk in the bottom of my bowl. "They had to go to work." I took my bowl to the sink and filled it with water. "Did you remember everything?" I got my boots out of the mudroom and sat down at the bar to put them on.

"Yeah, I think so, but I only have four harnesses, someone will have to stay up top." Billy sat down and checked his watch. "Where are Shawn and Heather?"

"I don't know. I hope Jon didn't take a turn for the worse." With my boots tied, I got up and went to the garage door.

"Where are you going?" Billy asked.

"To get my pack, I left it in the garage. Mom and Dad know we are going hiking and they know where, but they don't know we're going down a mineshaft, and I would like to keep it that way, especially after what happened last night."

"What do you mean?" Billy asked as I left to get my pack.

"Let's go outside and divvy up the equipment, and I'll tell you about Kristina breaking into my room," I said, coming back with my pack. "It was a long night."

"What happened?" Jo asked as I slung one strap over my shoulder and led the way outside.

I told them about the night before while Billy lowered his tailgate and jumped in the bed of the truck to push the equipment to the edge. He had everything we were going to need: rope, clamps, harnesses, helmets, and head lamps. I was impressed with his preparedness. We divided everything, making it as even as possible.

"I can't believe she broke into your house." Jo crossed her arms over her chest and leaned against the truck.

"What do you think she was going to do?" Billy asked, putting a thick coil of rope in his pack.

"I don't know, probably steal my dreamcatcher so Stalker could try to kill me. That was their original plan," I said, looking up at the sound of Shawn's Rubicon pulling into the driveway.

"Sorry we're late." Shawn jumped out of his Jeep and opened to the back door to get his pack.

"What took you so long?" Jo asked as Heather got out with two grocery sacks.

"We brought lunch." she held up the bags.

I shook my head. "I knew we were forgetting something." I smiled at Heather. "Thanks, I think I remembered everything but food. How's your dad?"

"He squeezed Mom's hand last night, but the doctors said that it could be an indication of anything." Shawn hauled me into a hug. "Are you okay after what happened with Kristina?"

"Yeah, I knew she would try something. She scared me. No one has ever come in through my window before."

"Are you pressing charges?" Heather asked,

"I think my dad is planning to. It's not really my call. I wonder if she's still in jail," I asked as Billy finished loading his stuff. "Are we ready?" I pulled my backpack on and adjusted the straps. Everyone nodded and put their packs on.

"Let's do it," Billy answered, and we started up the road to the trailhead.

There wasn't a lot of talk as we walked, everyone was lost in their own thoughts. I was thinking about Kristina and what would happen to her. Would she go to jail? Would they kick her out of Knights Inc?

When we hit the main trail, I remembered how scared I was the first time I took it. It had been one of the scariest moments of my life, but I'd been alone and totally unprepared for what I was doing. This time I was with my friends, and we had everything we needed. At least I hoped we did.

When we reached the new trail, we stopped. "Where did this come from?" Billy knelt and inspected the tracks in the dirt.

"That's what I wondered too." A knot of tension eased inside me when Billy confirmed that the trail hadn't been there before.

"You were right, Liz, this trail wasn't here last year or any year that I can remember." Billy stood up and turned around looking a little paler than usual.

"So, she's right?" Heather asked.

"Yeah, this is creepy." Billy stared at the ground again. "It doesn't look like anyone has been on it either, there aren't any footprints or anything." Everyone took a step back like it was going to bite them.

"We don't have to do this. It doesn't get any better from here." I shrugged as goosebumps erupted on my arms.

"No, we're doing this." Shawn took my hand.

"Yeah, it'll be fine." Heather adjusted the straps on her pack.

"Let's go." Jo took off down the trail and we followed behind her.

We were even quieter as we walked up the new trail than we had been on the old one. Even our shoes barely made any noise, almost like we were afraid we would wake a sleeping giant if so much as snapped a twig.

When the sounds of the forest stopped, and the twisted pines began to close in around us, we picked up the pace. It was almost like the air was heavier, pressing down on me, trying to get me to stop, to give up, not go on.

"How much further?" Billy whispered to me.

"I can't remember, I ran through this part," I whispered back as I looked from side to side, waiting for something to jump out.

"Running is a good idea." Heather started to jog.

We all followed her and the further we went, the faster we went until we were sprinting. After what felt like hours we finally burst into the clearing. I bent over to catch my breath and squinted up at the blue sky, thankful to be out in the open again.

"This is the scariest hike I've ever been on," Billy said through gasping breaths.

"No kidding." Shawn put his hands over his head and walked around. "Liz," he stopped in his tracks and spun around. "You're right. This is the same clearing as in your dream." He pointed to the mineshaft.

I walked to the opening of the shaft, stopping a few feet away from it. The dirt pile was bigger than last time and there was still no trace that I had been there the week before.

"Who did this?" Billy studied the dirt.

"That's what I want to know. The ground is dry enough. If someone was coming up here, we would see signs of them, footprints, trash, something." I backed away from the pile and took my pack off.

"This is weird." Jo took her pack off and sat it next to mine. "What do we do now? Whatever it is, let's get it done and get out of here."

"Good idea," Heather said.

"I think we should eat lunch then go down the shaft," Shawn said.

"I don't know if I can eat," Jo said, and Heather nodded in agreement.

"So, we wait until after we come out of the shaft and get out of here?" Billy opened his pack and pulled the rope out.

"Yeah, let's get this over with," Shawn said, opening his pack, and pulling out a harness. We spent the next twenty minutes getting ready to go down the shaft. Jo volunteered to stay topside, so Shawn, Billy, Heather, and I put on our harnesses then tied one end of the rope to the closest tree we could find. Unfortunately, it was on the far side of the clearing. We lost a lot of rope, but there wasn't anywhere else to tie it off and if all went well, we wouldn't need it anyway. We were using it more as a bread crumb trail than anything. Ready to go, we stood at the mouth of the shaft with our helmets and our headlamps on.

We were all staring at each other, afraid of taking the first step. We knew we had to, it was the whole reason why we were there, but peering into the inky blackness made my skin crawl and goosebumps pimpled on my skin.

"Let's do this." I took a step into the opening and let out a breath. The walls seemed sturdy even if they were covered in spider webs.

"Right behind you," Billy said, coming in after me.

"Everything is going to be fine," I heard Heather say, more to herself than to us.

The shaft didn't descend into the mountain as much as it ran parallel to the opening which made me feel better, there was less rock to fall on us if it caved in. Not that it wouldn't kill us, but it would be less work to recover our bodies.

The farther we went, the darker it became, it felt like our headlamps were working harder to give us the light we needed than they had before, and I wished there was more of it. After a few hundred yards our easy walk in the dark changed. The shaft started to descend so steeply I wasn't sure how we were going to maneuver it.

"Look at this." I moved to the side, allowing Billy and Shawn to see the descent we were about to make.

"That's why we have the rope," Billy said, rubbing his chin. "The way back up will be harder than the way down."

"Do you think it's safe?" Heather asked, looking over my shoulder.

"No safer than anything else down here." Billy threw the rope down the shaft and one by one we carefully went down backwards using the rope to steady us. It was closer to rappelling than hiking.

I was the last one down, and I slipped a few times almost falling, but I managed to regain my footing. I relaxed when I was on level ground again. "Well, that sucked." I dusted the dirt off my knees, waiting for someone to agree with me. When no one did, I spun around, and my mouth dropped open in awe. We were in a huge cave. "How did they do this?" I asked, walking over to the wall, and putting my hand on it.

The rock wasn't smooth like someone or thing had chiseled it out, but rough like the mountain had created the cavern. It wasn't cold to the touch as I expected it to be. It almost felt like room temperature, maybe a little cooler, but since I thought about it, the whole cavern felt the same way.

"No one did this. This isn't man made," Billy said, turning in a circle. "They found it, but they didn't make it."

"Who is they?" Heather asked standing next to Billy with her arms over her chest.

"Whoever made the trail and built the shaft. It was man made, but this." He held his arms out. "This is Mother Nature's creation."

The cavern was huge. My headlamp couldn't reach the far walls from where we stood. The ceiling was at least twenty feet above our heads with stalactites reaching down, some of them touching the floor, others hung between the walls and ceiling like a movie set. "This is crazy." Shawn grabbed my hand. "What do we do now?"

"Let's break into pairs and see what there is to see." Billy dug in his pack for something. "But let's mark our exit so we aren't stumbling around trying to find it later." He pulled out a glow stick, broke it, and laid it at the opening to the shaft.

"We'll go this way." Shawn pulled me to the right of the cave entrance. We walked around the semicircular cavern, searching for anything out of place, but all we found was dirt and rock. There weren't any other shafts leading out of the cavern and the thought of there being only one exit made me shiver.

"What are we going to do if we don't find the gate?" I whispered, not wanting Billy and Heather to hear me.

"Then we start looking somewhere else." He squeezed my hand and I wondered what we would do if they moved to Florida. I loved Shawn and didn't want him to move because I would miss him in my life, but it was more than that. If he left, I would be lost. I didn't know how long I would survive with my mark and no knights to keep Stalker and the other mares away.

"Hey guys, come check this out." Billy's voice echoed around the cavern.

Shawn's eyes lit up and he led me toward the sound of Billy's voice.

"Oh my gosh, I can't believe it," Heather said as we found them.

"What is it?" I pushed them out of the way.

I know they say when you find gold it's not all shiny and pretty like it is when you see it on jewelry, but what I was looking at had probably been polished for hours every day. The door was about five feet tall and two and half feet wide and solid gold. I took a step closer, it was closed tight and there wasn't a knob or handle. It was covered in symbols along the frame and in a spiral pattern beginning in the middle of the door. They reminded me of the rune on the pendant I had around my neck.

"Dang." I shook my head.

"What?" Shawn bent, trying to see what I was seeing.

"It's closed tight. How are we supposed to close it when it's already closed?"

"Did you think it would be that easy?" Shawn stood up. "Maybe we need to reseal it, not just close it."

"A girl can dream, can't she?" I leaned closer and squinted at the runes. "Yeah, maybe that's why it's closed."

"This is it?" Billy asked, reaching out to touch it.

"Don't." Heather grabbed his hand before he made contact. "I think it's exactly what we were looking for."

"The symbols on the frame and circling out from the middle. Does anybody know what language it is?" I pulled my phone out.

"No." Shawn hunched and got as close as he could without touching it.

"I have no clue," Heather said.

"Don't look at me." Billy shrugged his shoulders. "Are you sure this is the gate though? It looks closed."

"Yes, but I think Shawn's right." Heather pointed out a hairline crack. "It needs to be sealed."

Billy grabbed a flashlight out of his pocket and shined it around the frame.

"Can you see anything?" Shawn peered over Billy's shoulder.

"No, it's barely a crack." Billy turned his flashlight off. "What do we do now?"

"We document it and get out of here. Do you want to move?" I showed him my phone.

"Yeah, I'm going to keep searching. Maybe there's something else that will help us." Billy and Heather moved away so I could photograph the gate. I took a few pictures, one of the whole gate and some close ups of the writing. I glanced at the pictures and sighed.

"What's wrong?" Shawn looked at my phone.

"There's too much glare, I can't get the details." I put my phone back in my pocket and pulled my pack off my back. I opened one the outside pockets and pulled out the zip lock bag with my tissue paper in it.

Then I opened one of the smaller pockets on my pack and pulled out a piece of drawing charcoal.

"Are you going to draw it?" Shawn looked skeptical.

"No, I'm going to take a rubbing. I just hope I have enough tissue paper." I opened the first sheet.

"Do you think it's safe to touch it?" Shawn eyed the door like it was a rattlesnake ready to strike.

"I don't know but the information we need to close it might be here and I'm not leaving without it. Here will you hold this for me?" I positioned the paper a few inches above the door.

"Yeah," Shawn said, holding it while I rubbed the charcoal over the runes. "How did you know to bring this stuff?"

"I always have it in my hiking pack. You never know when you'll come across something like a grave stone, or Native American pictograms on a rock. I like to document that kind of stuff." I shrugged as I finished the first piece of paper. "You can let go now." Shawn let go of the paper and I carefully folded it and put it in the zip lock then grabbed a fresh piece and continued.

"That is a cool idea. Will you show me them some time?" he asked, and I thought it was strange we were talking about something so mundane while I was taking a rubbing of the gateway into the goblin dimension.

"Sure," I said, before concentrating on the rubbing.

I was just finishing with the last one when Billy said. "You guys, I think someone is on the other side of this wall."

"What?" I put the last piece in the bag and put it back in

my pack. I zipped everything up and put it on before Shawn and I went to find Billy and Heather.

They weren't far. Billy had his ear pressed up against the rock wall and Heather was standing over him with her arms crossed over her chest.

"What are you doing?" Shawn asked.

"Shh, listen," Heather said.

I closed my eyes and listened. At first all I could hear was the sound of dripping water and everyone breathing but then I heard something else. "Help us," they said, just like they did in my dreams when I first discovered the clearing with the mineshaft.

"We need to go, now." I backed up. I wanted to leave. We couldn't help them yet. I didn't know if we would ever be able to. I knew who they were, the people I saw outside the library window in the basement of the mansion. Stalker's slaves, I wanted to save them with every fiber of my being, but I didn't know how.

Shawn glared at me. "But they need help."

"I know but we can't help them yet."

"Come on Liz." Billy picked up a loose rock and hefted it to see how heavy it was. "We have to help them." He brought his arm back ready to hit the wall.

"Billy don't." I took another step back.

"What's the worst that could happen?" He hit the wall with the rock as hard as he could.

Chapter 41

When the rock hit the wall nothing happened, but I held my breath anyway. The voices on the other side of the wall became louder and they started banging on the layer of rock separating us. Billy brought the rock up and began hitting the wall over and over again while whoever was on the other side increase their banging until the whole cavern started to shake.

"We need to go, now." I half-walked, half-ran toward the glow stick marking the exit.

"Liz, no, they need our help." Billy called before one of the stalactites fell from the ceiling and shattered three feet in front of me, peppering me with chunks of rock. I stood frozen in place, staring at what was left of the rock and thanking God that I hadn't ran faster.

"Run," Shawn caught up with me, grabbed my hand, and pulled me behind him. We were almost to the exit when another stalactite fell and landed in our path. I shrieked and pulled away from him as we ran around it. I picked up the rope when we reached the tunnel and attached it to the carabiner on my harness while glancing behind me making sure Heather and Billy were following us. They weren't far.

"Climb." Shawn pushed me up the shaft. "I'll make sure they get out. We can't all go at once. "

I started climbing, holding onto the rope, and digging my feet into the soft soil at the bottom of the shaft, pulling myself up the slope one hand over the other, my feet trying to find purchase on the slick slope. After I made it twenty feet, I looked behind me. Heather was hooked up and gaining on me. Shawn was waiting for her to get some distance before he started, and Billy was hooking up his harness.

Shawn caught me looking. "What are you doing? Climb," he yelled, and I climbed as quickly as I could. The whole mountain seemed to tremble around us. Hand over hand, I pulled myself up the never-ending incline, blinking when dirt from above fell into my eyes. I was sweaty and shaking by the time I made it to the top. I offered Heather a hand when she reached me then we waited for Shawn and Billy.

"What are you doing?" Billy pushed me toward the exit when he reached us. "The shaft is going to collapse, go."

On level ground I sprinted. The opening wasn't far away even though it felt like miles. The light was just starting to change from dark to twilight when the ground under my feet began to shake. "Hurry!" I yelled, pumping my arms faster, trying to find more speed.

I burst out of the entrance, frantically looking from side to side. "Jo, where are you?" I yelled.

"Keep moving," Heather said, pushing me forward as she spilled out behind me, the boys weren't not far behind her.

"I'm here," Jo said, coming from the tree where the rope

was tied. "What's going on?"

Something in the tunnel exploded and the concussion of air pushed me off my feet as dirt rained down on my head. I fell, face first into the dried grass, and instinctively put my hands over my head to protect it from the debris showering down. I wasn't sure how long I lay there but, eventually, the dirt and rocks stopped falling from the sky and I rolled over and sat up.

"Is everyone alright?" I asked, blinking at the bright light and trying to find my friends. Everything was covered in a thin layer of dirt and rock and I watched four human forms slowly sit up.

"Yeah," Billy called. "Jo, where are you?"

"I'm here," she called, getting to her feet.

"I'm alive." Heather got to her knees then her feet.

"I'm here, but I think I twisted my ankle." Shawn grabbed his ankle, hissing.

I stood on shaking legs and tried to run, but my legs didn't think it was a good idea, so I walked unsteadily over to him. "Here let me see." I knelt at his feet. "Which one?"

He pointed to his left foot. "I tripped and twisted it when we were running for the opening."

I pulled his pant leg up and looked at his boot encased ankle. "I don't want to take your boot off, it will help keep the swelling down, but can you move it?"

He pointed his toes then twisted his foot from side to side. "Yeah, but it hurts bad."

"Let's see if you can walk. Don't put all your weight on it until you know it will hold." I put one of his arms over my shoulder and Billy grabbed his other one.

"On three," Billy said. "One. Two. Three." We lifted Shawn to his feet, and he took most of his weight on his good leg.

"Let's see." He tentatively put weight on his bad foot. "I think I can limp out of here," he said taking a few steps on his own with Billy and I close by in case it was too much.

"Okay, take your pack off. Then let's get the harness off you."

After we got his pack off, I had a minute to look around the clearing and my eyes filled with tears. Where the opening to the shaft should've been was a pile of loose dirt and rock. What were we going to do now? My only hope of surviving my mark was to close the gate and send the mares back where they came from. How was I going to close it when it was buried in the middle of a mountain?

I wasn't going to give up. *We would figure something out. We had to.* I wiped the tears from my eyes. *First, we needed to get off the mountain.*

"I'll see if I can find something to use as a walking stick." Heather went to the edge of the clearing.

"Don't go far," Billy called as he went to the tree the rope was tied to and started working on the knot. "Let's get out of here."

We gathered up our equipment and packed it into the four packs, we didn't want Shawn to carry any extra weight. Heather found a stick for him to lean on and Jo helped Billy put everything away.

Once everything was ready, we started down the trail. The trip down took a lot longer since we had to wait for Shawn. I didn't know what everyone else was feeling but I had to keep myself from breaking into a run until we reached the meadow and the main trail.

I checked my watch. "How is it already four o'clock?" I asked, digging in my pocket for my phone.

"What?" Billy asked and pulled his wrist up. "How long were we down the shaft?"

"I don't know, but it felt like forever." Jo took her sunglasses off to look at her phone. "What time did we leave your house, Liz?"

"Seven thirty, seven forty-five." I knew it was before eight. I remembered looking at my phone when we hit the main trail.

"There is no way we were gone for nine hours." Heather put her hands on her hips.

"Agreed." Shawn limped over to me. "You were right, Liz, there is something strange about the trail and the clearing. You didn't lose track of time the first time you went up there. It's the place." He put a hand on my shoulder and gave me a gentle shake.

I really wanted to say I told you so, but it was over, and they had already forgiven me. "Let's go. I'm tired and hungry, plus, we need to get ice on your ankle.

"I'm sorry, Liz, you were right," Billy finally said as we started down the main trail. "I shouldn't have tried to get to those people on the other side of the wall. This is all my fault."

"It's okay Billy, you were trying to help them. I want to help them too, I just don't know how." I shrugged and patted him on the shoulder.

"Can someone please tell me what happened?" Jo asked from

behind us.

Billy told her about finding the cavern and the gate then hearing the people on the other side of the wall. He told her how he tried to break through the wall and the resulting cave-in.

"The gate is buried in the mountain now?" Jo asked, crestfallen.

"Yeah, but we took pictures and Liz took a rubbing." Billy tried to sound positive.

"How is that going to help us if we can't get back to it? It's buried in the middle of a mountain." Jo sounded like she was going to cry.

"I don't know but at least we know where it is. If we can figure out what the writing on it means, maybe we can figure out how to close it." I stumbled with exhaustion as we hit the road and walked toward the house. "And there's a chance we won't have to be there to do it."

We dusted each other off the best we could before we went inside, then we got Shawn situated with an ice pack and his leg elevated in the dining room. We finally ate the sandwiches Heather and Shawn brought then I pulled out the zip-lock bag.

"What's that?" Jo asked as I opened the bag and pulled out the tissue paper.

"It's the rubbing I took of the gate."

"Where are the pictures?" Jo held her hand out for my phone.

"Here," I said, bringing them up and passing the phone to her. "They didn't turn out very good. The light sucked."

While Jo looked at the pictures on my phone, I laid out the tissue paper on the table, so we could see all of it. I stood back and wanted to cry. We had done it. We found the gate, and now it was buried under a mountain.

"What do we do now?" Heather stared at the table in awe. "Even if we figure out what this means, and it tells us how to close the gate, it's buried under a mountain."

"One step at a time." I took my phone back from Jo and took pictures of the paper. They turned out much better than the ones I took of the gate itself. "Step one, find the gate, we can check that off the list. Step two, figure out what this means, step three find out what we need to do to close the gate, step four figure out how to get back to the gate."

"Step five, close the gate and kill the mares." Jo smiled at me.

"Let's say we get everything lined out." Heather got up and paced around the room. "How are we going to get back to the gate?"

"We take our findings to the council and they can pay for the excavation to get back down there," Shawn said but didn't sound convinced.

"Let's back up to step two," Billy said, before taking a sip of his water. "How are we going to figure out what this means?" He waved his hand at the table.

"Research," Jo and I said at the same time. "I'll start on it tonight. See if Google images has anything that will help us translate it."

"I'll start searching the archives we have online." Jo drummed her hands on the table.

"We need to find Freeman's journal too. Maybe there is something on it in there." Heather stopped at her chair and sat down.

"Do you think we'll be able to do it?" Billy asked. "It seems like we are so far from this being over."

"I don't know, but I'm not giving up. I don't have a choice." I smiled at my friends. I was one lucky girl, who else had a group of friends ready to do anything to help them?

The home phone rang, and I ran into the kitchen to grab it. I read the caller ID after I picked it up from the cradle, someone from the mansion was calling. "Hello?"

"Liz? It's Jenny. Are Shawn and Heather there?" She sounded upset and I swallowed past the lump forming in my throat, worried that something had happened to Jon.

"Yeah, hold on I'll get Heather for you." I handed the phone over. "It's your mom."

Heather closed her eyes tightly like she was saying a silent prayer before she took the phone. "Hey Mom, how's Dad?"

"What?" Heather's head jerked up. "You're kidding, that's great." I glanced at Shawn who was staring at Heather with his mouth part way open. "Yeah we'll leave right now. See you in twenty." She hung up the phone and smiled. "Dad's awake."

"He is? That's great." I said, then clapped my hands and went to help Shawn put his boot on.

"He isn't a hundred percent, I guess he is having problems talking, but who cares? He's not in a coma." Heather went to the doorway. "Mom wants us at the hospital."

As soon as I got his boot on and tied he got unsteadily to his feet. "Okay, let's go," he said, his voice tight with pain.

"I'm waiting for you, little brother." Heather tapped her

foot on the floor with her arms crossed over her chest. "I guess I get to drive your Rubicon." Her eyes lit up and Shawn winced.

"Stop talking and go." I made shooing motions with my hands. "Call me when you can."

"I will." Shawn gave me a quick hug and kissed my cheek. "I love you. I'll call you later."

"I love you too. Go." Shawn limped out behind Heather, and I smiled. I went back to the dining room where Jo and Billy were talking quietly. "Okay, so I guess we have things to do."

"Yeah, we were just talking about heading home. It's been a long day and it's such a relief that Jon's awake." Jo got to her feet.

I was kind of bummed they were leaving but we were all filthy and tired. "Yeah, I need a shower. Why don't we plan on meeting for breakfast tomorrow?"

"Yeah, give me a call in the morning and we'll work it out."

After they left, I put away my hiking gear then went to shower. I had bruises all over my legs and arms from our race out of the mineshaft, but no blood. Once I was clean, I checked my phone for word from Shawn, but there was nothing. It wasn't a big deal, they probably needed some family time.

I spent the rest of my day enhancing the pictures of the rubbings I took and uploaded them to Google Image search. I found a few things that were close, but nothing was a hundred percent match. I gave up when Mom called me down for dinner, reminding me that we had to tell Dad about Knights Inc.

It went better than I thought. Mom started by telling him about Victor and how she didn't believe that he died of altitude sickness but by trying to put an end to the sleeping death. Dad didn't understand what Victor had to do with Knights Inc. I told him what I knew about the life Victor had before he met Mom, and that I had inherited his talent for dream walking. With Mom backing me up we explained about my mark and that the only hope I had for surviving was to learn to fight the mares and close the gate. He didn't say anything for a long time, only sat in his chair and stared out the window. After what felt like hours he got up and went to his man cave without a word and closed the door. Mom said to give him time, it was a lot to take in.

By the time we were done I could barely keep my eyes open. I still hadn't heard from Shawn as I went up to my room. I thought about calling him, but decided not to, he would call me when he could. I wondered what the clearing looked like in my dream after the cave in as I brushed my teeth. Would the shaft be caved in? What would the gate look like in the dreamscape? I took my dreamcatcher down with a plan in mind and climbed into bed.

Chapter 42

My dream began in the clearing and I shook my head. It looked exactly like it did when we left that afternoon. Dirt and debris covered the yellow grass and the mineshaft had caved in, the opening covered with dirt and rocks. I walked closer, wondering what it was going to take to excavate the gate when Stalker showed up. "You ruined everything," he yelled, and I swung around with my 1911 aimed at his head. "Now I have to start over." He walked toward me, limping slightly, and his head jiggled on his neck like a bobble head.

"You're the one who won't leave me alone." Keeping my eyes on him I kept my ears honed for anything that might approach me from behind.

"First, your boyfriend sends me back to my dimension for the first time in eons to save you, then you send me back. All the power I saved to cross over is gone, and now you ruined my tunnel. Why won't you just die like the rest of them?" He jumped at me and I pulled the trigger hitting him in the chest, stopping his forward momentum. He landed on his back but bounced to his feet effortlessly like he had landed on a trampoline, a bullet to the chest wasn't going to slow him down.

"No protection tonight I see, the twat finally did her job. Good, you can help me restore my power." He lunged at me again and I pulled the trigger. His head snapped backward and rested on his back so he was looking at the sky, his neck must have been broken. He put his hands to either side of his head and pulled it up to sit on his shoulders. "I want to show you what you caused." He walked around me with his hands up, keeping ten feet between us. He snapped his fingers and suddenly the clearing was filled with people.

They were from every era Twisted Pines had seen. There were Native Americans dressed in leathers, gold miners with suspenders and top hats, hippies with bell bottoms and peasant shirts, I even saw a Boy Scout. "What are they doing here?"

"These are my slaves; they are the ones who died before I could eat their soul. As punishment, they work for me." The goblin pointed to a couple chained together at the ankle as they used picks to break up the dirt where the opening to the shaft had been. I glanced at them, then back at the mare. My jaw dropped, and I did a double take. It was Victor and Stacy.

"You bastard." I pulled the trigger as fast as I could unloading my clip each bullet hitting him in the chest. He fell on his back and I switched the gun for an executioner's ax. I walked over to where Stalker lay, brought the ax behind my head, then let it slam down, severing his head from his body. I kicked the head into the forest and hacked the rest of his body to pieces. I didn't want him to come back anytime soon.

I turned around and found the slaves watching me. "You're free," I yelled, running to them. "I killed him. Run away and be free." Instead of running they just stared.

"We can't, Elizabeth." Victor ran a hand through his hair and frowned at the ground, refusing to meet my eyes. "We can only be set free when the gate is closed and all the mares who came through are trapped in their dimension." Tears leaked down my cheeks as he resumed his work. "I told you not to try. Now we have even more work to do." He shook his head and everyone in the clearing disappeared.

Epilogue

The next day I picked up Shawn at the mansion before we went to breakfast at the café. We were going to visit his dad in Spruce afterward, then we planned to spend the day together. Billy and Jo beat us there and saved us a table. We sat down and ordered coffee.

"Where's Heather?" Jo took a sip of her coffee, waiting for Shawn to start talking.

"She should be here any minute. She spent the night in Spruce with Dad, but she said she would be here." Shawn glanced at the door when the bell over it rang, and he smiled and waved.

"About time," Billy said, winking at Heather. "How's your dad?"

"Better, he slept through the night, and I could actually understand what he was saying this morning." Heather took the last seat at the table and signaled the waitress for coffee.

"What did he say?" Shawn's eyes brightened with the news.

"He wanted to know why I was there and not at home working." She rolled her eyes.

"What will happen now?" I glanced between Shawn and Heather.

"He must be feeling better then," Shawn balked.

"They are going to send him to Denver for occupational therapy. He can walk, but not well. His doctor said whatever happened to him, they still aren't sure what," she paused to roll her eyes, "gave him stroke-like symptoms, he will have to teach his body how to behave again."

"What does that mean for you guys and Knights Inc.?" Billy asked, glancing up from the menu.

"Dad's still in charge but is taking a medical leave of absence. We don't have to move or anything, but until he can perform his duties someone else will be in charge." Heather stared at her empty coffee cup like it was going to magically refill itself.

"Did the council pick someone yet?" Jo asked as the waitress came over to take their orders.

"Yes, I'll tell you in a minute." Heather glanced at the waitress then ordered her breakfast. Once we all ordered, and the waitress left, Heather picked up where she left off. "Magnus will run things until Dad is back on his feet."

"You've got to be kidding me," Shawn groaned, and I sighed.

"Darn." Jo took another sip of her coffee. "I was hoping my dad would get a chance to run things for a change."

"Let's hope Jon recovers quickly." I nodded. "Let's all send him positive healing vibes. Any idea what happened with Kristina?"

"Magnus bailed her out but is confining her to his house and is forcing her to spend all of her dream time with him or her mom." Shawn stretched his arms over his head then rested the one next to me behind my back.

"I know you were busy with your dad last night, but did you look for the latch for the basement door?" I relaxed into Shawn's arm.

"No, but do we still need to?" Heather leaned forward and drew her eyebrows together. "The gate is buried in under the mountain."

"I think we need to see what's in the basement. We know the gate isn't there, but I think we need to check it out. There might be something important down there."

"Okay I'll check it out later." Heather nodded her head in agreement. "Do you think Knights Inc. will pay for the excavation of the shaft if we find a way to close the gate?"

"We may not have to." I cringed thinking of Stalker's slaves.

"What do you mean?" Jo leaned toward me and Heather leaned back, crossing her arms over her chest.

"I dreamed of the clearing last night. Stalker was there, he was pissed. The shaft is caved in on that side too. He said he had to start over because of us. He has slaves, Victor and Stacy included, digging out the shaft." I felt horrible saying the next part. "It will be the second time they dig it out, but I don't think we need it."

Shawn pulled his arm away from me and spun in his seat. "What do you mean Victor and Stacy are helping him? Stacy would never. We don't need the shaft? How are we going to seal the gate?"

"They're slaves, Shawn." I rested my hand on his leg to calm him. "Stalker said if they die before he sucks out their soul, he takes them. There were people from the gold rush to the present day, moving dirt, working on reopening the entrance. I don't think it's the gate we found is the one we need."

"What do you mean?" Heather asked.

"I mean, why would Stalker care about the shaft if the gate is already open? He doesn't need it."

"Then where does that door open to?" Jo leaned forward.

"I think it leads from the dream dimension to this one."

"Once he has the shaft re-opened, all he needs is the power to open the gate and he will be real."

"How are we going to stop him?" Billy asked.

"We have time," I squeezed Shawn's hand. "I killed Stalker last night. He will have to come back from his dimension, then dig out the shaft, and replenish his power."

The waitress came with our food before anyone could respond and we sat silently while she put our plates on the table. "What do we do now?" Jo asked, looking at me for an answer.

I looked around the table at my group of friends; I had known Billy for my entire life, but I had only known Shawn, Heather, and Jo for a few months. It was funny how sometimes it didn't matter how long you knew someone before you knew that you could trust them with your life.

"Now, we find the other gate and send the mares back where they came from."

Dear Reader,

Thank you for reading the second installment of Knight Flyers. I hope you enjoyed it. You, the reader are the reason I write. I hope this story gave you a chance to escape your everyday life and take a walk in someone else's shoes.

This book was originally scheduled to be released at the end of 2018, that obviously didn't happen due to circumstances beyond my control and I'm sorry I made you wait so long. I hope that the third book will be released before the end of 2019 but I can't make any promises at this point.

I want to give a special shout out to my 'Critiquers' group on Twitter for beta reading this they are so full of amazing ideas. As always Leah and Amy, two of my favorite people in the world thank you for all the time you spend reading and correcting my spelling errors.

Last but not least I have to thank Jessica, she was my inspiration to write this book. She is my secret informant to young adult books and I couldn't have finished this book without her input.

Ann McCune

I live on forty acres in Northwest Colorado with two dogs (Ajax and Achilles), my amazing husband and an ever changing amount of barn cats.

I love to write about the Heroines Journey in the paranormal universe, because writing about everyday life is boring for me. I love taking a character who thinks she is weak and showing her how strong she really is.

When I am not staring at the monitor writing, I am staring at my Kindle reading, or spending time with my husband and animals.

Check out my website: AnnMcCune.com

Follow me on Social Media:

Facebook: @KnightFlyers

Instagram: ann_mccune

www.ingramcontent.com/pod-product-compliance
Lightning Source LLC
Chambersburg PA
CBHW071143100726
47908CB00002B/230